CHASING SNOWFALL

ANASTASIA WILDER

Published by Anastasia Wilder of Midnight Shadows Press on June 13th, 2025

Print ISBN: 979-8-9919091-1-2
E-book ISBN: 979-8-9919091-2-9

Book Cover by Emily Wittig Designs

Art Illustration by Valentina Soulsong

1st edition 2025

DEDICATION

To those who have the courage to pick up the pieces and start again.

Also, to the ride that has left me breathless, bruised, and turned on af, I hope you see this as the love letter it is.

TUNES & ART

Did you know Maverick and Charlotte's story starts in their short novella, Midnight Heatwave? It's available now!

CONTENT WARNING

Readers, please be aware that while this may not be the darkest book within dark romance, there are dark themes and sexually explicit scenes throughout. This book contains mature language, graphic violence, and subject material that may be disturbing. It is intended for readers who are aged 18 years and over. Please consider the below before reading, your comfort and care are paramount. Your mental health matters!

- Dark Themes

- Explicit Sexual Content

- Parental Loss – on and off page

- Grief

- Alcohol Use

- Panic Attacks

- Physical Abuse- off page, not between MCs

- Explicit Language

- Hunting & Field Dressing of an Animal

- Trauma

- Restraint by Rope

- Torture

- Physical Violence

- Gun Violence & Weapons

- Murder

- Gore & Corpse Abuse

Charlotte

CHAPTER 1

S trong, firm hands peel my heated and limp yet sated body off the island countertop. He throws me over his shoulder and gives my bare ass a sharp slap as he heads to the stairs and then takes them two at a time.

"Hey!" I giggle as I slap his ass in return. I'm in no shape to protest being carried. After that orgasm, I'm in no shape to walk; my thighs are like jelly. Best. Orgasm. Of. My. Life. God, the view from here is nice. My eyes take in thick, muscular quads covered in tight, dark denim and then rove up to his ass. An ass that's rock-hard and right at my eye level. I give it another pat. No jiggle, just granite buns, fresh from the bakery. Dare I say it could be America's ass? It's that perfect.

We get to the top of the stairs. "Where's your bed?" he asks huskily.

"On the right." What am I doing? What am I doing? What am I doing?!

In the span of a few hours—though really it felt like lifetimes—I feel like he's the first one to ever really see me, to know me. Like our souls were meant to find each other. I'm not even one of those people who thought I would ever have that kind of romance, but we just clicked. *Brain, please don't overthink this.* It feels like more than just lust at first sight. If it turns into something more, it's something more. I can't say why, but I trust him.

Which is why I suspected it might turn into this when I invited him in for coffee. I'm taking a chance that this could be more than just sex. He asked me to show him how I like it, how I want it—that's a kind of trust, a vulnerability I've never shared with anyone else. Not that any man from my past ever asked how I liked it. If I had told them I wanted them to put their hand around my neck, or restrain me so I couldn't move, or God forbid something even more scandalous, they would have run the other way, but not him.

He opens the door to my bedroom. With his long legs, he crosses the length of my room in just a few strides and drops me onto my bed with a thunk. I hear my rickety brass bedframe hit the wall. The screws need to be tightened, and I hope to God that this man knows how to break a bed. Welp. If I had any neighbors, they would definitely be side-eying me in the morning because I don't think they would be getting any sleep tonight. Thankfully, being on the corner means a bit more privacy, because the look in his eyes is pure desire.

He bends down, completely enveloping me with his frame, arms on either side of my hips. His hands grab my thighs as he sinks to his knees. "You are absolutely ravishing." Then, he grabs my chin with his thumb and forefinger to pull me forward for a devastating kiss. "Mmm. You taste so good, Charlotte," he says between kisses. "But you need to tell me exactly what you want me to do to you. This only goes as far as you want."

As far as I want. What do I want? I'm completely naked, and he still has his jeans and socks on. I want to tear them off, lick up and down every single inch of his torso and that V that dips below his pants. This man is so stunning, I swear to the heavens. And right now, he's looking at me like he wants to devour me...and like he wants an answer.

I am Charlotte Fucking Adler. I have managed the biggest hedge fund on the Eastern seaboard, almost died, and then started my life over. I am a badass. *I am a badass.* How hard could it be to tell the man in front of me, on his knees, that I want him to rail me within an inch of my life and keep doing it all night long? Preferably with all the toys I've wanted to try but never had the guts to use with any of my ex-lovers or ex-fiancé? That I don't want this to be a one-night thing? That he feels real? That I'm so tired of being tired?

"I—" *Good God, Charlotte, get it together.* "I want to try something new, something that scares me."

He still hasn't let go of my chin. "What do you want to try, sweetheart? I'll give you anything."

"I have a candle and some toys, and handcuffs." The words leave my mouth, and I can't take them back. This new place, where no one knows me or has expectations of who I am—was—is making me bolder. You know those moments that feel like the precipice of something greater? Something in my gut is telling me I can trust him. Maybe the way he jumped in to protect Quinn and I at the bar from that creep, the way he told me secrets while looking up at the stars as he walked me home from the festival; I *know* it wasn't an act.

"What a surprising, mysterious woman you are." The corners of his lips curl up, and he could give the devil a run for his money with that gorgeous face. Chiseled cheekbones and a jawline that's cut from marble, framed by wild and wavy light brown hair. "Where are these treasures, hmm?" He walks his fingers down my neck and through the valley of my breasts. "Should I go on a treasure hunt?"

My cheeks are flushed, and my mouth goes dry as I try to swallow. "They're in my bedside table. Second drawer from the top."

My eyes follow him when he stands and walks around the bed. I don't miss the bulge that's threatening to break through his pants. The only light source in my room is a small lamp on my dresser that's on a timer because I hate sleeping in the dark. When he opens the wooden nightstand drawer, then looks back at me, the warm light disappears in the valleys between his abs and his long lashes cast shadows on his cheekbones. A bit of shock shows across that beautiful face of his, and then he looks back at the drawer. "These are all still in their packaging."

Oh my God, he too thinks I'm a freak. I look to my feet and feel my stomach hit the first floor of my rental. This is the exact reaction that the guys I hooked up with in college, and even my ex-fiancé, gave me.

He must see the dejection in my facial expressions, because in two seconds, he's sitting next to me. "Don't do that. I'm just a little surprised to see them in packaging. You've never opened them. Going out on a limb here, but maybe you felt a little apprehensive about sharing that piece of yourself with others?" My shoulders slump, and I look at the floor. "Charlotte, I meant what I said. You are extraordinarily beautiful. I don't know who ever put the idea in your head to be ashamed that you want to embrace your sexuality, but I am not that guy. You're way too smart to listen to those assholes, right?" He puts his hand on my knee, and I look up at him. "Now, give me a safe word. If it gets too much, it goes too far, we stop right there. Or—we use red, yellow, and green, just like driving a car: 'green' means go, 'yellow' means you're close but don't stop, 'red' means stop."

"Okay."

"Red means?"

"Stop," I say.

"You say stop, and I stop right away. What do you say?"

"'Red' if I want you to stop."

"Good girl."

God, that does something to my insides.

He pulls me in for a kiss and lifts me to straddle him. Within a breath, he instantly calmed my nerves, and my core went molten for him. Respecting boundaries and pushing them at the same time? This man. The inside of my thighs rub against the roughness of his jeans, and his callused hands run up my back, the friction everywhere except where I want it the most. He stands up, and I wrap my legs around him as he turns us around and places me back on the bed. I bend my legs and position my feet on the bed. My eyes follow him as he gets out the candle and the French blue raw silk and rose gold handcuffs, both still in their packaging. He reaches into the drawer and pulls out a velvet black bag. *Crap!* Okay, that one makes an almost nightly appearance.

"What's in here?" Leaving the other items in the still-open drawer, he opens the bag and pulls out a sleek, matte pink vibrator with gold buttons.

I blush a bit, but with a confidence I didn't have a few minutes ago, I say, "That's Francis. He's helped me out a few times."

His dimples break on both sides of his face, the warm light from the lamp casting a larger-than-life shadow of him on the wall. Prowling toward me with the grace of a panther, treasures in hand, he says, "Move to the center of the bed." I do as instructed, and he rewards me with an appreciative grin, placing all the items on the foot of the bed, except the candle, which he unwraps. "Matches?"

I point to the dresser behind him with my foot. "On the candle plate."

He takes a few steps back, eyes never leaving me. He's making me feel like a work of art, like I'm beautiful. I know that I'm attractive, but in a basic kind of way. He's taking me in the way one takes in a Botticelli or Titian. I've never had anyone look at me the way he is right now.

He puts the candle on the dresser and starts unbuttoning his jeans. "Miss Charlotte, we are going to have so much fun." Running the match against the matchbox, the head ignites and burns brightly, illuminating his face and making those striking eyes glimmer. He lights the candle with the match and holds it for a few seconds. After a few more moments, he walks around to the side of the bed. "Green, like the grass?" he asks.

I nod. "Yes, please."

He holds the candle in one hand and then takes my breast in the other, rolling my nipple between his strong fingers. I close my eyes and lean into his touch. That's when I feel the first sting of the hot wax roll between my breasts, down my navel, all the way to my pussy.

Beep. Beep. Beep. *Ugh*. I hear the alarm go off, then a whimper. "Okay, bubba. Please, please don't pee on the floor again. We're going out right now." At the word "out," Finnley leaps off my bed and races down the stairs. I fly after him in nothing but a fluffy gray robe, trying like hell to get my boots on before we have an accident at the door. I fumble to unlock the deadbolt, the lock, the screen door lock, and then the door. Poor little guy; he's circling and trying to paw at the door. "One sec, buddy."

It's not his fault I'm bumbling like an idiot. I was in the middle of the best sex dream. Well, no, that's not true. Not a sex dream. It was a memory dream. Is that a thing? It must be, because it was a damn good memory sex dream. And one I wish I could scrub from my mind, just to get him out of my head.

And just like that, my morning has instantly gone to shit, and my anger could burn through all the snow on my back porch, in my backyard—hell, could burn the whole town. Fucking asshole.

Maverick "Ranger Rick the Dick" No-Last-Name. The one guy I've slept with in the past year and a half. I haven't seen or heard from him since the Summer Kick-Off Festival in May, and he's still got me dripping down my thighs. Last time I trusted my gut on men, I swear to God. What an asshole! I can't even bring myself to say his name, so my bestie, Quinn, and I usually refer to him as Ranger Rick. I know it's wild to think that way about a one-night stand almost five months later, but it felt like so much more...and it was the best sex I've ever had in my whole damn life. He made me feel so much—but really, more than that, he empowered me.

For the first time, I felt confident in telling a man what exactly I'd like him to do to me, and, Jesus, did he deliver! And that's what I get for sleeping with him on the first night. I haven't been remotely interested in another man since, because, in a town this small, there's no one else I would even want to consider. They would have big boots to fill because that man fucked like a champ and gave me a highlight reel to last my whole life, even if I hate the star of the show.

"Go potty." I point toward the empty spot of grass I raked off for Finnley last night. "Go potty, Finn." He just stands and cocks his head at me like, "What does that mean, woman?" I sigh. I go down the stairs and call him down to me. He comes right to me, sniffs around the patch, and finally does his business. I knew what I was getting into with a puppy. Mother and Father had several thoroughbred pointers growing up that they raised from birth.

He gives a yip, and I know he's ready to go in. The frigid early-October morning air leaves much to be desired in terms of warmth. He bounds up the two steps, already getting pretty good at the little trick I taught him: wiping his paws on the rug before heading back into the house.

Finnley is a German Shepherd mix—or we think he is, anyway. My boss found a small litter of newborn pups on the side of the road leading into the ranch, with no mom in sight. He kept going back with food and water for a week, trying to find her, but never did. He brought the pups to the barn and bottle-fed them for a few weeks.

The day Jasper brought the pups in, Finnley came right to me and never left my side. Jasper said it wasn't right separating a pup from his first love, so I kept him. His littermates went to neighboring ranches or farms because they're great working dogs. Finnley's been living with me for almost a month now, and we're still getting used to each other. He comes to work with me every day. He's almost two and a half months old, and he keeps me damn busy.

Entering through the back door, my small living room welcomes me, some rugs laid out over each other next to where I kick off my boots. It opens to the kitchen, where the clock on the stove reads 4:50 a.m. I groan, "I get another half-hour, buster." I feed him breakfast and check his water bowl before heading back upstairs. He jumps up on the comforter and burrows his way beneath the quilt just as I crawl back into bed.

I don't actually get to sleep for half an hour, but I lie there and mindfully breathe in and out, contemplating the choices in my life. Ugh... I'm still so mad at Maverick! I hadn't thought about him in a while—not really, anyway, until I ran into his friend Caleb at the store. Eh, I guess Caleb's kind of my friend, too, but I didn't ask about him. That would've been weird. Still, I definitely thought about him on the drive home, mostly because Caleb didn't mention Maverick, either.

Caleb and Kennedy got married two months ago. I didn't go. Maybe Maverick didn't come back for the wedding, or if he did, he sure didn't reach out to me. I'd already deleted all my socials just after I left Boston, but he still had my number.

And he didn't use it.

I am just about to fall back to sleep when Finnley climbs out of his tunnel and comes to lay his head across my chest. He snuggles so hard and makes the cutest damn little noises snoring. He knows exactly what I need all the time: hugs, pets, getting me out of my head—he just knows. I pet his soft, fuzzy puppy fur, give him snuggles, and put his ears between my lips. I make goofy noises and play with his paws and tail, all things to get him desensitized. He still smells like a puppy; I know that he's going to lose that scent soon. I've never smelled the baby scent that new moms go crazy over, but I imagine it's the same, and if not, then I guess I'm just crazy for this little guy.

The radiator is making a buzz that's the perfect white noise. *Do not close your eyes, Charlie. Do not close your eyes!* I give Finn a little pat on his butt. "Time to stretch, little man," I say, and he hops off the bed. With a grunt, I pull myself out of my comfy bed, swing my legs over the side, and slide my feet into my slippers. I walk across the hall to the guest bedroom that's really more like a home gym at this point. The only guest who has ever stayed with me is Quinn.

Flicking on the light switch, the warm, white LED lights that frame the far wall power on and illuminate the room. There's a small dumbbell hand weight set on the floor next to a yoga mat and a stationary bike. There's also a twin daybed. See? Technically, it's a guest room.

I'm in my PJs and see no reason to change into yoga pants and a sports bra when it just creates more laundry. Besides, I'm only stretching today and not going through a full workout. As a ranch hand, my work is very demanding on my body, and the best way to prevent injury is to stretch and stay limber.

I was lucky to find this house when I did and even luckier to have a steady paycheck coming in, so I didn't have to stay with the other ranch hands. My boss, Jasper, didn't mind that I wasn't staying on the property when I signed on at the beginning of summer. There are two women in the bunkhouse, so it's not like a frat house, but with everything going on, I need privacy. I wanted a place to call mine once I decided to stay in Silver Rapids for a while.

I sit on the floor and get into my flow. I focus on my breathing and try to think about my day. But my mind wanders to the way those luminous blue eyes looked up to mine from between my thighs, between long, languid strokes of his tongue. *Ugh, no, focus.* We're breaking in two new horses, and I have to help move one herd to another pasture.

Surprisingly, I love what I do. When I was coming through town, I stopped for some food at this cute diner and overheard a man chatting with the waitress at the table behind me about how hard it was for him to find reliable help. I didn't have any experience on a ranch, but I turned to him and asked him about the job. I love all animals, especially horses, and I rode English-style back home and knew how to care for and groom horses. I had absolutely no idea about cattle, a homestead, ranching, or anything like that, but he took me under his wing and showed me the ropes. The Economics and Business Data Analytics degree from Waverly University would not have helped me out here, but my weekly riding lessons and competitions did.

I am finishing child's pose when I look over to Finnley, who is napping in front of the radiator. "I'm hopping in the shower, and then it's time to get on the road." He opens his eyes but promptly closes them and gives a huff. I roll my eyes. What a diva.

I grab my phone off the charger in my bedroom, pull up my morning playlist, and hit "shuffle." It's a mix of '90s R&B, grunge alt, and pop from the 2000s. Tupac and Biggie in the morning just feels like the right move today. I connect to the Bluetooth speaker that sits on a shelf, and "I Ain't Mad at Cha" plays. I measure my shower length by how many songs play, and I'm just about to get out when *that* song comes on, and I'm instantly pulled back to Maverick fucking me against the wall and the vanity in this very bathroom, his thrusts matching pace to the song's rhythm. We spent all night tangled in each other—on the bed, on the floor, in here. Songs have a way of taking you back to a place and time, even when you'd rather leave the memory in the past. I reach for the phone and skip it immediately.

Fuck. Today is going to be such a long day.

Charlotte

CHAPTER 2

I get the coffee maker started with that sweet elixir of life. Jasper would say I "dress up" my coffee, but I'm just a girl. I get a knife from the drawer and open the Nutella jar, scoop up a big glob and run it around the inside of the thermos, and pour the milk into the frother. It's a bastardized version of a Maracchino from my favorite place back home. The café in town makes it just right; however, they aren't open this early. I still have to get dressed, but everything is ready—just need to run the frother while I get the leash and harness on Finn.

I don't bother with makeup or doing my hair most days, but I absolutely believe in skin care, so I put on a few serums and tinted moisturizer with sunscreen in it, as well as a heavy-duty lip balm. My waist-length blonde hair is already wild with curls, so I throw it into a braid to keep it from getting windblown.

It's going to be damn cold today, and anyone who's ever spent time outside out West will tell you to dress in layers because when the sun comes out and you're hauling hay across a field, you'll be grateful to take off a layer. So it's base layers, then jeans, then flannel, then socks.

I give a whistle, and Finn is at my side within a few seconds. This dog is so smart; my heart absolutely breaks when I think about what could have happened to him and his littermates if Jasper hadn't helped place them in homes. He loves working, and, just like me, he likes praise. I give him a scratch under his muzzle and say, "Good boy, Finn. That's a good boy. Let's go to work."

I flip the frother on and get him into his harness while the milk heats and goes all bubbly. He has a field coat and booties in the truck, too, just in case, but I don't think he'll need them today. I pour the coffee, grab our lunch from the fridge to throw in my pack, and lock up my little home.

The house was threadbare when I moved in, but Quinn and I shopped at all the thrift shops from seven surrounding counties. Anyone that knew the old me in Boston, with the high-rise apartment overlooking the Commons with the Carrera marble-top counters, custom paint acid-washed walls, and high-end fancy appliances, would fall over dead to see that I have to use a wrench to open my pantry cupboard. But those people have also never seen me happy, not really. You get really good at faking when you do it every day. So, that whole fake-it-'til-you-make-it? It can go the other way, too. It can make you think you're happy when you're dying inside.

I love my thrown-together home; it's a bit of cottagecore meets disco. I don't feel wholly safe anywhere, so, if I'm going to live under the radar, it should be in a place where the pieces tell a story. I bought the rug from a man whose grandpa owned a textile mill, and the design was something his grandma doodled. That's real—it came from a real person and not something from a big box store. Or the full tea set with service for ten that looked like my grandmother's I found for fifteen bucks at the flea market a few months ago. I brought some things with me from back East: most of my wardrobe, baby books that my grandparents made for me, small little art pieces I collected because I liked them—not because it would add value to my portfolio—and the teddy bear that my big sister gave me when I broke my arm when I was eight. All things that I was going to be dropping off at my storage unit, but after the incident at work, everything changed. I literally took what I had and ran.

I had a feeling things were happening in the wings that I could just barely make out in my periphery. So, I started getting things together to move. I didn't know that move would bring me to Wyoming.

"Get up, Finners." I open the door to the cab, and he jumps up to the floorboards, then to his side of the bench seat. No crystal ball told me I would end up working as a ranch hand in western Wyoming with a rusty, olive-green truck I named Verne. I sold my Range Rover in Pennsylvania and used that cash to get by until I found this job.

The sun is cresting across the horizon and waking up the world, the bright amber rays catching on the sagebrush in the landscape before me. The striations in the sky, from purples to dusky blues and soft pinks, cast a golden glow on the Tetons' snow-capped peaks in the rearview mirror. I'm waiting for the heat to kick on; sometimes it takes Verne a few minutes to get it cranking on high heat. There is the barest hint of crisp pine-perfumed air coming through the vents. I went from seeing the ocean every day to seeing a beautiful mountain landscape.

Dappled Stone Ranch is a thirty-minute drive on a good day with no snow or ice, but it's pretty slick today, so I'm taking it slow. I put new tires on the truck because I don't need to be that person with bald tires on a dirt road. I'm blonde, but not a dumb blonde.

One of the summer help guys installed a new radio so that I could stream from my burner phone. He kept trying to get me to install one with satellite stations because the stations can be spotty in bad weather, but I told him I like analog. It's true, though not for the reason he thinks, but rather because I don't need to sign up for anything with my name. The strumming of the guitar of whatever song is playing is perfectly tuned to the peaceful moments in the truck with Finn, surrounded by this untamed grandeur.

The road curves just before the ranch entrance, and I see "Dappled Stone Ranch" over the drive in a scrolling, wrought-iron sign above. A long dirt drive leads to the entrance of the house, about three-quarters of a mile off the main road. The corrals and stables on the left are near the house, and the bunkhouse is on the right by the open pastures. Coming to the estate, you see a sprawling log-sided home with the front all stone—granite, limestone, and slate. There's a large wraparound porch with rocking chairs and a table where I've played a few games of Go with Jasper.

The dirt road continues past the estate and curves around to the bunkhouse. Pulling along the fenceline, I park toward the rear where the kitchen is located. There's a fresh layer of snow on the pasture, and now that the sun has crested the treeline that surrounds the ranch, it glistens off the snow like Edward's skin. Honestly, Bella picked wrong, and I'll die on that hill. The snow crunches under my feet and Finn's paws, but it won't stick through the day.

The team likes to start their day by having their version of a morning huddle in the kitchen area; it hosts a map, and everyone gets their walkies and daily tasks from Ace.

The bunkhouse is a tight but clean space with bright bohemian and Western-flair decor throughout the house. The floors are hardwood and the rugs are worn. From what I could find out, Jasper's wife, Marie, was in the process of updating the space just before she passed away from breast cancer and he never had it in him to finish. That has to be one of the hardest things to do: bury the love of your life much too early. They had a son, but he's not in the picture. Jasper never brings him up and there are no family photos featuring a son. There are some photos up, though—you can tell Jasper loved Marie in those pictures.

Clint and Hank hunch over Finnley, and the ham is getting so many pets that he looks like he's smiling. The door opens, and I turn to see Jasper's tall silhouette blocking the light coming in from outside. "Mornin', y'all. We've got the day workers and Clint pushing the herd to the north lot after lunch. Hank, we've got your guys breaking in the new colt." He points to Clint and Hank. "You guys get with Ace if you need anything."

I bristle a little. I was expecting to help break the colt in. I try not to show the disappointment on my face. The low man on the pole shouldn't be complaining here, but Jasper said I had a natural talent with the younger horses.

He hasn't given me dismissal, but he isn't looking at me either, so I stay rooted in my spot, looking at the map of the property. I'm instantly in my dad's study, ten years old, getting dressed down after he praised Georgina for something trivial and told me I would be nothing but someone's trophy wife. My whole life tilted because that's what people said about my mother, and I would never be like her. My mother is the quintessential East Coast woman who went to school only to find a husband and become a kept woman. I've never seen her work a day in her life.

"You're thinking real hard, Lottie," Jasper says to me.

"Sorry, Boss," I say, a bit disheartened. "I was just looking forward to working with the colts."

"I know you were. You're damn good with those horses. But I need your help with something else today. It's a bit more, uh, strategic."

I know nothing about running a ranch, so I'm not sure how much help I could be. "I would help you with absolutely anything, Jasper. I hope you know that." In a few short months, this man has become more of a father figure than my own father has in twenty-six years.

"Let's get on up to the main house. This place has a lot of ears." He points to his ears and then looks over his shoulder and back at me and smiles. "I don't want the walls to talk. Come on, let's get some warm coffee. It's colder than a witch's tit out there."

"You don't know that, Jas. In my experience, witches are pretty hot.

It's the nuns you got to watch out for."

"Ain't that the truth."

He leads us out toward the side of the main house where the kitchen is located. You can tell a man lives here. Rugged, rough-hewn beams are exposed in the ceilings, the cabinets stained dark. All in stark contrast to the bright white walls of the kitchen. It's calm despite its ruggedness and reflects the man who is taking a seat at the long, living-timber table that takes up much of the kitchen.

"Lottie, we have a problem."

Oh no, I think. He's going to find out I'm more trouble than I'm worth and tell me to leave and not put him or his livelihood in jeopardy.

"Jasper, I'm so sorry. I didn't mean to cause any trouble—"

He interrupts me. "Whoa there, kiddo. You don't even know what I'm about to ask for."

He wants to ask me for something? I'm so confused. "Sorry. What?"

"It's not a surprise to me you've taken to this place so quickly. I knew you were a good egg the minute I met ya." I let out a breath I didn't know I was holding. "This place has needed a woman's touch for a long time."

I take a moment to look around the open-floor-plan kitchen and dining room, then through glass-paned doors into the living room. There's a solemnness to the house. Wide, expansive windows show the plains that seem to roll outward from the home. As though it were the pebble dropped into the lake to cause waves. Jasper has that kind of personality—larger-than-life, designed to make an impact, and so quiet you lean in to hear him.

"I could definitely help you spruce and update the house, but is this a strategic move?"

"Damn. No, not like that, although this is a pretty big evolution for Dappled Stone Ranch. I'm not changing the house; that's for the next man to figure out. I'd like to give you a promotion."

Charlotte

CHAPTER 3

"Okay, Little Miss Promotion!" Quinn squeals over coffee and cheesecake days after my meeting with Jasper. She waves me over to where she's sitting in the window of what used to be the old bank, but now it's the expanded home of the Flour Child, Caleb's mom's bakery and café. It's not fully remodeled, but the expansion will be open soon.

Quinn's long, dark curls fall around her flannel-covered shoulders. Her beautiful face is makeup-free. We abide by the "are we looking like homeless gremlins or cute?" texts before meeting up. Nine times out of ten, we look like gremlins, barely awake and just coming out of hibernation. She's sporting a green waffle-knit beanie from the bookstore she works at, a blue and green flannel, leggings, and duck boots with high socks. My girl looks amazing even when looking like a gremlin. It's giving gremlin chic.

Quinn went to school for communications and marketing, but she never had to work post-university. Her parents wanted to push for an arranged marriage. She's a transplant, like me. Actually, after I left, I turned into more of a tumbleweed that bounced around before I found somewhere I wanted to stay for a good while.

Quinn wanted to leave Dallas and escape the pressures her parents were putting on her. I absolutely understand that. She jokes that life at home would crush her soul like a stone crushes grain into a fine powder.

I would liken that to the vise grip my parents tried to keep me in. They didn't get me to agree to an arranged marriage, but it might as well have been. Corporate alliances are the same thing, just people building empires on the backs of women, literally. Ugh, just thinking about how close I came to marrying Julien makes me want to gag. Regardless, Quinn found her way to Silver Rapids. I'm happy she's here and I can call her my best friend.

"How does it feel to be leading the rabble? I'm going to get you a shirt that says 'Chaos Coordinator.' You can't wear it in front of Jasper, though. He's too nice; I don't want to upset him."

"He's a war vet who runs a cattle ranch pretty much by himself. I actually think he'd love it," I reply.

"At any rate, we love Jasper," she huffs and giggles.

"We do, indeed. It was kind of a shock. He took me into the main house, made me tea, and asked if I saw a future for myself." If I'd been asked that fifteen months ago, I would have said of course—moving up in the firm, getting married, kids, the whole deal.

Now?

My Magic 8 Ball says, "My sources say no."

"A future? Of course you have a future," Quinn says. *Only if they don't find me*, I think with an internal wince.

"He meant at the ranch."

"I know, silly. You seem to be really happy there. Would you want to do anything else?"

"Well, he asked if I wanted to work more on the business side. I didn't realize all that goes into running the day-to-day from the business side. I mean, I know it's a lot, but there's the politics of it. The ranch is successful, but he wants to add a second revenue stream. Wild timing, too, because I was thinking about approaching him about this idea I had."

"Ooh, tell me!" she says excitedly.

"Have you ever heard of 'eco-tourism' or 'glamping'?" I ask.

"Yes! I've done a yurt in the desert in Arizona and a few other places. Tulum was beautiful, but it's so touristy now!"

"Right. Essentially, I'd like to use some of the back property for that. There are so many people who would pay through the nose to experience this kind of life. I think that a few tiny houses built in the rustic style of log cabins, and a few yurts or tipis. I have to research a bit more on the structures between them, but from what I found preliminarily, the yurt might be the way to go in the winter—but we can have both, and folks can pick."

She's nodding along, and I can see her gears turning, too.

"They could also get training and work on the ranch, like doing the smaller things. Like that movie from the nineties. Only, we're not moving the cattle. Oh, and no kids or anything; only twenty-one and older."

"O-M-G, yes! Charlie, I bet people will love this! You could do an entire marketing campaign to reach snow and summer folk. When do you think you want to get it up and running by?"

I think for a second, then reply, "Depending on what permits and business filings we may need and how quickly we could either build or have the sleeping arrangements built, as soon as the new year, I think. Maybe that's being too loft. Even though the winters are rough, all the guys say this one is unseasonably warm, so that ground isn't as hard. So, by spring for sure, and we can start booking as soon as the plans and renders are ready."

"When do you think you'll share ideas with Jasper?" she asks.

"I was planning on doing it when I work next, or in a few days. There are some other ideas I want to put together for him." I wonder how to best pitch this. In my old world, I'd get a full business case together, do research, run through the known and unknown variables for risk, and get it together on a slide deck. I don't think he wants all that, but I will get organized regardless over the next few days I have off.

I am proud of this promotion; I love and crave praise. That's why I did so well at Seaside Financial Group. Give me a "good girl," and I turn to mush and work that much harder. If I ever went to therapy, they would probably tell me it's because I never felt good enough for my parents and constantly sought other means of validation. I'm sure I'll need a therapist—a damn good one—someday. For now, I just take it a day at a time.

"I'm proud of you, Charlie. I know this isn't what you thought you'd do with your life, but you're building a good thing for yourself here." She wraps me in her arms in a signature Quinn bear hug. "I don't know how I can help you, but if there's anything I can help with, you can put me to work."

She's squeezing me so tight, I gasp, "I can't breathe, Q."

She giggles and gives one more squeeze before she releases me. Her eyes shine with pride.

God, I feel like such a shit person. I hate that I lied to Quinn, Jasper, and everyone I've met here. I have always taken pride in everything I have earned. Adlers don't take handouts, and I am more than willing to work toward what I have, despite the nepo-baby persona people seem to project onto me. But the people here are so generous, and it makes it even harder that I can't be honest with them about who I am or the life I had before coming here.

I give Quinn a small smile, then we order the cheesecake flights—Caleb's mom's brilliant idea: heavenly cheesecake slices, a flight of four flavors. Mrs. Clark could put the finest bakery in Boston out of business. When the server comes by, I order bourbon pecan, apple pie, pistachio cardamom, and cookies 'n' cream. Quinn orders saffron rose, Nutella, peanut butter and strawberry, and pumpkin.

Cheesecake and coffee soon turns into girls'-time day drinking. We're a good bottle of champagne deep when we decide to pay our check and continue the party at my place. We both leave our cars and walk back, stopping at the market to get a bottle of rum. People think rum is a summer-only drink, and people would be wrong. Coconut rum and pineapple juice is never a bad idea; we even buy umbrellas and cherries. The drink is like a sip of summer sunshine in October.

The air is crisp, but it's not enough to kill the cheerful buzz we've got going on. There's light snow falling, but the ground still has enough heat to melt it on contact. It won't stick until probably mid-November. I love the snow. It has a quiet peace about it, falling gently around us, like living in a giant snow globe. October means the start of my favorite time of year: Halloween, followed by Thanksgiving. Honestly, it is significantly better than Christmas. For my family, Thanksgiving was like the unpretentious version of the holidays. Adler Christmas was always so stiff, and everyone tried to out-gift each other. But Thanksgiving at my grandparents' house involved tons of people and amazing food—all the best parts of Christmas without the gifts.

Fiddling with the keys, I hear Finn bouncing around on the other side of the door. Quinn is giggling like she's a damn elf working at a toy factory because it's taking me a second to get the door open. I'm trying to concentrate, damn it. I look at the human giggle machine next to me and quietly shout, "Shhhh!" and she laughs so hard she drops the goodie bag. Welp, thank God we bought a plastic bottle of rum.

"We haven't been this tipsy since Kennedy and Caleb's wedding shower!" she exclaims. "God, that was a great time. Well, except for the fact that I saw your eyes constantly scanning the crowd, looking for a certain six-three hunk o' man-meat that we call Rick. I can't believe he didn't show. What a shitty friend. Great party, though."

"Yeah," I say glibly, still trying to get the damn key in the lock. She would think it was a great time; she finally hooked up with Luke, and they've been in a situationship since. If she's happy, I'm happy.

Ah! Finally, we tumble into the house, and Finnley is there, licking at my face, greeting me like the bestest good boy.

"Hey, little man," I say between puppy kisses. "I missed you, too! Look who I brought home for you—Miss Quinn!"

He showers us both with love for a second, and before Quinn rolls around giving hugs to Finn, I smile at the thought and get a chill from a burst of wind through the open door.

"Come on, you two, let's get inside and warm up. Finn, outside." I stand up and go to the back door to let him out. I watch him run around in the small backyard while Quinn gets to work in the kitchen, making us drinks, and starts streaming our favorite Y2K pop favorites to the speaker on the TV.

Thinking we should probably get some food into us too, I pull up my favorite pizza place in town on my phone and place an order for a Kevin McAllister special for me and a veggie for Quinn.

The sound of the blender jars me, and I look over to see Quinn throwing ice and ice cream into a white mixture whirling around in the pitcher. Over the whirring, she says, "Pineapple Dream Smoothies!" Pretty sure she pours damn near half the bottle of rum into the blender. Yummm.

"I ordered us a pizza. You might as well spend the night; you have clothes in the drawer upstairs." I bring Finn back inside and get him situated with food and water. I didn't know how much I needed this day with Quinn until just now.

In college, I had some good female friendships, but they were husband-hunting the entire time. My older sister moved a few days after she graduated high school to California for university so I didn't have that fun time with her. But when I got the job at Seaside, it was time for the silly to end and it was only socially acceptable to drink outside the home at bars or over brunch.

I put on a classic film featuring our favorite problematic redheaded child actor, mute it so that it's just playing in the background, and happily accept a frothy bit of heaven from Quinn's outstretched hand, complete with an umbrella and a bendy straw.

We both get nestled into the couch, wrapped up with plush Sherpa blankets, and Finn settles between us. I take a second to appreciate the absolute genius of Tina Fey.

Quinn breaks the comfortable silence with a bomb: "Sooo, I have to come clean about something." She pauses. "I've been seeing more of Luke than I've been telling you." She buries her head in her hands. "Don't hate me. I know he's Ranger Rick's best friend, but we never talk about him, so I know nothing new about Maverick or what he's doing. And if I did, I would tell you. But also, we're not dating; it's just a casual thing for when we both have time. Only, it's been a lot more lately because you've been working so late, and I've had some free time."

I must be making a face because she says, "Oh my God, are you mad?"

"No, not that," I grit out, wincing. "Brain freeze." Then I rub my head and say, "I want you happy. We've not really talked about what you want out of your relationship with him. Or if you wanted one at all—you were pretty dead set on just hooking up. I didn't know you guys had been talking about something more."

"We weren't, until recently. And I was okay with it, but then he started reaching out more. I don't know."

"Babe, if you're happy, I'm happy for you." I absolutely mean what I say to her. Quinn has been my lifeline since I've moved here. I take another sip, slowly this time.

"I like him. But I haven't been in a quasi-serious relationship since senior year of high school. And, you know, I believe in making them work for it."

"Cheers to that!" We clink glasses and take a sip.

After about half an hour of yapping about gossip in town that she found out from working at the bookstore, the pizza delivery arrives at the house. Old ladies love to chit-chat around the fireplace and always share juicy gossip when they think no one is listening. I try to stand to answer the door but fall back onto the couch, and we both burst out laughing.

"I am drunk!" I declare. Standing back up, I shuffle over to the door and grab our food. "Let's eat at the island. Knowing me, I'll drip sauce all over the couch."

"Works for me," she says, and walks to get plates out of the cupboard. I love that she feels so comfortable in my home.

I look down at the island and flashback to my dream from a few days ago. I feel the words slip out. "He-Who-Shall-Not-Be-Named showed up in my dreams the other night."

"Whoa, what?"

"Yeah, it was hotter than hell, too." I groan, then bury my face in my hands and tell her about the dream. She knows all about the hookup because, the very next day, she called to check in on me, and I answered the phone in tears...over cooking dinner. He had been two hours late, and I knew I'd been stood up. She came over immediately. We ate the spaghetti carbonara I had made, because no way was that going to waste, got more than a little drunk, and watched baking shows to zone out. She even stayed the night.

"Oh. My. God. What? Spill! Wait! This calls for more alcohol." She gets up, runs to the kitchen to grab the pitcher, and places it on the coffee table after filling up both of our cups to the brim. She waits for me to break the silence.

I take a big gulp, then tell her all about it.

An hour later, we've eaten an entire box of pizza and drank the remainder of the pitcher. I will absolutely feel this in the morning. We decide to call it a night rather than start another movie.

She's drunk. I'm drunk, and I could really use some sleep.

"All right, let's get your bed situated," I say to her.

"I can just sleep on the couch. It's comfy here."

"Last time you fell asleep on the couch, you complained about your neck for two weeks. Let's get you into bed." I grab the blanket she's burritoed in and pull it so that she stands.

"Fine. But only because you bought a bed for me to sleep in," she protests, causing me to laugh.

We're climbing the stairs when my slippered feet almost make me fall backward—damn carpeted stairs. Who has carpeted stairs? Fuck being on the run; if my old boss really wanted to kill me, he could have just put carpet in my old apartment and watched me break my neck on the stairs.

We stop in front of her room, and I turn and say, "Bitch, I love you so much."

"I love you, you sassy bitch," she replies. "We should just get a compound with a vineyard and open an animal sanctuary."

"That sounds like heaven."

She wraps me in a tight bear hug. It brings a bit of a tear to my eye. I relish it. I feel so touch-starved. The only living things I touch are Finn and Betty White, my horse, but I think Quinn is contact-deprived, too. She doesn't even have a pet.

She turns to head into the guest room, and I call to Finnley, "Come here, buddy." He trots over, and as though he can sense it, he walks past Quinn's feet and jumps up on the bed. "Good boy. Auntie Q needs some cuddles."

She looks at me, frowns with her face, mouths, "Thank you," and makes a heart with her hands.

I blow a kiss and say, "Sleep tight," turn into my bedroom, and definitely do my damnedest to not have any sex dreams.

Maverick

CHAPTER 4

I can feel a bead of sweat spider-crawl its way down from my neck to my lower back, stopping at my jeans. We started building this fence before the sun came up, and now it's near three o'clock, and the Utah sun is baking me through my clothes. It may be late fall, and the air is getting cooler, but hard work is hard work. And at this moment, I can't wait to be done with this. I thought my days of being a cowboy were behind me, but when Jude broke his back this summer—fell off his horse training for a rodeo—I had to find some way to help him and the Cortland family.

I'm no stranger to life on a ranch or hard work. This was my whole life growing up, besides skiing, and I am painfully aware that if anyone found out that I was working at a ranch right now, they would look at me like I've grown a second head. I swore I would never work the life of a cowboy after leaving home. I was a skier. And if my whole fucking life hadn't flipped upside down right before the trials, I would've made Team USA. I'd love to make my way back there, but in the blink of an eye, I'm older and will need several miracles to get back to the team. And to be honest, I don't know that I even could.

For now, though, I'm trying to help my best friend and his family. The doctors have good hope that he can walk without his walker soon, but he's got a long road to recovery. He may never ride a horse again or do heavy lifting, but that's better news than what we were initially told when he first fell off Simba. Fun fact about Jude: he may be a bro, but he loves Disney.

I take a big breath and wipe my brow with my sleeve. Someone standing blocks the sun over me. I look up, and Jude's older brother, Sutton, has approached me. "I believe we're getting pretty close to the end of the fence up there. We just need to shore up, and we can get back to the house and get this weekend started! A few of us are going out tonight in SLC."

Yes—I need a night out, and if I play all the cards up my sleeve right, I'll find a pretty little thing to really play cowboy with.

"Works for me. Let's get this shit done. I need a night out," I say to him.

"That's the damn truth." He claps me on my back and walks over to where the wires coil around a spool, scoops to pick it up, and then walks to the next post. I like Sutton and the youngest brother, Hudson, but I've only recently gotten close to them.

Jude and I have been roommates in Park City since I moved out here a few years ago. We went to the same gym and started hanging out. He knew exactly who I was when we met, and it was nice to not have to work up to "Hey! I'm the asshole who fell off a hotel balcony, hit a tree on the way down, and fucked my life at training camp." He skied, too, but not competitively. The ski community out here is so small that if you're making moves and a name for yourself, folks will find out who you are kind of quick. Not to mention regional and national news coverage of it. Looking back on it, the number of people who track and watch the Trials and the Olympics overall—and feel like they know you or could do it better—is absolutely wild.

I need to power through this last stretch, and then I'm off for a few days. I'm not an employee, but the Cortlands pay me above and beyond what they should. Since the accident, Jude has moved back home, and I'm not delusional enough to think I could make rent on my own in our current apartment. I appreciate their help as much as they appreciate me helping them out on the ranch. So, it kills me to admit it, but I may have to get another job besides instructing this winter.

The tips are great, but the resort can only book employees for so many hours. Big families or private lessons with celebrities are the moneymakers. But most of the time, celebrities irritate the hell out of me because they feel entitled. When you're skiing, it's just you and the curve of the mountain; publicists, managers, and hype-men can't help you.

The rest of the team heads over to Sutton and me. Together, we knock out the fence within the hour. We get on our horses and ride back to the stables. I dismount Walter to walk him through the stable and to his stall, and, like clockwork, find Jude sitting on a wooden bench next to his stall with his walker in front of him.

He broke his back earlier in the summer. God, that day was so rough. It was one of the rare times that I hadn't wanted to leave Silver Rapids so soon. I wanted to see *her* that night, but Jude is my family. When I got that call, I had to leave. I'm so proud of his recovery and how much he's improved.

"Hey, trouble. How was it out there today?" he asks as he stands. I step forward and help him, then stop. His cranky ass has lectured me too many times that he "doesn't need help" and "needs to do this by himself." He grips his walking aid, brings it forward, and slowly rises to his feet. His mom put her bicycle basket on the front, so there's a cheery wicker basket with daisies braided into it that's got a beer, a horse brush, and a paperback sticking out of it.

"Eh, we got it done. Bro, I can brush Walter out. Why don't you just hang out with us for a while?" I motion to a small stool over in the corner.

"No, I've been on my ass all day. I need to move, and my mother and sister are acting like damn mother hens. I had to escape from the house," he replies. In the months since I've been helping the Cortlands, I've seen

Raegan, his sister, give him so much shit for falling off his horse, but she's also been there every step of the way, trying to help and make sure he's not pushing it so hard that he reinjures himself or is set back in his recovery.

I can respect that. I have firsthand knowledge of traumatic injuries and how long it takes to regain strength. For anyone, the process is long and arduous, but for stubborn assholes like Jude and me, it's downright torturous to expect us not to want to get back to top form. He was dead set on competing in the skijoring circuit this year to win some competitions and make a little money. There's not big money, but it's fun.

He is a rising name in rodeo, competing in calf-roping and saddle bronc riding. Calf-roping gets a lot of hate outside of the ranching community, but it has been a necessity to those working on a ranch or farm. You have to catch and restrain calves for medical treatment, branding or tagging, and check-ups. Now it's a part of competitions, celebrating the exacting technical skills that are needed to work on ranches. And bronc riding is basically an eight-second rush of adrenaline from a thousand-pound, fifteen-hand-high horse shot directly into your heart...and maybe your dick. I would take skiing down a double black diamond during the iciest conditions than trying to get on the back of a strong-willed, temperamental beast who hates to be ridden. No, thanks. Jude's a damn madman.

"Sutton mentioned there are a few guys interested in going out tonight. You comin'?" I inquire. Since the accident, he really hasn't been interested in going out. The doctors have cleared him for light activity and it would be great for him to blow off some steam, but I get the feeling from the look he just shot my way that he isn't interested in going out to the bar tonight. The last time he did, his body language was off; I could tell that he was uncomfortable.

"Nah. I think I'm staying here."

"No way, guy. I'm calling bullshit; you just said you wanted to get out of the house. Shake off that dust and have a few beers."

"I don't want to be the crippled guy in the bar," he says reticently.

"First off, don't say crippled. You have a temporary, limited-mobility impairment."

"Semantics."

"Second, who gives a fuck! Let's get you back into the world of the living. There were some buckle bunnies looking for you the last time we went out. I'm sure some would even play nurse and lick you back to health."

"Ugh, if I say yes, will you promise to never say shit like that to me again?"

"I could say yes, but I don't want to lie to you."

He sighs and bows his head, his longer-than-usual hair falling forward over his brow. "Fine, but if I'm not feeling it, I'm out."

"That's all I'm saying."

He's quiet for a while, still brushing Walter. I'm opposite him, brushing Walter's other side. He breaks the silence by asking, "What about you? Are you still hanging out with Naomi?"

At that, I groan. Naomi was a casual hookup. We've been nothing more than friends with benefits; I have never considered dating her. To be honest, I haven't reached out to or seen her in a while, and the last time I saw her, I said as much. I don't understand why people drag it out. If you know it's not a fit, why try to make it work? It's not fair to the other person in the relationship. She wanted it to be more, and after this summer, I knew I wanted something more, too—but not with her. She called me an asshole and said that I would never amount to anything. I didn't think it would hurt as much as it did, but she knew me enough to know that was the one thing to piss me off. I said to her, "Tell me something I don't know, Naomi." She got huffy and stormed out of the apartment in my favorite band tee. Am I the asshole because I just want my shirt back?

This summer ruined me. I haven't looked at any woman the same since.

"No, I told her I wanted something different with someone else. She called me an asshole, and that was that."

"Dude, that was cold."

"I didn't see the point in drawing it out. All it was was blowing off steam for me, and I thought that's what it was for her because I took her at her word, but it wasn't."

"I mean, I get that, but Naomi was so damn hot. That tight body and long brown hair...mmm. Someone's going to wife that one up real quick."

He's right. Someone will, and hopefully they'll be perfect for her. She's utterly and completely vapid. But hey, I subscribe to the idea that everyone deserves happiness.

"Yeah, hot for sure, and she knows it. I just want something more substantial."

"Whatever happened this summer really made a mark on you." He grins. "I should say, 'whoever happened.'"

He knows all about Charlotte; he was beholden to hearing it while resting in the hospital. After all, he was the reason I couldn't go back to her that night, like I had planned. I was his emergency contact at the hospital, and I thought she would understand that he is basically my brother, and I had to come back to him. I texted her as much, and she never responded. She left it on read. As fiercely as she protected Quinn from that drunk guy at Bart's, I thought "found-family" loyalty would resonate with her.

We spent the most amazing night together. I walked with her after she wanted to leave Bart's and took the long way back to her place. A few hours walking together under the summer moon, I feel like we talked about everything yet nothing at the same time, and I knew—I knew we would be perfect together. I didn't learn about her parents or where she came from, but about the goodness in her spirit, peeks into her soul. She let me teach her things about her body, pleasures she wanted but never experienced, and she gave herself to me completely. I've had good sex, great sex even, but I've never been locked in with a person before.

Those fleeting moments gave me the slightest glimpse of what a future could be with her. I thought the connection between us was undeniable, however unexpected it may have been. Sure, I wasn't looking for anything with anyone when I found her, but that simple conversation and the hours after, when I gave her every single thing she wanted, left me spent. I went to work that day with the biggest smile on my face. I left her in bed, looking like a damn temptress, and I wanted to say, "Fuck the responsibilities; I want to spend the rest of the day balls-deep in the most beautiful woman I have ever met."

She played me, though. I think the whole "I never do this" was an act, and I played right into it. Or she wasn't okay with what we did, or the way I edged and then brought her to so many orgasms when she told me explicitly that was what she wanted. I believe in consent. We weren't drunk; she was eager and wanted to explore her sexuality. We went over safe words, and if she said "Red," we stopped immediately. What a chump.

"Whatever." I sigh and continue, "I want to go out and find someone to play cowboy with tonight."

"Attaboy, there he is! Are you headed home first?"

"Yeah, I planned on meeting you guys there. I need to get home, talk to my manager from the resort, and shower. I smell like ass and horse."

He scrunches his nose and moves to sniff in my direction. Waving his hand in front of his nose, he agrees, "Bro, you stink. Get the hell out of here. I'll finish up."

I lift my arms and give a sniff test. I don't smell that bad. "You sure?"

"I'm good. Go ahead. Let me have a few moments of peace out here before I head back to the hyenas."

I laugh. "I don't know, they aren't so bad. They give a shit about you."

I walk behind the horse, clap Jude on the shoulder, and stop to put the brush on the shelf outside the stall. Walking from the stables, I pass the main house, nearing the rear barn where we park. This ranch is smaller than what I've been on before. There are some day workers getting ready to leave, too, and I nod goodbye to them as I jump in my Jeep.

I cannot wait to take a shower when I get home. But I want to squeeze in a quick cardio session first; no point in showering before a workout. I've got my gym bag with me, containing a fresh set of shorts and a tank for running. Driving back toward home, I get off at the exit and pull into the garage next to the building. I switch out my work boots for the running shoes in the trunk before grabbing my bag and walking over to the gym next to the apartment. The few seconds I'm out of the truck in the cool air raise goosebumps along my arms and legs. Now that the sun is down, it's damn cold.

I get to the sleek entrance with its black walls and bright white lights and scan my key fob. I may be tight on extra cash, but I refuse to use the gym at my apartment building. For all the other amenities it offers, they skimped on the gym equipment, so I joined the fancy gym next door. There are a couple of bigger influencers that work out there, but I try to keep to myself and get through my set. I spent so much of my life training that it's nice to keep my body in the shape it's in, but I don't need to add much more muscle. As it is, I'm as bulky as I've ever been since working with Jude's family. For a downhill skier, I was taller than the average athlete with my six-foot-three frame, but I had the speed, and that was all that mattered. Well, that and good knees—until my injury.

Thinking about skiing, I text my boss at the ski resort to check in. We've been in good communication throughout the summer, but now that the season is about to start, we'll have kickoff meetings and get updated on new or changed policies for the resort.

> Hey , Ollie, I wanted to check in and see if there have been any updates about when the season kickoff might be?

No reply when I put my bag into a locker and change into my workout gear. I pull out the headphones I always keep in there and start a playlist that matches my running pace with a good BPM.

Walking to the wall and then stretching, I see a beautiful woman at the barre going through exercises, watching me, but I'm not trying to get involved with anyone here. Hooking up with women I've met at the gym has never worked out well in the past. Uncomfortable, I break eye contact and head over to the treadmill to get some miles in so I can get home and get ready for a night out with my boys.

After a solid set and sitting in the sauna for a good steam, I feel like a renewed man. The wooden benches that line the room are empty. I pour a scoop of water over the stones and watch the steam billow up. Climbing to the highest bench, I lay the extra towel down as a pillow, stretch across the pine planks, and take some deep breaths to clear my head.

I've missed the rigors of training for something. Skiing pushed me to do something beyond myself, gave me a reason to push myself to the limits or beyond what I thought I was capable of. In the gym or on the mountain, you lose all notions and clear your mind of the surrounding bullshit. I'm in the gym damn near every day of the week, but not because I train to ski competitively; rather, because I still need to be in good shape to navigate the mountain for hours on end while instructing.

Jude used to join me in the gym most days, except days he worked, when he said that working a ranch was hard enough. He's not wrong. I think that's why we both wanted to skijor this year. It's the perfect marriage of our passions. He didn't want to just rodeo and work the ranch; he would race with me.

In some ways, I feel like the only thing I used to have time for was training. The only reason I have friends is because I already had them growing up. I missed the early part of my twenties and the college experience because I was singularly focused on skiing...and not disappointing my dad.

At the end of all that, what did it really get me? I don't talk to my dad, my mom is dead, my skiing career tanked, and I am a glorified babysitter for a few hours a day.

Damn, get out of your head, Bennett.

I need some drinks. I need some time to just let loose. And, honestly, I really need to get laid.

Charlotte

CHAPTER 5

I t takes two days to recover from the Pineapple Dream Smoothies and to prepare a full business proposal for Jasper to review. I prepared many of these for my old managers and directors, but this one feels so much more impactful. Maybe because it seems more personal? My past proposals were much more high-dollar, high-visibility projects to the firm and to my future, yet this one feels much more weighted, probably because I'm more invested in the success of this side of Jasper's business. He doesn't have disposable income the way some of my old clients did. At least, I don't think he does. From everything I've seen, he lives pretty simply no matter what he does, even if the homestead is on the bigger side.

What we do will help supplement the income to Dappled Stone and help Jasper retire so he doesn't have to work so damn hard. I know he wants to work, and I'm not sure who he even has to leave the legacy of the ranch, considering he's no longer talking with his son. But that is none of my business and it isn't my problem to deal with. I have to make sure I've run down all these numbers for projection and start-up costs appropriately.

Depending on how the conversation with him goes and whether we can negotiate pay terms with vendors, we could have the project up and running within a few weeks. The construction labor could come from the hands; there are no permits required beyond business filings.

I've been staring at my computer screen for an hour. It hasn't changed, and the proposal hasn't written itself. Finn comes over and nudges my leg. "Okay, okay. Let's get some food." I look out the window in the guest room and find that it's dusk. *Shit.* I've been at this all day and completely skipped lunch and dinner. I probably could have kept going if my poor dog wasn't insistent on being fed. I look down at my legs, and he's sitting, but his tail is whipping back and forth, knocking into the plants.

Groaning a bit from the stiffness that's taking root from not moving and just rotting in front of the computer screen, I get up and damn near fall over because my foot has absolutely fallen asleep. A change of scenery always helped when I was stuck on an idea at the office; maybe I need to get out of the house. After I get Finn some food, I determine we should go for a run.

I look down at him. "Food, then a run." He immediately sprints down the hall.

Finn scarfs his food down—I need to get him one of those slow feeders. I'm getting some kind of dinner together for myself when the sound that all dog owners know comes from the living room. Oh, no, no, no. Blech—Finn throws up his dinner all over the carpet. I hang my head, while he cocks his to the side as if to say, "Sorry, Mom, but I'm still hungry."

"Let's get you outside so I can clean this up," I say. "Bud, you've got to slow down. No one is taking away your food."

I disinfect where he puked and get some new food out for him. Then I make a note to see if I can have the feed store in town order a slow-down bowl for him. Sitting on the floor while he eats, I refill his food bowl a bit at a time so he slows down. "No run today, I think."

After I make sure he's better, I head to the ranch to make my pitch to Jas.

I get to the main house and walk up the steps, paper presentation in hand, my secondhand laptop ready and loaded with a presentation. Knocking on the front door, I wait for him to open it, but Jasper calls from the barn door, "Charlie!" I turn to him. "This way, kiddo," he directs, then returns inside the barn.

Maybe he wants to review it in the barn office instead? I muse. That works for me. I'm ready for this!

I walk into the barn and see Ace brushing his horse. "Hey, Ace."

"Heya, Charlie. He's in the office," he says.

"Thanks." I nod.

"What's that you got there?" Jasper points to my clunky laptop and folder.

"My presentation about some business ideas. Are we not reviewing that today?"

"We are, but let's talk about it out on the range."

I smirk and shake my head. I should have known that he wouldn't have wanted a fancy presentation. He wanted to talk it out first.

Jasper gets into the driver's seat of the UTV, and we set off. The smell of the trees, the sounds of the birds in the sky, and the view of cattle grazing in the field...all of it puts a pure, genuine smile on my face. The trail goes through a copse of trees and opens onto a private target range I know like the back of my hand.

A white sign with red lettering reading "Private Property: Range in Use" is staked next to a worn wooden bench. A large tote with a combination-style lock sits under a black pop-up tent that's staked into the ground. It holds notebooks, extra rounds of ammo, headphones, safety glasses, everything we need.

There's a spray-painted line spanning about thirty feet that Jasper sprayed over the last time we were here. Before that, you could barely make out the lines. Four lanes are spread across those thirty feet, with overturned milk crates as seats. I go to the second storage tote, the one that has the papers, grab a few bales of hay, and take them out to the designated target markers: one at twenty-five, fifty, and a hundred yards respectively, first for my lane, then his. The hundred-yard target is for rifles, but we haven't worked our way up to that yet, so we're just working with my Smith & Wesson 642. I'm comfortable with my revolver, but not overly confident.

Before working here, I never thought I'd ever shoot a gun, let alone have one of my own. Jas took me to the outfitter where he goes, and we picked one together. I wouldn't say I'm clumsy—other people might, but I wouldn't. I wanted something that didn't weigh a lot so that I could easily lift it, one that wouldn't get snagged when I pulled it out of the holster and had a lower likelihood of me firing it accidentally.

The first couple of times I fired at the paper targets, I did not expect the recoil, and that was just with dummy rounds. But after Jas said we could move to live fire, we focused on the way I grip the butt, my stance, and how I ground myself to the grass, my breathing, and how it affects the way I grip. I had to accommodate how I position my arms a little differently because of my boobs. "I don't know what it's like to shoot with those things on my chest, so we'll find something that works for you," he had said.

Now, he says, "Lottie, let's hear what you've got for me today."

"While we're shooting?" I point to the ear protection I've got around my neck.

"Eh, we'll shoot after." He's sitting on the bench, rubbing at his chest. "Pull up a crate."

So I do.

Charlotte

CHAPTER 6

"Are you going into town for Mrs. Wright's grand reopening? That's tonight, isn't it?" Jasper asks as we get up from where we are lying on the ground. I dust the dirt off my chest and stomach and swipe my hands over my jeans to get the dirt off my legs, too. Jasper does the same. I know he's no spring chicken, but over the past few months he seems to have really aged. Not his mind, though; that's still sharper than a knife.

I look at Jasper and smile. He loved my proposal. That feeling is damn near the best thing I've felt in a long time.

"You know it is. If I didn't know any better, I would think that there's something between you and Mrs. Wright," I say, and wiggle my eyebrows at him. "I see the way you ogle her tarts. It's the same way she ogles your buns."

He blushes and shakes his head. "No, no. It's not like that. She's got great tarts, though." He laughs and adds, "The key lime–passion fruit one is *mmm*." He makes a chef's-kiss hand gesture.

"Can I say something?" I ask, passing him a water bottle from the table next to me.

"You're going to whether or not I give you permission, so out with it."

"It wouldn't be a bad thing. You and her? You could use someone to spend time with, and she's sweet."

"I don't think that's a good idea." He says it in such a way that it's final.

I don't know why he would be opposed to it; she seems like a charming woman. But he knows the history of everyone here far better than I do.

It makes me sad, though. I've come to love and cherish this man more than my own father. He's the kind of man that any child would dream of having as a father. Man, I wonder why his kid doesn't talk to him.

"Fine. Just one thing—one thing." I put my pointer finger up. "I wanted to let you know that I've noticed."

"Noticed what?"

"That you've been limping a bit, nearly favoring your left side, and I saw you grabbing at your shoulder. And there's no one up here but yourself and—" I pause. "And if you need anything, you call me. Promise me. You've taken me in and treated me far better than my own father. I would hate for something to happen to you." I don't tell him I overheard him taking a call in his office when I was getting some things from the pantry closet last week. On speakerphone, the doctor had said, "Oncologist referral," and I walked away. That was none of my business and I would never invade his privacy like that.

If he has an inkling that I know something is wrong, he's not going to tell me, and that's fair enough.

"If I had a daughter, I would hope she would be as amazing as you, kiddo. I'm here for you, too." He looks like he's about to say something else when he gives a huff. I hope I didn't speak out of line with him. "Let's get back to the house so you can get on the road."

We're silent on the drive back, but it's comfortable. I take in this beautiful land sprawling out all around me with the afternoon sun's rays on my face. I feel at peace with the decision I made to stay here.

When we get out of the UTV, he says, "I wouldn't turn down a treat if you wanted to bring something back for me tomorrow," and nudges my elbow.

I smile. "No problem, Boss."

The drive home goes by in a blur, which is crazy. I don't really remember it. Though I know I didn't, what if I hit an animal? I wasn't even paying attention, but my eyes were on the road the whole time.

I pull into the driveway with just enough time to let Finn out, get his dinner sorted, throw some dry shampoo in my hair, and change. I rush upstairs, grab a clean pair of pants and a sweater, then snag my makeup bag from the counter before letting Finn back in.

Whatever makeup I can manage in the truck will have to do—maybe just some mascara, lip stain, and a little blush. It's a far cry from what I'd wear to an event back home, but hey, you do what you can, right?

"Mama will be back soon, baby!" I call out to Finn before rushing back to the truck.

Without any major traffic violations, I get to Main Street fairly quickly and see that Flour Child is jumping! I was not expecting so many people to be inside when I rounded the corner to the bakery. Caleb and his mom went all out with this.

I don't remember hearing from Quinn that it was going to be a full party, but damn, maybe I should have dressed up a bit more. They have the local newspaper here for coverage of the event. I recognize the photographer trying to grab photos before the sun goes completely down. When I first got into town, he kept asking me out, and he tried again right after the festival. That was post-Maverick, and I had no desire to be around men. The biggest TV station in Wyoming is in Cheyenne, on the opposite side of the state, and I doubt they would send anyone out here for the reopening of a bakery. No matter how beloved it is by the community.

I call Quinn on speaker. Verne's engine is loud as I drive down the busy street. He's not fancy; in fact, he's basically a dinosaur, but I love that about him.

She picks up just as it goes to voicemail. Her twangy drawl answers,

"Bitch, where are you?"

"I'm trying to find a parking spot. Every single spot on the street is taken. I should have just walked. Oh, there!" I pull into a spot—well, technically, I think it's a spot. There are no signs prohibiting parking. I check for a fire hydrant, too, and don't see one. "This has to be a spot, right?"

"I don't know. I can't see you. I think it's okay. Come on, they're about to cut the ribbon."

"It'll be a sec; I am a few blocks over. The place looked like it was packed," I tell her.

"It is! It is so cute. Luke and his crew did a fantastic job with the renovations. And a heads-up, Luke, Caleb, and Jake are here. Ranger Rick is not, but wanted to let you know they are."

"It's fine. My issue isn't with them. It's with Ranger Rick. They didn't lie to me." I walk around the corner. "Ah, I see you." I disconnect our call, and she runs to greet me with a hug. She almost lifts me off the ground, and we walk back arm-in-arm to the café.

"Damn, girl." I squeeze her arm.

"I know, I've been enjoying the access to the gym in the apartment building," she says. Quinn radiates good vibes, and my girl loves a reason to dress up, even in our small town. She's got more curves than a switch-back mountain. If I didn't know any better, I would swear she wears shapewear under everything, but she's just built like Jessica Rabbit with chocolate-brown hair and warm, emerald-colored eyes. It's fifty-something degrees out, but she's in an ivory, short, ribbed sweater dress with thick black tights and flannel boots. Meanwhile, I'm in some fleece teddy bear pants, a thin brown sweater, and a quilted vest. I definitely went with the cozy look, and she looks like a million bucks.

I feel even more underdressed when Luke comes out behind her and says, "Ayo! Now it's a party. Heya, Charlie." He's wearing black jeans, a crisp white button-down, a black vest, and a cowboy hat.

"Hey, Luke."

He steps up to give me a fist bump. I've come to terms with the fact that he and Quinn are in a situationship, and whatever they do is for them to figure out. She's happy with it. I've also come to terms with the notion that just because he's friends with Maverick doesn't mean they're the same. So, for now, he and I are cool.

"Congrats on this," I say, motioning to the café.

"Thanks. It's all the crew."

"Ah, don't listen to him, Charlie. Wait 'til you see the inside. He drew all of this up for Mrs. Wright, and it looks just like the drawings."

I look over to him, and I think her words of praise made him blush. Red is creeping up his tattooed neck to his ears.

The sun has set, but some uplights shine from the window boxes, showing off the new sign and the updated interior nicely.

The bank vault and the deposit boxes can be seen from the arched cutout that leads to the expanded seating area. Mrs. Wright and Luke went with varying shades of creams, greens, warm browns, and black for the color scheme, and it feels very organic with the exposed brick, with a bright buffalo watercolor painting along the far wall and gold accents throughout.

Caleb and his mom are speaking with someone, but I catch his eye, and he gives me a smile and a nod. He calls Luke over to join them, and after he excuses himself, I watch Quinn give a little, contented sigh.

The whole town seems to have come out to celebrate. There's an acoustic singer and guitarist set up on a small, raised platform near the bar area. I remember Caleb mentioning a space for open mic nights and that kind of thing.

The singer is killing a rendition of a Stevie Nicks song, and the guitarist is adding his own flair to it. And damn, he's fine. There's something beautiful about someone doing what they love with passion.

Quinn catches my look toward the singer and guitarist. "They're good, right?"

"Where did Caleb find them?" I ask. "I haven't seen them around before."

She's encouraged me to get back out there since the fiasco with Maverick, but honestly, I think that was my cue to keep my head down and focus on me.

"Let's go check out the band and get their socials."

"I told you, I don't do social media," I mumble. And for damn good reason. I have always been a private person, but I felt pressure from Mother and her publicist to have a picture-perfect life. It was a reflection on her if her daughters didn't show how perfect their life was. It was exhausting to live up to that kind of pressure. Right after the announcement of my engagement to Julien, I stopped posting and just kind of abandoned it.

Yet another reason to abandon my socials: that's how I found out he was cheating on me. More than one woman DMed me to tell me he was just with them. And when confronted, he said they were jealous of what we had and that he only had eyes for me. Against every instinct in my gut, I believed him. We were always together, and I didn't think there would have been time for him to cheat. But when I messaged the women back, it was always during working hours or on trips. It's horrible to say, but I wasn't even that heartbroken because I realized I wasn't in love with him anymore—or maybe ever. I broke off our engagement with little fanfare. I tried to give him the ring back, but he was so indignant that I ended up keeping it. It's at the bottom of the jewelry box with my fun costume jewelry. It was a five-carat, perfect emerald-cut solitaire. Beautiful, clean lines, but not my style at all, and I think he knew that. But, like everything else, our relationship was about him, not us.

Also, I don't want a single person from my old life to find me. My old boss, his goons, my family—everyone can stay far away from me. I shiver a bit when I think about how connected Allister is with the Irish Mob. Though the connection was only through screens and friends of friends, when I came to him with the accounting errors I found and went back to work, and he did nothing about the issue, I kept my eyes and ears open. Surely somebody besides myself would have noticed. A few weeks before I left Boston, I saw him at a restaurant with Brady, a known enforcer and hitman. I did my best to stay away from him at that point and tried to work from home as much as I could. I've always had good intuition and felt in my bones that something was wrong after that. The vibes were not vibing, and I started packing things up and going through the motions.

Quinn rolls her eyes and holds her phone out to snap a selfie of us.

"You're not going to share that, right?" I ask her.

"I know the rules, even if I don't understand why." Bringing her hands up, she makes air quotes and says in a mocking tone, "'No sharing on social media. My life depends on it.'"

"Yes, exactly. I'm not being overly dramatic or trying to be cryptic, I just can't tell you why," I reply.

"Okay, fine. But I want to post a faceless shot, so let's grab a drink and cheers."

The bar doesn't have a line, so we grab a drink. An Old Fashioned for her, and a Manhattan for me. Turning to the singer and guitarist, we hold our drinks out, and Quinn snaps a photo. She puts a filter on and posts it. The guitarist notices and gives us a wink and a smile, acknowledging us.

The singer, with her sultry, raspy voice, says into the microphone, "Okay, ladies and gentlemen, Ezra and I are going to take a quick break. At the request of Mrs. Wright and her staff, please enjoy the bar and the baked goods!" Everyone claps, and they leave the stage.

Ezra. He looks like an "Ezra." He wears a faded band tee with rolled sleeves and a pair of jeans. I notice he's got on a pair of Converse and not cowboy boots; that's kind of out of place around here. Especially as the temperatures cool down—no one is wearing canvas shoes.

He catches me looking at him and gives me a warm smile. And, shit, he's walking straight toward us.

He clears his throat and says, "Hello, ladies." His voice is deep and silky. It's the kind of voice that wraps around your entire body, and the kind that, if he whispers your name, would make you shudder. He says something else, but I don't hear him.

"Sorry, what?"

"I said, 'Excuse me,'" he repeats, then motions to the bar. And then he just stands there.

"Oh! I'm so sorry. Of course." I move out of the way.

Quinn watches this interaction with a smirk. I feel a blush take over my face and neck, then spread all the way down to my feet.

"Quinn, let's go find Luke," I suggest, then whisper to her, "That was so embarrassing! Why didn't you pull me out of the way?!"

"I'm letting you have a fun meet-cute with that guy. Ezra's a fun name."

"I don't need a fun meet-cute." I don't need a meet-cute at all.

"You need to get back out there. It's hard to do that when all you want to do lately is work."

I love working. It gives me a sense of purpose. I have a stellium in my sixth house that rules work and routine.

I sit with that for a second. I am definitely in need of a damn good orgasm, and with all the toys I have, I know how to get myself there in seconds. But a long, drawn-out night with a man could absolutely do me some good.

We find Luke standing next to Caleb, Kennedy, and Mrs. Wright.

"Your man did a fantastic job with this, Q," I say conspiratorially.

"I know, right? I mean, no, he's not my man. We're just friends."

"Yeah, mm-hmm." I elbow her. "You don't look at him like you're 'just friends.'"

"We're both happy with where things are right now."

"If that's the truth, then I'm happy for you. Do you think you would ever want to do marketing for Flour Child or help him with marketing his business?" I motion toward Luke.

We continue to watch people approach our friends and congratulate them on the renovation reveal.

"I've thought about it, but I don't think that mixing business and pleasure, or whatever this is, would be a good idea."

"I can respect that. But you have such a creative way of thinking and seeing things; I think you should think about it. When I shared the business proposal with Jasper, he loved the idea of the marketing. I told him I got a lot of that from you."

"Aw, I'm so glad Jasper liked it. I know we've only been in each other's lives for a short time, but I hope you know I only want good things for you. And since you've started with him and taken on the additional responsibilities he's given you at the ranch, you've changed, in a good way. Like, you've turned into a savvy businesswoman."

God, I hate lying to her.

"Yeah, it's been good. And I know you want good things; I want those for you, too." The alcohol might be making me emotional at the moment, but I add, "I don't know that it matters the length of time you know someone, whether months or decades—your soul knows when it finds someone it's meant to find. You're my soul sister." I look into her forest green eyes, now rimmed with silver, and see she's gotten a little misty-eyed, too.

Wrapping her arm around my middle, she pulls me into a side hug and squeezes. "I love you so much, Charlie."

Luke, Kennedy, and Caleb come over to us. Mrs. Wright says, "Okay, gang. Let's get a cute picture for the mantel before everyone leaves. Caleb, give me your phone." He hands her his phone, and everyone scoots together.

"She doesn't have any social media, does she?" I whisper to Quinn.

"Yes, but it's only ever pictures of baked goods and latte art."

"Okay."

"Say, 'Flour Child'!"

We do, and she takes a few photos of us.

"It's still pretty early in the night; I could have one more drink," Luke says to Quinn. "Can I get you anything?"

"Yes, we can definitely have another drink. Right, Charlie?"

"I have no plans; let's do it," I say. "But I need some food. I have tried none of the new pastries."

"What are you girls drinking?" Luke asks. Quinn tells him our order, and I peek over her shoulder to see that Ezra is still at the bar, talking to the bartender.

He notices me and says something to the bartender, shakes his hand, then comes over to me and says, "Hey, I'm Ezra. Sorry if I seemed like a jerk earlier; I just needed some water." My God, that voice! He should be the singer. I notice there's no Western accent, though; if anything, maybe a hint of Midwestern.

"No, I'm sorry. I wasn't really here, ya know? I'm Charlie."

"Is that short for Charlotte?" he asks, which is kind of weird. What else would it be short for?

I laugh. "It is, but no one uses it."

"I like 'Charlie,'" he says. He smiles and crosses his arms across his broad chest.

I do my best not to let my gaze linger on his veiny arms or hands.

Or the way his biceps look in that rolled-up T-shirt. He's got a pleasant smile, too, just a touch of stubble with full lips and white teeth. Nice amber-colored eyes and thick but groomed brows. But, God, the way I love men with veiny arms.

"You guys have a great sound. I haven't heard you guys play around here before."

"Thanks," he says. "This is our first gig in town, but hopefully not the last."

The singer comes up to him and says, "We start in two."

"Okay, Isa."

"Charlie, hon," Quinn calls to me, causing me to turn around, "we are thinking of Bart's after. Sound good?"

"Uh, yeah. That's good with me."

She nods and gives me a cheeky wink.

"Well, I have to get back to the set. It was nice to meet you, Charlie. Maybe I'll see you around." He sticks his hand out to shake, and I take it.

I don't know why I say what I do next, but the words "You should come out to Bart's after. You know, if you're not busy or anything" come out of my mouth as I walk away from him and head back toward my friends.

"I'll be seeing you, Charlie."

I don't turn around. Leave them wanting just a little, am I right?

"Mrs. Wright," I say, giving Caleb's mom a hug. "This is wonderful. Congratulations!"

"Ah, all I did was pick some paint samples. Caleb and Luke did the heavy lifting." She moves her kind gaze to her son and my friends, who are over by the door. "You guys headed out?"

"Yeah, is that okay?"

"Oh, please, dear. You guys go have fun." She gives me a light squeeze.

"Ah! I have a little package for you to take to Jasper."

"Yes! God, he won't let me in the door without some goodies."

She goes behind the wraparound workbench and comes back with a white box tied with a black-and-white-checkered ribbon. Unless she's changed the packaging, she made it fancy especially for him.

I smirk and take them from her. "Thank you."

"Don't mention it. Now, get out of here. And don't let those boys in that box tonight. Those are special."

That's it. I will not be happy until I get these two together.

I walk out the door and tell the group, "Guys, give me a sec. I need to drop this off at the truck."

Quinn is on her phone, and the guys are looking at Caleb's phone. Everyone is attached to the damn things.

Quinn notices me and says, "All right, all right, all right! Let's get goin'!"

"I need a drink," Luke says in his deadpan way.

"Me too, guy," I say. We walk to the bar, and I think I wouldn't mind if a certain guitar player comes to find me. Life has to start again at some point, right?

Maverick

CHAPTER 7

I t was damn good to get out tonight with Jude and his brothers. He wanted to stay out, and I'm sure as shit not going to be the one to tell him no. It was hard enough to get him to come out with us! But it was just an onslaught of bar after bar after bar.

With his general swagger and personality, he won over a lot of sponsors on the rodeo circuit. But that also means the man is enjoying the female attention that comes with it. He's a playboy, and the man loves a buckle bunny.

I was like that when I was young, training. I didn't have time for a relationship, and it turned into just sex with whomever I was hooking up with—great sex. But just sex. Sex has merely been something I associated with a good time, definitely not intimate, typically no cuddling or anything beyond what's deemed un-asshole-like.

Tonight, there was no shortage of girls I could have brought home, especially since Jude has been staying with his family while he recovers from his back injury, but I just wasn't into it. As much as I wanted to get my dick wet tonight, I found reasons not to pursue any woman. Shit, there were two of them who flat-out said they both wanted a good time. I pointed them toward the guys.

I wouldn't say I want to settle down, but when I get the itch to get with someone, I'm reminded why I'm so damn unlucky with the opposite sex. Sometimes, I feel like that just gets to be a little much.

The boys wanted to hit up one more bar. I wanted to get home and crawl into my bed.

The air is chilled and blowing through the parking garage of our apartment complex, whipping my scarf around. I button my pea coat and then stuff my hands in my pockets to keep warm.

I climb the stairs up to our floor, my blood pumping and warming me. As I get to my floor, I reach for my security key fob on the key ring to let me in. As soon as I get into the apartment, I feel my phone vibrate. Then again. And again. I pull it out to see what's going on, and the "Gold Not Silver Rapids Bros" group chat is popping off.

Caleb: You guys, look at the space! We had a full house tonight.

Luke: Dude, I was there.

Garrett: It looks great. Congrats, guys!

Yes, you guys def gave it new life. Congrats.

Caleb: Yeah, I know you were there, Luke. The other two were not. Go dance with Quinn.

Luke: It's hard to go to dance when my phone keeps buzzing. Damn group chats.

Caleb: You could mute it. You CHOOSE not to. You love us too much.

You guys are probably in the booth, sitting across from each other.

Caleb: *sends pic* Actually, no. We're about to watch a certain someone take a ride on Brutus.

Luke: I still haven't told her bc you're one of my best friends, but you could and probably should come visit and just casually drop in on a night where we're all together.

I told you, it was just a summer thing. She has moved on.

Caleb: But you didn't.

Garrett: You came to the damn Middle West and were still heart-eyes for the girl. I'd be happy to shoot my shot, bro.

Caleb: Other guys around town have heart-eyes now, too… you snooze, you lose, bro.

I don't want to know anything about what's going on with her.

Fuck. Fuck. Double fuck. I know she's there. I've known she's been in Silver Rapids this whole time. They know I don't want to be kept up-to-date on the comings or goings of Charlotte. But maybe that's what best friends are for—to love you and to piss you off by helping you face the truth. I've known them all for so long and we text all the time, even if it's just about trivial things.

Garrett's in Ohio working as a corporate accountant; he stayed there after going to Notre Dame for lacrosse. He comes home when he can, but I know he loves his life away from this place too. Like me, he too felt stymied. Caleb, Luke, and Jacob are still in Silver Rapids, so they would see her regularly. And that's just the thing—I've asked them repeatedly to leave me out of whatever she's got going on.

Exhibit A of why I have no desire to date. I damn near caught feelings for a woman I knew all of twenty-four hours. I know there are stories of people who fall in love in that amount of time, and this is not that. But I would be lying if I said she didn't completely enrapture me. Enough so that I was dumb enough to believe the bullshit she spewed to me about "I'm not usually this kind of girl."

Lies—utter nonsense. She certainly didn't suck my dick like someone who wasn't experienced. I mean, who has a damn treasure trove of sex toys in their nightstand, still in their packaging, just waiting to be tried out?

I got played, and by the time I went back to Silver Rapids, she had already moved on. I told Luke and Caleb not to mention me, especially because Luke doesn't shut up about her best friend. I'm not trying to come between whatever they've got going on, but I got fucking played. I cannot think about this chick another minute. And yet, the universe keeps putting her back in front of my face.

I look at the picture Caleb sent...again. She looks hot as fuck, though—even in her casual state.

Like every other woman, she left before she ever really knew me. All the women in my life end up leaving me somehow. And if she ever asked about me, surely someone told her enough to make her stay away. Especially since the whole town treats me like a pariah—the same town I'd have to return to if I wanted any kind of relationship with her.

Mom and Dad worked damn hard and sacrificed so much for me to get as far as I did, to ski in the Olympics. Such a waste—a lot of time and even more money. I was already named on the team roster because of my finishing time at the Grand Prix. I worked my ass off to get high enough in the standings to get named early. Mom never got to see that, though. She didn't get to see me race in the later years at all. She died when I was twelve.

I was to leave for the Games within the month and was training with other teammates and hopefuls. I needed to stay sharp, supporting the guys who were still battling it out. Staying close to the team wasn't required, but it helped build camaraderie. I've known a lot of these people since I was a teenager. It's competitive, but I wanted my friends to do well. In a stupid moment, I got drunk and was looking out at the mountain, lost my footing, and fell off a damn balcony. A third-story balcony. And I hit a tree. My entire career went up in smoke, blown in just a moment because I got sad my mom wasn't there to see my dreams come true.

Obviously, I was dropped from the team. Not because I was drunk, but because of my injury; I lost my sponsorships because I was drunk. You have to carry your own health insurance, and the team covers you while you ski with the team. But because I wasn't at camp or participating, and was training on my own with my personal coach, it took a lot of persuasion and him pulling every single favor he could to have the team cover the costs of my rehabilitation.

He couldn't do anything about the loss of sponsorships and what came after, though. Media fallout; my image was ruined. It didn't matter that I could have rehabbed and returned to the sport. Nobody wanted me afterward, and my coach, by the grace of whatever gods, was able to get me an instructor position.

My entire life—what had consumed my every waking moment—gone in a stupid accident. Hours of my life, every day, every weekend while the kids were having fun, I was on my way to and from the mountain. It was all over.

What morbid shit to think about before bed.

I turn on the TV and slink onto the couch. In a world where there are hundreds of channels, I can't find anything to watch.

"Ugh." I groan out loud and slam the remote on the coffee table with much more force than necessary.

I fill a glass with water and take it with me to my room. As I'm brushing my teeth, I get a text from Dad. He's always been a night owl, but there's no way he would know I'm up, so he probably meant for me to see this first thing in the morning.

Dad: Hi son. Mrs. Wright and Caleb had their re-grand opening. You should call or send a nice note congratulating them.

I know. Caleb sent me photos. I said congratulations.

Dad: But not to Mrs. Wright.

I had planned on sending a card later this week.

Dad: That would be nice. I bet she would appreciate that.

Dad: Or, you could come home for a visit. Or just to claim what's yours. Or work the land.

I have a job I like, Pops.

Dad: Teaching kids and rich tourists how to ski

the bunny hill isn't how we saw your life going long-term, kiddo. Your mom and I always hoped you would grow to love the ranch. We hired a new ranch hand, Charlie. Real smart, lots of big ideas for this place.

At his mention of Mom, I immediately close my messaging app and turn my phone on silent. Good for Charlie; let him run the place. I want nothing to do with Silver Rapids. I brush my teeth and check my phone one last time before I put it in sleep mode. One more text from Dad.

Dad: I love you, son. No matter what you do or where you are. Good luck on the slopes this season.

Thanks.

I don't deserve anyone's love, least of all the man who has sacrificed so much so that I can "teach kids and rich tourists" how to ski.

I fall into a restless sleep and end up staring at the ceiling for the better part of the night.

Charlotte

CHAPTER 8

"**L**et me get your dinner together, sugar," says Janice as I pay for my dinner at the Bluebird Diner. The diner is a true mid-mod, quintessential gem. It has a retro interior, but it's original, not designed to resemble an old-school diner. The counter stools are chrome and sky-blue glitter vinyl, and they spin! I love that whenever I come in, it feels like stepping into a slice of Americana.

I did not have the strength to cook tonight. And the soup du jour is brisket tortilla. I know the soup rotation like I know the back of my hand. It's nice that I can count on it being consistent. They have staples like chicken noodle and the five-alarm chili every day, but whatever they put in this brisket tortilla soup is addicting.

I look out at the truck. Finn's sitting in the front seat, looking out the windshield, tracking my every move. What a good boy.

Kennedy, Caleb's wife, is working behind the counter and talking with Sheriff Hayes. I go over to say hello while I wait for the soup and a slice of caramel apple walnut pie. "Hi, Kennedy, Sheriff Hayes. How are you guys doing?"

"Hi, Charlie!" Kennedy says. "I haven't seen you in a hot minute, darlin'. Sheriff Hayes was just telling me that there have been a few break-ins lately."

"Hi, Charlotte. You making sure you staying safe? Locking the doors and keeping your curtains or blinds closed when you're not home?"

Sheriff Hayes asks.

"Oh, no. That's awful. I keep everything locked up tight." I nod. "Just break-ins? No one has gotten hurt, have they? I haven't heard of anything happening." The hairs on the back of my neck are standing up, and a horrible sense of dread sinks to my stomach.

"Could just be drifters. But they'll find out real quick that Silver Rapids folks don't like to be tangled with. I'd be real careful, though, Charlie. It happened not too far from where you stay. With break-ins, they case a neighborhood or a street before moving on. You make sure to keep an eye out. You see somethin', you say somethin'. And keep a piece on you, if you have one."

I pat under my arm where I keep my handgun tucked in its holster beneath my coat. I've never had to fire it at anything other than practice targets, but if a bear, cougar, or some other predator ever came after the cattle or chickens, I know I could take the shot if I had to.

"Good, that's good," he says.

Janice comes over with my soup and pie. "Here you go, sweetie."

"Thank you," I say to her. "You guys have a good night. I will be careful, Sheriff." I wave as I walk out the door into the night.

It's been three weeks since I reviewed the proposal with Jasper. After I tear into this food, I need to research more on the exterior and interior of the cabins. I want them to be perfect. No, I *need* them to be perfect—a balance of modern sustainability with the wildness of the West, the open sky, the mountains, and the wide plains. I was excited about breaking in the colts, but I am even more excited about this because I get to own the project from start to finish. I just have to get some food in me first.

"Come on, little man. Let's go." The rusted truck door creaks open and catches in the wind. It flies open, and I send a little thanks to the spirits because I didn't have an extra hand with my bag and the food.

Finn jumps out of the truck on my side, and I push the door closed with my butt. We walk up the driveway to my cozy little home. He's playing in the snow when he goes rigid and stares at the house. The screen door is slightly ajar. I'm not expecting a package, and anyway, the mail carrier usually leaves my packages on the swing. Maybe someone new was delivering today?

Walking up the stairs of the porch, I don't see a package, but I do see wood splinters on the welcome mat Quinn and I painted. *Oh, no.* I pull the phone from my pocket and call Finn over, heading quickly back to the truck. I'm not about to be the girl who dies in the first fifteen minutes of the movie.

Sliding into the driver's seat, I dial 911.

The operator answers, "911. What's the nature of your emergency?"

"Hi, I live at 434 Hill Street in Silver Rapids. The front door of my house has been busted open and I think someone has broken in."

"Okay, darlin'," the man on the other end of the line says to me. "Just stay calm and stay with me. Are you in a safe place now?"

"Yes, I went back to my truck. Should I drive away?" *Breathe. Breathe. Breathe.* Oh, my God. Sheriff Hayes said no one got hurt, but what if they're looking for something? What if they're looking for some*one*? "I think I'm going to go back downtown."

"No, you can stay there. I've alerted a deputy, and they're on the way to you. You're lucky; they're only a few blocks from you. Just stay with me."

"I'm freaking out. I'm freaking out." I'm crying; Finn is sitting on my lap, trying to calm me down. I focus on my breathing and pet his fur.

Soon, I hear the sirens coming, and the man on the phone is still talking, but I can't hear.

Sheriff Hayes's truck and a squad car with its lights and siren on pull up to the street. He gets out of the truck and a woman gets out of the car. He walks to me and she goes up to the house.

"The sheriff is here," I tell the operator.

"Okay, ma'am. I'm going to let you talk to them. Good luck."

I open the door and shut it before Finn can jump out. I lean against the truck because my knees damn near give out.

"Charlie, I didn't think I'd be seeing ya so soon. I'm so sorry. My deputy is checking out the house now to make sure there's no one in there. Okay?" the sheriff says.

I can't say anything, so I just nod my head while tears stream down my face.

The deputy comes out and walks over to us. "There's no one inside, but they left quite a mess. It looks like they turned over a bunch of stuff, but only you'll be able to tell us what they took, ma'am."

"Okay."

"Charlotte, I'm going to go talk to Deputy Ellis and call dispatch. Just stay right there, all right?"

I nod and sob silently into my hands. My first thought is that I am so glad I brought Finn with me to work. My second thought is that they've found me. I don't know how, but they've found me.

I dial Quinn's number; I've memorized it by heart.

She picks up on the second ring. "Hey, baby girl. What's—"

"I need you. Can you come?" I'm nearly in hysterics.

"Of course! Where are you?"

Sobbing, I can barely get out the words. "I'm home. Someone broke in."

"Oh, fuck. Sweetie, I'm on my way. I'll be there in five minutes. Are you okay?"

"No. I'm freaking out." I'm shaking so hard my teeth chatter.

"Okay, okay. Stay on the phone with me. Let's just breathe in and out."

Someone knocks on the window of the truck, and I scream.

"What?!" Quinn says.

I look out and see Sheriff Hayes motioning for me to get out of the truck.

"Okay, well, we got two things. We can have someone out here to help put a lock back on the door. It looks like they used a crowbar to get in. But also, a man was found trying to break into the Morgensterns' house a few blocks over, and Bill wrestled him and knocked them out. Damned ol' fool." He gestures up the steps. "We can walk through the house with you right now."

"I don't want to go in there." I shake my head.

"No problem. You don't have to go in right now, but we are going to need a report for all the things that were stolen. And you'll have to get it together for insurance. But, Charlie." I look at him. "You don't have to do that right now."

"I called Quinn Langley; she's on her way over."

"All right. It might be good to stay there tonight or for a few days. Or maybe you can stay at the ranch for a little—"

"Charlie!" Quinn calls as she gets out of her car. I run over to my friend and fall apart all over again. "You poor thing! What kind of asshat does this?!"

The deputy says, "Hi there, Quinn," as she walks to where we are gathered on the street.

"They think they caught the guy at the Morgensterns' house," I say flatly. I'm hollow, void of any kind of feeling except terror and dread.

"Oh, thank God." Quinn looks at me. "Honey, you and Finn are going to stay with me while we get this sorted." She stays in an apartment above the bookstore on the corner of Main and 5th Streets. "Let's just get you an overnight bag, and we can get pizza and get drunk tonight."

I nod. "Thanks, Q. I'm, uh, going to take you up on that," I say. I'm exhausted; this just took all the wind out of my sails. "But I don't want to leave all my stuff in the house without a lock, though."

"Oh, honey, we can call Luke, and he can come secure this place." She looks to the deputy, whose name I still don't know. "Is that okay?"

"Oh, yes, I can stay here until Mr. Draper gets here."

"Q, can you get my stuff, though? I don't want to go in there." Tears start falling again.

She hugs me even tighter to her. "Babe, I got you. I got you. We'll get properly drunk tonight and come back to clean another day."

"I can stay with her, Quinn, if you want to go grab her a bag."

"Baby girl, I'll be right back." She walks over to where the sheriff and another deputy stand by the porch, taking pictures. I know I'm shaking a bit, but on unsteady legs, I push off her car and go let Finn out of the truck. He jumps out but doesn't leave my side as I walk back to lean against Quinn's Lexus. Then I think, *Fuck it*, and slide to the ground to gather Finn into my arms.

"I'm sorry," I say to the deputy. "I never got your name."

"Oh, I'm sorry." She sits down next to me. "I'm Deputy Avalon Ellis. We met briefly at Caleb and Kennedy's shower, but I didn't look like this." She motions to her uniform and copper hair in a bun.

"Oh! Yes. You're friends with Kennedy. I'm sorry, I'm not really here right now."

"You just had a serious violation of privacy and trust. I wouldn't be here either." She gives a sympathetic smile. "I would be a puddle on the ground crying, so just standing or sitting upright seems like a feat, if you ask me."

Quinn comes out of the house with two giant bags and my rolling suitcase. "You do not need to go in there. I got everything you'll need for a few days and then some." She pulls me up and gives me a hug with tears in her eyes. "I'm so, so glad you weren't here, Charlie." She squeezes me so hard, her petite frame damn near lifts me off the ground. "I texted

Luke, and he'll be here within half an hour. He had to get some lumber for the door. On the way out, Sheriff Hayes said we don't have to stay. Let's get you warmed up and get some tequila in ya."

I do not deserve her.

"Thank you, Q." I lean my head against hers. Turning to Avalon, I say, "Thank you, too. I'm, uh, sorry I didn't recognize you earlier."

"Don't sweat it."

"Hey, Sheriff Hayes, I'm going to take our girl to my place now, mmkay?" Quinn calls over to the sheriff.

"One sec." He walks down the steps and crosses the small yard to hand me a card. "That's my number. If you need anything, call me. I'll have a report that you can share with your landlord, but you likely won't need it. I'm sure word is going to spread to everyone in town, including him."

Oh God, I do not want any attention on me, especially not with this.

"Thanks." I reach out and shake his hand, but he doesn't let go.

"I think you should tell your boss about what happened and take tomorrow to figure out your next move. Jasper would understand if you needed to take some time."

"I'll, um, think about that." I need this job; I can't just not show up for work. I'm not salaried, so I only get paid when I work. The sheriff is right—I'm sure Jas would hear about this, and I would want it to come from me—but not tonight. No, tonight I want to get drunk, take a shower, and cry. Maybe get drunk in the shower while crying. What is my life?

I wake to a text from Jasper the next morning.

Jasper: Do not come in to work today, Lottie. I saw Sheriff Hayes and heard all about it. Take the day. Also, there's a new arrangement that we need to discuss when you come back to work.

I'm coming in today.

Jasper: No, you're not. I don't have anything for you here today.

Boss, I'm okay. It'll help me focus on something else.

Jasper: If you really want to do something, you could start packing up your things in boxes because this new arrangement has you living in the back cottage so you can be here full-time.

I'm stunned. I don't want a handout.

Jasper, that's really so generous of you, but that's not going to happen. I like having my space and my house.

Jasper: This is part of the new work arrangement. You're going to be puttin' in the hours and here more with the project, and this solves the issue at hand. Unfortunately, I will not be taking no for an answer.

Quinn comes into the living room in pink plaid flannel pajamas, her hair wild, squinting her emerald eyes. We hit the tequila hard last night, and I definitely had a really nice, long cry in the shower, which would explain the pounding headache, except I don't know if it's from the tequila, or crying, or having my little semblance of peace completely shattered.

She sits on the floor pouf next to me and puts her head on the armrest of the sofa. "Baby girl, I hurt so bad," she says.

"Jasper is making me move into the cottage on the property."

"Good! That's good."

"But I didn't want to live on the property, and I feel like I would never see you anymore." I take a deep breath to try and center myself. "I'm trying to do this myself."

"Sweets, we're going to be old bitties together, telling the other how hot we used to be. Jasper just wants to help you. I think this is a good idea."

"I guess it's what the universe wants for me. Even with my gun and all the practice I've had so far, I don't think I want to stay in the house."

She's stroking her hand across my head while I look up from my makeshift bed. "I think you're meant to be on the ranch. Everything has led you to this moment. The spirits want you there."

I groan and roll over toward the back of the couch. "Ugh, I did not want to spend today packing."

"Babe, it's a new moon. A perfect start for a new project and to set intentions, kind of perfect for this energetic shift in your life. We can close out this chapter and start your new chapter on the ranch with a new moon ritual and cleanse our auras."

I'm into the metaphysical and spiritual, but they've never guided me the way they guide her. I roll back over and look at her. "You really think this is the right move? Literally?"

She giggles. "Yes, and besides, you don't really have a whole lot to move."

"But I finally felt like it was my own little place."

"Release what no longer serves you, baby. I feel like this is a good sign."

She glides her hand down one arm, casting off unseen energies clinging to her, and then again on the other side, as if she's cleansing herself.

I know she's right. I feel as though what I've been working toward and what I've been running from is leading me here.

"Fine, but you, my love, are helping—after we eat some breakfast."

"Deal."

We spend all damn day packing up my little house on Hill Street. I was only here for a short time, but it makes me melancholy as I pull away from one of the first places that felt like home.

I've been in the cottage along the far property line for two weeks. Quinn and I had packed everything and arranged it in basically the same placement I had at my house. She's back tonight to help me get the last bit settled. We put on some Stevie Nicks, pull oracle cards, and sit on the porch in the rocking chairs to enjoy the moonless sky full of stars, cuddled up in blankets with mugs of hot chocolate.

I thought that Ace would have an opinion about me moving onto the property, but he was really supportive. He and the guys even pitched in and got me a housewarming gift: a vintage etched crystal vase stuffed with flowers. Being here has felt so much like family. The transition has been a lot smoother than I could have ever hoped for.

Ace, Clint, and Hank have been teaching me to rope cattle. I practice on a metal sculpture that resembles a calf. I'm not great with a rope, and I get tangled up every time I go to fling my wrist and release, but they haven't given up on me.

Jasper has been amazing. We're putting resources into the project, and we finalized the internal and external designs of the eco-cabins. I have never felt so supported at work. Permits for temporary dwellings and the business filings have been submitted and are in the approval process.

With that stage completed, I've been able to spend more time with Jasper and learn more about the business. He comes to my cottage, and we play chess almost every night. We've been working through an inspection process to join a co-op and he's been telling me about his life here as a kid growing up. This life is slower, more intentional. It feels like this time here is healing parts of me that spent so much time worrying about everyone else and what they needed or wanted before my own needs. And now? It's just slower and more deliberate. I'm waiting for him to show up for the night, tea and biscotti from Mrs. Wright ready.

I had to go pick up the cheesecake for tomorrow's Thanksgiving dinner. Jasper gave everyone the option to head out on Wednesday and come back on Saturday, but most wanted to stay here, relax, and enjoy their days off. For those who stayed, Jasper has an all-team Thanksgiving dinner. That just makes me respect him even more. The cattle will be fine in the field for a few days.

We're having slow-roasted brisket with pulled pork, mac and cheese, greens, and I was shocked to shit when Ace said he was making the cornbread. He had several chairs and tables brought up to the house from storage this morning. Ace also mentioned that Jasper loves apple pie, but Flour Child was sold out, so I got caramel apple walnut instead. It's close, right?

Charlotte

CHAPTER 9

The steady beeps of the monitors hooked up to Jasper set a rhythm for me to breathe in and out to. Breathe in for four, hold for four, breathe out for four, hold for four. Repeat. It's hard to believe that this man has only been in my life for a few months, but in that short time, he's become more of a father to me than my own. He's come to love me and truly see me more than the man who should have.

After our Thanksgiving dinner, he started coughing up blood, and Ace raced him to the hospital. Ace tried to call, but after the bottle of bourbon I shared with Hank and Clint, I had to go to bed. He showed up early the next morning to tell me, and I've been basically living here for the last two days.

There is a reading light next to my chair that emits a glaring, bright white glow. Even though the shade is rolled down, I can tell that the sun is trying to cross the horizon and is slowly creeping its way through the world, telling everybody to wake up. But how can I wake up when this is a nightmare?

Good men shouldn't die this way, surrounded by machines, with no family, no warmth. That's why I couldn't leave when they told me it was time to go after visiting hours the past few nights. The nurse knew I wasn't family, but said that I could stay as his "daughter." He had an emergency contact listed from when he last stayed at the hospital years ago. While he was still conscious, Jasper asked them to call the number listed. I'm not family, and I do not know who it is, but I hope they come.

He's still sleeping when the charge nurse comes in to take some vitals. I unfurl myself from the sleeping chair to sit up a little straighter and ask her, "How is he doing?"

"It's hard with these things, dear. With the cancer so advanced, sometimes the body just needs rest, and sometimes it's close to the end," she says, but not unkindly. Just a matter of fact, something she sees every day: people leaving this Earth, people being born.

She gets his vital information and records it on the computer.

"Has there been any success in getting in touch with his emergency contact?" I ask her.

"I thought you were his daughter?"

"Uh," I stammer. I don't want to flat-out lie to this woman. But I am not saying anything that's going to get me kicked out of this hospital room. "Um—"

"She is; in all the ways that count," Jasper rasps out. He's got the bed controls in his hand, raising the top half into an upright position.

"Jas!" I say.

"Then, no, ma'am. We've not heard yet." Of Jasper, she asks, "Are you feeling up for some breakfast?"

In a typical Jasper way, he replies, "I'd love some bacon and a Bloody Mary."

"The bacon I can get you, but the booze? That would be a trick or two. How about some water or juice instead?"

"I'm just playin', darlin'. I don't drink vodka. Maybe a whiskey and some oatmeal with brown sugar, chocolate chips, and some thick-cut bacon."

"This isn't a bed-and-breakfast, but I'll see what I can do." She looks over to me from her mobile cart. "If he needs anything, push the red button on the side of the controls." She points to the remote control in

Jasper's hand. "That notification goes to the main station, and we'll be back here right away."

"I think we'll be okay for a little while longer yet," Jasper says.

She nods to Jasper, but to me, she gives a stern look as if to say, "Call immediately if something changes." Then she packs up the cart and wheels it out the door toward the patient across the hall.

"Heya, Lottie. What are you doing here?"

"I couldn't leave. I told them I was your daughter, but I'm pretty sure they know that I'm not. How are you feeling?"

"Like death."

I choke out a sob that's like a laugh, too, tears escaping. "That's not funny!" I don't do well with these types of situations. I laugh at the worst times, or don't have any emotion at all. Which one is worse?

"Lottie, it's how I feel. It has been for a while. I was diagnosed a year and a half ago. I wanted to fight, but three different doctors said it was too advanced. There was an option for experimental treatment, but it was in Cleveland. I'm not leaving my home to go to Ohio. My life is here."

"What's left of your life. You don't know; it could have worked, and you could have still come back here. Or maybe it's not too late. Could you still take part in the trials? I can stay here and take on some more—"

"It's hard for you to understand. And that's okay. The world is still young and new to you," he says. "But the world, it's not been kind to you. I know, kiddo."

Sobbing, I wonder how he can just give up on his life. "You don't know."

"Yes, I do. Look at me. I have something to tell. I've wanted to tell you for a while." He pauses. "And I know it might not have been the right thing to do, but I wanted to know who I was working with. That day in the Bluebird, when I hired you. I had a feeling that you needed help."

"Jasper, what are you talking about?" I blink away more tears.

"Charlotte Clara Adler, twenty-five, of Boston, Massachusetts. Daughter of Ellen and Bruce Adler, owners of Seaport Real Estate Group. Top of her class at Waverly University in Economics and Financial Analysis... Graduated at twenty years old. Younger sister of Georgina. You lived in a fancy high-rise condo that overlooked the Boston Common, and you were engaged at one point. You wanted to be an interior designer, but ended up going into finance. That's where it gets muddy. You were on the fast track at Seaside Financial Group. A big muckety-muck. You're damn smart, Lottie. But you left there quick, fast, and in a hurry. You damn near have more money than I do saved up."

"How do you—"

"I figured something real bad had to have happened for you to come all the way out here, looking lost as a person could be. You paid the waitress in change that day. That truck of yours is damn near falling apart. You live damn modestly in that little house. I don't see a trace of the girl with fancy clothes or the watches, or Range Rover. It was hard to find your old Instagram, you know?"

"Jasper, you don't understand." I hesitate. My entire world went sideways in the last sixty seconds. "How did you know all this about me? Did you tell anybody? This is really bad. I have to—" I move to stand. He puts a hand out to stop me.

"One of my best friends is like a brother to me. He's a government contractor. His job is to find people. I asked him to look into you."

"But all I told you was my name. How did he get the rest of it?"

"Lottie, when you spend your youth in the Army, you focus on the details. I got the number from your license plate. He pulled a trace to a junk trader in Pennsylvania. And he hacked those records and found a sale in Pittsburgh for your Range Rover. The rest was pretty easy for him to find after that."

"Why?" I think I'm in shock. I stand up. "If anyone knows where I am—"

"Don't worry, honey. He knows how to make it so that no one will know where you are. Your secret is safe here; you don't have to tell me what happened."

"Oh, my God. They're going to find me. My boss at the firm—"

"They're not going to find you. Owen is good at his job. Someone would have to see you with their eyes in order to find you. He deleted all traces of you after you left Boston. You went on quite the road trip, didn't you, little one? North Carolina, New Orleans, Texas, Missouri, then here." He says this all like he's not talking about my life over the past sixteen months. It's not surprising how calm he is. That's his nature.

"There's a reason you stopped in this town. I think it was to help me. Having you at the ranch these last few months has made me so happy. Hell, even teaching you how to shoot. There were ulterior motives there. I want you to be able to take care of yourself." He looks to my hip. "Do you have your gun on you?" I nod. "Good. I always thought I was going to share this with Reid, but he hasn't been home in a while. He never wanted this kind of life. I hope that he's happy doing what makes his life right. Sharing my knowledge of what I've spent my life doing means it wasn't for nothing—that someone will know how to run things after I'm long dust in the ground."

"Oh, Jasper!" I reach for his hands.

"This life is a hard one. Lonely too. Always worrying about something else's needs before your own. But it brings a sense of purpose to make sure the livestock are well taken care of. That we provide something to them in return for their lives."

He starts coughing, and I go to get him some tissues.

"I believe all this happened for a reason, Lottie. Even if we don't know what it is just yet."

He's right; the sense of purpose I've found while I've been working here has helped soothe parts of my soul I didn't think could be saved. I have lived so much of my life while in the dark. Scared of every single time I would come home from the ranch to someone waiting in my house. Or every time a car turns a little too slowly in front of the drive. Or, fuck, just waiting in the shadows while I'm out in the pastures.

I can't catch my breath; I'm shaking from the realization that someone knows me. My hands have gone cold, despite the warmth in the room. I dig my nails into my palms when I make a fist and then release it over and over again.

"Lottie, it's okay. Come here." He's got his arms—hooked up to the IV and machines monitoring his vitals—outstretched, inviting me for a hug. This man is dying, and he wants to comfort me.

I have never known comfort like that.

I go to sit on the bed, careful not to jostle him too much, and give him a hug.

That's when it really comes pouring out. I cry and cry and cry. I cry for me, for a life that wasn't really what I wanted but was a life I could live with. I was too scared to stand up to my parents and pursue what brought me joy. I chased a paycheck instead. I cry for what my life could have been. I cry for Jasper.

I don't believe in God. Could the concept of God exist? Sure. Maybe. I disagree with what we call the existence of something more. Spiritualists, religions, mathematicians, they all call it something different but don't deny the existence of something. I believe in spirits and in following the signs the universe puts in front of you. I know I found him. All the horrible things that have happened in the world have led to this moment.

He's patting my back while I'm falling apart. Breathe in for four, hold. Breathe out for four, hold. Repeat.

Honestly, I don't know how long we sit there, just hugging.

I pull my arms away slowly so I don't bump his IV. I take a big breath in and sigh.

I see I left tear stains on his gown. "I'm sorry. This is a lot. I'm not usually a hugger." I sit back further. "Thank you." I breathe.

"No, Charlotte, thank you. I haven't had a proper hug in a long, long time."

It baffles me why his son would ever want to leave this place, or him.

"Now. I need you to make some notes; this is important. I'm the one with the business proposal this time."

Over the next two hours, he explains that he wants me to take over the day-to-day operations of Dappled Stone Ranch. That he believes in me and my ideas to bring the ranch into the next evolution of what it could be.

"The lawyers have all the information they need from me. When the time comes, you just need to sign the paperwork. They have some contingencies in place depending on if my plans for the land work out the way I hope. And if not, they'll know what to do."

"No, this is too much. I—" I'm kind of dumbfounded right now. "I can't accept that, Jasper. That's your life's work. And there's still so much I don't know about the ranch other than what we've been working on. I can't." What is he thinking? I don't even know where to start unpacking this, or what this means for me. I don't even know if I can or should stay.

"Knock knock," says Quinn. I texted her to sneak in some pastries and bacon from Flour Child and the Bluebird. "I have treats for Mr. Bennett. And a coffee for you."

The three of us play cards and cribbage for a while before Quinn has to get to work.

Jasper falls asleep after dinner, and I doze off at some point, too.

The night nurse comes back in to get more vitals. The steady beeping doesn't even register in my brain anymore.

It's been such a long day. A long couple of days, truthfully. Quinn has been looking after Finn and is staying at the house with him when she's not at the bookstore.

"Sweetie, we're winding down on visitor's hours," the nurse tells me. "You can go home and come back in the morning if you'd like."

Jasper rouses. "Lottie, go home. Give some hugs to Finnley and sleep on a proper bed. Take a shower; you look awful."

"You're one to talk, old man."

"I know it."

"You're sure you're going to be okay?"

"Yes, I'm not dying tonight."

I give an exhausted sigh. "That's not even a little bit funny."

"I wasn't tryin' to be," he admits. I know he has had a much longer time than three days to process what's going to happen, but it makes me lament over the time he's spent knowing about this and not telling anyone. He's a strong man, but that can't be easy. "Listen to me—go home. There's nothing you can do here but worry, and I don't want to watch you do that."

Ah. That's it, then. He wanted to do this alone. Maybe he wants some privacy?

"Okay." I stand up and squeeze his hand. "I'll be back first thing in the morning."

Maverick

CHAPTER 10

I'm just walking into my apartment with both hands full of groceries when I feel my phone buzz in the pocket of my coat. Whoever it is will have to wait a few minutes.

I hear the ping letting me know they've left a voicemail, but honestly, after this day, I don't want to talk to anybody. And the only people I talk to know to text me, so it's nobody that I would normally talk to anyway.

I put the paper bags of groceries on the countertop before the handles break off. After I unpack the cold items and put the dry goods into the cupboards, I make dinner. I appreciate all the new appliances and the way everything has its place. It's so different from how my childhood home was, with vintage and estate pieces. I got in trouble if I broke something because it was important or an heirloom, and I get that, but when Jude and I moved in together, we definitely had newer apartments in mind.

I know this is cliché, but I don't always love steak. Growing up on a cattle farm means you have beef every which way possible. But tonight, for whatever reason, a steak looked delicious. I roast some carrots and broccoli with lemon and Parmesan cheese.

I open the sleek cabinet door and pull out my favorite whiskey. I pour a few fingers into a cut-crystal glass from a decanter Dad got me when I turned twenty-one. It has a "B" engraved right in the center. It was the one time I can remember sitting down and having a drink with Dad.

We were in the living room. There was a fire, and it was snowing so hard outside, but it was sunny—typical crazy April Wyoming weather. It looked like we were in a snow globe.

I had just had another knee surgery and couldn't get up and down the stairs, so I was sleeping on the couch for two weeks. I think I spent more time with him during those weeks than I have since I was in high school. We watched every single '80s and '90s movie in existence during that time. I made them more outlandish just to see if he would leave, but he never did. The walker I had to use helped me to be mobile, but Dad was there every time I had to take a piss. I couldn't turn around without him lurking somewhere, either in the kitchen or the office, or my makeshift bedroom.

That was just before the other accident. Before I lost the sponsorships and everyone just "knew" that I was going to make it to Team USA. Damn near the whole town donated money to my training fund. I know Mom and Dad had money, but most everything they made from the ranch went back into the ranch or my college education. Even though I went to Colorado State University through their online program, it was still expensive. They didn't want me to have loans, and I was training every single minute I was awake.

I've got a few more days at Jude's ranch until I transition full-time to work at the resort. My boss sent me a message letting me know that I'm not on rotation for the ski school yet. Maybe I can get a few more days in at the ranch in the meantime.

I get an incoming text from the guys back home.

Caleb: We miss you, Mav!

Luke: You know, it's a hell of a lot easier to get on your nerves when you're home. You could visit us sometime, you know?

Hardly, I think. The last time I visited, I damn near fell for a woman. And the ensuing mess was not enough for me to want to pursue her after that.

I almost turn my phone on "Do Not Disturb," but realize I should check the voicemail.

Over the speaker, it plays: "Hello, this message is for Reid. My name is Kelly from Silver Rapids General. You've been listed as an emergency contact for Jasper Bennett. We've left several messages. We'd like you to call us back as soon as you receive this message."

Several messages? I haven't gotten any fucking messages. Eh, I don't think, anyway. But I go to my deleted messages—I cleared everything out this morning—and, sure as shit, I have five messages from the hospital under a suspected robocall number.

Fuck! Dad is in the hospital and has been for three days. No one from the ranch thought to call me? Fuck. It's almost 8 p.m. and a five-hour drive home, if the roads aren't bad. It's not where my mind should go, but I just spent like $150 on groceries. I'll have to charge gas on a credit card to get there and back, and maybe take the groceries with me so I'll have something to eat at the house. Or freeze what I can? I don't really know because my mind isn't making sense of anything right now.

The hospital should have a nurse on duty, no matter the time, so I call the number the nurse left while I get an overnight bag out from my closet and pack a few changes of clothes and some essentials and get my travel kit together. I've got enough for two or three days. I doubt I will need anything else.

"Hello, Silver Rapids General Hospital. How can I direct your call?" answers a man with a far-too-chipper tone of voice for this time of night.

"Yeah, I'm looking to get information on a patient, Jasper Bennett. I missed a call from the hospital earlier."

"Certainly, I'll route you to the ICU. One moment."

Intensive care. Why would he be in intensive care?

The hold music is atrocious. It's the same at every doctor's office; the corporate Muzak does nothing for anyone except make them throw the phone against the damn wall.

"Hello, this is Kelly. How can I help you?"

"Hello, Kelly. This is Maverick Bennett. You left a voicemail for me regarding my father, Jasper Bennett. Can you tell me what's going on?"

"Certainly—however, I'll have to confirm I can release information to you. His chart lists Reid as an emergency contact."

"Yeah, that's me. That's my middle name."

"Oh, well, sir. We've been trying to reach you—"

"I know. I didn't get your messages, and this is the first time I'm able to call you back. What's going on with him?" I ask, irritated that this woman thinks she can make me feel bad because I didn't call her back sooner.

"I'm so sorry to tell you this, Mr. Bennett. But your father collapsed at work and was brought in three days ago. He has been diagnosed with stage four lung cancer. I'm afraid that he does not have much time. He's asked that we reach out to you to make you aware. Mr. Bennett will be moved tomorrow to palliative care. He has a DNR and has started end-of-life care." She pauses. "Sir, are you still there?"

"Um, I—yes," I say and sit on the corner of my bed.

"Sir, if I may suggest, if you would like to see him in person, I would recommend you get to the hospital in the next few days."

"Uh, okay."

"Is there any message you would like to leave, or would you like me to transfer you to his room?"

"No, that's okay. I'll be there as soon as I can."

"Very good. Goodbye, sir."

I slide off the bed and sink to the floor. And for the first time in a long time, I cry.

I sit there for a long time, just looking at the same spot on the ivory carpet, replaying every single conversation with my dad that I can remember. All the way back to childhood. I want to get up and go to him. But I'm paralyzed to this spot on the floor for hours.

I have to get up now.

I pick up my bag, get a cooler bag from the linen closet in the hall, and pack up the groceries I just bought, along with some ice packs to keep it cold and a few water bottles and energy drinks for the road.

It's nearly 2:00 a.m. by the time I get my stuff into the back of the Jeep and get onto the highway. I text Jude.

> Hey, I'm going out of town for a few days. I just got a call from SR General. My dad is in the hospital, and it doesn't look good. I don't think you're coming back to the apartment anytime soon, but I locked everything up. Can you make sure Walter is looked after?

> Jude: My man, I am so sorry to hear that. And of course. Have you talked to your dad yet? I know you guys aren't close, but try to call him and check in?

> We haven't talked in months. He texted the other day. "Wish you would come home soon. But I know it's a fool's hope. I have a new head ranch hand that's been real nice to have helping me. Have a good season, son."

> Jude: Did you respond???

> Yeah. I said, "Thanks."

I see bubbles pop up, indicating that he's typing something, and then they go away, then pop up again. Then nothing. He doesn't respond.

I didn't know what to say back to my dad other than "Thanks." What was I supposed to say? "Sorry I'm such a fuck-up." Or, "Sorry I didn't live up to your, or anyone else's, expectations." Or the one I would never tell anyone, ever: "Sorry, I want to come home"—if for no other reason than to repair any kind of relationship we had.

I can't really think about any of that right now, and yet that's all my mind wants to wander to. I don't need the GPS to tell me how to get home, but I turn it on all the same. And a playlist to keep me from falling asleep. I need something to distract me for the next five hours.

They'll all be sleeping, but I text the guys from home.

> I'm on my way home. My dad is at SRGH. They said to get home ASAP. I don't know much more right now, but I'll keep you updated.

Then, I toss my phone into my bag.

It took almost six hours, with the weather, to get here. I pull into the parking lot of the hospital. It's full already. It'll be cold enough to leave the cooler bag in the car, but I bring a water bottle and one of the energy drinks with me.

I spent a lot of time in this hospital with Mom when she was sick. But I'm not exactly sure where my dad is, so I stop by the registration desk.

"Hello," I say, my voice hoarse from lack of use. "Can you tell me where Jasper Bennett's room is?"

"Let me see." The woman at the desk looks up his room number in her computer system. "He's on the third floor, room six. You'll take the second bank of elevators past the fountain, go up, and then turn right."

"Thank you."

I walk toward the elevator to find the hospital is busy at eight o'clock in the morning. Pushing the button triggers so many emotions rushing into me. This is the same button I would push when I would come visit Mom after school. I knew it was coming then; I expected it. This? I didn't expect the call this time. I bounce on my toes, waiting for the world's slowest fucking elevator.

Getting on, I try to slow my breathing, form a game plan for what to say to him when I see him. You think that I would have done that in the hours of driving up here, but I couldn't focus on anything. It was almost like I was numb.

I get off on the third floor and head right. The smell of disinfectant and the sterileness of the sage-green and mauve wallpaper along the walls hit me again with a feeling of pain. Mom was on this floor for a little while. I remember Dad taking me shooting after a particularly hard visit. It was like he knew I had so much rage, so much anger, that I had to let it out. Not even skiing or being on a mountain could quell what I was feeling. My mother was being ripped away from me. And now, my dad is too.

The nurse at the desk stops me. "Hello. Can I help you?"

I'm really not trying to be an asshole, and even though I could find the room on my own, I say, "I'm looking for room six."

"Ah." As if a light goes off, and she's remembering who the patient in room six is, she says, "It's the third room on the left."

I nod in acknowledgment and keep walking.

The door is closed when I come upon the room. *Breathe.* I try to peek in through the small glass window, but there's a curtain wrapped around where the beds are. The kind you usually have drawn when you're sharing a room. I thought maybe I could see him before I went in, and I'd know exactly what to say or do. Well, that plan went to shit.

I don't knock on the door. I slowly open it and hear the beep of machines and my dad talking with someone. A doctor or nurse, maybe?

Pulling the gray-green speckled curtain back, I don't know what to look at first. My dad, who looks absolutely awful, hooked up to a bunch of machines and monitors, or to the woman who, in no uncertain terms, looks like she would rather I be dead: Charlotte Fucking Adler.

Charlotte

CHAPTER 11

J asper's taking a sip of the whiskey I snuck into my water bottle. I put it in one of the white styrofoam cups they give you with the best ice nuggets in the world. That's the only thing good about hospitals.

The nurse gave him a dirty look when she smelled it on his breath. He's dying—what does it matter if he wants to eat ice cream for days on end or get drunk while he's in the hospital?

He waved her off after she got a little huffy.

Before I went back to the ranch, I stopped at the store and picked up his favorite bottle of whiskey. I know he has bottles at home, but it didn't seem right to get into the liquor cabinet and bring him a bottle. I also bought some sunflowers, put them in a canning jar, and brought them to put on the window ledge. The view of the mountains is stunning, but even a man might like flowers every once in a while.

He said something that broke my heart even more than it already was. "Nobody has ever given me flowers besides Marie. Thank you, Lottie." Then I started crying again.

For being the ice queen everyone always thought I was, I have been more emotional the last few months than I ever have in my whole life. I think it's because I could never show emotion, let alone *have* emotions. My mother showed no sort of feelings toward my sister or me. How she never showed that she cared at all that my father was always sneaking around is beyond me. But that's what the people expect of an Adler:

perfection. At almost every cost.

Yet another reason my life out here, while unexpected, has been my saving grace.

"Have you given any more thought to what we discussed yesterday? I know it was a lot to throw at you, and I wanted to tell you earlier, but the timing was never quite right. How do you tell someone, 'Hey, I know you're in a bad way and that's why I pay you in cash,' or 'Hey, I'm dying of cancer'? That's not a great segue into riveting conversation."

"I get it, but Jasper," I scoot closer to his bed, and the chair grates across the floor, "I wish you would have told me sooner. We could have found some options or worked together to—"

"Lottie, there's no use going on about the past; it's not going to change. What I can do is ensure the future of my ranch is in the best hands—that's you, darlin'."

I give an exacerbated, frustrated sigh and slam my head onto the bed. "Argh."

He pats my head. "All right, get your notebook out. The little one you always carry around." The man is so goddamn observant. "I've been making a file with all the important stuff to know: who to go to, what to file, and when. You'd likely call it an SOP." I laugh at that. He would of course know that I would call it a standard operating procedure. He continues, "I've also talked with Ace about this. That man agrees and has no desire to go round and round with the circus anymore. He'll be the one to help you find your feet."

I am still trying to wrap my head around this. Jasper believes in me. It's a great feeling, but damn if I'm not terrified.

"I also thought you would appreciate this. You'd be a bit more off-grid when you take this over, as well. I had it drafted so that an LLC would be the managing partner; your name wouldn't be on anything public-fac-ing, but it's filed away with the bank, lawyers, and muckety-mucks."

That is so damn thoughtful. At every turn, I feel, in my experience, that people are mostly out for themselves. This man may restore my faith in the goodness of people.

I'm looking at his face now. With some wrinkles around his eyes and the gray of his beard even more prominent because he hasn't shaved in a few days, he looks so tired in a way he didn't just two weeks ago. Or maybe, now that it's really coming—his death—he doesn't have to pretend anymore.

Looking into the eyes of a man who has done and lived so much, I ask, "Jas, why me?"

"Because you've shown more grit and determination than most people around here."

I sit with that for a second and have to disagree. I laugh. "Hah, I appreciate that, but there's no way that I have any more grit or determination than the other folks around here. It's not an easy life living out 'in the West.'"

"You're right, it's not. I know it wasn't what it seemed, but it looked like you had a pretty nice life. You left and tried to make a start here. Hard as it is, you found this life, and it chose you back. Don't get me wrong, there's a lot of good people around here, but they're from here. They know what it means to be from here. You? You're working on it. And anyway, I'm the boss for a little while longer."

"Yeah, Boss, you are," I quip, and we both laugh.

"I'm tired. I think I'm going to rest a bit more. Make sure they wake me when breakfast comes."

"God forbid you miss a chance at bacon."

"Live your best life while you can, Lottie."

Jasper falls asleep, and I start reading a book that Quinn left here for me. It's the second in a dark romantasy duet that is Dramione-coded. It's angsty, and the hero doesn't just come in and save the girl; she saves herself. I can't handle real life right now, so escaping into a fantasy book will definitely help me escape this reality where a good man is dying. Sure wouldn't mind a hero swooping in to save me from this.

I'm damn near done with the book when I hear Jasper's voice.

"Hey, Lottie."

I look over to him, but his eyes are still shut. "Yeah?"

"In case I can't say it later, thank you. For everything."

I reach over to push his hair back off of his forehead. "No thanks needed. And anyhow, I'm the one who should be thankful—"

I'm cut off by someone coming into the room and pulling the curtain back.

"What the fuck are you doing here?" The man's eyes track where my hand is on Jasper's head.

No. No fucking way. Maverick enters the room, and I am just about to lose it.

"You!" I shout at him.

"What are you doing here?!" he snarls again.

"Reid, calm down. This is Lottie. She's the ranch hand I told you I hired over the summer. She's been a big help."

"Dad. What are you talking about? You said his name was Charlie."

"No, I said the ranch hand's name is 'Charlie,' which is true, but I usually call her 'Lottie.'"

"I don't care what you call her. Why is she here?!"

My head ping-pongs back and forth between the man who has become like a father and Maverick.

"Your name is Maverick..." I pause and emphasize, "*Bennett*?!"

"Yes."

"Oh, my God."

"You two, uh, know each other?" Jasper looks between us.

"Yes," we both say at the same time.

"Jasper is your dad?" I point to Jasper. "This man is your father?"

"Why? Did you fuck him on the first night, too?" he asks instead of answering my question.

"Maverick Reid Bennett, watch your damn mouth!"

"Ew, no!" I turn to Jasper. "Eh, sorry, Jasper," I say, then, turning back to Maverick Freaking BENNETT, "No, I'm not sleeping with your father." I shudder, then cross my hands across my chest at the accusation and get so fucking mad that I am pretty sure steam is coming out of my ears.

"Then what are you doing here at eight a.m.?"

"She works for me, I told you."

"I don't see the rest of the crew here, just her." Maverick points a finger at me.

"Hey, I don't know what the hell you're talking about, but I have been here for days. Days! I heard the nurses say they left you message after message. Stars above know that you're way too busy to call or text anyone back. What have you been doing that you're so busy that you can't get to your dad's bedside while he's in the damn hospital?!"

"I was working! And the number that called went to spam blocker."

"A likely excuse," I admonish.

In the background, I can hear the beeps from Jasper's heart rate monitor getting closer and closer together. A nurse rushes in, the one who got huffy earlier this morning. She yells, "Okay, I'm going to need you both to leave if you can't calm down. This yelling is not good for the patient."

Oh, no. I look over to Jasper, and he's got his eyes closed tight.

"Shit, Jasper."

"Dad," Maverick says and rushes to the side of the bed opposite me.

The monitor evens to a more steady rhythm, but I feel like I might be the one to have a heart attack.

"It's okay," Jasper says to the nurse. "I think I know what's been going on."

She says to Maverick and me, "I'll let you two figure it out, but one of you has to leave."

What? I mean, okay, so Maverick is his son. And NO ONE told me. The guys had to know who his father was. I don't know if Quinn knows.

I need more than a minute to sort this out.

"I'm, uh, going to leave you guys to catch up, Jasper. I'll drop by the barns and see what Ace has got going on and if I've missed anything. Call me later if you need anything or want me to come back. Okay?"

"Lottie, I'm sorry about this. But we'll talk later about everything."

I give him a hug and kiss his cheek. He hugs me back. I feel it to my toes. "Bye, Boss."

I grab my stuff and don't even look Maverick's way when I walk out the door.

I park along the fenceline to the main barn and see Ace. He gives a whistle, and I wave.

"Heya, Charlie. I just got a text from Jas. He said you might be out of sorts. Something about you and Mav getting into it, eh?"

"Um, yes, actually. I didn't know that Maverick was Jasper's son. It's not like there are pictures of him or anything around the house."

"I didn't realize you knew 'im. He hasn't really come around much, and no offense to Jasper, but he's not exactly everybody's favorite."

"What does that mean?"

"I think it's best that he or Jasper tell you. But I will say, he put his dreams in front of everything else and left Jas in a bad way here."

I don't really know how to interpret that, but I'm damn sure going to ask Jasper tonight when I get back to the hospital.

"Okay, fine. Let's talk in the barn; it's cold as hell out here. I'm not dressed for a walk right now. I was expecting to be with Jasper all day. There's a bag of my clothes in the lockers. I could run up to the bunkhouse and put another layer on."

"Nah, let's get to the barn. Finn would probably like to see ya."

We walk back toward the barn. He walks ahead and opens the door. "Thanks," I almost say, "You don't have to do that," but think against it.

"There's no beating around the bush here, because there's not much time. Did Jasper talk to you about taking over the operations here?"

"That's what I like about you, Ace, you just get right to it. Yes, he did. I don't really know what to say or do at the moment. That's not very capable, is it?"

"You may not feel ready, but you have a team. There's an entire team here ready, and," he emphasizes, "more than capable to help you run this place. Jasper trusts you; that's more than I can say about a lot of other people. You know him now, but Jas does not trust easily. He sees 'it' in you. I do too. And so does the crew. You see this place differently, and what it could be, not just what it is."

I swear Ace's words are going to make me cry.

"And besides, it's not like we're letting you go." He gives me a wink and a pat on the back. "Let's go to the bunkhouse and get the crew together. Jasper gave me instructions, while you were away, to explain the situation to them. Not surprisingly, they're all on board. You've entrenched and wiggled your scrawny ass into the heart of everyone here. Except maybe the new guy, but he's only a day worker, and I'm sure you'll figure him out."

I breathe slowly, mindfully. Lately, I feel that all I'm good for is converting oxygen to carbon dioxide because I can't get my feet beneath me. But—and a big but—maybe this is supposed to happen. I love my life in Silver Rapids. I love what it could be here.

The bunkhouse is lively, and the crew is gathered for lunch. Most of the time, we take lunch into the field or eat when we can, but everything is thrown off with Jasper in the hospital, and I guess this is where I can help. Before, I would have pulled my team together for a regroup and planned new strategies to attack and find the solution to our problem. This is no different. I am good in a crisis. *Except when the crisis is your life.*

Right.

Ace whistles, and everyone settles. "We all know that Jasper isn't coming back," he begins.

I almost choke on a swallow, trying not to cry again. I look at the team and see all of them, every single one, has silver lining their eyes. Hardened men and women, cowboys, lamenting the impending loss of the man who has worked this land with them.

"And he's made damn clear his wishes. Charlie is going to be taking the helm to take the ranch to the next level. You already know about the changes we've started to make to the property with them cabins, but I'll tell you this now: any one of ya that have an issue with this, you're free to leave now. This is the wish of a dyin' man, and I'll keep it."

"We're gonna miss the boss, but he saved my life," Hank says with his twang. "And Miss Charlie, if he says you're the new boss, you're the new boss. I'm staying, if you'll have me."

"Me too," Clint says, crossing his arms. A chorus of "Me too" and "I'm staying" sounds off from around the room.

I'm overwhelmed with emotion; with the support of the team I'm so proud to be a part of. "I want everyone to know that I'm not trying to change what it is that we do, but to make it better. But I will need your help. That's for damn sure. I'm still so new at this, and you all have a lifetime of knowledge. I'm just a sponge, ready to soak it up."

"I'm not sure what the plan is for Jasper, but we're going to keep y'all updated," Ace says.

A bunch of solemn faces look back at me.

"His son," I bristle, "is with him now, but feel free to give him a call and see if you can get in to see him. I'm sure he'd like that," I say. "Ace, head up there first; I'll get dinner going with the crew." I know it's Ace's night for chow, but I want him to go see Jasper.

"Yes, sir, Charlie." Ace smirks as he tips his cowboy hat at me. "You seem to be real good at collecting the hearts of the ill-tempered."

I smile and nod at his words. "They seem to find me." I laugh.

After dinner in the bunkhouse, I take Finn for a run around the property. Normally, I wouldn't feel so free to run in the open, but I believe Jasper. If he said that Owen could wipe my trail after Boston, that means, for the first time in almost a year and a half, I don't have to look over my shoulder.

But I keep my promise to Jasper. I take my gun with me and strap it to the shoulder holster under my jacket. Though it was awkward to learn how to move with it, now it feels pretty normal.

Maverick

CHAPTER 12

Bright sunlight floods the room, and the heaviness of what's to come presses down on every available surface.

"So, Charlotte is Charlie and Lottie?"

"And sometimes, kiddo, you're a first-class asshole. That was terribly rude, and your mama and I raised you better than that."

"Dad." I pinch the bridge of my nose and pace the small room like a caged animal. "I don't know how it escaped you to tell me that her name was Charlotte. The guy you've been referring to as 'Charlie' all summer is Charlotte?"

"Son, I've been saying lots of things. You just don't always hear them." Dad sounds exhausted. I turn from looking out the windows at the mountains to face him. His eyes are studying me, and he sports a smile, thin and tired. "The only thing I've ever wanted for you was for you to be happy. Your mom hoped you'd settle down, but you have a wild spirit. You were meant to be wild, a maverick. But together, we hoped you may find that wild spirit would want to settle down at the ranch. Then you got good at skiing, and then great. And then we realized that our hopes and dreams aren't yours and that all there ever was was your happiness. That's all. Always."

I swallow down the emotions threatening to escape. He's never said anything like this to me before. He's always been honest with me and said what he meant, but this—this is raw.

We play a game of cribbage with the set that Charlotte left. We talk about everything and nothing. He's won several games before we realize it's dinnertime. The intervals of beeps are like a buzzing insect; they fall into the background, but I don't know how they expect him to rest when they're always coming to check on him.

The nurses have come into the room to give him different medications and check vitals. They should let him rest and recover a bit before they release him to go home.

"When did they say you can come home?" I ask, and he covers my hand with his. I look down at it. It used to be so big and strong, and now it's wrinkled and weathered with age from working in the sun. But it's still his.

"Kiddo, I'm not going home. Well, I am, in a way; she's my home. I'm going home to your mom. I have missed her every single day, and I can't wait to get my arms around her."

"Dad. Stop. What are you talking about? Of course you're going home." I scoff and stand up.

"Reid, stop pacing. Come sit with me for a bit and just be still." He pats the covers, and I go to him. I sit on the bed like I did with Mom, but I was twelve when I tried to hug her and climb in the bed with her. I can't do that now with Dad.

"No. No, I don't know why you're just giving up."

"You'll always be the best thing I've ever done. I've been with you every single step of your life, and I'll always be here." He taps my chest. "Taught you all I know in this world so you can be ready to experience it for yourself."

A night nurse comes in, takes his vitals, and gives him some medicine to ease the pain.

I walk out to the nurse's station after Dad has fallen asleep. Sitting there is an older nurse with gray hair near her temples, the rest a natural red color. "Hi, ma'am. I'm Jasper Bennett's son. He's in room six. I know—" I can't say it. "I know he made it clear that he would not be released, but is it possible to leave a note? Can we have the nurses and staff coming in be just a bit more gentle? That's my dad in there."

"Oh, sugar. I'm so sorry." I can tell by the look in her eyes she means it, but they're still words she must have said hundreds of times. "I'll leave a note."

"Thank you," I say wearily. I go back to the convertible chair and set it up as a bed. There's a pillow and blanket on the windowsill. I fluff the pillow before I lay down.

I smell her as I finally drift to sleep.

The next morning, the nurses come in a bit more gently. The woman who kicked out Charlotte is in the room with us when she gets a call on the hospital phone. Dad's still sleeping. She says, "Oh, honey, I'm sorry. But right now, it's best if he only has one visitor at a time. You can call us a bit later to check. Mm-hmm, okay. Bye, bye."

"That was your 'sister.'" I must look like a damn idiot because I have no idea what the hell this woman is talking about. "The pretty blonde who was here yesterday."

"Oh, uh, right, Charlotte?"

"Mm-hmm." She eyes me up and down. "Well, I told her we could only do one visitor at a time. You two looked like you were going to kill each other, standing over my patient. Who should focus on other things."

Charlotte! I can't even think about what all of this means.

"Mav?" my dad says. "You're still here?"

"Yeah, Dad."

"That's nice. Can you help me up?"

We both go to him, but I say to the nurse, "I got this."

She nods, gives a thin smile, and walks out of the room.

I help him to the bathroom and then get him settled back in bed. Dad and I play more hands of cribbage. He looks a bit more weary, though the hum of the hospital is less glaring than it was yesterday.

I set up the chair closer to the bed on the side that lets the staff have better access to him.

We're both looking out at the snow-capped mountains and having a conversation about one of my very first races when he says, "Remember the first time I took you to Vail to race?"

"Yeah, I was so scared, and you said, 'You'll get it done.' So confident I would not chicken out."

"That's one of my favorite memories. Your mom was by my side, and my kid had two wooden planks strapped to his feet, about to fly."

We both fall in and out of naps, surrounded by the warm light of the sun. The snow clouds loom off in the distance, threatening to roll in quickly. "I love you, Dad," I say, almost in a whisper.

He taps my hand in response, and I drift off to sleep.

My eyes were only closed for a moment, but when I wake, my father's hand is cool over mine.

I call, scream for the nurse. She says he's at peace and has a DNR, so there's nothing they can do for him. They could have, I think, but he signed the form. He could have tried some type of treatment. He could have told me sooner, not like this, not when we didn't have enough time. There wasn't enough time.

I'm an orphan. I have no one left on this Earth to give a shit about me or what I do.

There's paperwork. I hear nothing they're saying. I hear nothing at all. I go to my Jeep, get in, and scream and scream and scream.

I send a chat to my boys, both in Utah and the "Gold Not Silver Rapids" chats. Caleb, Luke, and Jake all come over to the house and give condolences. All the crew, even Charlotte, have given theirs as well, but it was short and clipped. They lost their leader, their friend. But I lost my dad. Suppliers and vendors have sent flowers and baskets and plants. He was so well-loved and respected, judging by how many people have reached out. Charlotte hasn't said but a few words, as if trying to stay clear of me. Honestly, I have too much to say to her, but not enough energy.

I know Dad didn't want anything fancy. He said that when Mom died. I texted my boss at the resort that I had a death in the family, but he hasn't responded, and to be honest, I haven't really cared. Days pass, but I'm not really here. I'm stuck in my head and wishing like hell I could turn back time.

Caleb and his mom offered to help me arrange things, and I have to go into town to meet with folks about the service. My parents weren't religious, not conventionally, so we arrange for a graveside burial under the willow where we buried my mom and dad's parents.

Mrs. Wright has done this before. When Mom died, she helped Dad with everything because she had just done it for herself when Mr. Wright died.

"Do you have a suit, dear?" she asks.

I do, but it's at the apartment. "Yes, but it's not here. I'll have my roommate bring it when he comes later this week," I tell her.

"Okay, that's good. Is there anything you need, sweetie?" she asks. I don't think this woman is carrying a Time-Turner in her purse, so I just shake my head. "Oh, Maverick. You were always the most sensitive of all my boys." Then, she pulls me into her arms and gives me what I need. I really just needed a hug.

We bury Dad under the willow behind the house on a sloped hill where wildflowers bloom in the spring. Right beside Mom and my grandparents. There are three headstones etched with names and dates. I don't really remember my grandfather, but my grandmother died just after my mom. And then it was just Dad and me. There are a few rows of white padded chairs with people from town sitting in them. More people surround the gravesite in a circle, listening to the preacher say some words I don't hear. People I haven't seen in years—friends of Dad's, teachers, police and firemen, other ranchers. They nod when they see me looking at them.

I hear the snow and the wind, though. It's coming down softly but steadily, and it's cold. I'm wearing a pea coat that's a bit too small for me now, but it was in my closet, and I needed something besides my suit coat to stave off this bitter cold. In winter sports, you learn to love the cold, because if you don't, you'll just be miserable. But today, it's cutting me to the bone.

In front of me is Dad's casket, with the American flag draped across the coffin. A photo of him sits on an easel next to the casket with white roses across the top. The sun is shrouded behind thick, gray clouds. Like the sky is mad at the earth and is withholding any bit of golden warmth from the sun. I hear a few people gently crying, but the sound that cuts through the snow and the wind is Charlotte's sniffling.

She's standing next to Quinn, directly opposite me. I would think she's purposefully ignoring me, but it's as if she doesn't even see me. Her black dress is cut to just below her knees and has long sleeves, under which she wears nude stockings and black cowboy boots. She has a shawl wrapped around her shoulders, looking like it's a tapestry or a woven blanket, almost. I feel like I've seen it before. She looks so different from the woman I met over the summer. That woman was shiny and big-city; the woman before me now looks like she's spent her life on a ranch. The wind blows a strand of her blonde hair across her face, and I want to push it behind her ear.

I shake my head to clear that thought from my head. Her arms are wrapped so tight around her as she sobs, looking like she's holding on for dear life. Her beautiful face, more tan than I remember, is blotchy and stained with tears.

I hate that she's here. I hate that she lost someone special, too.

My guys are here, too. All of them. My framily, the friends that have become the only family I have left, has shown up for me.

The flag that was draped across the casket is being folded and held over the gleaming wood while a bugler in the distance plays "Taps" and a firing party of seven men fires shots into the gray sky. I look up, and it's stopped snowing. One. Two. Three. At the last shot, I wince and close my eyes.

The preacher indicates the end of the service and invites me to join him. There's a bowl of dirt that's been put on a small table next to the photo stand, dirt that was excavated from this spot. I reach in and grab a handful—tiny grains pressing into my palms and settling into the crevices of my fingers. I squeeze it hard, feeling it weigh heavy in my hand.

In my head, I say, *Dad, I'm so sorry. I'm so damn grateful for everything you've given me. I miss you already. Please give Mom the biggest hug and kiss from me.* I squeeze my eyes tightly shut, but a tear escapes. I throw the dirt onto the casket and hear it hit the wood with a soft thud, the scattered grains of soil sliding across the smooth surface.

I don't stay to watch anyone else say their last goodbyes. I trudge through the snow, back to the house. The wake is being hosted in the main house, where the food is laid out on our long dining table. I go straight past it to the liquor cabinet and pull a bottle of whiskey out. I open the ice maker inside the door and get two cubes, then pour four fingers into a rocks glass that matches my set.

People come in and mingle, sharing stories about Dad. There's some classic rock playing, my dad's favorite. Mrs. Wright tries to get me to eat, but I have no desire for anything.

I leave before another person tries to give condolences, and I slip out to the barn, taking the bottle with me. The guys notice and follow me out. We get extra chairs from the closet and post up in the office in the barn. They stay with me as my heart cracks—as it cracks like ice.

Maverick

CHAPTER 13

I wake up on the couch with a blanket thrown across me. I look at my watch, and it reads 6:38 a.m. Ugh. I had the good sense to take off my suit coat and white dress shirt before passing out. The smell of cedar and old hay dust mixes with the bourbon from last night. Sutton—or maybe it was Luke—had gone and got us another bottle from the house after we finished the first. My head hurts, but not from the alcohol; all the emotions running loose in my head cause more damage than the whiskey ever could.

I throw the blanket off, fold it up, and put it and the pillow in the closet. The guys said they would check on the house before leaving. I check my phone and see texts.

Luke: House is empty if you want to go get some sleep in your bed.

Caleb: Mom put the leftover food in the fridge. She said you have to eat it within three days.

Garrett: I'm so damn sorry I couldn't make it, Mav. You know I would have been there if I could.

I know, man. It's ok. Thanks, guys, sincerely.

I see Charlotte and Ace in the field working, and I don't bother to tell them I'm leaving. My overnight bag's contents are scattered over the floor in my room. I don't really know what the hell I'm supposed to do now. I just feel like I can't stay here. My new life is back in Utah; my job and the season are about to start at the resort.

I pack up the overturned bag and get a thicker sweater from my closet, throwing it on with a fresh shirt and a pair of sweatpants from my dresser. Dad always kept the room the same, even after I moved out, and all my stuff stayed right where it was. Almost like he expected or assumed I would come home someday.

I grab a plate of whatever Mrs. Wright left for me, along with a fork from the drawer in the island and a water bottle. Another five hours in the truck. I sigh and shake my head, then get on the road. I get to the Idaho state line and feel hot all over—I need to crack the window. I stop to get gas and try to just feel the wind in my hair, keep my eyes on the road, listen to whatever comes on the radio, anything but focus on the thoughts I'm trying desperately to keep from entering my brain.

It was a blink of a drive because I'm home already. I drop the bag on my bed, change into base layers, and grab my gear bag and skis. I don't bother unpacking because I just want to get on the slopes. I definitely don't want to go to my mountain to ski; I don't want to see anyone. So, I head to Alta. For the people who know, it's one of the best mountains around; it's just about the snow, not dripping with luxury like where I work. I'm only going to get in a few hours, but that's fine with me.

I text the Cortland boys.

> Hey, I'm back at the apartment. Grabbing skis and heading out. Depending on when you get home, let's get together.

> Sutton: We're home already, guy. We didn't stay and left after you crashed. Hudson is still sleeping, I think.

> Jude: We should def get together when ur back.

It's been a few hours of skiing off-piste; I wanted to get knocked on my ass for a bit. I'm on a lift to get over to a groomer when I feel my phone vibrate. The groomers are well maintained, and in the morning when you get the first tracks, they look like corduroy. But right now, they're torn up with fresh tracks of skiers and snowboarders.

My earbuds read a text to me.

> Ollie: Hi, Maverick. I heard about your dad. I'm so sorry, man. And I know it's not the best time, but we're at capacity, and we're not bringing back any other instructors this season. I can definitely put in a word for you at the other resorts or let you know if we need folks later in the season.

"Fuck!" I yell into the sky. I did not need this right now. I had no plan other than to return to instructing.

Just like that, I have nothing left: no job, no family, nothing. *Fuck!* I hang my head.

I text him back when I get off the lift and navigate to a spot where no one can run into me getting off the chairlift.

> That's disappointing to hear, but let me know if something comes up. I'd love to come back.

I put my phone away and ski for another hour, just to get worked up. Maybe it's better just to head back to the apartment. I call Jude when I get to the car, and he picks up on the second ring.

"Hey, guy. I got some more shit news, man," I say in lieu of a greeting.

"Eh, what's going on?"

"Oliver just texted and said they aren't taking additional instructors, and that was going to be my primary source of income besides working at your place. What the fuck, man!"

"So, uh—" He stutters a bit. "Fuck, shit, okay. I did not want to do this today, but maybe it's supposed to happen this way." My stomach sinks and feels as if it's being dragged behind my truck, bouncing along the road. "I'm moving home. I'm moving back to the ranch while I rehabilitate. Mav, I'm so sorry. I'm trying really hard to get back on the circuit next season, and I need to save money, too. I'm so sorry, man. But you could get another roommate! That way, it's not all on you for rent and stuff."

Somewhere, someone is laughing at my avatar because I pissed off everyone.

"I think, though—and take this with a grain of salt and a lime, man—but I think you should at least think about moving back home, too."

I cannot believe I'm fucking hearing this. Jude—God love him, he's like my brother and I only want what's best for him, but goddamn.

I'm silent, stewing about this for so long that he asks, "You still there?"

"Man, I'm just—" I don't finish the sentence.

"I know. I do. That's why I think you should go home and reset. Figure out your next move."

Home. I don't even know what or where "home" is right now.

"I want you to get healthy and get back to doing what you do, Jude. I just didn't expect this."

"Mav, I'm sorry."

"I mean, I wouldn't have to pay rent, but I would have to find a job. The whole fucking town hates me, so that should be interesting, but

I'll, uh, I'll figure it out. What's your timeline for moving out of the apartment?"

"Well, I called the office to see about breaking the lease already. Just to have all the options and know what the next steps are once we talked. They wanted thirty days, but they had so many people interested that they would accept a fourteen-day notice, and we could get our deposit back."

"It sounds like you have your mind made up about this. And real talk, I don't know how I was going to make it work besides getting a bunch of part-time jobs. And if you're going on the circuit, you won't even be home most of the time besides your offseason." I don't say anything for a moment. "Things happen for a reason, right?"

"Trust in that, man."

"What about the apartment? We have to pack it up. I mean, I do. Save your back."

"Shut the fuck up. We'll come over and pack it up."

"All right, thanks."

"Are you still wanting to get together?"

"Tomorrow, man. I just want to go home and rot. Maybe we can pack up the apartment a bit. Bring some boxes."

I'm tired even though I didn't push myself today. The stress of everything is just getting to be too much right now. My muscles ache, my throat is raw and scratchy, and I've got a headache the size of Utah.

It'll be nice to sleep in my bed for the first time in a week, even if I just stare up at the ceiling counting sheep or all the many ways I could have been a better son.

Sleep finally comes around 2 a.m., but after tossing and turning, I get out of bed at 8 a.m.

The guys walk in at ten to find me on the couch, just staring at a blank TV.

I start pulling stuff out of the closet and my dressers. I become painfully aware that I don't have a whole lot of stuff to pack up. The apartment came furnished and it's sad that, all of a sudden, my whole life can be packed up into a small trailer.

We pack up everything that's mine except for some clothes and toiletries, all stuff that can fit into a weekender bag.

Sutton grabs a beer from the fridge and sits down with Jude on the couch. "I'll be up in a few days with Walter and whatever doesn't fit in your tiny-ass Jeep. I can bring it up with the trailer."

"Thanks, man, I appreciate that."

"What's the plan for tomorrow?" Jude asks.

"I got a call from the lawyer asking for me to let them know when I'll be at the house. They'd like to do the reading of his will. There's no reason to put it off any longer," I say.

We have another beer, and they head out. I'll get another night in the apartment. We decided the guys are going to take the mattresses to the farm. Everything else that didn't come with the apartment will get donated.

I'm not ready for what's to come, but in Dad's words, "You'll get it done."

I called the law office when I was driving back to Silver Rapids. They're meeting me later this afternoon.

The pines that surround the house are dusted with snow; they look like Christmas trees, or maybe that's just me projecting because the holiday is next week. If I'm honest, being alone in that big house during the holidays makes me want to rage. The last time I experienced Christmas in that house was about two years ago. Last year, I spent it with the Cortlands. Maybe I can get the guys to come over for a guys' night.

Parking the truck up next to the house in the spot that was usually reserved for Dad, I grab my two bags out of the cab and walk up the steps to my childhood home. I feel like I'm coming home with my tail between my legs.

I punch in the code for the front door and stomp my feet on the welcome mat before walking in. The house is clean, but it smells stale. I've been in the house since Dad died, but when I cross the threshold and shut the door, the impact of what this means hits me like a linebacker sacking a quarterback. I fall back against the door, sink to the floor, and take several big breaths. Choking down a cry and blinking back tears, I let my head hit the door behind me.

After several minutes, I head upstairs and drop off my bag in my closet. Fuck, this feels so weird.

I'm the only living relative Dad had left; he was an only child, and my mom's family is gone, too. I don't know if it's a formality, but I have to imagine that all of this is left to me. Right?

I take a shower before the lawyer gets here in just a half-hour.

I hear the doorbell ring just as I pull on a crewneck sweater over a green long-sleeved thermal. I open the door to see Dad's lawyer, Kelsey Buchanan. And Charlotte.

"What do you want?" I ask Charlotte. I don't mean for it to sound so rude, but even to my ears, it rings like a slap.

"I'm not sure; Ms. Buchanan asked me to meet her here."

"Mr. Bennett, I've asked Ms. Adler to join us this afternoon. We could do the reading separately, but it would save time to do it all together."

My jaw is clenched so damn tight. I have no idea why Charlotte is here.

As a witness, maybe? I open the door further and motion for them to come in.

Kelsey pulls out a thick, yellow envelope and moves over to the dining table.

I should ask if I can get them a drink, but I don't.

"Please," Kelsey says, "get comfortable. Would you prefer the office, or perhaps the couch?"

"Office," I say at the same time Charlotte says, "Couch."

"Eh, how about we go to the table?" The lawyer motions to the long table in the dining area. Sunlight slanting in through the windows illuminates the space. My mind wanders to why Charlotte would have an opinion either way on where we do this.

The lawyer has jet-black hair, amber eyes, and hair as straight as a pin. In her kitten heels, wide-leg denim pants, and a blazer, she walks into the open-space kitchen area. By comparison, Charlotte looks like she just came in from working in the pastures—dark jeans and a Carhartt jacket, a gray sweatshirt peeking out from under the hem. But I get the feeling that even though they may be worlds apart on the outside, they both have the look of women who are cunning and smart as hell.

We sit down and settle as Kelsey pulls out two large envelopes, which land on the table with a thud. "This is the last will and testament of Jasper Eugene Bennett, signed and notarized on September fifth of this year."

"To his son, Maverick Reid Bennett," she reads, "Jasper Eugene Bennett leaves the full deed and responsibility of the Bennett estate, including land, buildings not of the Eco-Tours portfolio, and any remaining assets."

Does that mean just the land? I wonder.

Kelsey continues, "To his friend, Charlotte Clara Adler, he leaves the controlling interest of Bennett Enterprises, including Bennett Cattle and Dappled Stone Eco-Tours. As well as Ms. Adler having access to the property and the dwelling that she currently occupies for as long as she wishes."

Charlotte sits across from me. She's got streaks of dirt on her high cheekbones. Her cowboy hat shades her eyes from the light streaming into the kitchen, but I can see her blue eyes go wide.

It's so quiet in here, you could hear a pin drop.

"However, per Clause eight-B, the division of the assets is contingent upon cooperation by both parties. Should both parties not successfully engage in joint operations for a period no shorter than twelve months, it will nullify the inheritance, and all assets revert to the Trust, which lists Flying Horses of the West, a 501(c)(3) organization, as beneficiary. They pair military and former pilots suffering PTSD and at risk for suicide with a horse companion and a place to stay, if needed."

"Wait, what?" I say. "Wait, you're saying that we—" I motion between Charlotte and me, "have to work together?"

The lawyer nods. "Yes, that's correct."

Charlotte shakes her head. "I think there's been a misunderstanding."

"Ms. Adler, according to this, you have the controlling interest."

"Wait a damn minute." The world is spinning too fast, and I feel like I'm just catching up. "She gets the business, and I get the land. And unless we work together for a year, we both lose it all?"

"In its most simplified explanation, yes. Mr. Bennett was very explicit in his instructions."

"Did you know about this?" I look to Charlotte.

She's quiet and looks down at the table, at the document in front of her, a twin to the one in front of me.

"You did?!"

"He told me last week in the hospital," she says, looking at me—not defiantly, but not shying away, either. "But he said that his son had no interest in running the business. I didn't know he meant you."

I am fuming! "Can I contest this?" I glance at the lawyer, who wears a look of professional blankness that comes from years of watching people implode.

"You can, but I'll warn you now, this is airtight," Kelsey says flatly.

My jaw tightens, and I clench my hands into fists. "What am I supposed to do for money if I have to move back here?"

"Finances will be available for business operations, but not personal. Should you have a need for a position, you could likely get one with your new operations manager."

"I am not working for her." I point to Charlotte. "She's not going to be the one to sign my paychecks."

"Actually, the accountant would be the one to run payroll for the organization. But, yes, Ms. Adler would be the one to direct your daily activities if you should become employed with Bennett Cattle or Dapped Stone Eco-Tours."

My expression must be murderous, because both women stare at me with looks of trepidation.

"I'll start the transition plan and have it drafted by next week. You'll both receive account access for business needs, along with a continuation of payroll for Ms. Adler in the way previously arranged, by cash. Congratulations to you both. I truly hope you find a way to make it work." Kelsey stands up and smooths her hands down her jeans, then looks between us. "Good luck."

Charlotte has the good sense to take off on the lawyer's heels.

Me? I'm left sitting at this table, feeling my dad is playing one last trick on me.

Charlotte

CHAPTER 14

It's been two weeks since Jasper's death. Two weeks of seeing Maverick Fucking Bennett every day. It's been two weeks of hell. It's the feeling of sorority hell week all over again. Maverick is doing everything he can to haze the shit out of me. Never mind that I've been here since May, working with his father and the entire team, while he's been playing cowboy on somebody else's ranch.

Walking one of the colts from the arena to the stables, I see Maverick leaning against a fence post, looking out at the cattle in the pasture. I feel like a cloud is just hanging over me, and not because of the gray skies.

"You know, I've been thinking about what this land would be worth, or what it could be if it weren't a ranch," I hear him say to himself. He must be talking to himself because there's no one around, and I sure as fuck don't want to talk to him. We haven't exchanged a kind word, except for when I gave my condolences at the funeral and he grunted and walked away.

"I don't think you were thinking grand enough when you suggested the eco-cabins," he says, then turns to look at me.

"I know you're not talking to me." I am so mad, I feel like I could launch myself forward and claw his eyes out. His dad and I have worked damn hard to change the trajectory of this place. We wanted it to be sustainable, to let people see what life on a real, working ranch could be.

"Oh, I'm talking to you. No one else here helped persuade dear ol'

Dad to turn acreage into a damn glamping retreat. As it is, I was going over things with the accountant. I need you to clear things for me before making big purchases."

"Any purchases I've made have been for the ranch and upkeep of this place. I have purchasing authority. If you have a problem with it, take it up with the accountant. Or Ace. I'm sure he'd love to straighten it out with you."

"I bet he would."

I keep walking the colt to his stall to brush him, but say loud enough that he can hear me, "Turns out I'm the one that signs that paycheck after all."

Just then, a Silverado truck with "Cortland Farms" printed on the outside pulls up with a single horse trailer and honks. The colt bristles, but doesn't pull too hard.

Maverick says nothing as he walks past me to greet the man getting out of the truck—who is hot as hell. Strong jaw with the perfect amount of stubble and a mustache. He tips his baseball hat to me when he sees me and offers a blinding smile, but I do not have time to even think about getting to know any of Maverick's other friends. It's bad enough that the guys I thought were my friends lied to me the whole damn time.

I'm working in the barn when they bring a new horse into the stable. I'm assuming it's Maverick's. We have a quarantine stall, so if a horse gets sick, it can be separated from the others. You can't just stick a new horse into a barn; you have to make sure they have time to quarantine and then introduce them to the other horses safely, usually letting them hang out with a fence dividing them. If you force it, there can be aggression from other horses, and that creates bigger problems.

I pop my head out of the stall belonging to Ace's horse, Candy Cane, and lean against the door. I watch them load the new horse into the quarantine stall. He's a beautiful appaloosa, and a gelding, thank God.

He's a beautiful chestnut color with a white blanket and chestnut spots along his hind quarters.

I walk over, and while I don't have the intent of heckling or interacting in any way other than to see the new horse, Maverick is ready to give me attitude.

"What do you want?" He looks at me with such disdain.

I really don't want to engage and wish that we could just work together, but I say, "He's beautiful."

"He's handsome, rugged—not beautiful," Maverick replies with a grunt.

"Males of a species can be beautiful," I retort.

Maverick's friend's eyes volley between us.

"Ma'am, you're beautiful," the stranger says.

"Ugh, Sutton, this is Charlotte."

"Hello," I say, a bit sassily.

The horse comes up to me and sniffs my pockets, his head hanging over the dutch stall door. Ahh, he's after treats already.

"What's your name, beautiful boy?"

Sutton answers while Maverick just glares. "This is Walter."

I roll my eyes. "You can't help what your parents name you, can you, Walter?" I pull my hands out of my pockets and let him sniff. He nudges me with his nose. "I have a peppermint. Can he have one?"

Maverick studies me and says nothing, but nods once. He watches me warily.

I slowly put my hand in my pocket and pull out a mint. The crinkle of the wrapper makes Walter perk his ears, and a smile crosses my face. "You know what this is?" I unwrap it and open my hand. He snatches it gently with his lips, then crunches it between his teeth. I wipe my hands on my jeans. He nudges my pockets again. "That's all I got, big guy. Maybe another time."

I look at both men, then walk away without saying another word to either of them.

As I return to Candy Cane, I hear Sutton say, "Hot damn, man. She doesn't seem that bad."

That makes me smirk.

For the rest of the day, I don't have any other interactions with Ranger Rick. He'll always be Ranger Rick to me, the nickname he told me about over the summer. It was a nod to him wanting to be an adventurer. I thought it was cute at the time. But now? It's just a reminder that he's a dick, Ranger Rick the Dick.

I see Sutton take off when I head back to the cottage.

It is feeling homey, my little place, though sometimes when it creaks or the wind blows hard and rattles the windows, it freaks me out a bit.

It's late when I finally get into bed. The salt lamp on the dresser emits an ember-like glow. Since the break-in at the other house, I don't like sleeping in the dark. Quinn got me this lamp and a little cow stuffie, which have helped a bit.

I'm only asleep for two minutes, I swear, when I wake to Finn's barking. He's alerting and circling, pointing to the window. I groan. The clock says 12:37 a.m. Only an hour and a half of sleep.

"Ugh, Finn. What?! There's nothing out there. Go to sleep, bud."

He whines and jumps down from the bed. With a huff, he goes to the living room.

Fuck. I'm still wide awake after five minutes. I flip my pillow to the cool side, hoping it helps put me back to sleep.

I hear something, a rhythmic beating—thump, thump, thump.

What in the world is that? I slip my feet into my slippers and pad across the floor to my bedroom window. I pull the curtain back and twist the blinds open to see where the noise is coming from.

I see a large bonfire and several headlights not too far off in the field next to the cottage that's usually reserved for rotating the cattle. That motherfucker! He's throwing a party in the field next to my cottage?! Why the fuck wouldn't he have a party up by the main house?

In the light of the fire, I see Maverick with a bottle of something in his hand, with guys I can only assume to be Luke, Caleb, and someone else huddled around him. I grab my field coat and trade out my slippers for boots at the door, and let Finn come with me. Once outside, I can hear the loud rock music blaring from the truck's speakers.

I trudge through the field to get to the fire and the assholes around it. I see it's a makeshift firepit made of patio paver stones. Yep—around the fire lurk Luke, Caleb, and the man I saw helping Maverick move his stuff in earlier, Sutton. I look at Luke. "I see you come prepared."

He at least has the good sense to look embarrassed. He runs his tattoo-covered hand through his caramel-brown hair. "Heya, Charlie. We weren't keeping you up, were we?"

"As a matter of fact, yes."

"We're sorry, Charlotte," says Caleb from where he's sitting on a log.

"You can say that again," says Sutton. "I'm sorry we're keeping you up."

"You didn't tell us anyone was staying in the cottage, Mav," Luke says to Maverick.

"She's not anyone," he says snidely. "Just a ghost, haunting the property."

Luke snorts. "Eh, she's haunting you, but I wouldn't say—"

Maverick interrupts, "Do not finish that sentence, Luke Draper."

Sutton and Caleb laugh.

Facing me, Luke says apologetically, "I'm sorry, Charlie. I didn't know you were staying here, or we would have kept it closer to the house."

"Don't apologize; this is my land," Maverick snaps. "I can go or do whatever, wherever I want."

I walk up to him, about to smack him or, at the very least, shove his drunk ass, when Caleb intercepts me.

"We'll pack it up, Charlie," Caleb says, then whispers so that no one else hears, "He's just having a hard time with everything. He doesn't like change."

I don't care, though. He's been an insufferable asshole and I've had it! Pointing at Maverick, I say, "I know your dad just died, but that doesn't give you the right to be a fucking asshat all the damn time. Good Lord!"

"Yes, you can call me 'Lord,'" he says smugly, getting so close I can smell the alcohol on his breath. Ugh, he smells like a distillery.

"How much have you guys been drinking?" I look to Luke.

"He was like this when we got here. We thought some fresh air would help, and he said, 'Let's go to the party field.' And, well," he opens his arms and looks around, "this used to be our old party field growing up."

"I see. Well, I can see how that would be confusing, but seeing how Jasper left running the ranch operations to me, I don't want to have more 'parties in the field.'"

"Well, Charlie, I mean, technically," Maverick hiccups, "this is my land. Just sayin'."

"I never thought you'd be a sloppy drunk," I spit at him. "Guys, please get my 'landlord' back to the house."

"Jeez, Mav, you just love pissing people off," Caleb says as he tries to get Maverick into Luke's truck, from which Luke grabs a giant bucket of water and some sand, then smothers the fire.

"Can the rest of you drive?" I don't see any beer cans or bottles anywhere on the ground, but maybe they've thrown them in the truck beds.

"We're okay. He's the one who was knockin' 'em back," Luke says. He thumbs over toward where Ranger Rick is sitting.

"I'm doing a Seventy-Five Hard, so no drinks for me, ma'am," Sutton says, flashing a smile.

Uh, I'm not in the mood to be called "ma'am," especially by one of Maverick's friends.

"Cool. Well, good night, guys. Caleb, give my love to Kennedy. We need a girl's night soon."

I enter the bunkhouse, where everyone's gathered for the morning meeting. My eyes don't linger, but Maverick looks like shit. Good! I put some extra chipper in my voice as I say, "Good morning, folks! I'm going to be walking the property with the contractors, but I will have the walkie with me. If anyone needs me, holler. Ace is going to be working with you on what's next."

"Holler?" Maverick pipes up from where he's posted up by the lockers.

I try. I really do. I try not to let him get to me. I think about not acknowledging him, but that won't help the situation. Ace said we should try to present a united front to the hands.

"You may be the owner, but you don't have an actual job, right? So, as a courtesy to your dad, yes, you can work here. But you're going to actually work. Feel like mucking stalls?"

"As a courtesy to my dad? Please. I'm a better cowboy than any of these guys. I wanted to get away from here—sue me."

Ace must have had enough of Maverick's shit, too, because he says, "Maverick's too pretty to be a cowboy. Isn't that right, Mav?" He laughs, and a bunch of the older crew join in. There's definitely no love lost between them.

"Didn't you know?" I interject. "Our friend, Mav, was a hand at his friend's family's ranch. Sutton's family, right? He worked there instead of helping his own dad. Doesn't seem really like someone you want in charge of the land, does it? He doesn't even work his own land."

Maverick's eyes darken as he glowers at me, and the room goes silent. *Oh, shit.* Did they really not know that he was working somewhere else? Is there, like, ranch code or something, and I just broke it?

"What would you know about loyalty? You're just a ghost. Here one day and gone the next."

"I'm not fighting with you. Ask Ace what he needs you for today."

I walk out and let the door slam behind me, but not before I hear a thud. Like flesh on flesh. I don't turn around, but have an idea that Ace may have just socked Maverick. What an insufferable bastard. I take a few breaths and try to calm my racing heart. What is it about him that gets under my skin?

After meeting with the contractors and checking in with Ace, I tell him I'm going into town. I need a drink, and maybe some pistachio ice cream. Something. Anything to make this day better.

I wander past the Book Nook and see a few people in there, so rather than going in to bitch about my crap day with Quinn, I send her a text and tell her I'm going to the Flour Child for some sweet treats and a spressie.

Caleb sees me and comes over to where I'm paying for my ice cream and éclair. "Charlie!" he says. "I'm so sorry we kept you up. I knew you were staying on the property, but didn't know about the cottage. Otherwise, we would have stayed in the main house." He looks at my ice cream and the clear clamshell containing the éclair. "Can I get you a drink? On the house. Go have a seat, and I'll bring you anything you want."

Normally, I wouldn't take a free drink, but I'm just pissed off enough. "Espresso martini?"

"Perfect. Classic or something fun?"

"Classic, please."

"No problem, take a seat."

I stare out the window, replaying the embarrassing moments with Maverick from this morning, and it's all bullshit. My phone vibrates with an incoming text from Quinn.

Quinn: We are so busy; I can't get away right now.

It's ok. I would be shit company. I'm stewing over Maverick's shit.

Quinn: Ewww.

Not his actual shit, weirdo. He's making this transition so much harder than it has to be. I know he's sad about his dad. I'm actually heart-broken about it. I never wanted to be enemies. I wasn't exactly happy to have to see that the man I was pining over was shaping up to be a grade A asshole.

Quinn: We need to get you over a new man, or under.

Maybe I'm playing this wrong. Maybe I should try to play it aloof, like him? He's making it seem like this is just a game.

Quinn: Ooh, yass, bitch. A fire with fire kind of

thing. I say either pretend like he doesn't exist, or make him jealous just to fuck with his head. What about that one guy, Ezra? Hell, just go have some fun with the guy, and who gives a shit about Maverick? Live your life, bitch.

"Hey, Charlotte." It's only when I hear someone say my name that I look up and see Ezra. Speak of the devil. "I said your name a few times." He laughs and gives a brilliant smile. "Where were ya?"

I slyly put my phone in my lap. I do not need him to see his name on my screen. "Hi, Ezra! Eh, I'm not sure." I laugh it off.

"Ha! A daydream vacation. I like it."

"Something like that. How are you doing?"

"Good, yeah. I'm finally getting settled into town."

"Oh, I didn't realize you were moving to Silver Rapids. That's great."

"Yeah, I've been trying to get acquainted with all the local things. I saw your friend at the bookstore. She said you might be here. I had a thought."

"Ah, yeah? What was that?" *Damn it, Quinn.*

"I was thinking maybe you wouldn't mind playing tour guide to a new resident?"

"Um, you know. I'm still kind of new here myself," I lie. I've lived here for a few months and know all the things that someone new should know, but I'm really not trying to spend time around men right now.

"Then we could explore together. Maybe hit up the Bluebird Café on Friday night? If you're not busy? I've had dinner there a few times, and the food wasn't half bad. Or the bar, Brad's?" Ezra's honey-colored eyes are bright, and his full lips stretch out in a smile.

Maybe Quinn was right—maybe I just need to get out and "live my life, bitch."

"Bart's," I correct him. I look up to him and smile. One date; I could do one date. "Actually, I could play tour guide on Friday. Say eight o'clock? We could meet at the bar."

"Perfect. Can I get your number? You know, in case I get lost on the way," he teases.

I could do a date, but I don't want to give him my number, even if this is a burner phone I add minutes to. If things go well, then I would give him my number, but how do I say that without coming off like a damn crazy woman? "How about I give it to you if you find your way on Friday? Gives you a reason to explore the town a bit more."

"That's an excellent incentive. I'll see you Friday."

I determine that Ezra seems like a kind soul.

"See you Friday." I smile politely and hope this date goes better than the last.

I text Quinn back.

You bitch. You sent him here?

Quinn: I knew you were in a bad mood. Are you guys getting together?

Yeah. Friday at Bart's.

Quinn: Yasssss! You just show up and look like your fabulous self. Well, I mean not your ranch self, your 'dress like an east coaster' self. I'll take care of the rest.

Nuh uh. What's the rest?!?!

Quinn: Customers just came in, ttyl! Kisses.

I shake my head. Why do I feel like I just got played by my bestie?

Maverick

CHAPTER 15

This week has sucked so much ass. Charlotte has given me the hardest time transitioning to the ranch. I know Dad left the running of the day-to-day to her. But she doesn't know a damn thing about running a cattle ranch, and when I try to even talk to her—no, just look at her—she shuts me down and gets ready for a fight. I know I'm pushing her buttons, but hand to God, I don't know what Dad was thinking. She may have a fancy-pants economics and analytics finance degree, but she sure as shit doesn't know anything about running a damn ranch.

The speakers on either end of the stage and above the bar reverberate with the bass thumping with the beat of the music. There are so many bodies in Bart's tonight that I can hardly make my way to the bar rail to get an order in with the bartender. It's normally not this crowded, but it's Christmas, and ski season is just about to kick off—with that, an influx of people has flooded Silver Rapids...and Bart's. All I wanted was a fucking drink with the guys.

I take a breath and navigate to the rail, careful not to get in a fight in the meantime. On a normal day, I hate people—let alone strangers—touching me, but today, especially, nobody better even think about bumping into me. The smell of peanuts on the floor, the bass, the fog drifting from the DJ and dance floor...it's the stereotypical country western bar. I should have stayed at the house and drank whatever Dad had stashed in the cabinet.

"What will do ya?" asks the bartender when I finally get up to the rail.

"Double whiskey, rocks," I yell back to her.

She looks like she's about to ask what kind, but my face must say, "Does it look like I give a fuck?"

I take my phone out of my pocket to see three missed calls and texts from Luke and Caleb in our group chat.

> Luke: Bro, we're in the bar in our usual corner. Grab a drink and get over here.

> Caleb: Where are you? You said you were on your way over an hour ago.

> Luke: You better not be sulking in the house, you miserable asshole.

Miserable asshole indeed. I roll my eyes and slip the phone back into my jeans as the bartender comes back with my drink. I hand her my credit card.

"Keep it open or close you out, darlin'?" she asks.

"Keep it open and bring me another one of these." I lift my glass, and she nods. Nothing has gone my way in days, months—fuck, it's been years since the scales tipped in my favor. While she is making my drink, I look at the mirror lining the back of the bar. Behind the bottles of bourbon, tequila, vodka, and everything in between, I can spot Luke in his black cowboy hat where he said they'd be.

"Our corner" is raised a few steps off the floor and hosts some tall cocktail tables with stools and a built-in corner booth that we have always gravitated to. I wouldn't say we kick people out of the spot directly, but we discourage their presence just by being obnoxious assholes.

Luke is surrounded by people, but I can't exactly make out who. The only reason I can see Luke is because he's six-foot-four and standing up with his phone to his ear, scanning the room. I can feel my phone buzzing in my back pocket. *Jesus, man, I'm coming.*

The bartender returns with another glass of burnished liquid gold. She gives me a sly little smile. She's a pretty girl with short blonde hair and green eyes, and I bet she flirts to get better tips, but I am not interested. Not right now, anyway. Maybe I just need to get Charlotte Adler out of my mind with someone else. A night of meaningless sex just to shake the woman out of my thoughts. She's everywhere I turn now.

It's not fair to the woman, but who knows? Maybe whoever it is would be down for a night of blowing off steam, too. Everyone is free to make their own choices. I won't judge, even though everyone seems fine with judging me. Everyone thinks I'm an asshole; no need to change their minds about it now.

I won't think about the fact that in the shower this morning, leaning against the cool tiles, I reminisced on a night that somehow feels like both only months and a lifetime ago. Charlotte on her knees, water from the shower dripping down her body, her perfect pink lips taking my dick down her throat, my hand in her hair. I came harder this morning than I have in a damn long time.

I won't think about that at all. My dick, though—he's thinking about that now. Before walking away from the bar, I adjust my pants. The last thing I need is for my friend downstairs to make an appearance.

I take a sip of whiskey, the smooth liquid stinging on the way down but settling with caramel and vanilla on my tongue. The bartender comes back and lingers a little while longer, wiping down the counter space in front of me. As tempted as I am, I don't really have a desire for blondes tonight, or maybe ever again. I give her a slight shake of the head as I grab both of the drinks and turn around to fight the crowd.

I literally run into Garrett.

"Mav! Hey, guy." He tries to give me a hug, but I have two drinks in my hands. He knocks his knuckles to mine, then puts his hand on my shoulder. "I'm so sorry I couldn't get back for your dad's funeral last month. I wanted to so bad, but the firm literally told me I couldn't take the time off."

"I know. I told you, it's okay."

"How are you holding up?"

"I—I don't know," I say. "It's hard, you know? Because I see him in every direction I turn on the ranch. People who hate me are coming up to me and telling me how great my dad was and asking if I need anything. It's just fucked. And this thing with Charlotte is..." I trail off.

"I can't even imagine," he says.

I'm the first in our group to have lost a parent. But I had all the guys beat when I was twelve; now I'm truly an orphan. I nod because I don't really know what to say.

"I'm going to get a drink. Do you want another one?" Garrett says, then looks at the whiskey I'm double-fisting and laughs.

"No, man. I'm okay."

"Okay, I'll see you in a sec. Everyone is back there." He points to the corner where I saw Luke in the mirror.

"All right," I reply as I head that way. I know I have a "fuck around and find out" face on because people part easily around me as I head back to the corner.

With Luke's back to me and his big frame blocking sight of other people in the booth, not a damn thing can stop the shock on my face when I call his name and he twists, moving just enough for a blonde curl of someone sitting in the booth to show.

Fuck. Fuck. Double fuck. I wanted a drink with my bros. I sure as shit did not want to see her outside of the ranch. I know it's a small town, but this isn't the only bar. I was here first. I don't care that I left and came back; this place was mine first.

"Luke," I say calmly. He didn't say that Quinn—or Charlotte, for that matter—would be joining us tonight.

"Hey, man! Where the hell have you been?" he says and moves over a bit to reveal Quinn and Charlotte, both dressed to the nines. Then he sees my face and winces just slightly.

Garrett comes back with two bottles of beer and has a smile on his face when he says, "That didn't take nearly as long as I thought."

"Ohhh, shit," Quinn says under her breath, but still loud enough to hear. "Charlie, let's go grab a drink...or two."

Charlotte doesn't move. She just bounces a sequin-covered leg to the beat of the song, staring me down. Who wears sequin pants and snakeskin boots? This is Bart's, not the snobby, high-society bars where she's from.

"Ladies, grab a round on my tab," Luke says. He goes to help Quinn and Charlotte stand by offering a hand to each of them.

As she passes Luke, Quinn says, "Thanks, sugar," and pats him on the butt.

"Thanks, Luke," Charlotte echoes, giving him a small smile.

I back up several steps, allowing them space to get out of the wooden enclosure and descend the steps from the platform. She doesn't even glance at me as she passes. *Fine.* I didn't want to see her here tonight, anyway.

Do not watch her leave. Do not watch her leave. Do not watch her leave, damn you.

Technically, I don't watch her leave, but I can see her blonde hair weaving in the mirror's reflection.

Luke's eyes, though, are honed in on Quinn. I give him a nudge and he says, "Sorry! I know, I know. I didn't know they were going to be here."

"Yeah."

"For real. Quinn said that she would not be staying long, anyhow; it's just us tonight."

Caleb piped in, "Quinn said she wasn't expecting to see us and that she'd be leaving soon. She's just here for moral support."

"I don't want to talk about them. I just wanted a few drinks with the guys."

"Great! We have shots!" Caleb cries out. I think he's had a few already. "You three are behind."

"I'm good, buddy. I've got two sippers right here. I'll catch up if you slow down." I laugh.

I'm in no mood to let the antics of the blue-eyed fiend distract me from this time with them.

"No slowing down tonight, bro." Caleb all but shoves a shot in my face.

"Fine," I reply.

"Yes! Bottoms up, bro," Luke says.

Garrett and I each take a shot glass from Caleb's outstretched hand, clink, and shoot it back.

The girls have been gone for quite a while. Caleb is two sheets to the wind, singing along to every single song that's playing. If he had half a brain, he should have gone into music in some capacity. But he didn't think choir would have been the right look. As it is, he always knew he was going to help his mom run the bakery. He plays the piano and the guitar pretty damn good, though. He taught himself through YouTube videos.

"You know, they are probably running up your tab," I say to Luke.

"Ah, let 'em. I told Q this morning—" He pauses. "I got that contract to build the annex on the school. Besides just getting us all together, that's why I wanted to come out tonight to celebrate."

"Ayooo. That's fantastic, guy. Good for you!" I reach out and bump his tattooed fist.

"About damn time people see what a badass builder you are," Garrett says, clapping.

"Fuck yes, Luke!" Caleb whoops. Right before he falls over on the bench.

I notice Jake's absence. Caleb only ever gets like this when his brother isn't around. He doesn't like to see Caleb get drunk. "Where's Jake?" I ask Luke.

"He's at the bakery. There's a new employee that's caught his eye, based on what Caleb was telling me when I picked him up from Flour Child."

"No shit?"

"Yeah. It would be great for him to find someone to connect with."

Caleb picks this time to chime in. "He needs some lovin' in his life. Mom was talking about him maybe wanting to move out by Dad. I think that would be so hard for him, but in a good way. I don't want to lose my little brother."

Caleb: my emotional, happy drunk, ladies and gentlemen.

I try again and fail not to look for the blonde and brunette making their way across the room. I see them at the bar now. Quinn is talking to the bartender, and Charlotte is turned, facing our corner. I know my eyesight's not Superman-strength, but I swear I can feel her looking back at me.

My dad.

I cannot believe the move he pulled, and to what end?!

She is now the manager of the entire ranch and Dad's portfolio.

Luke can tell I'm pretty hot about something. I haven't told them yet what my old man has decided about the fate of the ranch. Now is as good a time as any.

"I'm so damn happy for you to get the annex bid, guy. You've been building your business and been on your shit. You're going to get so big, you'll be turning down jobs soon."

"Thanks, bro. It means a lot to me," Luke says, and puts a hand on his heart. "How are you doing, though? You look like shit."

"Don't pull that punch, please."

"We've never pulled punches. If anything, we punch harder. I'm so fucking happy to have you home, but you've been different. I don't mean since the last time you were home. You are still a broody fuck, but you seem disconnected from everything."

"Well, I've got news, too. I didn't want to share it because I didn't want to believe it." I pause. "Dad updated his will and trust. Charlotte will now be the primary interest holder of the ranch's business operations and will manage the day-to-day operations of Dappled Stone Ranch and its financial portfolio. And I will be the owner and deed holder of the property."

"I'm sorry. Jasper did what?" Luke asks. "That's why you've been an insufferable dick lately?!"

"That actually makes a lot of sense," Garrett says.

An "I agree" comes from Caleb, who is still lying on the bench.

Luke and I swivel our heads to look at him.

"What the hell?" I ask.

"What? It does. Charlotte's been in the café sharing all the stuff she's been doing with my mom and I. From a business perspective, she's killing it. And she's not bad with the horses and has been learning so quickly."

I just give him an indignant huff. "You're cut off."

"It makes for good business," he slurs. "Don't be mad because you can't hit it now because she's your boss."

"What?" I ask.

"She's your boss. You're going to work the ranch, right?" He sits up straight at that. "That's hot! Like forbidden lovers or some shit."

"Bro, I'm definitely going to shoot my shot now. You'd have a sexual harassment suit on your hands." Garrett is too happy about this.

"Not to throw more fuel onto this," Luke adds, "but Quinn said Charlie was meeting up with someone tonight, so I don't think Mav is getting into a forbidden-lovers situation, Caleb."

"Eh, excuse the fuck out of me? Say that again?"

"I don't know who, and it's none of my business, but you're my best friend."

Caleb squeaks, "Excuse?"

"One of—one of my best friends," Luke corrects. "And whatever happened over the summer, maybe it was just the one time, and maybe that's for the best. You'll have to work with her, at the very least if that's what Jasper wanted, and you're planning on staying here, so just let it go." He turns to Caleb. "She would be his boss, though, huh?" Then he starts to laugh and pat me on the shoulder.

I can't actually believe what I'm hearing.

Charlotte Adler is not my boss. Charlotte. Adler. Is. Not. My. Boss. I still own the ranch, even if I leave.

I find her again in the crowd, dancing with Quinn. Is that dancing, though? They're just bouncing around and singing along to some pop song.

Luke has turned around and is watching them, too. He's got a grin on his face.

"What about you and Quinn, then? That's a thing?"

"It's a thing...I don't know, man. We get together when we can. What plans does she have to stay here? I haven't asked her, but I don't want to leave. She said some shit about her parents wanting her to go back to Dallas. She turned down access to her trust fund when she said, 'No.' I couldn't give her a life that she was used to, even if it ever did turn into something serious."

"I highly doubt that. She seems smitten as hell with your ass."

"If she's good with it as it is, I am, too. If it's meant for me, it'll come to me. Don't chase, Mav. Attract what you want." His eyes are still on his prize, currently dancing with my "could have been."

"You and your manifesting," I say. I must admit, though, it's working; Luke's doing great.

Looking back at the girl who has been haunting me everywhere I go, I see a man approach and put his arm around her waist as she dances. It's fine; this is fine. I don't care. She can do whatever she wants, and I can, too. If she wants to whoop it up with that clown, who am I to stop her?

After several minutes of watching them, I reach for my other drink, only to see that Caleb currently has it in his hand. I pinch my brow. "Ugh, dude. For real, you're cut off."

"Last one!" Caleb shouts.

"Here, have a shot," Luke says as he hands me a drink.

I sling it back and slam the glass on the table. "Not cool, Caleb Wright." I scowl at him.

A few more country songs later, the DJ's voice plays over the speakers, saying something about finding a dance partner, and then plays some R&B song.

Caleb jumps up and says, "Ooh, I love this song! Let's go dance!" We're on the club hits now, so there are even more people on the dance floor.

"Is that going to be a problem for you?" Luke asks me.

"Why would it be?"

"Because you look like you're about to go ballistic. You're way too calm after that bombshell news about the ranch."

"I'm fine. And to show you how fine I am," I turn to Caleb, "let's go boogie, bud."

"Here we go," mutters Luke.

"Fuck," groans Garrett. "I just got here; no fighting."

We don't go right to the girls on the dance floor. We first make a stop at the bar. Another drink and a water down before we make our way to them.

Charlotte is glistening with sweat. From behind her ears, I see a bead trailing down her neck and curving between her breasts, which are definitely out on display in her white, deep v-neck, short-sleeved shirt. It's so thin, it might as well be tissue, and it's plastered to her body. I can see her black bra and her peaked nipples. I don't care that she looks damn good. Those sequin pants hugging every sinful curve of her body.

Fuck. Watching her body move with such fluidity, her hands above her head, is a sight. And the peek of skin showing beneath her shirt? It's also sweaty. It reminds me of the scene I was jacking off to in the shower this morning.

No! Stop thinking with your dick! She is going to make your life a living hell.

I watch a hand snake across that stomach. A hand that's not mine—that's the reality check I needed. Nothing like a bucket of "doesn't belong to you" to bring you out of a daydream.

The hand is inching up her shirt now. Absolutely not. The guy is basically grinding his dick on her ass.

She's clearly loving the attention, because a sly grin breaks across her face, and she opens her eyes and looks right at me.

I don't react; I just kind of stand there and swing back and forth while Caleb and Quinn dance. Luke went to get some waters, and here I am looking like a goddamn idiot, watching Charlotte bump and grind with some guy.

She turns in his arms and gets up on her tiptoes to say something in his ear. He lifts her up a bit in a hug. I've never seen the man before, which I guess isn't a surprise because I haven't been home long, and even then, it's been months since the festival, and I wasn't paying attention to anyone but Charlotte. He's not hideous—tall, broad shoulders, blond hair, a bit of stubble on a strong jaw. He's wearing jeans, boots, a cowboy hat, and a way-too-tight black T-shirt. So, maybe most would see the appeal. Me? No, I do not.

She's got to be talking about me because his eyes snap to meet mine, and he gives me a smile. *Yeah, go ahead and smile, asshat.* I just smile right back. I'm not bothered. Nope. It's fine. And it's fine because I already had her. She's already screamed my name from midnight well into sunrise.

He's nodding when she pulls away from him and balances on her feet. "Thank you!" she says to him. He takes off his hat, pulls a handkerchief from his pocket, and wipes the sweat from the brim before placing it on her head. He might as well just have pissed on her. Around here, that's claiming rights.

He brushes against my shoulders when he tries to make his way past. I damn near check him back. But my eyes track to Charlotte. And Quinn and Caleb are playing like they're not watching or listening.

"Charlotte," I growl.

"Oh, hi!" It's the first thing she's said to me all night. She has venom in her voice. "I didn't see you there."

Absolute bullshit. I step into her space. "Do you know what you're doing?" I flick the brim of his hat.

"Yes, sir. I'm just having a good time. My date went to close our tab."

Mmm—"sir." If this were any other situation, that would do it for me.

"No, you don't know what you're doing because you're just playing cowgirl until something better comes along."

"That's not fair or true, you asshole."

"I'm the asshole? I thought you were better than a buckle bunny."

Pointing to the hat she's wearing, I ask her, "You know the saying, 'You wear the hat, you ride the cowboy'?"

"I have. Who cares? Maybe I want to ride the cowboy!"

"Him? Really, Charlotte?! Do you even know him?" I point my thumb toward the bar where the douchebag scampered to as soon as he saw me behind her.

"I didn't know you. And now that I do, I don't want to. Bye, Ranger Rick."

Infuriating woman. "Stop calling me 'Ranger Rick'! You had no problem remembering my name when you were moaning it for hours. You'll have no problem remembering it when you cash those checks I sign, either."

"That's where you're wrong, Ranger Rick." She leans in to whisper, her mouth so close to my ear that her breath tickles the hairs on my neck. God damn, she smells so good. The whiskey hasn't killed my senses so much yet that I can feel it to my toes when she says, so low that I have to strain to hear her over the music, "I'm the one in charge of the ranch. And while you own the land, you don't have a job. So I guess that means you're not going to get paid. And because your dad put everything in a trust, you're not going to get it until the lawyers say so." She gives a little hmph and boops my nose right before she sashays away.

Damn it to all the hells in all the worlds. I turn around to see her walk up to the guy and put his hat back on top of his head. He pulls her into his embrace and nuzzles her neck. She pushes him back just a bit, as though trying to be playful, but I know this girl, and she likes her space. But, to my surprise, she offers him her hand and heads back to the corner where my guys are.

I try to catch up to her, but Bart's is even more packed now.

I hear Luke say something, but can't quite make it out. I catch up just in time to hear Charlotte say, "Guys, this is my friend, Ezra. We're heading out, but I wanted to say bye first."

"Ezra, it was nice seeing you again. Y'all have a great time!" Quinn says.

"Hey, Ez. You guys have a good night." Caleb gives him a fist bump. A fist bump! What in the damn hell is going on here?! I will definitely be asking him how and what he knows about this guy.

Whoa. That means Charlotte's talked about this guy before. He's not just a random hookup. What the hell?

"Nice to meet all of you. I'll make sure Charlotte gets home," he says.

My eyes go right to Charlotte, and she's looking right at me. Daring me to say something? To make a scene? I don't move a muscle. Okay, not true. Pretty sure my jaw just ticked from how hard I ground my teeth at his statement, and maybe my fist clenched.

"Night, guys," Charlotte says, then looks up at this asshat she's about to leave with and smiles. Smiles with full teeth, not a smirk.

He leads her away with a hand on her back.

I turn to Quinn to ask 101 questions when Luke steps in front of her. "Hey, man. Take a breath," he suggests, his hands up. "You knew you both were going to have a run-in outside the ranch eventually, and we're all here having a good time. Let her have hers." Leaning in closer, he adds, "But leave Quinn out of it. They're best friends, and she's not going to give up a peep, and you know it."

The rest of the night is a blur. Somewhere between Caleb pushing more shots, Garrett suggesting we do karaoke, and me hanging my head out the window for fresh air, I can't remember a thing.

When I wake up, I feel something poke into my back. My legs, too. My head and my neck. I try so hard to peel my eyes open—try and fail because they're crusted shut. I can feel a slight draft; I'm freezing, and I feel like shit. Am I on the side of the road? I might be dying.

I try blinking again and feel my eyelids slowly peel away from each other. Only to reveal the bane of my existence sitting and watching me intently.

"Ughh, should have left me dead on the road," I slur.

She holds a pair of scissors up, then opens and closes them quickly.

Okay. Okay, now she's got my attention.

She lowers the scissors to my bottom half. I look down to see my fly is open, and my dick is sticking out of my pants. "Wha—?"

Snip.

I scream, and then pass out.

Charlotte

CHAPTER 16

I double over with laughter. I'm laughing so hard my sides start to hurt, and tears are streaming out of my eyes. Seriously, I almost pee my pants. I can't believe he actually passed out. I grab the bucket of water off the stool and dump it over his head. With how cold it is, it should wake him up. Not cold enough that he would die of frostbite, but close.

"Wha—?" Steam immediately billows up when it hits him.

Yup, that woke him up. Serves him right for letting Walter out of his stall. The horse had enough sense to stay in the barn, luckily.

"Fuck!" he exclaims. He's still flat on his back, sprawled out on the hay, when he pats down his groin area, lifts his hands, and then freaks out again. "Oh my God, where is it? We need to get to the hospital. Put it on ice."

I reach down for the hot dog that I put into his pants and dangle it above him. "Are you looking for this?" I ask, and, in the most savage move ever, I take a bite out of it. "Mmmm."

"Jesus Christ! You're fucking crazy. That's my dick!"

"Oh, Ranger Rick, if only your dick was this tasty." I throw the rest of the snipped hot dog at him, and it lands on his chest before rolling off onto the horse bedding, where it immediately gets gross and covered in hay. "Now get up—we're having an all-hands meeting, and it would be nice for the guys to see the new 'Property Owner' there. Then, you're helping drive the cows to a different paddock." I throw his coat at him, turn on my heel, and walk out.

The crew already resents him, so I don't have to work harder for that, but they really don't take kindly to idiots letting their horses wander in the barn; it's dangerous. And Ace made it pretty clear that the old-timers feel a kind of way about the "absent" son being gone for so long and suddenly coming back to the ranch. I guess they noticed that he never visited except for holidays, or that he tried to convince Jas to sell the land. They worked the land; they were the ones to stay through the hard times. And the newer and younger folks respect the old-timers, especially Hank and Clint. We have a small team, but so far, we've been blessed with no drama between them. Dappled Stone Ranch is more than a job; it's like a family.

I felt bad for a minute—everyone processes trauma, loss, and pain differently. And I know this is the last place Maverick wants to be. He made that perfectly clear this summer. Given everything that's happened with the death of Jasper that brought him back here, it's likely not changed. But nothing is going to excuse his dickhead behavior.

I overheard Hank say that Maverick was a threat to their way of life, to everything they've built. I find it hard to believe that he would intentionally work to see this place fail, or at least I want to believe that. It would go against everything he shared with me that night over the summer.

It was just a night—strangers sharing things they don't dare speak to their friends and family. I didn't put it together that his resentment of his family was because of the ranch; he never said what his family did or who they were. We didn't ask or tell any details about our families. I thought we would have had more time to get to know each other.

Jasper trusted both of us. But he knew I needed this job, what it provided me. Maverick may need the land to make peace with whatever demons are following him. It's not that Jasper chose one of us over the other, but he trusted us to figure it out together. Whether or not we like it. This wasn't my doing, but Jasper is so important to me that I'm honoring his last wishes, no matter how much Maverick wants me to quit.

Maverick looks like shit. Ace has him loading and unloading the feed and hay because the pastures are mostly brown, grasses mostly dead. What's left is going to die off quickly because of the early dustings of snow we've been getting. I started at Dappled Stone when it was mostly green and lush; now it's cold, gray, and brown.

"Wow, Ace." I approach my friend and stand next to him, watching Maverick work. My boots sink a bit into the mud. The freeze and thaw cycles are brutal on the paths and areas along the fencelines. "You weren't kidding about putting him through the paces. Thank you." I'm not evil, but Maverick has done nothing but make my life hell since he's come home.

Maverick flicks his ice-blue eyes in our direction, sweat beading on his brow. Too bad—this is work that still needs to be done. He's skipping assignments, doing small things that are disrupting the flow for everyone here. I mean, who fucking reorganizes the barn? He doesn't respect what I've done here, and though I've only been here for months, when the team is as small as ours, you learn all the jobs quickly. It's not like I had no barn or horse experience. I spent all of my free time with my horse; it was better than being at home with my parents, and Georgie was always dancing.

Since the funeral, Maverick has made it his personal mission to challenge me on every single thing and stir up the crew. I know he's hurting, but I'm not the only one paying the price of his strained relationship; the ranch is, too. And now Ace is having him do the grunt work.

"Yuck it up now, Charlotte. I don't care how many hours you've worked on this land—my name is on the deed. You're really just a ghost, aren't you?"

That's it; the heart of it. I shift my gaze to Ace and say, "Work him hard. He needs the paycheck. I'm done for the day."

He gives me a conspiratorial smirk and says, "Yes, sir, Charlie."

I giggle and pat the railing of the fence before heading to the barn to charge the walkies and check on the records, make sure there's enough feed and supplies. I'm great at compliance paperwork; that's the part Ace was all too happy to have me take over.

Since Jasper's death, Ace has been letting me fly solo to make decisions, and then will come in and we review it together. I was so scared that he was going to abandon me when Jasper's wishes were read. But he said, "We both know I don't need a fancy-ass title to know who's really in charge." I smiled and gave him a hug. That's all Ace needed. He's a good man for the ones he cares about.

Quinn is unpacking the biggest box of smut I've ever seen. The Book Nook boasts the scent of old pages and fresh paint. Quinn and the owner, Viviane, painted it earlier this week. Two large, second-hand chairs face each other by a wall-mounted electric fireplace, a coffee table between them. I feel that Luke's design influence is changing the look of this place, which is great. They've always had a great selection of books, but it was missing something.

Last night after the interaction with Maverick, I wanted to have a good time with Ezra. I really did, but I didn't feel a spark. I think it's because I was so angry at Ranger Rick that I couldn't be present with Ezra. We went to the small distillery in town for a cocktail and he walked me back to my truck. We struggled to keep a conversation going. Duds.

"Ooh, this one is about vampires and fae!" Quinn exclaims. "It's supposed to be so good! The MMC is like seven feet tall and wields shadows."

"Mmm, a Shadow Daddy. I need something less angsty, though. I have enough angst with Maverick being in such close proximity every day."

"Hmm, you could go with historical romance."

I shake my head.

"Then it's a rom-com for sure, darlin'. I'll pick one out while you pick up our food next door."

My stomach likes that idea because it rumbles as soon as she mentions food. "What did you order?"

"The usual, but new cocktails. I took Mrs. Wright a few of our new arrivals this afternoon and told her you were coming over to help unpack books and hang out. Then she said dinner was on the house! I love her kind heart; she's been kind of sad since Jasper passed."

"She's such a sweet woman. I love the people in this town."

"Me too. Everyone's so damn nice!" she says in her twang. "Ooh, the drink Caleb invented—I sampled it the other day, and it was so damn good, Charlie. It's a sassy espresso kind of cocktail. Espresso, Licor 43, whiskey, citrus peel, and cinnamon—an 'Old Carajillo,' he called it."

"Yes, fuck yes. Please, I need a drink after this day." I stand and walk to the door, the overhead bell jingling. I swear, this job has aged me a bit because I'm sore in places I didn't used to be. And it's not from the sex I'm not having with anyone, just rough wear on the body. There's a serious lack of sex.

The sky is already dark since the sun is behind the mountains, and the streetlamps are buzzing around me. Flour Child is literally next door to the Book Nook. I don't know how Q does it. The scent of cookies, fresh bread, and sandwiches lingering all day long—I would constantly stuff my face.

I push the door open and wince inwardly; my arms are sore from moving boxes and from work today. I hear a familiar voice coming from the bar area, and my eyes track right to him.

Shit. Ranger Rick is sitting at a table with Caleb and Luke, balancing on the chair he's tipped back away from the table, an amber liquid in his glass.

He must feel my eyes on him because he looks at me, and his eyes darken.

Play it cool; don't let this asshat get under your skin. Get the food and drinks, and put distance between you.

Caleb stands up from his chair and walks behind the bar, then waves me over. "Hi, Charlie! I've got your order ready."

I ignore Maverick completely and walk over to Caleb. I hear a thwack and the screeching of a chair against the floor. *Sweet Jesus, just please leave me alone.*

"I'm not in the mood for your shit, Ranger Rick." I bet he's regretting telling me that was his nickname growing up.

He laughs heartily, like he just heard the funniest joke in the world, while I stand at the counter, looking at him like a damn fool. He leans in so that only I can hear him whisper, "Are you stalking me?" It sends shivers up my spine, not because I feel threatened, but because my stupid, traitorous body is responding to his clean scent and the sparkle in his eyes. I should not be turned on by the violence this man could bring, given all my past trauma—but, fuck, the lack of attention my pussy's gotten lately is so damn evident.

"All set, Charlie. Say hi to Quinn." Gods, I could kiss Caleb. He holds out a large paper bag and a drink carrier with four drinks in to-go cups.

"Thanks, Caleb," I say as I take our dinner and slowly walk my fine ass away from that annoying, infuriating, handsome-as-hell pain in the ass.

As I open the door, I sneak a peek at him, and he's still got that grin on his face, his gaze lifting from my ass.

"See ya at the office," he says, his voice cutting through the other noise in the café.

I open the door and Quinn says, "Luke just texted me this picture of you and Ranger Rick. He's standing awfully close. Want me to go knee him in the nuts? I would, baby girl."

I let out a sigh. I might drink all four of these damn cocktails by the time the night is over.

Maverick

CHAPTER 17

I sit down on the leather couch with another drink in my hand and stare at the fire, watching it crackle and pop. It's nice having a fireplace; none of my other places had them. The way the fire dances soothes something in me. It's nice sometimes just to sit with my thoughts. To replay all the mistakes I've made. Most recently, Charlotte tops that list. I can't help but get under her skin the way she's gotten under mine.

The house creaks a little, as if urging me to snap out of my mood. Or it's just an old house, the earth settling.

My phone's been buzzing all night. I don't know why he's picked tonight to call nonstop, but without having to look, I know it's Owen. Before I talk myself out of it, I pick it up.

"You know, I am not above getting on a plane and coming out to Wyoming, you little shit."

I laugh, mainly because I know he absolutely would. It's only out of respect for the fact that I need space that he hasn't already.

He continues, "Figured you must have hit your head hard enough to forget how to answer the damn phone. It would have been a wellness check."

"I should have sent you to voicemail if you were just going to give me shit the whole time."

We fall into conversation about the ranch, what he's been up to, and the difference between coastal winters and winters in the West. It's bullshit, but I let him carry the conversation. He's the only family I have, and he's not even my blood family. How pathetic is that?

Ultimately, the conversation finds its way back to Dad. It's why I haven't answered his calls until now.

I take a big breath and push it all the way out. Maybe it's the whiskey, maybe it's the interaction with Charlotte, or maybe it's just time.

"I stayed away from here for so long, and all these memories are flooding me," I confess.

"That's only natural, Reid."

Reid—after Owen Reid. He and Dad were closer than brothers; they were each other's wingmen. Dad called me Reid and Owen is the only one left to call me by that name.

"Well, it's why I stayed away from Dad. I can't explain it—but I always thought he blamed me, resented me. For Mom. For the Olympics. What a waste I turned out to be." I almost sob. "They sacrificed so much for me."

Owen's quiet, letting me fill the silence, then says, "Mav, you were twelve," no pity or judgment in his tone.

I sit up straight. "It doesn't matter. You know, I can see my mother so damn clearly in my mind right now? I can see her walk around the corner from my parents' room into this very room and yell at me for having my shoes on. The way she smiled at me, even when the pain got to be too much from the medications and cancer making her weak. Or how I begged her to come outside one more time to see how much snow had fallen overnight, and she finally came to the porch, and her face lit up. 'You know what that means, sweetheart? You get to ski on the hill after chores.' The hill was literally a mound of dirt that Dad used the backhoe to create in the pasture closest to the cottage. She started coughing real bad and Dad had to come out to carry her back to their bed. She died that night." A tear, hot—so hot it boils and must leave a trail of seared skin—falls from my eye.

Owen doesn't say anything. He just lets me get out all the things I haven't been able to voice but think about almost every day.

"I think about that night with the guys and what happened all the time. Especially when I'm out on that back pasture. What could have happened if you and Dad weren't home? How different so many lives would be."

"That ain't your fault, either. You are a good man, as much as you protest and sulk. And you care, and that's what makes you so angry. You care, and you wish you didn't."

It's my turn to be silent; I just sit there with what he just said.

And Owen? He doesn't rush me. "How's life at the ranch been? What about your housemate? How's she doin'?"

"Every day's a damn dream over here at the Dappled Stone."

"Fall in love yet?"

"Ha!" I bark out. The sound breaks and shatters the silence against the walls. "That's something you definitely don't have to worry about. I just don't know what he was thinking, leaving this place for me. Or having Charlotte run it. Why would he do that?"

"You're rolling out the welcome mat, I bet."

"Something like that. She doesn't want to be here, so I'm just making it easy for her."

"You've always hated anything that feels like it's got teeth. That one is a firecracker; she'll bite back."

I almost say, "Tell me about it," but the words get caught in my throat.

We hang up after he tells me what he can about work and the old sailboat he's restoring. We have amazing sunsets in the mountains, but in North Carolina in the Banks? That view is damn nice, too. I sit back on the couch and watch the fire die out.

Charlotte

CHAPTER 18

Turns out that building these damn cabins in the middle of winter is exactly the headache you might think it is, even with the warmer-than-average temperatures. And yet, here we are—me and my crew of semi-willing ranch hands. The general contractors got everything settled with the foundation and framing to code, along with the roofing. The doors and windows are being installed now.

Jasper suggested we use Draper Construction, Luke's company, for this project. When I approached Luke about it, he was honest and recommended another construction company. He gave me the name of a general contractor who has experience building tiny homes and who understood we wanted to have a focus on sustainable and eco-friendly materials where possible and where code allowed.

Despite who his best friend is, I like Luke. He's been nothing but helpful as we've been building the cabins. He's been an excellent resource to lean on.

Clint must have been a builder in a different life and has taken a special interest in this project. I'm so grateful for him! I had him work with the contractors to make sure the windows he's installing are perfect. Not that I don't trust him, but being that these are temporary dwellings, we have to carry insurance, and I want everything perfect. I had Clint install windows and doors on a cabin first, then had the contractors inspect to make sure he had it down perfectly.

I tried to explain it was just as a precaution, and he said, "Charlie, I haven't done this in almost twenty years. I want them guys to go over this with a fine-tooth comb. I don't want to find no fleas after, you know?" Once he had it installed, the GCs said they were good to move on to the flashing around.

Today, I'd like to have the structure sealed up. It feels like a race to get this done, I think just because it's nearing the end of the year. It will be a symbolic start to the new year, a good cutting-off point.

I step over a pile of lumber and call out to the crew, "You all deserve some whiskey after this!" Walking up to Hank and Clint, I ask, "What are the plans for the new year?"

They share a look and give me smirks; sometimes that's all I get from them. Ranch hands are a different breed. Sometimes I get a full belly laugh—other times, I get a smirk and a grunt. And they mean the same thing.

"I'm staying here," Clint says.

"Me too," Hank adds.

"Well, I hope you guys get some type of rest over the next few days." Just then, my phone rings, and I see Ace's name on the screen. "Enjoy the next couple of days, guys. Don't do anything I wouldn't do." I turn away from the guys and flip open my phone. "Hi, Ace."

"Charlie, I'll be up at the construction site soon. Was checking to see if you needed anything from the office?"

"No, I'm good. You don't have to come over unless you want to watch Hank and Clint. As it is, the guys are almost done." It's 4:00 p.m., and the sun is fading quickly. We're in that time of year where the black sky consumes everything, and right now, it's dictating how much light we have to work with to get this last cabin settled.

"All right. I'll get the evening feed and headcounts started with my guys while we get them in the barn."

"After you guys get them settled, are you taking off for New Year's?"

"Charlie, you know damn well no one is taking off for New Year's. But it's nice you offered."

"I tried to keep Jasper's traditions."

"We get that, but it's the first year without him, and it's just different. I think the crew wants to work." I start to interrupt, but he continues, "Let them. If someone wants to take a day, let them. But let them work through it if they want to, too."

Resigned, I say, "All right. Then I'll see you in the New Year."

"See you tomorrow. Hey, Charlie?" There's a pause. "Sleep in a bit; you look like you need the rest."

"Shit, you should take the week then, buddy!" I reply.

He just laughs.

I text Quinn.

> Nothing crazy tonight. The guys are working tomorrow, and I want to work with them.

> Quinn: Eh, didn't you give them the day off?

> Yeah, but no one is taking the day. It's important to me that they see I'm in this, too. So, maybe a movie, girl dinner, and Prosecco.

> Quinn: :salute emoji:

An hour and a half later, Quinn's knocking on my door. I let her in and see she's got a giant overnight bag with her! When she walks inside, the wind blows in a dusting of snow. It's damn cold, single digits.

"Q, what the hell do you have in there?"

"Cold weather essentials: spa socks, face masks, Prosecco—well, kind of. It's bubbly wine. And frozen pizza." She then pulls out her tablet.

"And this baby is loaded up with episodes of *Bridgerton*."

Bless her! I don't get Wi-Fi this far away from the house, and even then, we use Starlink for internet in the offices in the barn and the house.

I preheat the oven, and we get our makeshift spa-bar station set up on the coffee table in the living room. We take the pillows off the couch and lay down blankets.

We put lotion on our feet and then the spa socks. I even turn the extra space heater on so that it blows toward our toes. It's like our old nights together when I lived in town. I miss the random nights we could get together. I've been so focused on the ranch that I feel like I've neglected her.

I give her a hug. "Thank you! I didn't know how much I needed this."

"Oh, baby girl, I've missed you so much! But I am so damn proud of all that you're doin'!"

"I've missed you, too! I know it seems like I'm not here," I motion between us, "but I am. I'm just...trying to make something bigger than myself."

"I know. That's why I'm not mad; I'm proud of you—of us. I'm taking on more work responsibilities and think I may be making some boss babe moves of my own soon."

"Fuck, yes. Can you tell me or are you going to edge it out of me?"

"I think I'll make you squirm a bit in your seat. But it's all good things." She laughs and pulls out another bottle of sparkling wine. "Charlie?"

"Hmm?" I look over to where she is now in the kitchen.

"I know, you know?"

Wait, what?

"Eh, know what, Quinn?"

"I know that you're hiding somethin'. Kind of big or bad or maybe both? And I've been going over in my head what it could be that you wouldn't tell me. All I could come up with is that it has to be scary as fuckin' hell or maybe dangerous." She pauses and smiles at me, but there is heartbreak in her eyes. *I am such a shit friend.* "But whenever and only *if* you're ever able to tell me, you know I'm here for you. You can't scare me away, baby cakes."

I swallow the lump in my throat and nod solemnly. "I don't deserve you."

Uncorked bottle in hand, she walks back to our pillow fort and sits across from me, refilling my glass. "Babe, we deserve every happiness in this world. Don't let whatever's eatin' you stop you from trying to find what shred of happiness you can find. All right?" She clinks the vintage juice glass against mine and I promise myself to try and find happiness where I can.

"Okay, enough Sad Sally shit. I wanna dive into a regency romance and be swept away by a lord for a few hours."

We devour two frozen pizzas, bottles of cheap bubbly, and fall asleep with masks on our faces.

In the morning, I have every intention of sleeping in. But months of getting up at 4:30 a.m. have my internal clock reset to this new life.

Quinn knows she can sleep in and stay as long as she wants even when I have to work. I leave Finn cuddled up with her on the couch.

The energy of the day has me itching to start this year off right. I'm outside every day for work, but rarely do I get to be outside because I want to be. And today, I want to take Betty White for a run, just me and her.

It's 5:30 a.m. by the time I hop in Verne and head to the stable. Not fifteen minutes later, I'm already regretting not staying in when Maverick walks in and heads straight to Walter's stall.

Maverick

CHAPTER 19

Happy New Year? It's just another day. The bitter cold doesn't bother me so much as the feeling of knowing this is my first year without a family. Admittedly, I thought about going to Bart's to tie one on with the guys. Garrett's still in town until the end of the week. But when it came time to go out, I had zero desire. So, I texted the boys and told them to be safe and have a good time. Then I told them to come over later tonight for a chill guys' night.

The urge to get out and enjoy the snow is always there, a presence in my life—much like the way people feel spirits or angels with them, only my guardian angel is being out in the wilds with the snow. If I have to work today, there is not enough time to get to the closest mountain to ski, but I could definitely get on top of Walt and just roam.

It's not that early, and I know the crew isn't taking the day off, so the overhead lights in the barn don't alarm me. But I can smell the faint scent of something rich, creamy, woodsy, like sweet butter and honey, and nuts. In a stable, the smells of hay, dust, and manure are usually overwhelming unless you're used to it. But this familiarly potent scent, whatever it is, hits my nose, and it's sensual, like a caress enveloping me. I've smelled it before and my brain finally catches up.

The hair on my arms stands on edge. Our two female ranch hands, Jemma and Billie Jean, wouldn't wear perfume to work. Which means that Charlotte's in here.

I take another breath and close my eyes. I open them to find her staring at me from Betty White's stall, strapping the horse's belly buckle tight. There are daggers in her eyes. "Did you see me come in here? It's a bit early for you, isn't it?"

"Please. I have better things to do than to watch outside my window and hope you walk by, Charlotte. You have packages on the porch, by the way. Might want to get those before they accidentally get lost."

"Don't even. I'll get them later." She continues to tack up Betty White with those annoyingly assured hands, fingers making quick work of the buckles. Betty White is a magnificent horse—a Tovero, with gold markings. Maybe that's why she went with the name Betty White, because while she is white, she's also golden—a Golden Girl.

I watch her pull Betty out of her stall, and she catches my stare.

"Didn't think you'd be up before noon, if I'm honest," she says as she walks past Walter and me. "But I guess some perks come with being the owner. Why are you even here?"

I stroke the soft skin of Walter's nose and give him a peppermint. "Don't worry about her, she's just bitter," I tell him.

It's not even 8 a.m. Couldn't make it a few hours into the new year without someone giving me shit.

I continue tacking up Walter and lead him out of the barn. I see hoof marks going to the east, so I set off to the west.

I'm thankful I don't see her while we're out. Upon returning, I love on Walter and give him some hay, oats, and water, after which I put leftover peppermints in the office. There's a bowl of them for the horses. Not that I'd let Charlotte see, but I sometimes sneak them to Betty.

The guys texted while I was riding, saying they were on the way. They're stopping at Flour Child for pizzas and the liquor store to pick up beer. We're watching some football and playing poker.

I walk up the stairs and see the brown packages and the thick envelope sitting on one of the Adirondack chairs. It's petty as fuck, but I bring them in with me. If she wants them, she can ask nicely. I chuckle to myself, "Say please, Charlotte," then drop them off in the office.

After the quickest shower I can manage, I hurry downstairs to tidy up, but beyond the laundry basket in the mudroom, you'd never even know I was here. I was always a "tidy" kid, but that's how Mom and Dad expected me to be. We were always on the go, and the mess just caused stress when we had to run out the door and I couldn't find something last minute.

I get a fire going in the fireplace and make sure there's enough ice in case we want something other than beer. I hear a single honk out-side—Luke. I open the door, and he's got the music playing so loud in the truck I can hear it from here.

He shuts off the engine, and the boys all pile out of the truck, beer, pizza, chips, and the box of poker chips in hand.

"Maverick! You ready to have your ass handed to you tonight?" Garrett laughs as he gives my hand a slap and a fist bump.

"That was a damn fluke last time." I laugh. "Where's Jake?" I ask.

Caleb says, "He's in love, guy. He's working overtime and hanging out with Gracie."

"Nice. At this rate, he'll be the next paired off before any of us." I laugh again and shut the door.

The guys don't laugh; there's a beat of silence, like there's a joke that I don't quite understand.

"Let's eat. I'm starving," Garrett says, breaking the silence.

"You're always starving. Don't they feed you in the Midwest?" Luke punches him in the shoulder.

"Please," Garrett guffaws, "I'm still working out three to four times a week. When was the last time you saw a gym?"

"I lift timber and have a physically demanding job; I don't sit behind a desk crunching numbers for the man all day long."

Garrett just smirks and winks. "That's not all I crunch."

Caleb has the sense to get the beers into the fridge and hands one to each of us. "Cheers, assholes."

I miss this. With the guys——the people who really know me—I can just be myself.

We sit at the breakfast nook table instead of the long dining table in the kitchen. Pizza boxes and bags of chips are strewn about. Several beers and some terrible hands of poker later, something on the porch catches my eye.

The guys notice the look of concern on my face and turn their heads in the direction of the large windows overlooking the front porch and out to the eastern pasture. There's nothing I can see from here now. But then the lock on the door clicks, and the door opens.

Charlotte pushes inside.

"Eh, this is a private party," I say to her. I take in what she's wearing: new boots, skintight jeans that are hugging her curves so closely that I don't even know how she got them on, a cropped cashmere turtleneck sweater that exposes the slightest sliver of skin, and a puffy vest. Despite being completely covered up, she looks sinful as fuck with her cheeks flushed from the cold and her golden curls wild. Why does she have to be so beautiful, though?

"My invite must have gotten lost in the mail. Same with my packages."

Shit. I told her to come pick them up, but I didn't think she would come get them tonight.

"Heya, Charlie," Luke says. He sees and works with her the most because of Quinn and the cabins.

"'Sup, Luke."

"Did those windows go in okay?"

"Yeah, they looked great. Thanks."

"No problem, I'm glad."

I'm losing my shit because he really shouldn't be helping the enemy. But then, doesn't it benefit me in the end? I don't know; it's all very damned-if-I-do-and-damned-if-I-don't at the moment.

Garrett stands up and says, "Damn, Charlotte, consider yourself invited."

"Hmm," she says as she walks over to the table. "What are you guys playing? Ooh, Texas Hold 'Em. I couldn't; that's okay. I've just come to get my packages and a bottle. You don't mind, do you, Ranger Rick? Jasper used to let me get a bottle when I was out because he didn't like me going into town for something he had a bunch of."

I watch her walk from the nook to the liquor cabinet, and I swear to God, she's practically strutting down a catwalk as she pulls out a bottle of bourbon and a jar of candied cherries from Italy. I can feel my blood boil because, hot damn, her ass in those jeans. I want to bite my fist, but I shake my head and get that thought out of my mind. I look over to Garrett and his eyes are lasered in on her ass, too. Caleb and Luke share a look between them and then look at me with shit-eating grins on their faces.

"These cherries are my favorites," she says as she reaches to the back of the cabinet, and as she bends over slightly, the sweater creeps up her back. "Do one of you mind opening this for me? It'll make it easier to do it when I get back home. Last time, I cracked the damn jar open."

Garrett stands up and walks over to her. "I can get that for you."

I can't watch this. I walk to the office and get her packages. I accidentally drop the one on the bottom of the stack. I get a peek at the shipping address, and the sent-from address snags my eye. I almost drop the damn thing again. Sex toys? She shipped sex toys to my house?! Doesn't she have enough? She had a treasure chest in her dresser over the summer.

My body goes hot as I remember exactly how she looked as I used her pink toy on her—as she watched me push it in and out of her body. She came on it and then asked to lick it. Charlotte Adler is kinky as fuck.

I can only guess what's in this box, and I have a very active imagination. In my sex-addled brain, I rush back to the kitchen, not sure what I'm expecting to see, but it certainly isn't Charlotte licking cherry juice off the side of the jar. She's got a small droplet of red liquid on her chin, and Garrett wipes it off with his thumb.

I clench my jaw so hard it pops.

She smirks at me over Garrett's shoulder.

My brain is saying, "What in the hell is going on?" and my body is saying, "Mine. Mine. Mine."

"Ah, perfect," Charlotte says to Garrett. "Thank you! I really need one of these tonight."

A full-blown blush splashes across my face.

"I'll get out of your hair." She crosses the room to take the packages from my hands when I don't move—my legs seem to have rooted in place. Before leaving, she says, "Enjoy, guys."

I remember Garrett saying he called dibs however many months ago the second he saw her. He's still looking at the door when he says, "Goddamn, you are the biggest fucking moron, Maverick."

Luke and Caleb double over with laughter.

Me? I'm still left wondering what in the hell just happened. I lose the rest of the night and Garrett again takes all our money.

Charlotte

I hadn't known it was guys' night at the main house last night. I saw Luke's truck, but that's nothing new, so walking in and seeing all of them there? My God, I couldn't have planned it better if I had tried. So what if I put a little more thought into what I wore to get my mail and packages? On the off chance he saw me, I just wanted to look extra good. I didn't think he would hijack them off the porch so I would have to ask him for them.

When I walked in, his eyes left a burning trail on me as they swept up from my feet to my eyes. But then, so did Garrett's. I don't want to get Garrett's hopes up, and I knew it was cruel to intentionally flirt with him, but seeing Maverick get flustered was so damn worth it. His jaw was clenched so hard when Garrett opened up the cherries and I licked up the side of the jar, catching the juice. That was an accident too; I just didn't want to get any on the floor.

Did I want the whiskey and cherries? Absolutely. Could I have drank vodka instead of whiskey tonight? Yes. Did I have to take the cherries? No. Jasper always let me raid the cabinet when I wanted something to drink. But tonight? Means to an end. I'm glad I could interrupt Maverick's stupid guys' night.

I have no way of knowing if he actually peeked at the senders' names on my packages, but I damn hope he did. Then, he would have seen that I ordered something from a well-known sex toy company. His face was flushed when he came back into the room, holding my boxes of goodies! Quinn ordered me two books, while I got some skincare and a new temperature-play vibrator.

The ride into town and to the grocery store takes me past my old house. I give a little wave and continue on to get some shopping done. It's gray and cloudy—I love when it's moody outside. I'm going to get some good reading in when I get back to the cottage. I intend to curl up with a fuzzy blanket and Finn and dive into my new romantasy.

I haven't really had a chance for any workouts, but I still do yoga pretty regularly. My food choices, though? I need more fresh fruit and veggies. I definitely think that being on a cattle farm has increased my meat consumption.

I pull my shopping list from my back pocket and pop in my headphones. Bopping along to some throwback tunes I have saved to my flip phone, I enjoy just wandering the aisles and looking for blue cheese dressing for a wedge salad. It sounded so good when I was making my meal plan. I also need to find some artichokes. I'm in the right aisle but can't reach the very last jar of artichokes on the top shelf, pushed all the way back, and I'm thinking about stepping on the bottom shelf when a man says, "I can get that for you."

Ezra's watching me with a smile on his face when I turn around. "Need some help?"

"Hi. Yes, please."

He reaches up with ease and grabs the jar for me. His smile reaches his amber eyes. He looks good: the sleeves of his button-up are rolled up, paired with a sherpa vest and jeans. He hands the artichokes to me, and when our hands touch, I expect some kind of electric moment, but I feel nothing. "Here ya go."

"Thanks."

"What are you making with artichokes?"

"I like them on a charcuterie plate and just to snack on." I notice he doesn't have a cart or basket. "What are you getting?"

"Just some essentials."

Okayyy. "Ah." I nod my head.

"Actually, I know you're shopping for groceries. Obviously," he laughs nervously, "but would you want to have dinner with me tonight? I had a great time with you when we hung out last."

Would I like to get dinner with him? I feel bad because he's so nice, and the stupid shit with Maverick is just that: stupid. I'm not doing that again. Maybe this would be better; I'm in a better headspace, for sure. And after Julien, then my one night with Maverick, I want safe, nice. Right?

"Yeah, okay. That'd be nice. Did you have a place in mind?"

"Ten Pennies? I haven't been there, but I heard it's nice."

I've been to Ten Pennies once with Quinn when we took her brother—because, in his words, he "wasn't eating at a retro diner or a bakery four days in a row." He's just as interesting of a conundrum as Quinn—and it's the nicest place in Silver Rapids. That isn't saying much, but I'm not expecting Michelin or James Beard Award-winning chefs to prepare meals for me table-side anymore. Lately, I'm happy with Parmesan and buttered noodles.

"Okay. I know where it is. What time are you thinking?"

"I can come get you at seven?"

"No, that's okay, I can meet you there."

"Are you sure? I don't mind."

"It's okay. I forgot to bring something into town for Quinn," I lie. I don't want anyone knowing where I live now.

"Okay. Then I'll see you at seven."

"See you." I walk toward the check-out line and turn around to see if he's still there, but he's gone.

I stop by the bookstore before I head back, just briefly to give Q the juice. I can't say I'm surprised to see Luke there.

I heard about Luke before I met him. Quinn told me all about this insanely beautiful, tattooed man who kept coming into the store to buy romance books for his mom and nana. Then I found out from Garrett that Luke was the one reading them. Poor guy turned redder than a beet. I told him I'd keep that secret.

The bell dings, and her eyes lift. She sees me and squeals. "Happy surprise seeing you, darlin'."

"Q, I saw you two days ago."

"Every day I see you is a good one."

"Hey, Charlie," Luke says.

"Hey." I give him a "bro" nod.

"Why do you have to torture him like that?" he asks.

"I don't know what you're talking about."

Quinn shrieks, "Oooh, tea?"

"Your bestie waved a red flag at Maverick last night, flirting with Garrett."

"Charlie! You did what?" She feigns surprise.

"Whatever. Maverick needs to get over himself."

Luke gives me a knowing look, but I just meet his smirk with my own and pop my hip out.

"Just sayin'," he mutters. "Consider yourself warned. That saying from that eighties movie—'You mess with the bull, you get the horns'—that should be Mav's motto."

I shrug, nonplussed.

To Quinn, he says, "Enjoy your lunch. I'll get these books to my mom."

I raise my eyebrows, then look at his hand clutching the books and smile conspiratorially.

Quinn goes over to the chairs by the fireplace, and I follow. "I have a date with Ezra tonight. Ten Pennies."

"Oh, honey. I thought you didn't feel anythin' with the last one?"

"I don't know. I don't want to not give him a shot because Maverick was being a dick and threw me off my game. If nothing happens tonight, then we can be friends."

"That's fair. Okay, now tell me about last night."

I'm dressed up—well, for Silver Rapids, I'm dressed up—and feeling pretty good when I get a spot right in front of the restaurant just before seven o'clock.

I spot Ezra at the bar, his face illuminated by the candles along the rail.

He smiles and walks over to me. "Hi!" He gives me a hug before I can react. "She's here," he says to the hostess.

The young girl walks us to a booth along the wall, the furthest away, despite several other open booths.

It's not busy, but it's lively. There's jazz music playing over the speakers, just loud enough that you would have to lean in to hear someone talk.

"Maybe after dinner, we could grab a drink somewhere else, too? Still up for playing tour guide?"

"Yeah, maybe!"

Dinner is painfully dull. He does most of the talking, and I quietly but intently listen to him tell me about his life. We don't have anything in common, which isn't always bad, but there has to be something!

The server comes over to the table, asking if we would like dessert, and before he can say anything, I blurt out, "I'm so full. Dinner was delicious."

She looks to my empty plate and then Ezra's plate that he's barely touched. "I'll get you the check and a box," she says.

I feel bad that I cut dinner short, but I don't want a second cocktail anywhere. After Ezra settles the check, we walk toward the door.

I say, "This is me," and motion to Verne.

He walks me to the driver's side of the truck and moves like he's going to give me a kiss.

"Thank you so much for dinner," I say, stepping back toward Verne.

A look of hurt and rejection crosses his face, but I stick out my hand, and he shakes it.

"Anytime. We'll have to find another time to play tour guide."

"Yes, next time." I smile, thinking maybe we could be platonic friends. I could stand to add a friend to my life, but I can't help but get the feeling that something about him unsettles me.

On the drive home, I remember what I have waiting for me. I can still read a bit, take off my makeup to hydrate, and have a DIY facial. There's also the other fun treat waiting for me. And even though I knew I wasn't going to hook up with Ezra on the first night, I could still have an orgasm. That wasn't a line to Maverick—I never hook up on the first night...except with him, that one time. And look where that got us.

I try so damn hard to get my head right once I'm home and in bed, but do I get that O? Even with that new toy? Sure don't.

Charlotte

CHAPTER 21

I'm sitting on Verne's tailgate, swinging my feet, talking with Ace about getting the insides of the cabins' drywall hung. Finn jumps up and puts his head on my lap. I absently pet his head and scratch behind his ears. His ears perk up before I hear a sound, but a few seconds later, a truck I don't recognize drives down the main entrance. At that moment, Maverick comes out of the house, walks down the stairs of the porch, and sits on the bottom step. He doesn't say anything—just sits there.

The truck pulls up next to mine and Ezra gets out. What the hell? How does he know where I work? I told him I worked on a ranch, but didn't tell him which one. Did Caleb or Quinn tell him?

"Hi, Charlie! I hope you don't mind me just showing up here."

"Um, hi, Ezra." I glance at Ace and give him a pleading look; he can tell something is fishy about this.

Ace steps in and says, "Actually, we were just about to go talk business with some of the hands."

Ezra reaches into his truck for something, and my heart lurches. What does he have? He pulls out a small bouquet of mixed flowers and walks them over to me. "I had a nice time with you last night." He tries to lean in for a hug and, just like last night, I step backward.

I look over to Maverick, feeling his eyes boring into me. "Oh, thank you so much. These are lovely."

Oh my God, this is so awkward. Our date was okay—nothing special—and there was maybe a spark? Ezra is so nice; I just wasn't into it. I might be persuaded to go on another date, but that's the least of my concerns. I know I didn't tell him where I work.

Ace smirks. "Come on, Boss. We have a tight schedule to stick to."

"Right. I'm so sorry, Ezra. I have to go, but I'll give you a call."

"I'd like that," he says. He pushes his long hair out of his face and wraps his hand around the back of his neck. "Sorry to just show up out of the blue."

I laugh nervously. "Not a problem." I walk backwards, keeping pace with Ace. "I'll call you soon."

I watch as Ezra gets in his truck, pulls out and turns the truck around, and leaves. The hair on the back of my neck is standing up.

Maverick gets up from where he was sitting and walks toward us, but I turn away. "Thanks, Ace."

"Do we need to worry about that one?" he asks.

"I'm not sure."

Maverick walks past us and huffs.

Ace says, "I'm going to let you deal with that." Then, he walks toward the doors at the other end of the barn.

"Thanks again."

Maverick, in Walter's stall, is pretending to look for something. I walk to Betty's stall and sneak a peek at him; his face is beet-red, and not from the sun.

Ooh, shit. I think Ranger Rick is angry.

"It must be hard to sneak away to get some, eh? You have to invite him here to the property?"

"I have never invited him here. I don't know how he even knew where I worked or lived."

He doesn't let up. "Is that why you're so mean? It's been a while." He walks out of the stall, and I step forward to meet him.

It takes everything in me not to punch him in the mouth. I grit my teeth and don't say anything back. I'm not trying to give him more ammo. I just want to get on my horse and ride for a bit.

"Yeah, I bet the more you miss it, the meaner you get."

The flowers are still in my hand, and I take them into my truck's front seat. When I return to the barn, Maverick has already saddled up Walter and left.

I walk over to Betty White's stall and say, "What a mess, Betty."

I'm so over this day. Whatever gods I pissed off, they're out for me today because things just continue to get worse. The scent of Maverick is carried to me on the frigid winds whipping through the open door—vanilla and oak with a touch of cinnamon and honeysuckle, like the best whiskeys. That's what he smells like, and, just like too much whiskey, it can make you sick.

I put away my tack against the wall, and he goes to put his on the wall opposite. It makes sense why Betty White and Walter have tension; their owners go at it every time they can. I slough off my coat. Despite the cold, I'm burning up. Maverick is making so much noise, the way a man does when he wants you to know that he's putting away dishes or laundry, slamming every cupboard or door.

"Why do you have to be so loud? Just put your shit away like a normal person!" I exclaim. I tried to tell myself that I would not let his bullshit get in the way of what I want. I wasn't so sure that I wanted this when Jasper first told me he wanted me to manage the ranch, but in the time

I've been at the helm with Ace, it's been fulfilling finding that purpose and balance between using the land to raise cattle and, further out, to supplement with the glamping.

"Honestly," Maverick replies, "because right now I want nothing more than to get you all pissy."

"Why? Is this because of what you think you saw? I told you, I didn't know he knew where I worked, or why he came to find me, or give me flowers."

"I don't care what you do or don't do with your time. But if you think you're going to be spending your time with a guy named Ezra, you're delusional. How do you know he's not some crazy guy stalking you?"

Why would Maverick say that? Why would he even fucking care? He's made it perfectly clear that he can't stand me and doesn't respect me at all. He showed that hand when he humiliated me in front of our entire staff.

Yet the notion makes me pause. I absolutely thought it was strange the way Ezra showed up here with flowers—uninvited, and when I hadn't even told him where I worked. The one time we went out on a date, we met up somewhere neutral. I don't trust anyone to give them my address.

"You don't get to have a man show up to MY property and give you flowers," Maverick says and crosses his arms. The movement pushes his biceps out. Even under the flannel he's wearing, I can see the outline of his arms. "A man who you don't even know."

"We're not a couple. We're not anything. I live here too. We are business partners, at best. And I use that term loosely because a 'partner' never would have said that I have no business being here in front of our entire team. Or that sooner or later I would just leave in the middle of the night like I have all the other times when things get hard. You have no idea what I have been through or who I am!"

He crosses the aisle dividing the sides of the barn in just a few strides. "Oh, sweetheart, I know exactly who you are. You're the one who will be leaving here soon. On to find the next victim in your schemes. You are a liar and a cheat!"

His words cut me to the core. I have been as honest as I can with everyone; what I haven't shared has been withheld to keep them safe. And to keep me away from Allister. I've built a life I can finally be proud of. I'll do anything I can to keep from being dragged back to Boston or, worse, six feet under in the middle of a Wyoming valley.

"I am no cheat. I am a lot of things, but I'm no cheat!" I spit back at him. "This might surprise you, but I didn't even want to take this on. I never asked to be the one in charge. What the hell do I know about running this place?! Nothing, except for what I've learned here. But I'm trying and doing the best I can, and you're not helping me. The one person who should give a shit if I drive this place into the ground!" I scream.

"I know team building, I know hard work and dedication," I continue. "I know business! Not cattle! But I'm here asking you to be civil with me so we can get a decent working relationship. Because I'm scared of letting all of them down. They believe in me!" I point back to the pen we just came from. "I'm scared of failing, of ruining this legacy your father left me. And you." I poke him in his stupid and ridiculously muscled chest. "I'm scared of my own goddamn shadow sometimes, for reasons you'll never know or understand. And I'm terrified, terrified of going home."

All of this comes pouring out of me—this confession. I feel like everyone has always thought I am so put together and have a solution for everything. But I've been putting on a front for years: of being the perfect daughter, having the perfect relationship, living a picture-perfect life. I've built walls so high to keep a fortress around me, to make my parents proud. And damn, if that doesn't do a number on the psyche. I am so tired, and I've literally put my life on the line.

"You know what? No, I'm not doing this." I turn on my heel and start to walk away.

He is there in an instant, gripping my wrist so tight it hurts. I don't care. I yank it out of his hand—or try to, anyway. All that does is bring me closer to him. Tears threaten to spill out, and I lift my chin to the roof of the barn, my throat burning. With Maverick this close, I'm surrounded by whiskey. His sapphire eyes are glaring into me, and his mouth is set in a hard slash.

I try to pull away again, and this time he lets me. I almost stumble backward. He reaches like he's about to keep me upright but lowers his hands.

"You already know everything you need to know about me. I'm not going to be able to make you change your mind, and I don't fucking care enough to try to now! You know when I would have cared? Over the summer, when you didn't call or bother to text me. I really liked you. I would have really tried with you. You're just like every other man; you got me flat on my back once, and that was enough for you." I cross my arms over my chest.

"I DID text you! I texted you while you were still dripping with my cum, Charlotte!"

I scoff. "Now who's the liar? I didn't hear a single word from you! At least be a man and admit you didn't want me beyond that night!"

Now he looks angry. "I texted you before I even left your street." He's putting on a good show, that's for damn sure, pacing with his hands on his head, looking like a caged animal. "I told you to get some rest and that I couldn't wait to see you for dinner."

Now I'm getting angry. Why is he lying straight to my face? Tears were already brimming, but I wanted to at least wait until I was in the comfort of my own place to release them. They're freely falling now.

"Stop!" I cry. "Just stop!"

He grabs my shoulders. "Or you could stop pretending and admit that I wasn't good enough for you. I'm too big of a fuck-up for you. I'm good for one thing, and that's a good time." He grabs me by the throat. "Isn't that right?" His eyes look devastated as he says this, but the set of his jaw and his posture show just how tense he is.

I am scared of a lot of things, but I'm not afraid of this man. Do I want to knee him in the balls? Yes—but he doesn't scare me. "I never thought that. I had a smile on my face the whole damn day, a smile that you gave me. And not because of the orgasms! I met a man who made me want to live after being afraid for so fucking long."

"What are you so afraid of?" He's so close.

"Of them finding me."

It happens so fast. He lightly squeezes my throat and brings me to him for a bruising kiss. I am kissing him before I know which way is up, and I'm dizzy before I come to my senses. I bite his lip hard and push him. Then I do something that he said I would do.

I run.

Maverick

CHAPTER 22

I'm stunned for a second to be kissing this infuriating woman. What the hell am I doing?

And now she's running. Of course she is, just like I said she would. But I'm not letting her go. Not this time, not without answers.

I chase after her across the gravel. She's already in her truck, slamming the door shut, locking it just as I reach the passenger side. *Damn it*. I yank the handle anyway, uselessly.

My Jeep keys are still in the house. Too far, too slow. But—the side-by-side: those keys are in my vest pocket. I dig them out, adrenaline flowing. *Please, please let there be fuel in this fucking thing.*

I jump in, crank it, and send thanks into the ether that it has a full tank.

Charlotte is headed to the back of the property line where she lives. It's been a long time since I've been there. It was to be a mother-in-law cottage, but my grandmother died before the construction was finished. She was older, but I think the heartbreak of my mother's dying is what actually killed her. She died of a broken heart.

The cabin has always reminded me of my mother. Everything around here is tied to memories that are too painful.

The pathway isn't lit, and it's slick as hell out here. The UTV's tires aren't gripping the gravel because of ice. I can feel it start to slide. That's when I see Charlotte's old-ass truck in the middle of the field.

Shit.

I slam on the brakes and damn near lose control myself. Pulling off to the side of the road, I can see the ice patch ahead; she likely hit that and it caused her to slide all the way over there. I park and run over to her truck. I fall down, bare hands slamming into the snow. I climb to my feet. The snow is up to my ankles here, but I trudge over to her.

I finally get to the driver's side door and try to open it. "Charlotte, unlock the door." Looking through the frosted glass, I can see her shaking, tears rolling down her high cheekbones and falling onto the collar of her shirt. *Damn.* I remember that night in the summer; she was on the verge of having a full-blown panic attack.

"Charlotte!" I bang on the window, trying to get her to snap out of it. "Come on, Charlotte, come back to me. I need you to open the door."

I knock on the window repeatedly. The lights from the UTV shining from behind us cast her in a shadow, but the moonlight reflecting off the snow illuminates the shape of her lips, which are trembling.

I hear the faint click of her manually unlocking the door. I immediately open it and reach in for her.

She reacts to me trying to grab her. "No! Don't touch me, don't touch me."

"Hey," I pull my hands back, "it's okay. It's okay. You're okay."

"No, Maverick, I'm so fucking far from okay. But I'm trying to be; I'm trying so hard."

"Let's get you home. Did you hit anything with the truck, or just slide?"

"I'm not sure; I don't remember."

"That's okay. I don't know if we should try to drive the truck back to the road."

She's silent, still shaking.

"Can you try to start this thing up?"

She reaches for the ignition to start it, but it doesn't kick over. *Shit*. We can't look at it now, but we can in the morning. The wind is whipping pretty hard, even though there's no snow in the forecast for tonight.

"Come on, we can leave it and have the guys pull it out and look in the morning. Did you get hurt anywhere?" I look over her body and don't see any blood or broken glass.

"I hit my head, and my chest hurts."

"Yes, that's pretty common. That means that the seatbelt did its job and kept you in place." The seatbelt is still strapped across her chest and lap. What with the cold, in a few minutes, the adrenaline drop will hit her pretty hard. "Charlotte, I need you to get out of the truck."

"I can't move."

"I'll leave you out here to freeze if you're going to purposefully be ridiculously foolish."

"Fine."

"Let's go, Charlotte."

"I'm fine; I'll walk to the cabin in a minute."

My feet and hands are freezing, my pants frozen from falling in the snow, and I'm only wearing a vest. This woman is so damn exasperating! "You'll freeze. It's another mile. You surely don't want me to win by freezing to death, do you?"

"It was never about winning for me. Just leave me alone."

That's fucking it. I reach in to unbuckle her seatbelt, her personal space be damned. I'm cold, and she's just being stubborn.

"Let's go." I take the keys out of the ignition and throw her over my shoulder. I leave those hideous flowers in the truck to die.

"What are you doing? Put me down!"

She's trying to kick her legs up, but my arms are banded tight across them. Her fists are pounding into my back. It's so cold that my ass is already numb—so pound away, sweetheart.

"Maverick! You asshole! Put me down!" She grabs my hips and bites my ass.

Fuck. I felt that. My hand cracks hard and fast across her ass cheek. It actually hurts my hand, so it has to get her attention.

She cries out into the crisp air, "Ow!" the sound reverberating through the night. She doesn't stop punching, but she doesn't bite me again.

I throw her into the side-by-side, and she kicks at me. She connects her cowboy boot with my shin.

"That hurt," I tell her.

"Good, maybe you shouldn't have manhandled me."

"It's too cold for this shit." I lean in and whisper, my lips barely brushing her ear, "You told me you wanted it rough. Remember?"

"I meant in bed. That ONE time. I didn't ask you to rip me out of my truck!" She looks like a toddler with her arms crossed over her chest, but despite her tantrum, I'm not letting her walk to the cabin.

"You may need your toes someday," I say.

I walk behind the vehicle to get in, and then zoom off to her cabin. The ride is tense, with her simmering over on her side and me with my balls about to fall off on mine.

The small cottage is nestled in a copse of aspen and pine trees, somewhat protected from the elements, the branches swaying and creaking in the frigid wind. I remember helping Dad with the interior construction when I was a kid. It was one of those projects that I recall so vividly, and yet there are other times with my parents that I can barely remember. Like parts of my childhood are just missing.

When we pull up, Charlotte's arms are still crossed, her hands tucked in her armpits. The icy air has painted her face and ears an angry red. She shouldn't have taken off her coat in the barn. The keys to her truck and the cabin sit heavy in my vest pocket. I debate giving her space; I would want space. But I don't really care what she wants right now.

Deciding not to give her a choice, I get out of the UTV, walk up the few steps, and notice the planter boxes in the windows and the pair of rocking chairs on the small porch.

"Hey!" She catches up to me. I open the door, and she tries to block me from entering. "You can't just barge in here like you own the place."

"Don't I, though?" I'm curious to see the cottage now. If it's the same as I remember.

"No, you don't own this cottage. Your father gave me this tiny little piece of land. You got the rest of the ranch!"

"Well, then, neighbor. Have a cup of sugar?" I ask, my tone dripping with sarcasm. I push across the threshold and take a few steps inside. She huffs and moves to stand in front of me while I take in the space.

I walk around her yet again and put the keys on the stone countertop. It's a small space, but Mom and Dad designed it to be understated, beautifully appointed without being over-the-top. Lots of natural touches throughout. It looks nice and lived in. Charlotte's brought some of the furniture and rugs I remember seeing at her house, along with the decor. It looks like what I imagine boho coastal meets cowgirl would look like—eclectic, but the colors are all kind of the same, muted.

"Pass your inspection, neighbor?" she demands. "I don't have any sugar, but thanks for stopping by. Please leave."

Ha. I won't be doing that.

Walking back to where I know the bathroom is, I cross to the tub. I run water until it's warm, but not too hot, then flip the bath lever to let the tub fill.

"Finnley can sleep in the house tonight. You can get him in the morning when we sort out your truck and this mess." I motion between her and me.

"Maverick, I'm tired. I don't know what your game is with this, but I just want my space."

"I know. Get in the bath; you need to warm up."

She sighs, resigned to do what I ask for a change. If what she said about my dad knowing about her situation is true, then he definitely kept a file on her. He has a file on all of his employees. I want to get back to the main house and tear it apart until I find out exactly what has her so frightened and who she's desperate to stay hidden from.

"Thank you for the bath and for keeping Finn for the night. But we need to talk about the barn."

"Which part?" Does she have the balls to ask me about the kiss?

"You didn't text me. I believe you think you did, but I wouldn't lie about getting something from you. At any rate, I feel like if you really wanted to get in touch, you would have. And you didn't." She sounds utterly defeated.

I look over at her and take in the set of her shoulders, burdened with whatever demons are weighing her down, the shadows that have now darkened her normally resilient and brilliant blue eyes.

"I know what I did. I don't really care if you believe me; it's not really a new concept for me." My tone is icy, evidently cutting her just as hard as the wind blowing outside. But it's a lie, and I think we both know it.

It was one of those things we shared in the early-morning hours of that night, staring at the constellation of fake stars on the ceiling of her small rental house near downtown. The words we shared with each other, as complete strangers, may have been the most honest words I've ever spoken aloud. And maybe it's better that she doesn't trust me, because the way she looks right now, with her full lips pouting and the anger in her eyes, is better than her looking haunted and sad.

"We have a long day tomorrow. Get in the fucking bath. I can't have you getting sick." I walk past her and straight to the door, ready for this day to end.

She calls out to me as I slam the door hard enough to rattle the windows, "We are not done with this conversation! Maverick!"

I mutter into the inky black sky, "We might as well be, because I don't go 'round in circles."

My jeans are soaked, caked with dirt, and there's water in my boots that sloshes between my toes with each heavy step I take away from the broken woman inside that cabin.

The crunching gravel under the UTV's tires and the whirring of the engine break the silence of the night, but the sound of Charlotte screaming about "them finding me" is loud in my mind.

If I'm honest with myself, we can work through the issue of her not getting my texts. I don't know who the hell I was texting over the summer, but when I connect with her tomorrow morning, if the numbers don't match, then they don't match. I have a hard time believing I transcribed a number wrong, and it's actually a valid number, but if so, some asshole out in Massachusetts could have saved a lot of fucking headaches with a simple "wrong number, dickhead."

If I'm honest with myself, deep down to my bones, I know she felt a connection that night, too, and wouldn't have ghosted me. That's why she's still so angry. If I'm honest with myself, I know it would take a lot to terrify a woman like Charlotte into fleeing the only life she's ever known to find shelter in the mountains—which makes her statement even more troubling.

Dad wouldn't have changed. He was an officer who flew Apache helicopters. Dad was methodical and calculating. He kept a file on every person he brought on as an employee, regardless if they were a day worker or lived in the bunkhouse. There has to be a file with her background and information stored in his office, and because he was old-school about certain things, it would be paper and not electronic.

The house and barns are quiet when I park and walk up the stone steps to the front door, which I unlock with a passcode and not a physical key. Dad replaced the lock a few years ago because I was always leaving the keys somewhere else and couldn't get into the house. I punch my birthday into the keypad, the lock disengages, and warm air floods my face when I open the door.

I peel off my boots and flip them upside down, melted snow dripping out, socks next because, even though this is my house now, I feel like I might still get in trouble for tracking in mud or dirt onto the floors or carpet. Mom kept this place spotless, and call it habit, but I don't want to traipse sodden sock prints to my bedroom. I can't bring myself to sleep in the master bedroom on the first floor. Maybe I never will; I'm still just an interloper, so I take the stairs to my childhood bedroom and go straight to the shower.

The hot water can sometimes take a minute, so I turn it on as hot as it will go and shut the door to the bathroom. I could use a good steam; I miss the sauna at the gym. Sloughing off my dirty clothes, I lay my jeans to dry a bit on the bench in my closet and discard the rest into a pile on the floor.

I adjust the temperature of the shower before stepping into the stream, but the warm water stings my skin. Good. I was purposefully mean to Charlotte today—in front of the crew, which definitely didn't win me any points with them. So, when I'm gripping the base of my cock, I definitely don't have the right to be thinking about the fact that she might be naked in the bath right now, with bubbles sluicing over her tight, toned body.

No, I'm definitely not thinking about her. I can lie to myself; I've been doing it long enough.

When I come, my forehead against the tiles, her name doesn't leave my mouth, but I scream it in my mind.

Turning off the water and stepping onto the bathmat, I stand in the shower, breathing in the steam. I dry my body and put on a pair of blue sleep pants and socks before heading downstairs.

Creeping into my dad's office, I feel like a kid again, except Dad's in the ground and now it's my office. This still feels like an invasion, like I don't belong here. Part of me thinks I'll never get past this feeling.

The office has a large, L-shaped desk situated close to the window overlooking the front pasture. It's dark, but I can see the light above the door leading to the barn glimmer in the night. Where the rest of the house is bright and whitewashed, these walls are painted a warm brown, except the wall with the glass door that leads into the office, which is a deep blue and lined with bookshelves. There's a worn, tufted leather chair in the corner with a blanket draped over the arm and a reading lamp overhead. The filing cabinets are made of worn wood that matches the desk. I start there first.

In the movies, when a parent dies, you have all these hoops to jump through and mountains of paperwork; that didn't happen for me. Dad knew this was coming. He had everything he needed for the lawyer. It makes me mad all over again. I wish he would have told me sooner. I don't know what I would have done differently, mainly because I wasn't given an opportunity to do anything. Would I have come home? I don't know. I left because I felt a weight on me that was crushing, but if I had known? Maybe. Now I'll never know.

I find a key for the cabinets in the top drawer of the desk. Not very original, but Dad would never have let anyone break in here, anyway. There are security cameras all over, and his mantra was "shoot first, ask questions later." The Army training he went through equipped him with the knowledge of how to incapacitate and shoot a target while still keeping them alive, but not allowing them to move.

Also, no one would be stupid enough to break into Jasper Bennett's property. He was essentially a hero in Silver Rapids. When he came home, the folks in town practically gave him the keys to the town. I'm not bitter about what my dad worked hard to achieve. He's one of the biggest influences on my training: work hard, or don't do it at all. But sometimes that's an impossible task to live up to.

The top row of cabinets contains the ledgers of livestock records, full of birth and health information, receipts of sales and purchases made, and information regarding feed and inventory—everything needed to maintain business operations. The second row has historical data regarding the pasture rotation schedule, safety compliance, financial records, taxes, and permits, but no information regarding employees. Where else would such files be? I know he had files. I accidentally walked into a meeting about him firing someone once. He and Ace talked about it afterward and said that he put it in the employee files.

There's a small cabinet built into the desk. I try to push in the locking mechanism and give the top drawer a tug. Thank the stars—it's unlocked.

Jackpot. All of what I need should be here. Employment and pay data, background check information. Nothing too crazy—some guys have a history of run-ins with law enforcement, some don't, but it looks normal to me. I find her file; it shows that Dad made cash payments. Why the hell would he pay her in cash? I keep reading through her folder and find emails between Dad and Owen talking about Charlotte. Then, I find a kind of CIA-level background brief on her—like, down to her food preferences and shoe size. Things Owen would be privy to.

What. The. Fuck?

Why would Dad have reached out to Owen for information about her? I return to the email exchange and read every single line.

She wasn't kidding when she said she was afraid of going back home. Charlotte has a retrieval contract on her life. The money man for the Mob wants her dead or alive.

Maverick

CHAPTER 23

I've been reading the file for an hour, and I'm no closer to finding out what is going on with the woman who has invaded my life so thoroughly. I sure as shit am not a detective, but I can try to put together the pieces.

From what I can tell, she had a high-profile job: a senior financial analyst who managed a large portfolio for a hedge fund firm, which came with a pretty hefty salary. If the data that Dad has is correct, she's a millionaire, and that's not even counting money from her family. The report didn't go into detail, but she has several personal investments independent from her family, too. Owen said they were influential in the Boston area and beyond with all their real estate properties.

The woman in the one-bedroom cabin in the back of my property has millions of dollars…millions, with an s. Why the fuck is she working for cash on a ranch in the middle of Wyoming? Why not just take her money and go into hiding somewhere easier?

What do they have on her? Better yet, what does she have on them? And why the hell does she stay here?

Her lack of social media definitely makes sense now. I think back to the morning after I left her. I didn't know her last name, but I tried to search on socials and found nothing.

I push away from the desk and run my hands through my hair. I thought I knew this woman, thought I could read her like a book, but

I know nothing about her. I thought she was after money when I saw her in that hospital room with Dad. Thought maybe she knew who I was and was trying to weasel her way in somehow. But unless she's an Oscar-worthy actress, she was just as shocked as I was.

I know the ranch is profitable, but as things go, Dappled Stone is not a big player. We sell beef to high-quality restaurants all over the country. I would never admit this to her, but her idea of eco-tourism to supplement income is sound. I don't even have a choice at this point; it's happening regardless, but it could help offset the operational costs of the ranch.

It's irrational, but there's still a part of me that doesn't want her here. She's going to end up leaving, anyway. But there's an even more irrational part of me, a part I won't vocalize, that realizes she doesn't have anywhere else to go, and that part of me wants to claim her.

I close the manila folder full of Charlotte's secrets and see a number scrawled in Dad's handwriting on the inner flap. It's a phone number. I take my phone out of my pocket and enter the number into a message. I don't know whose number it is, but I Google the area code, and it's from Pittsburgh. It could belong to anyone.

If it's 10 p.m. here, it's midnight there. I decide not to text it immediately and take a picture of the folder instead. I have to think about how to handle this, and I don't want to do that right now. What I want to do is go knock on the door of the cabin until she opens the door and tells me what the fuck is going on.

Does Quinn know about this? Luke said they've gotten really close. Would she dare tell her best friend? She must have told someone. She mentioned an older sister. Has she tried to contact her?

A million questions are running through my mind. I came in here looking for answers, only to get more questions. I leave the folder on the desk and sneer at it, like it's personally offended me because it has provided no actual answers, and walk over to look out the window.

I don't even have Charlotte's number to call or text her. If what she said about not getting my texts is true, she wouldn't receive anything from me now, as it is. Which is a completely separate issue. Who the fuck was getting my text messages?

I should get dressed and go over there. Instead, I go to the liquor cabinet in the kitchen and pull out a bottle of 10th Mountain Bourbon. Dad got turned on to it when he tasted it while I was training in Vail. It became one of my favorites to steal from his stash. Besides being a damn good whiskey, it was inspired by the men of the 10th Mountain Division near Vail who fought in World War II and brought skiing back to the States and inspired others to strap wooden planks to their feet and conquer mountains.

Tipping a hefty pour into a rocks glass, I sit in front of the unlit fireplace and take a long sip. The warm, amber liquid soothes as much as it burns as it makes its way down my throat, leaving a taste of honey on my tongue.

The house is too quiet; I hate it. At the apartment with Jude, we always had something on in the background—music or TV, something. I have a small TV in my room upstairs, the same one I had when I lived here. We never lived in luxury, but one thing Dad never skimped on was the TV, as he loved watching football when he wasn't taking care of this place, Mom, or me. And when he had downtime, he sat right here and watched the games on the giant TV across from me.

The remotes are in a stone bowl on the coffee table. I put on a streaming service and search for my favorite comedy show about a family who loses all their money and goes to live in a town they bought as a joke. It's not dark, it doesn't take itself too seriously, and the humor is perfect, exactly what I need to decompress. I take another sip from my glass and sit back.

I'm still reeling from what I just learned about Charlotte, and, frankly,

I still don't really know that much about her past. That night we shared together, we talked about our dreams and our future, not about the details of our pasts, the pain there. Though now it seems her future, her life, depends on her ability to stay hidden from these people, whatever the reason may be. And, inexplicably, her life is tied to mine—and this ranch—if she stays here.

Do I want her to stay here? A few hours ago, I wanted her so far away from here. Now, though, I can see the protection this place gives her. The anonymity someone might need. But that doesn't mean I want her here with me.

The house is freezing; I should put on a shirt or sweater, but go to the linen closet in the hallway leading to Mom and Dad's room. I open the heavy wooden door and get a waft of my mother's old perfume. There are a few bottles of her favorite right at eye level, and it socks me in the gut. I'm an orphan. Both my parents are dead.

My throat goes dry, and at this moment, Mom is here, next to me. I'm overwhelmed with memories of her chasing me around the house, of picking flowers for her and of her putting them in a small glass or vase, even if they were weeds. It's been years since she died, but I still feel her absence. I got really good at compartmentalizing and never letting emotions show. Was that my way of protecting myself, and maybe Dad? If he saw I wasn't sad, saw I was okay, he wouldn't worry about me, and he could focus on himself.

If I gave any fucks about myself, I would try to get into therapy, but I don't need someone to tell me something I already know—that I'm fucked in the head and I'll never have a healthy relationship with anyone until I can have one with myself. So, instead, I drink, I ski, chasing a feeling to fill me and make me whole again.

I don't want a quilt; I want a fluffy blanket, and there's a down comforter in a bag on the second shelf from the top. The bag won't come down, even when I yank on it. I get a chair from the dining table and climb on top to pull it down. Is this thing weighted? It feels like it's stuck on something. I give it a yank and pull it so hard I almost topple off the damn chair. The bag comes flying out, along with a fabric box with metal corners that clatters to the floor, its contents scattering all over the hallway.

God damn it!

I push the chair and comforter away and bend over to pick up what's fallen out. Pictures.

Pictures of me, clippings of newspapers, and magazine articles from almost every age. Baby pictures, pictures of my first time on skis, high school with the guys, even recent articles from after the incident at the Trials. Dad collected all of this.

I was never upset that there weren't pictures of me up on the walls. Dad got kind of weird after Mom died and took most of them down. Like he was too heartbroken to see her, and he needed to pack them away. We never talked about her—he didn't ask, and neither did I. I don't know if he ever saw or dated anyone; if he did, he kept it quiet. I wouldn't have minded—it had to be hard to lose your wife when you're in your forties, with so much life still ahead of you.

I'm so disoriented at the thought of my dad saving these. I stayed away for a reason—we fought all the time. He wanted me to take over the ranch, and I wanted to not feel stuck under his shadow for my whole life. In the end, what good did it do, anyway? I'm still under his shadow in a way I'll never outgrow, and I'm still alone.

I pick up another picture. I was maybe twelve years old, with a crooked grin and my dad's arm slung around my shoulder, rifles in our hands. We were at the shooting range practicing on a target deer. He was still teaching me how to hunt, gun safety, and the responsibility of taking a life. We were going to get my license so I could hunt big game with him.

He taught me that there was a balance in life, that even though we raised animals with the purpose of killing them, we should respect them and the land. At that age, I couldn't comprehend why I was okay with raising cattle, but not with hunting elk.

I wanted to make Dad proud. We sat in the blind for hours. I blew the bugle, waited for a bull to come, and lined up a shot perfectly. I pulled the trigger, and it went down—a huge, six-point elk. Dad loaded it onto the truck and said that it was our responsibility to make sure that it didn't go to waste, so we field dressed it there, cutting out the organs and leaving them for wildlife to consume. Then we drove it into town for the butcher to process.

Dad brought home the meat a couple of weeks later, and I couldn't eat it. I couldn't eat Bambi's cousin. I faked a stomachache and went to my room. He came up after me and said, "We both learned lessons in this. You value life differently, and I learned I pushed you too hard. How about we just shoot at paper instead of animals? Want a frozen pizza instead for dinner?"

When I wasn't skiing, training, or in school, I was with him. All of that changed when I went to high school and started hanging out with my friends. I haven't been shooting in a long time because there hasn't been a need to. But with everything surrounding Charlotte, I wonder: could someone come here and hurt her?

I gather the rest of the photos and put them back in the box. I can't focus on the TV right now, and upon looking at the clock in the kitchen, I find it reads 3:27 a.m. Sleep is calling me—I turn off the TV and head up to my bedroom with the box of photos in my hands.

I lay in bed all night, replaying a million memories in my head, and don't get a second of sleep.

Charlotte

CHAPTER 24

My hands are pruney and I still haven't washed my hair. Maverick all but threw me in this bathtub to warm me up, and that worked, but now I'm freezing again—I can't blame it just on the bath going cold. I've been here so long, the bubbles are gone. I can see the dirt and grime from the day settled on the bottom of the tub.

I hear my stomach growl from beneath the water and move to stand. It's so late; I really shouldn't eat anything. I reach for my towel on the hook next to my navy blue, silky robe. The clawfoot soaking tub is so big that I have to lean against the wall for support to get my leg out. A bathmat catches the water droplets falling freely from my body as I start the water in the shower stall. I just need to wash my hair, get some protein in me, and try to sleep.

A quick shower and a cheese-and-salami snack later, I'm in bed, wide awake. For hours. Maverick's hot and cold possessive behavior, the weirdness of Ezra showing up today, and the absolute madness that overtook me when Maverick and I were fighting in the barn play on a loop in my mind. Come to think of it, I'm pretty sure those flowers were left in the truck when Maverick put me over his shoulder.

Stars above, Maverick. What a mess! The way he kissed me should be illegal. He kisses with his whole body, and it melts me to my boots. That kiss was hot enough to scorch the earth beneath me, even if it was only for a moment. He knew that was a way to get me out of my head—grab me by the neck and kiss me. It scared me. I was never this girl before, scared of everything. But now, knowing there are people out there searching for me, hunting me, has changed my whole mindset.

I'm so done with being afraid all the damn time. I hoped this was going to be a place I could just rest for a bit. Even though he kissed me, Maverick's made it damn clear he wants me gone. But I promised Jasper that Dappled Stone would have a future. I suppose Maverick and Ace could run the ranch just fine, though he would probably let the yurts and cabins go to waste.

I am sick of running, almost more than I am of being scared; it's exhausting.

What happens if I don't leave? Like, what is actually the worst thing that could happen? Maverick realizes I could help him, and we wouldn't be romantically involved. And we could just co-exist in the same space together with separate lives. Or, we could end up trying to kill each other in the end.

I still have so much that I want to do here. I want to see it through. Surely, we can be civil and talk about this in the morning. For now, I just want to get some sleep—preferably without nightmares, but those still haunt me a few nights a week. My sleep schedule is so broken. I swear, I want to get railed so hard that I forget my name and can finally sleep through the night. I wouldn't even have to cuddle; he could go on his way, and I would just sleep blissfully.

I'm really not in the mood to get myself off tonight, though, so I slip my weighted eye mask over my eyes and count sheep until I finally doze off.

Bang, bang, bang. I try to move, but my arms are by my sides under the covers, stiff from last night's cold. Bang, bang, bang. What is that?

I throw the covers aside and rip off my eye mask. "What?!"

I know who it is before my feet even hit the floor. I push them into my slippers and shuffle to the door.

It is so bright, the sun shining through the curtains and illuminating the living room and kitchen. It takes a moment for my eyes to adjust, and while I fumble for the locks, I can hear Finn on the other side of the door. Then I hear Maverick mumble something to him—"Your mother takes her sweet-ass time opening this door. Doesn't she know it's freezing out here?"

Yes, well, when you wake someone from a dead sleep, it takes a second to process.

His hand is raised to knock again when I open the door. He almost knocks me in my face, but steps back.

Finn runs past my legs and goes straight to his stuffie. It was already cold just opening the door, but when he runs past, he brings cold air in with him; it sends shivers up my spine. I can feel goosebumps break out across my arms, and my nipples pebble. I'm in nothing but a thin strapped silk cami and short silk tap shorts.

I look at Maverick and, like a heat-seeking missile, his eyes go straight to my nipples, pointing from underneath the navy fabric.

I fold my arms across my chest and glare at him. "What?"

He's stunned for a moment. "Uh, wanted to drop Finn off. And—"

He looks down to my toes and up my bare thighs, coughs, and brings his eyes up to mine. "You should get dressed, or put something on; we need to talk."

"I was sleeping. You know what you should be doing right now? It's only seven a.m. It was my day off."

"I couldn't sleep, and I wanted to talk to you," he says flatly.

"Ugh, for fuck's sake! Come on. It's fucking cold, and I'm practically naked. Just hang out here while I get dressed." I motion to the small couch along the living room wall.

"Where do you keep the coffee?"

"You're not making yourself at home in my house."

He walks over to the cabinets and starts opening all of them, searching for the coffee.

"This isn't funny. I didn't invite you over for tea."

"Oh, but I've got tea for you. Get dressed. I know how to make coffee."

I give an exhausted sigh. *Whatever.* I have nothing to hide, and if he wants to make the coffee, then fine. I walk to the bedroom and shut the door, look in the mirror, and, yep, sure as shit, my cami is sideways and my nipple was practically peeking out to say hi to him. I groan.

Stripping out of my pajamas, I pull an outfit from my chest of drawers—a simple one, because I don't know where this is going, but enough layers to stay warm. I put boot socks on over my leggings and a purple flannel over my long-sleeved base layer with a built-in bralette. I am not getting dressed up for this asshole.

I open the door and hear Finn squeaking his bunny stuffie. It was the first thing I bought him, and is still his favorite toy. Stopping in the bathroom, I smooth my wavy hair, pull it back into a messy bun, and brush my teeth. It might seem counterintuitive to brush your teeth before coffee, but I would rather have coffee breath than morning breath. Ick.

Maverick is in the kitchen talking to himself, but I can't make out what the hell he's saying. I leave the hallway and round the corner to see him wrestling the bunny out of Finn's mouth. "Just let go, and I'll throw it," he grits out to my dog.

"Finn, drop it," I say, and, like the good boy he is, Finn drops the bunny at Maverick's feet and looks at him expectantly.

"Why wouldn't he do that for me?"

"Because he's my dog."

He doesn't respond; he just leans against the countertop and scowls at Finn. I look to where he's playing on the carpet in the living room and whisper, "Good boy."

The coffee pot is percolating, and the brew smells so damn good. I get the beans from Flour Child, a balanced cinnamon and hazelnut blend. When you mix it with a dollop of Nutella and some whipped cream...ugh, so good.

Returning my attention to Maverick, I ask, "What is going on? Why are you here so early? Couldn't wait for round two?" I know I'm being bratty, but honestly, I give zero fucks. Today-me is out of fucks.

The coffee maker dings, signaling that it's done brewing. I walk past him to where I keep the coffee mugs and get a rush of déjà vu. Only, it's not, not really. I made him coffee in my old house. On the night that started all of this. I shake my head to jar myself out of whatever reel was about to play in my mind and start the motions of making coffee.

I keep the Nutella next to the coffee mugs. It's the only time I use it, so it should be where I need it, despite Quinn saying it should go into the pantry. I rummage in the fridge for whipped cream and half-and-half.

In the windowpane's reflection, I can see Maverick watching me; it's unnerving. I remember every single thing about that night, including how he takes his coffee—black, like his heart. Yet I ask, "How do you take your coffee?"

"You don't remember?"

"How could I possibly remember how you like your coffee?"

He scoffs and looks right through me. "I bet you do. I bet you remember a lot of things." He definitely woke up and chose violence today.

I swallow. "Nope. Light and sweet?"

"Black."

Blech. Gross.

"Black it is." I pour him a cup and slide it over. I finish making my fancy coffee and get a twinge of sadness when I remember how Jasper used to call it my "dressed-up" coffee.

I stop to think about Maverick and how he's doing—how he's *really* doing and not this aloof persona he's trying to sell to everyone all the time. Jasper wasn't my father, and I miss him terribly. Surely, Maverick must be having trouble. I almost ask him, but we are not friendly like that, so I say nothing, refusing to be the first to break the silence. I walk over to the small, two-person dining table and sit down in one of the wooden chairs.

"That's still not coffee. That's sugar impersonating coffee with some caffeine."

"Mmmm" is all I say in response. I take a sip and damn near burn my mouth. *Let's just give that a second to cool.* Putting the mug down, I rip off the Band-Aid. "What do you want to talk about?"

He walks over to the chair opposite me and pulls it out. It screeches across the wood floor. A manila folder appears from inside his coat. "I want to know why my dad had this in your employee file." He slams the folder down on the table, jarring me and shaking my coffee.

He doesn't know that I've seen it before. That night, after he showed up, Jasper told me to go look for it in his office. "I'm sure you read it. Do I have to spell it out?"

"I think I deserve to know what the hell is going on. It's not just you anymore. It involves the ranch and, therefore, me."

I'm a bit stunned. I didn't look at the situation like that—how my problem is now his, too.

"I...just give me a second."

"You've had enough seconds."

"It's not every day that a man discovers your secrets!"

Now it's his turn to be shocked.

"I don't know how else to explain except from the beginning. Because I'm sure there's something I can't remember or that my mind has blocked out, but this is what I know," I begin, and then I tell him. I tell him everything.

I tell him how my father got me a coveted position at Seaside with Allister and how prestigious the firm is. That I would be set to take over the company at the right time if I played my cards right. I knew my father was a client at Seaside. Allister would come over for holidays and parties, for Christ's sake! I was making moves and working with the right clients, building mine and the company's portfolio.

I was there for two years before I started noticing things that were fishy. Some portfolios were going up when they made the wrong investments, and others were going down. The consulting fees for some clients were astronomical, and others were consistently being waived. When I asked about it, they made it seem like this was normal for long-standing clients when they had terrible months. But the clients weren't having terrible months; they were making record returns, and they were transferring a great deal of money to offshore accounts. My father's proximity to the board and executive management meant I had easier access to them than most people just out of college and starting out at the company would.

I connected the dots, analyzing data records with what I knew was happening internally. One day, I noticed my computer glitched and was stuck on a report I was analyzing. It shouldn't have been a big deal, but the client wasn't mine. It was a colleague's, and I had no business review-ing it. I think that's when the internal security team started tracking my movements. When my screen would glitch. I wanted to report it to IT, thinking I was just being paranoid, but I decided against it.

That was around the same time I noticed my boss coming to dinner more with my family. I had my condo that I owned, but dinners with my family were an expected and regular thing. My then-fiancé would join, as would my sister's boyfriend. We were, from the outside, a perfect family.

No one knew I knew Julien was cheating on me with his secretary and countless others, besides my mother. I didn't even tell Georgina. Mom said not to make a scene; that "it happens," but what beautiful babies we would make. Once we were married, I could have an affair if I wanted to, too. A mother should never say that to her daughters, especially when she knows what it's like to have a husband who cheats on her. Julien and I didn't live together, though he kept insisting, and both he and my mother pushed for a date for the wedding. I broke up with him privately and couriered his things to his building.

I was lost and felt that I needed something different. I started packing things up to put them into storage while I sold my place. I didn't care if I lived in a small studio; I wanted something different. Almost all of my stuff was already packed up. I was out with my friends one night, just wanting to be normal, when I saw my boss out with people known to be in the Irish Mob. It was a small bar in the financial district, and I overheard him talking about someone looking into records that they weren't supposed to be, and that "they needed to be taken care of." He didn't care how, but reiterated that "she needed to go away in order for business to maintain operations."

I knew then what was going on. I had enough evidence to take what I needed to the SEC or FBI, or whomever, to make this go away. But I didn't know how to do that. You can't just ring the FBI up and say, "Hey!

My boss is in business with the Mob, and here's the proof."

I tried to play it cool and went to work one day. Then, these two guys blocked me from getting into my car at the valet stand. I didn't know who they were, but they tried to get in my car, and I just took off. I had a bunch of stuff already in my car because I was in the process of moving to a small apartment I had found. That's why I still have some stuff from home. The boxes were filled with my favorite things that I wanted first in my new place.

I was so scared. I called my father and heard my boss in the background; they were at the country club together. He was with Allister, and I couldn't trust him not to tell my boss what I said. So I went to the ATM, took out as much cash as I could, and ran. I have been running ever since. I can't use my ATM or credit cards because they could find me. Same with a phone—I got a burner flip phone that didn't require a name. I sold the Range Rover for cash and got the truck instead. They can track everything.

I tell Maverick how I took random jobs to pay for rent and gas. How I didn't know what I was looking for when I ended up here at the ranch, but that his dad offered me a job and practically saved my life.

I've never been as emotional as I am now, my tears just flowing out. I run out of breath and am shaking by the time I finish. When I say, "Your dad saved me," I gaze into his blue eyes, bluer than the brightest sky, hoping he understands how big of a leap I just took, what I just trusted him with: my life. It feels so goddamn good to have someone know the truth.

He says nothing for several long seconds. His carved jaw ticks, and he clutches the edge of his seat, his hand between his legs. Faster than a snake, he pulls me out of my seat and onto his lap, then buries his face into my neck, squeezing me to him.

Maverick

CHAPTER 25

I feel her whole body shake, and her breaths are uneven. She is so small beneath my hands, splayed across her back. Her hands are in my hair, grown longer than it has been in a while, and fuck, it feels good.

"Hey, breathe with me. In for four and hold for four, then out, remember?"

She gives the slightest of nods. "I remember—everything."

"I know you do," I say playfully, the corner of my mouth just below her ear, at the softness of her neck where her pulse is beating so wildly. "Breathe."

She does box breathing for a minute, and after another, her breathing has stabilized. After another, I can't be sure that she needs me holding on to her at all; it's for my own fucked-up benefit. I've been wanting to get my hands on her since the night she showed up at Bart's for her date. There is no reason to lay any type of claim to her, but I don't want anyone else to, least of all the asshole named Ezra. I loathed the way his hand touched her bare stomach and meandered up under her shirt, the way he felt he could touch her. She may end up leaving Silver Rapids, but while she's here, she's mine.

I give her the lightest of kisses and then push the pad of my thumb against her lips, as if to trap my touch there a little longer. I try to give her this comfort without being a complete dickhead. My cock does not need to make an appearance right now. But damn it, her body feels warm, and her legs are bracketing mine. The last time I had her thighs around me feels like a lifetime ago, not mere months. Our bodies were slick with sweat in her tiny brass bed, and I was moving so slowly in and out of her, trying to wring out the last bit of her orgasm. We were different people then; we had fewer complications then.

"Maverick?" she asks quietly, still gently playing with my hair. "Did you really text me?"

"Is that your question?"

"Yes."

"Yes, I texted you. I sure as shit texted somebody, but you're telling me you didn't get any messages? When I left your house, I texted you. I went home and helped my dad because his new help got the day off." I chuckle. "I didn't know it was you I was covering for. I texted later that evening, telling you I had to go home because there had been an accident."

"Wait, what?" She bristles.

"My roommate in Park City, he got thrown from his horse. It fell on him, and he broke his back. I was his emergency contact. I got the call and had to go."

She stands up, lifting off of me. "Wait, what?"

Is there an echo in here?

"I texted that I would not make dinner after all and asked to meet up the next time I was in town."

"So you wouldn't have even been here for dinner, anyway?" She sounds pretty pissed.

"No, but I texted. Jude is like my brother, and he—"

She puts her hands up with her fingers spread wide and shakes her head, like she doesn't want to hear me. "So, it didn't matter anyway. I mean, yes, I'm sorry about your friend. But it was actually, in the end, a one-night stand," she says with indignation in her voice, shaking her head.

Doesn't she get it? I had to go home to see him; we did not know at the time how bad it was.

"Charlotte, it wasn't like that. I wanted to see you again. I had to go."

"It doesn't matter; it's what it is. It's fine." I can hear the hurt in her voice. "It was one night—it's not like someone finds their soulmate from a one-night stand."

God damn it. I want to shake some sense into her. But she just dumped all that trauma and gave it words.

"Don't do that," I say. "It meant more to me than that. It wasn't a cheap night that meant nothing."

She walks away from the small kitchen and into the living room. I almost think about telling her I came back a week later on the "off chance" that I would run into her. I surprised Dad, and that was the last time I saw him before the hospital. He asked if I wanted to do dinner, and I blew him off to find her. That's not on her; that's on me. I have to live with that.

Fuck it. I tell her, "I came home a week later. I didn't want to just come over to your house because you didn't text me back. Maybe it was just a one-night thing for you, and that would have been fine. I wanted more, but that would have been fine. Dad kept asking over those two days if I wanted to do dinner at the Bluebird, and I blew him off."

She whips around. "Mav—"

"I'm not saying that's on you; I'm saying that I wanted to find you. And I did." I breathe. "I did. You were walking on 5th Street, walking toward the bakery, and this guy opened the door and put his hand on the small of your back to lead you in."

"I don't even know who you're talking about. There wasn't anybody after you. I don't remember—" She stops, then asks, "What did he look like?"

"I don't know—tall, tan, muscly, had his ribs out with a side slit shirt and a ball cap on."

"Oh, my God. Did you get a good look at him?"

"No, I just watched you talking with him. You didn't notice me on the street. He opened the door to Flour Child and I saw you smile at him when you walked past him and he put his hand at the small of your back."

"God, you're an asshole. I really wish you would have had the balls to come and say 'hello' at least!"

"Why would I interrupt you on your date?!"

"It wasn't a date! That was Quinn's brother! He came to visit her over the summer. He was just being nice!"

I scoff. "What?"

"That was her brother, Cash. But damn, if that was enough to put you off of chasing after me...well, then it's probably for the best nothing developed. I just told you: my mother told me it was okay to have an affair. My ex-fiancé regularly cheated. I want someone to chase me, someone who will fight for me. That's not you, though."

I say nothing. I would fight for someone, the right one, if she existed, but my head isn't in the damn clouds, and she's going to end up leaving. *Right—keep lying to yourself, dumbass. She is the right one; she's the only one you think about. You've turned down women practically throwing their pussy at you because you only thought about her.*

"I'm sorry, Maverick. For whatever or whomever hurt you so badly that you don't feel you deserve to be happy." She steps farther away, but I step closer, invading her space even though it's clear that she needs some breathing room.

Crowding her against the table next to the sofa and the wall, I don't stop until she's completely boxed in. God, she smells good.

She shakes her head as though she can read my thoughts. "You have a chance to be happy. I can never truly be with anyone like this. To ask them to sacrifice a stable life for me."

"Did someone hurt you?" I ask.

It takes a second for her to understand what I'm asking. "No." She looks down and away from me. She's lying, I think. Even though she trusted me with everything else, that doesn't mean she would share that kind of trauma.

I'm far from an honorable man, but there are some things that I would kill someone for. Thinking about those things makes my blood boil, and I take a few steps back.

I don't tell her that any man would drop to his knees and worship her as a goddess. That it's the least she deserves after the last year and a half. That I would be that man—but a part of me knows I don't deserve her. We can barely have a civil conversation now. And if I ever learn that someone did hurt her like that, they would never find a body on this property. I know how to hide something that doesn't need to be found.

"I don't need your pity. I don't want anything. Actually, that's not true. I want to know who the hell I was texting. Because I don't have your number."

She walks into her bedroom and comes back with an old-school flip phone.

I pull my phone out and say, "What is it, then?" She tells me the numbers one by one, and I enter them exactly. It's not the number I had texted, thinking it was hers. "Well, shit. I just sent you a text from my number." I push my hair back with my hand.

She looks down. "That one I got. The other, I never got." She hands me her phone. The only text threads she has are with Quinn, Ace, my dad, and Luke.

"You didn't delete it?" I ask.

"No. I never got it, I swear."

I hand her phone back to her.

She closes the phone and puts it in her back pocket. "You should have had dinner with Jasper. He told me that his son came home unexpectedly and left just as suddenly."

"You probably know all about my relationship with my dad. It was complicated. After my mom died, we just drifted apart. And after a while, that was the norm, and then feelings morphed. I wanted to have a relationship with him, but I didn't know how to re-engage. You wouldn't understand, but I had a reason for staying away and distancing—my dad blamed me for my mother's death."

"What?"

"He didn't have to say it, but I knew he did."

"No, Maverick. I don't believe that. He loved you." She walks over to me, and it's my turn to back up.

"He could love me and still blame me."

"Why? That doesn't make sense."

She moves closer to me and moves to put her hand on my shoulder. I don't need to be coddled and placated, and I back away before her outstretched hand can touch me. She flinches at my rebuff.

"Jasper didn't think that," she says, like it's breaking her heart to say it. "He told me how much he loved you."

She didn't get the damn texts.

She sighs. "Can we just be friends? Start over?" She sticks her hand out to me and says, "Hi, I'm Charlotte, aka Charlie, aka Lottie. Depending on who you're talking to."

I take her hand and say, "I'm Maverick Reid Bennett."

"Nah, you'll always be Ranger Rick." She laughs.

"I fucking hate when you call me that." I'm still shaking her hand. She looks down at our clasped hands and back at me.

"Okay, truce. Can I have my hand back?"

I drop her hand like all of a sudden it was burning me.

"In the spirit of a truce, do you want to visit another cattle ranch? My friend's family, the one who broke his back, they wouldn't mind a visit. This weekend maybe? I could stand to get back and see the race in town."

She considers, and says, "Okay, that would be great. Get to see another operation."

I go to leave, and when I'm on the porch of the cottage, I have to check my phone. I scroll all the way back and look at the number I texted thinking it was her. The last few numbers are transposed.

I take a screenshot and send it to her. She responds immediately:

> The devil is in the details, Rick.

Maverick

CHAPTER 26

I'm in the house when I see Charlotte get out of her truck and head to the barn. She agreed to come to Utah with me to check out the skijoring competition and another working cattle farm with immediate access to the manager of the property. She also agreed that she could stand to get out of here for a few days. It's not a vacation so much as a work trip? Yeah, right.

I text her as she walks her horse out of the barn with Ace.

> I'd like to leave this afternoon. Does that work for you?

> Charlotte: The event is tomorrow, right?

> Yes, but I'd like to check in on Jude and see some folks tonight.

She has a damn flip phone, so I can't tell if she's read it or is responding. Ten minutes later, she replies.

> Charlotte: Ok, but I have to drop Finn off with Quinn.

You know, you could leave him here, right? The crew could watch him.

Charlotte: I don't want him to sleep in the barn…and I don't want anyone to have the code to the cottage or the main house.

Ok, that's fair. We can drop him off no problem.

Charlotte: Thanks. I'll be ready in about three hours, maybe sooner.

Leaving in three hours puts us on the road by eleven o'clock, with enough time to get to Salt Lake City and out to see Jude and his family's ranch. I miss his crazy ass. I had my own damn reasons for working at their ranch over the summer—did I deserve the punch from Ace? No, but there's something to be said about his loyalty to my father. The fucker didn't have to punch me, though.

I call Jude to give him a heads up on our arrival time.

He answers after the second ring. "Maverick, what's up, bro?"

"Hey, guy! Charlotte and I are planning to get on the road at about eleven. That would put us to you around five p.m., assuming no issues. We can come straight to the ranch before we check into the hotel. I'd like to get her a tour and get her in front of Sutton so she can talk to another ops manager. Then dinner, drinks, and going out."

"You don't need to get a hotel; you can go back to the apartment. Oh, but there's nothing in your room besides an air mattress."

"Eh, I appreciate that, but I think a hotel is probably best."

"Best for privacy, at any rate," he chuckles. "What's the plan for the rest of the weekend?" he asks, a sly tone in his voice.

I'm not taking that bait. "Besides catching up with you guys, watching the competition, having dinner, and going out with you guys. We've got to get back here on Sunday. It would be nice to do a Cortlands' Sunday breakfast, though."

"For sure, Ma would love to see you." He pauses for a beat. "And meet your lady friend."

I groan. "She's not my lady friend. She's my business partner."

"Yeah, right. She's the one you didn't shut up about for weeks and the one you sulked over for months. You think I didn't notice you didn't mention a single other girl over the summer? Please, guy. You're my best friend. I know you better than you do. Isn't she your boss now, too?"

"I'm not even going there. Don't say that shit in front of her." He laughs, so I say, "I'm fucking serious."

"I'll see you in a few hours, then." Still laughing, he hangs up.

Fuck. This will be good for her, but likely fucking torturous for me.

I pull my phone out and text her.

> I'll have my things packed up in the Jeep. Come up to the house, or lmk when you're ready to go, and I'll come get you.

Charlotte: Fine

This woman. Snow is starting to fall, and though it's not supposed to be a long storm, I don't want to get stuck on the roads. I walk to the cabinet and grab the bottle of headache reliever to put in my bag. I definitely think I'm going to need it.

When I see her K10 is still parked near the barn, I know she hasn't left to get her stuff from the cabin.

Opting for comfort on this trip, I pack jeans, sweatshirts, thicker flannels, and some cold weather gear. The drive isn't terrible; it's just long. I decide on a matching gray sweatshirt and joggers, one of my favorite blue beanies, and loosely laced boots.

My phone buzzes with a text from Charlotte.

> **Charlotte: We're ready. Will be at the house in just a minute.**

I have some water and snacks in a small cooler and a large thermos of coffee. I wonder if she's bringing anything. Did she ever go on long road trips growing up? Should I bring more food, just in case she didn't? I grab some more grapes and cheese out of the fridge, and an apple, too. I don't know why the thought of being within touching distance of her for five hours has me nervous, but it does.

Looking out the window at the snow that's slowly falling, I'm lost in my head and don't hear her knocking on the door.

"Maverick!"

Shit. I zip up the cooler and walk to the door. "Sorry. I'm sure you have the key code to get in here." My dad would have given it to her.

"I do. But I haven't used it since Jasper—" She pauses. "It's your house now."

"Oh," I say. "I have snacks." I lift the cooler to show said snacks. "You ready?"

"Yeah, just let me grab my stuff and Finn's dog bed."

Finn is in the truck bed, standing up against the walls, but doesn't get out until she whistles for him. Good boy.

She moves to the back of the truck bed and reaches in to get her bags, which I take right out of her hands. She almost protests, but I say, "We might get weather later, and you'll have no desire for wet clothes."

She mumbles, "Thanks," then walks to the passenger side to open the back door for Finn. "Up, boy," she says to him as I open the rear driver's side door and get our bags situated.

She gives me Quinn's address to put into the GPS. I pull onto her street and see a familiar black Ford F-150 with a silver "Draper Construction" decal parked in the street in front of a small brick house. Quinn is standing at the end of the drive with Luke.

I pull alongside the truck and roll down my window. Looking at Quinn, then smirking at Luke, I meet his eyes when I say smugly, "Luke, didn't know I'd see you today."

But, honestly? Good for him.

Charlotte hops out, grabs Finn's bag and dog bed, and crosses in front of the truck. Giving her friend a hug, they squeal like they haven't seen each other in months.

"Hi! Thank you, Quinn. I'll be back on Sunday to pick him up." To Finn, she says, "Be good for Auntie Q." To Luke, she gives a nod and a look—not necessarily unkind, but definitely a look.

He laughs as he comes up to the window. "Good luck, Mav," he says and pats me on the shoulder. I know he's referring to more than just the farm visit, too.

Luke then says to Finn, "Come on, boy. Let's let Mom and Dad work their shit out."

I'm going to kill him.

He pats me on the back and walks away before either Charlotte or I can say a single word.

Quinn, giggling, waves over her shoulder. "Bye, friends! Play nice." With a sassy wink, she pats her leg and Finn runs to her side.

I hear a huff from the other side of the Jeep and sigh.

"What kind of tunes?" I ask without looking at her.

"Whatever you got queued up is fine, I'm sure."

"What do you—"

"Seriously, I like everything. Whatever you want; it's your truck."

Five hours later, we're both hoarse from singing along to hits from the '90s and '00s, with some more recent stuff thrown in, but Pop2K gets me every time. I know I had some type of anxiety before, but after the first half-hour, Charlotte started humming along to a song, and then I did, and next thing I knew, we were just singing like we're on our own version of *Car Karaoke*. We made one stop at a gas station in Lava Hot Springs for a quick restroom break, and I filled up even though the meter showed just slightly less than half a tank. I will never run out of gas if I can help it; I can thank Dad for that one.

We're just outside the small town where the Cortlands' ranch is when I text Jude:

We're 15 minutes out.

Jude: Ok. We're in the northern pasture, but you can go up to the house. Ma's there, and we'll be on our way in about 20. Unless you want to meet us out here? Keys to UTVs are in the usual place.

We'll meet you out there. We've been in this truck for almost 5 hours. We can walk a bit.

I slip the phone back into my sweatshirt pouch. I turn down the music and tell her, "Jude is out in the pasture. We're going to meet him out there, and he and Sutton can show you their facility and how he runs the operations."

"Sutton is the older brother, right? The one who you guys were drinking with that night?"

"Yeah, sorry about that. That was him. He's a good man. Raegan is Jude's younger sister by a year, Hudson is the baby, and then there's Sutton and Mrs. Cortland. Their dad died a few years back."

"We didn't talk about this, but where are we sleeping? At the house?"

"No, I got us two hotel rooms in town. It's a historic hotel, but it's not fancy or anything." I add, "I don't think the boss would approve of spending unnecessarily on the Ritz, right?"

"Right."

"So, I know Dad left the assets to both of us. You have a bit of breathing room now, right?"

"That's not my money; the only money I have is what I get paid from the accountant, and even then it's only cash. I'm not changing anything from how I was living before." She looks down at her hands resting on her thighs. "For me, besides having some new responsibility for the ranch, nothing about my situation has changed."

"Maybe we can see if the bank can add you—"

"No. Nothing with my name."

"Okay. No problem," I say, hearing the panic in her voice.

"Shit, at this point, I feel like I should use an alias, anyway. But I didn't want to lie to your dad about my name. Though, what would it have mattered? He and Owen would have found out I was lying."

"That's a fair point."

We pull into the Cortlands' ranch, Blazing Star Ranch, and I drive up to the main barn where the key box is. No one is around to ask what I'm doing here, not that it would be a problem. They tend to run this place with a smaller crew than Dad preferred at our ranch.

"Okay, let's get going. Grab your gloves and your coat." I reach in the back for my own gloves and a vest.

She looks at me and giggles to herself.

"What's got you giggling?" I ask her.

"You."

"What about me?"

"You look like a gym bro who's trying ranching for the first time."

"Sweetheart, I've been doing this my whole life. I could do this naked."

A pretty shade of pink creeps up her neck to her ears, and it's not from the cold.

Walking past her and into the barn, I grab a walkie talkie from the ledge and the keys to the remaining UTV parked outside. "Come on."

We make it to the pasture in no time, and I call Jude on the two-way, asking for his location. When he responds, we head his way until I see the other vehicle and call the guys over.

"Sutton, you remember Charlotte. Jude, this is Charlotte Adler. She's the, uh, new—"

"Manager at the Dappled Stone Ranch," she quickly finishes when I stumble over the words. "Nice to meet you. Thanks for letting me come check out your place." She gives a pleasant smile and reaches out to shake their hands.

"Well, we don't have much time, so, let's get out there, eh?" Jude motions for her to walk with him.

I follow, looking at Sutton, and hang back just slightly, letting her ask them all her questions. They answer every single one. We're out for about an hour when Sutton and I head back to the side-by-sides.

He was eyeing her up and down the entire time she was out with Jude, working with pregnant heifers and cows.

"She's a natural, Maverick. She's got good instincts. Give her some time, and I'm sure she'll settle in. And you still have Ace, right?" I nod, my gaze not leaving her. "Then you guys are in good shape. Keep what was working, and the rest will come." Out of the corner of my eye, I can tell he's keenly watching her, like a predator looking for its prey.

"Yeah, she actually brought it up on the drive—that she would be interested in shadowing a bit more over the year and letting him take on more in the business. Succession planning or something. He still hates me."

"It could only help to stack in that department. If you're trying to get back to skiing or anything else, you'll need someone who can run that place like clockwork without you. And she may want someone else to help assist."

I sit with that for a second. It's been such a shitshow since Dad died that I haven't even given stock to what I want.

The sun is setting and offering its last bit of light. Something catches in the glare, and I look to see Jude and Charlotte heading back our way, engaged in their own conversation. He's walking a lot better since I saw him last.

"How do you attach the rope to the saddle?" she asks.

"Through attachment points on both sides of the saddle, then they meet behind, hooked with a climbing-strength carabiner, and then attach a rope for the skier. It doesn't impede the horse at all. I can show you tomorrow."

"I can't wait to see the rigging."

"It breaks my heart that we aren't in it tomorrow," Jude says, looking at me but still talking with Charlotte. "Your boy, Maverick, promised he was going to compete with me this year. Even if there's no glory, just the joy of saying he did it. He'll ski anything, but—"

"Are you able to ride yet? It can take a while to recover from an injury like what you suffered," she asks, and then instantly regrets it, covering her mouth with her leather-gloved hands. "Oh, my, I'm sorry. That is absolutely none of my business."

Poor Charlotte looks ashamed that she asked such a personal question.

It's funny to see when her proper side comes out. It may seem like she's being bashful, but it's the way she was raised—all proper and shit.

"It's okay," Jude assures her. "I'm not ready yet. The doctors said I could ride in a few months, but I might not race or ever compete in any rodeo events ever again. But I'm going to prove them wrong. I'll get back there."

"Oh, no. I'm so sorry. I used to compete when I was younger in jumping and I loved it so much. It would be so hard to know that I couldn't do it again if I were still competing." She reaches out and puts her hand on his shoulder. It doesn't mean anything, but the way he looks at her unsettles me.

I notice Sutton watching me and turn to him. "'Sup?"

"Yes, it's so sad Mav here couldn't keep his promise to Jude," he says, his tone dripping with saccharine honey.

"Couldn't you still do it if you wanted to?" Charlotte asks, looking at me.

"I—uh, yes. But it was supposed to be with him, our thing." I slap Jude's shoulder, pulling him closer to me and out of proximity to Charlotte.

Jude, never one to miss a beat, says, "You know what? Charlotte, I bet you could pull Mav down a street, right?"

"Ha! She'd sooner run me over on the street, either in her beat-up truck or with Betty White."

"Hey! I'd never do that to BDub. That would traumatize her." She laughs, and it's infectious; Sutton and Jude join in. "But I would. If that was something you really wanted to do, I would pull you down a snow-covered street behind my horse." She says it casually, but her shoulders are pulled back and her chin is raised ever so slightly, like she's trying to be brave. Maybe she is—could this be an olive branch, or is it a ploy for something else she has planned?

She's here, though; she wanted to see a working ranch other than Dappled Stone and she is here putting in effort with them. We agreed to be civil, and if she wants to do it, who am I to say no?

"I would," I consent. I don't say anything else, but I see Jude behind Charlotte, grinning like the goddamn Cheshire Cat.

We skip out on dinner with the Cortlands and venture out to go get checked into the hotel. We stayed out on the ranch until well past sundown, and judging by her shivering, she's got to be cold.

"There is a Thai place next door to the hotel, and we can place a pickup order when we check in. If that's good with you?"

"Yeah, okay."

I pull into the parking lot that's a block behind the hotel, off the main drag. The wind is whipping pretty good when we get out of the car. Snow flurries blow from the main street and reflect the overhead lights, the world looking like white glitter has bombed it.

It's early in the season for a skijoring competition, being that it's November, but the snow machines are in place, blowing into the street, and the course designers will have a backhoe pushing the snow into the right places.

We get out of the truck, and I grab both our bags. "It's supposed to dump snow tonight. The weather's perfect for tomorrow."

"Dump snow?" she asks, her teeth chattering.

"A large snowfall is a 'dump' in ski terms." She laughs. I continue, "It sounds gross. But it's a good thing. I like big dumps and I cannot lie."

The last bit I say in the style of Sir Mix-a-Lot. It earns a toothy smile from her. I haven't seen her smile in a while, not that I've given her any reason to. If I think about it, I haven't smiled lately either. At least not since before Dad died.

"Fuck it, I'm running," she squeaks and shakes her shoulders in a shiver. Then, she takes off at a sprint, running toward the street.

"Damn it!" I give chase after her. I almost take myself out on a patch of ice but luckily don't fall. She rounds the corner, and I lose sight of her just for a second—I immediately want to put eyes on her. I know she's a grown-ass woman, but she doesn't really know where she's going. Now that I know people are actually after her, I feel uneasy not knowing where she is when she's not on the ranch.

I round the corner just in time to see her head into the Thai restaurant. She's laughing when I catch up with her. "Sorry, I couldn't be out another second in that. I don't normally mind it, but I have nothing on under this." She motions to her body. She's wearing thicker leggings, thick socks that go up past her boots, a long-sleeved thermal, and a puffy hip-length coat.

Instantly, I think of her naked underneath—which, okay, everyone is naked under their clothes, technically, but I know what her body looks like bare: perfect breasts with rosy pink nipples and flared hips that are perfect for gripping. I look her over from her toes up to the beanie on her head, taking in her expression when she realizes that I'm imagining her naked.

"I mean, like, base layers! I don't have base layers under this," she clarifies, practically tripping over her words.

I try not to make a big deal about it or embarrass her, so I laugh it off, even though I was the perv, acting like I could see her vagina through her leggings. "It's okay; we're all nude under our clothes." I point to a decal on the wall with an animated bowl of noodles, and it breaks the tension between us.

We place our order with the server. I get tom kha gai soup, summer rolls, and pad see ew while Charlotte gets a spicy red curry with chicken and white rice. It takes about ten minutes for our order to come out, during which she asks questions about Sutton and Jude.

Where did we meet? I met Jude skiing. How long have we been friends? Almost six years. Are they with anyone romantically? That throws me for a loop, but I give a non-answer and say they don't really share their sexcapades, so I'm not really sure about Sutton, but Jude is a bit of a tomcat who doesn't like to be tied down. Why would she care? Does she fancy one of them? I knew my instinct about Sutton making eyes at her wasn't misplaced!

"Order for Maverick."

"Thanks."

I hold the door open for her as we walk back into the glistening snow globe. The snow is really coming down now and the backhoes are moving the snow around to build the race course. Charlotte looks like she's in a trance, watching them build the course. Like she sees it, but isn't really looking.

"Let's get in before the food gets cold."

We walk through the rotating brass and glass door and are greeted by a young man working the front desk. There are Christmas trees, a ton of warm Christmas lights, and evergreen decor all throughout the lobby. There are vintage wood cabinets with mirrors—an updated, sleek look mixing with the historic elements of the hotel and well-designed new fixtures that give it an eclectic vibe.

"Hello!" the young man calls. "Checking in?"

"Hi, yes. Maverick Bennett—I have a reservation."

"I'm going to run to the restroom real quick; do you need me for anything?" Charlotte asks.

"No cards, remember? I'll put it on one of mine."

"Thank you," she says. "Sir, where are the restrooms?"

He points to an area just beyond the elevators. "Just behind there."

She nods and takes her bag with her.

We already talked about the bed situation: I was able to get a two-bedroom suite, so we decided we were fine to share the one bigger room.

I hand over my ID and credit card for the reservation. He goes through the rigamarole about checkout and the free coffee in the lobby.

"How many keys?"

"Two, please."

He gets us sorted and hands me our keys. "Room 614 and your parking pass. It's a corner room with a view of the lake and the north end of the skijoring race course. You'll leave that in your car window to make sure you get a parking space for tomorrow."

"Great, thanks," I murmur, though I'm not really paying attention to what he says.

I head to the elevator bank to wait for Charlotte. I just want to shower, eat my noodles, and pass out. When she comes out, she walks over to me, and we're companionably silent as we take the elevator up to the sixth floor. When we get to the room, I pull one key from its sleeve and hand her the other. I wait for the pad to turn green when I tap the key to it before stepping inside and holding the door open behind me. I can't find the light, but she flips it on when she walks further into the room.

"Uhhh, what's this?" she asks with shock in her voice.

I walk from the hallway to where it opens up into the room. There's a single king bed in the large room.

"I have no idea." I walk over to the desk in the corner and put the food down, along with my overnight bag. "Uh, I didn't do this. But we'll get it sorted, no worries."

I get my phone out to call down to the front desk and put it on speakerphone. "Hi, this is Maverick Bennett. You just checked my business associate and I into room 614."

"Yes, I remember. How can I help you?"

"This room only has one bed."

"Yes, sir, it's a king room."

"But I asked for a two-bedroom suite when I called and made the reservation. I definitely asked for two beds and a door separating them." I glance over to Charlotte, who looks horrified at the prospect of sleeping in the same bed as me. Okay, point made.

"Let me look at the system; one moment." He puts me on hold.

Charlotte looks uncomfortably at me and then at the bed. Then at the arched mirror on the wall next to the bed.

The receptionist comes back on the phone. "I'm so sorry for the inconvenience, Mr. Bennett, but this is the only room we have available as we are completely sold out for the events this weekend and we don't have any rollaways left. I will leave feedback for the manager that the reservation type was incorrect. Unfortunately, there are no other rooms available, and I know that all other nearby hotels and lodging are sold out because of the skijoring competition and festivities this weekend."

Well, fuck.

Maverick

CHAPTER 27

I turn to look at Charlotte. She looks pissed. "I didn't do this."

I don't say that I don't mind it, because if I did voice that out loud to her, she probably would lose her shit.

"Look, I can sleep on the floor tonight, and then tomorrow night I'll stay over at the ranch. It's not a big deal."

"That's not fair to you, either. Maybe they'll have a cancellation for tomorrow night, and we can ask in the morning."

"You take the bed, just give me a pill—"

"Mav, we can share a bed. We've slept together before." I laugh, and she blushes and says, "I mean, that too, but, God, we've been asleep in the same bed before. It's fine."

She hasn't called me "Mav" since we slept together.

There's a small desk along the exposed-brick wall, surrounded by an expanse of windows that allows the streetlights to shine into the room. I drop our bags onto the bed and take our food over to the desk.

"We can do the thing with pillows if you want—put 'em between us so that we can stay on our side of the bed." That gets a laugh out of her. "I promise to stay on my side of the bed." Another laugh.

"Don't worry, I'll keep my hands to myself," she says.

Speak for yourself.

"Pssh, yeah right—you know you'll be cuddling me come morning."

I don't look to see if she is amused or giving me the side-eye. I just walk over to the food bag and tear into it to get my noodles and soup out—but then I hear a huff and a giggle. Satisfied, I say, "Let's eat."

Other than the desk, there's the obligatory cuck chair, and those always give me the creeps, so I motion to the chair at the desk. She sits while I lean against the side of the desk. We split the order of summer rolls, and I devour my soup in just a few spoonfuls. Handing her the container filled with the red curry, our fingers graze, and my eyes immediately flash to hers. I wouldn't call it lust, but there's something charged in her blue eyes, and her lips part with a gasp. I pull my hand away like she just electrocuted me and take my noodles over to the bed.

"Yummmmm," she moans as she takes her first bite of her curry. "This is so good."

My dick twitches in my sweatpants at the sound of her moan, and I have to readjust how I'm sitting. Great, now I'm not hungry for just noodles.

We eat in silence for a few minutes before I reach for the remote and try to find something to watch to quell the roaring in my head encouraging me to say something, anything—but I'm afraid my mouth and my brain are short-circuiting because of the noises coming from the woman at the desk. I find something on Create, of all things. It's a channel by PBS. A host is giving travel tips about Phuket and Bangkok.

"Seriously, this curry is amazing." She swivels in the chair, kicking her feet with a flourish as she turns. "When did you find this place?"

"I love Thai food. I try to find it whenever I travel or visit new places. This is one of my favorites I've found."

"Have you ever been to Thailand?"

"No, but I'd love to go one day. You?"

"Nope," she says. "But it was on my bucket list."

Was—like her hopes and dreams from before all of this just disappeared.

"I think you should keep it on the list."

"Sometimes I think I should just chance it and move. Live off-grid and be peaceful. I don't know if I'll ever truly feel safe and know peace again. I'm always looking over my shoulder. Even if Owen said he could wipe my trail so that no one could find me, I don't think that feeling will ever leave me."

She's not a stray dog for me to adopt, so I shouldn't feel the overwhelming need to provide shelter for her, but I do—I want to be the one to provide that for her. When the fuck did she go from my enemy to the one I want to protect? When the fuck did I let my guard down?

"I think you should keep it on the list," I repeat. "We can try to figure out the rest." We? When the fuck did we become a "we"? I am so fucked. She looks at me, her mouth forming an O shape. "'We' like the team at the ranch and Owen, not like you-and-me 'we.'" I cough.

"Are you a shower-in-the-morning or at-night kind of guy?"

And now it's my turn to be shocked. "I'll shower tonight. We've got an early morning if we're trying to get to the ranch first thing and then get back here to watch the competition."

"I'm finally warmed up. I'll shower tonight, too. But you can go ahead first. I wanted to stretch a bit; I'm really tight."

"Ladies first."

"No, you go ahead. I want to digest my food and then stretch a bit."

"Okay, then." I grab my food containers and put them back in the bag, then into the garbage container. Since she mentioned it, I realize I feel stiff, too, but with the energy in the room right now, maybe a cold shower is best.

Thank God I brought pajamas! I was supposed to have my own room, and I usually sleep naked. I grab my toiletry bag, sleep pants, and leave her to do her stretching. Definitely not thinking about her lithe body doing downward dog and how flexible she was when I moved her body around like a rag-doll.

After the fastest and coldest shower ever, I brush my teeth and get situated for bed. I open the bathroom door and find her still stretching, her hands reaching between her spread legs with her pert ass in the air.

I cough, almost involuntarily. "Shower's free now, if you want to hop in."

Her eyes open and find me staring at her. She unfurls herself to stand and shifts her weight back and forth as she continues to stretch. "Okay, almost done."

I take my dirty clothes and fold them to go back in my bag. In the mirror by the bed, I see her continue to stretch and hear her make some breathy sounds. She peels off her thermal, revealing a lacy bralette underneath. Charlotte puts the shirt in her bag and grabs her stuff to take into the shower. She pulls out some aqua-blue satin fabric—I have no idea what it is, but if that's what she's sleeping in, it's going to be a long night.

I pull a chump move and pretend to be asleep by the time she comes out of the shower. I'm facing the mirror, so when she opens the door, I quickly close my eyes. I left the lights on so she could see where she was walking, but I'm still an asshole because I open my eyes and see the bundle of blue is actually a nightgown with a lace hem and the tiniest little straps. It looks like she's wearing water, the satin reflecting the lights in the room and hugging her curves. I don't hog the entire bed, but I am so curious to see if she puts a pillow barrier between us.

I close my eyes again and will my heart rate to steady and slow down. She turns off the lights, and the bed dips slightly when she climbs in. To her credit, she doesn't cling to the side when she gets in, either. She rolls onto her back.

"I know you're playing possum, Maverick. I told you I wasn't going to tentacle you in your sleep."

My cock thickens against my thigh at the thought—he definitely doesn't want to go to sleep now. "Good night, Charlotte."

"Good night, Mav."

I eventually fall into a deep sleep and wake in the morning with a jolt, my eyes flying open to see a mess of blonde waves and some light peeking from behind the curtains. Breathing in, I inhale the scent of pine and smoke. The corners of my lips turn up—Charlotte used my shampoo. The most primal part of my brain—and my dick—screams, "Mine, mine, mine!" But she's not. I have to keep reminding myself that I have no claim to her and that, just yesterday, she said she wanted to leave.

Through my chest, I feel a thump, thump, thump that doesn't belong to my heart. My right arm is banded tight across a silky material and a body that isn't mine. An arm is resting lightly atop mine, holding mine in place. Her breathing is deep and even, a sure sign Charlotte's still asleep, which means she hasn't felt my dick poking into her, my knees bent right behind hers. I want to stay here for just a minute. I don't know that I've ever cuddled anyone without sex before. This must be a dream.

What the fuck are you doing? This is not your style. Pull your arm slowly away and get up.

She takes a big breath and wiggles her ass closer to my crotch; now my dick is firmly wedged between her ass cheeks. And if the thigh-high slits on the nightgown were any indication, there's nothing but two pieces of fabric separating us. *Fuuuuck.* I pull away my hips and gently tug my arm out from underneath hers. *Wake up, Maverick.*

I snag my watch on her nightdress—I forgot to take it off last night—and that does it. She goes rigid, meaning she's awake, and she knows. Now she's death-gripping my hand.

"Maverick," she grinds out.

"Hey, I woke up like this. You were holding my arm in place. Can I have it back?"

She immediately lifts her arm, hops out of bed like I just told her there are bedbugs in the mattress, and crosses her arms. I push myself up on my knees and sit on my haunches. Goddamn—what she's wearing is positively sinful. I take in the swell of her breasts, now pushed up over her arms, her strong shoulders, the curve of her hips, the slopes of her calves. She's put on more muscle since I last saw this much of her skin.

I cock my head to the side, smirking. "What were you planning on getting into this weekend, Charlotte?"

"I like to sleep in nice things. I wear flannel every day, okay?" she spits out.

"Okay, Little Bird. No complaints from me; you could even wear it more."

"Little Bird?"

"You're like a bluebird day after a big snow. Not a cloud to be seen, brilliant sun in the sky. It's beautiful and clear; you can see out for miles."

She drops her hands to her sides, and I can see her peaked nipples beneath the fabric. God, I want to suck them. I can't get up because she'll see just how much I enjoyed that cuddle.

"We can call that a reverse cuddle. I tried to pull my arm away when I woke up, but you were holding on tight, Little Bird. I guess I was right; you cuddled me in the morning."

"Ugh!" She stomps away to the bathroom, and thank God. I stand up, go over to the window, and open it just a crack. Enough to welcome a cold burst inside to deflate my dick.

I take my chance while she's in the bathroom to change into my clothes for the day. We'll be outside all day, but can come back here before the competition if we need to.

"Hey, fair warning, I'm naked out here," I call out to her.

"Let me know when you're settled!" The closed door muffles her reply.

I'm mostly dressed when I knock on the bathroom door. "Hey."

There's a noise, like she was leaning against it and then stood up. She unlocks it and cracks it open. "Hi."

"It's not a big deal, but we could have saved this awkwardness if you would have just told me you wanted to use my body for some cuddles." I laugh, and she pulls the door wide and tries to push past me, but my arm snaps out and stops her from crossing the threshold.

"At least be a grown-up about it. I need to get dressed."

"We've got an early morning, Charlotte. We didn't even need an alarm clock; your butt wiggled and woke me up well before my watch vibrated." I let her pass, turning my neck to look over my shoulder. "Oh, I love the way you smell with my shampoo in your hair." I step inside the bathroom and shut the door to get myself together.

"Fucking asshole," I hear her mutter from the other side.

I don't care why she used my shampoo—maybe she forgot hers—but she'll have my scent on her all day, and that makes it hard to breathe.

I give her a few minutes to get dressed and settle with the fact that, on some level, however unlikely, she feels safe with me. She was able to drop her guard for a night and let me in, even if we didn't fuck like heathens all night.

"Ready or not, I'm coming out." I gave her like ten minutes, so she has to be dressed by now. I pull the door open, and she's sitting at the desk, looking ready to go. "Ready to roll?"

"Yes, but—" She hesitates. "Thank you. I haven't slept like that in a really long time." She sighs. "Like, a realllly long time, and I didn't have nightmares of some faceless man trying to hunt or kill me."

Well, fuck. That's a lot to unpack. "You're welcome. I was just giving you shit earlier. I'm glad you got some rest."

I glance at my watch: 6:07 a.m. I motion toward the door and grab the cooler bag that's got water bottles and snacks for the morning, along with my hat and gloves.

"Can we stop and get coffee in the lobby?"

"Yes, fuck yes," I reply. We grab a fix, one of her "dressed-up" coffees, then step out into the sunshine. I turn my face to the sky and close my eyes. The sun instantly warms my exposed skin. I breathe in the cool air and open my eyes when I exhale. I bring my head back down and find Charlotte studying me.

"You're more at ease when you're not at home. That's a real thing, isn't it?"

"More than you'll ever know."

"I'm sorry," she says quietly.

"For what?"

"That you wanted more, and now you're back at the one place where you wanted to disappear from."

"It's no different from your situation, only reversed," I muse. "I'm glad you can find some type of reprieve there. It's not bad all the time. But then I think of all the bullshit I put my parents through, all the ways I let people down, and it gets suffocating. I'm never going to change people's perception of me, and I'm okay with that, but to be surrounded by reminders of it—to live within the same four walls your whole life—that feeling will take some time to get used to."

"Hmm," is all she says. Our walk to the truck is made in silence, as is our drive to the Cortlands' ranch.

I park along the fenceline just next to the barn and find Sutton, Jude, Hudson, and Raegan waiting for us.

Sutton, always the first to step up in any situation, approaches us. "Good morning, Charlotte. You didn't get a chance to meet our younger siblings, Hudson and Raegan, yesterday."

They put their gloved hands out, and puffs of steam leave their mouths when they greet her.

"Nice to meet you! I can't stay long, but I had to meet the woman who's been keeping Rick in place!" Raegan says eagerly. Her eyes bounce back and forth between Charlotte and me.

"God, Rae!" I grunt.

"Nice to meet you, too. Please call me Charlie."

Hudson, the idiot, is openly ogling her. "Nice to meet you, Charlie, ma'am." He tips his cowboy hat to her. I punch him in the shoulder, and so does Jude.

"Oooh, you're trouble. I can tell," Charlotte says to him.

I give Jude a look, and he redirects, stating, "All right, we only have a short window of time before the competition in town, so let's get it done. You two ready?"

"Yep," she says in a brighter tone than she uses with me.

"Giddy up, then. Charlie, you're with me," Sutton says as they walk to the horses.

Jude and the rest of us walk to the ATVs.

"Bro, you've got drool on your chin," Jude jabs. To Hudson, he taunts, "And you, it looks like you're about to piss on her—knock it off. That woman would eat you alive."

"What a way to go, though," Hudson says.

"I have to agree. I am an equal-opportunity appreciator, and she's way too pretty for you, Rick," Raegan says from behind me. She's got a magnetic energy that draws people to her—men and women can't help but be captivated, both by her charm and beauty. Because she is beautiful, with her long black hair and gray eyes that match those of the rest of the Cortland kids.

I never, ever went there, but I can see the appeal. I also know that I could never keep up with her; she turns over dates faster than milk going bad.

I turn around and glare at her. "Don't start, Rae."

"Ooh, shit. You really do like her," she teases. "Rick has the hots for the boss! I could steal her from under your arm, and you wouldn't even know what happened, Mav."

I hang my head. God damn—they are not going to let up. The Cortland siblings are like my siblings, and they will tease me mercilessly like I'm one of their own. The sun won't be the only thing beating down on me today.

Maverick

CHAPTER 28

Five hours later, we're done for the day and are packing into our trucks to get back to town. The sun is shining high, and there are only a few clouds peppering the sky, but not so much to melt the snow that fell last night. We've got to get back to town to see the opening ceremony parade. Rae made fun of me for weeks when I didn't get a big, souped-up truck like everyone else; I wanted the Jeep truck. I didn't—and still don't—plan on being a rancher for the rest of my life.

We pull off the gravel road leading away from the ranch and turn onto the main road. I reach into the cooler bag behind Charlotte's seat to pull out two water bottles. I hand one to Charlotte, and she takes it with appreciation.

"Thanks." She gulps it down, her slender neck moving with each swallow. "Phew, I was thirsty. I definitely didn't drink enough while we were out there."

"You have to be careful; staying hydrated is important!" I say it more harshly than I meant to, and I wish I could take it back the second the words leave my lips. I'm not trying to be a dick, but it comes out so naturally, my default setting. After this morning, waking with her in my arms, my emotions are all over the place, and seeing her ride off with Sutton just made my blood boil.

"I know that! I'm just saying." She crunches the water bottle down and screws the cap back on.

I don't apologize for the outburst, but I tell her, "I know...you should just be careful anyway."

We're a good hour behind the gun here because we didn't leave the ranch on time. Rae was showing Charlotte how they balance tradition with practicality, and it was more important that she got to see that firsthand. On a smaller ranch, you do everything. We have a few more hands than they do, so she may not have to adapt everything she learned today, but at least she could see it being done.

With our parking pass, we are able to snag a spot but have to go around the back way because the street is now a race course. Jude and the rest of them will have to find a spot in the blocks behind and will have to walk to get close. The lot attendant waves us in, and we find one of the last spots. I park, and can hear the music blasting from the speakers on the main street.

Charlotte grabs the bag out of the car.

"I can take that," I say.

"I know you can, but I got it."

I let her carry it because she wants to. "We have at least fifteen minutes before they meet up with us. Want to go up to the room for a second? Grab some more water and smash some more of that food from last night?"

She makes a little moan and throws her head back as she says, "God, yes, that curry was so yummy."

Walking on the sidewalk, the salt crunches beneath our feet. We push through the rotating door and hurry to the elevator to take us to our floor. She doesn't mention stopping at the front desk to see if there are any more rooms available for tonight. And if she's not pushing it, I'm not either. I would sleep next to her again, maybe pay attention this time and see just how far that slit up her nightdress goes.

"I saw some serious fashionistas down there! I didn't know it was going to be like this. I feel seriously underdressed in my flannel and Carhart jacket."

"Not everyone dresses up."

"I brought a top, just in case."

"Just in case of what?"

"I don't know, in case there was a hotel bar or something and it called for it."

"I wouldn't change into anything fancy or sheer; we'll still be outside the rest of the day."

"Okay, I'll save it for after—we can run back up here and change."

We're back down in the action within a few minutes, and Charlotte is about to see her first taste of skijoring.

Charlotte walks out of the hotel and toward me as I lean against a pole holding up the snow fence. "That was the coolest thing I've ever seen! I'll definitely need to go thrifting with Quinn so I have something cool to wear next time."

"It's such a rush, isn't it? Full-on Cattle Ranch Wife Chic isn't a look for you, though. With the fur coats and Pit Vipers, no, you need to dress the part if we're doing this. Cowboy hat, fringed chaps, the whole thing. I like this cowboy hat, though," I say, inclining my head to indicate the hat that wasn't on her head when she went up to the room to change.

"Guys!" Rae runs up and puts her arms around our shoulders. "We're going to the bar, and you both are joining us."

"That's not a—"

"Oh, I could use a drink to warm me up!" Charlotte exclaims.

"Your first drink is on me, sugar," Rae says, and they slip away, arm in arm. Rae turns back and winks at me.

My jaw is on the floor. She absolutely did just steal her away from me.

"Hudson went off with some chick," Sutton says, coming up behind me with Jude in tow.

I'm watching Charlotte's round ass walk ahead of me. She and Rae are talking animatedly. I'm glad they're getting on, because Charlotte could use some friends in the business. Beneath the hem of her field coat, there's a peek of pink above her jeans. She's wearing a pair of wedged boots, or some kind of boot. They're not cowboy boots, that's for sure.

Sutton says, "You're hittin' that?"

Jude sniggers.

That means Jude hasn't shared my secret that it was Charlotte who I was—what? Heartbroken over? Was I heartbroken? No—disappointed, sure, but not heartbroken. At any rate, Jude's a real one.

"No," I say sourly.

"Oh? Okay. You're just pining then. If she's turned you down, would you mind—"

I turn on him. "Fuck yes, I mind." I point my finger at him. "Hands to yourself or in your pockets, and you can jerk off, but you don't touch her."

Jude's laughing, and Sutton just looks like he's going to enjoy pushing back on me.

I take a step into his space, and even though we're the same height, I square my shoulders. "Stay away from Charlotte," I say, my voice low and deep.

"Funny, Mav, Charlie doesn't seem to know that she's your girl or that you've laid some claim to her. Maybe I should go ask her myself if she has your brand on her somewhere?"

My jaw tightens and my hands ball into fists at my sides. I will not hit Sutton. I will not hit Sutton. I will not sucker-punch Sutton. Forcing an exhale from my nose, I try not to engage; he only wants a reaction out of me, anyway. "Go ahead and ask her. You and I both know she won't be interested." Not waiting for him to respond, I walk away in the direction the girls went.

I wonder if she would be interested in Sutton; he could be exactly what she needs. But, if I'm honest with myself, I'm the one she's going to be with. Since she bared her soul to me in the cabin kitchen, I've known that she was it for me. It may just take her a second to catch up with that. Fuck—that would be something if she ever let me brand her.

"Mav."

I turn around and wait for them to catch up.

"I'm glad to see you have something worth fighting for," Sutton says.

The tension eases from my body and I feel less like a goddamn caveman.

Jude slaps him across the arm. "You're waving that red flag in front of him—knock it off. But for real, if you want it, Mav, she's going to make you work for it."

I take that in and ponder what it means to have to really put in the work. I've never had to do that before—but I can.

Like a homing beacon, I catch sight of Charlotte's blonde hair turning into the bar up ahead.

That uneasy feeling of having her out of my sight settles over me again. I'm not trying to cage her; she's had enough of that in this life. I keep my cool, stay with the guys, and turn into the bar. I've been here a few times with them over the summer.

Actually, this is where I met Naomi. It was just a casual fling for me, but I know she wanted more. That was just something I couldn't give her. And when I told her as much—well, let's say she didn't take it well.

All things considered, the bar is a little sleeker than the impression the outside gives. It's got clean, black lines, gold hardware, glass tabletops, and a mercury-glass bar.

The girls are already at the bar by the time we get there. It's crowded, but not packed, so I really don't have an excuse to get so close to Charlotte except for the fact that I want to. Leaning into her, I ask, "Getting enough shots for everybody?"

Smug as fuck, Rae pipes in, "Actually, I have her first drink, Rick," and shoots me a wink. "You can get the second." The innuendo isn't lost on me; she's implying that I can have her sloppy seconds.

The bartender returns with the girls' shots and a drink. They clink each other's glass and take the shots back in one go, slamming the empty glasses back on the bartop.

Rae went for the obvious and ordered them both whiskey. My Little Bird may think I never pay attention, but I spy some rosemary along the bar next to the other garnishes. When he comes back, I ask the bartender for what I know happens to be her favorite drink. She made a comment on the walk home about how much she loves herbs in cocktails.

I order a few waters, as this could last all night—luckily, Mrs. Cortland's Sunday brunch may be the best hangover cure in the world. We also have a five-hour drive home.

I get the drinks and find Rae and Charlotte on the dance floor, bouncing along to whatever god-awful music the DJ's playing. I hand her the water, and she takes it with a smile and a wink.

God, that wink. I make a "come here" motion with my finger, her drink still in hand. She cocks her head to the side as if to say, "Make me." What a brat. I mouth, "Come here." She huffs, and then takes the ten steps to stand in front of me. I hold up her drink, the rosy lemon that she and Quinn liked so much. I think I got the recipe right, based on what I can remember from months ago.

She notices the rosemary and the slightly yellow shade of the drink, and her face breaks into a smile, a wide one that stretches from ear to ear. "Is that for me?"

"Mm."

"I can't believe you remembered."

"The exact recipe is fuzzy, but it's close."

"Thank you, Mav."

Again, Mav—not Maverick, not Ranger Rick, not Dickhead. Mav.

She takes the drink, and our fingers touch. Her beautiful, full lips turn up on one side to give me a barely-there smile, and then she turns away to resume dancing with Rae.

Sutton and Jude are occupied with some locals. I never truly felt like a local when I was here, like the dark gray storm cloud from Silver Rapids seemed to follow me wherever I went and warned people to stay away from me. I stay with Rae and Charlotte on the dance floor, looking like a right fool.

The girls are dancing pretty provocatively, and I'm not inclined to intervene at all. I love watching Charlotte dance, her body swinging with the rhythm. I don't even mind when Rae puts her hands on Charlotte's hips; I know Charlotte is mine.

A few hours and a few shots later, the girls are still on the dance floor, only we've moved to a corner, where they've claimed a high-top table, tossing their coats onto the chair that sits opposite me. There is a heat vent right above the table, and considering that it's late January in Utah, you can believe it's cranking. So much so that the girls have visible beads of sweat dripping from behind their ears. I track a bead winding its way down over Charlotte's collarbone and in between the valley of her breasts.

Fuck. Before my brain can catch up, my feet are walking toward Charlotte and I pull her backside into me.

She doesn't turn around to see who's grinding their dick up against her, and that makes me irrationally angry. She'd let just anyone get this close to her?

"You're not being very careful, Little Bird," I growl in her ear.

"I knew it was you, Ranger Rick; your eyes haven't left my ass in hours, except to look at my tits." She still hasn't turned around. She just keeps dancing to the beat. "And as it is, I hardly doubt my new friend Rae would let just anyone touch me." I hear the smile in her voice. She turns to face me, but my hands never leave her body. "Don't get the wrong idea, Maverick. It's just a dance, right?"

I don't say anything. I just let her move her hips to the beat and hold my stare on those beautiful blue eyes.

She's the first one to break and look away. "Rae, I need a break. Where's the bathroom?"

"I can show you," Rae yells over the music.

Chicken shit. I smirk and watch them walk away. I go back to the table and take a sip of water. I'm done drinking tonight. As it is, I only had three drinks.

I look for Sutton and Jude. They would have texted or found me to tell me they were leaving, but I don't see them. I spot Naomi talking with some people, but she doesn't see me. I heard her name announced earlier, as a rider in the competition, so I'm not too surprised she's here. I don't want to make it awkward, and I don't know how she will react if she sees me, so I put my back to her, really not wanting to engage, and pull my phone out.

Jude: Bruh, she's probably already over your ass.

I just don't need the drama, and with Charlotte, I'm not trying to have a scene.

Jude: Yeah, ok.

Where the fuck did you disappear to?

Jude: By the bar, I just saw Charlotte and Rae order another shot.

Ok, I'm in the same spot where the girls stashed their coats.

Jude: Incoming. Incoming!

I don't see it until it's too late. I hear a familiar female voice call my name, but with the music, I can't make out if it's Rae or someone else. I would have recognized Charlotte's voice.

But I turn to find Naomi in front of me, all smiles.

"I wondered if I might see you here. I saw Sutton and Jude at the bar. How've you been?" she slurs.

I hope she has a good time, but this is not my mess to clean up. "Hey, Naomi," I say, looking for an escape.

"It is sooo good to see you. You're looking good." She steps into my personal space. I try to keep my distance by putting my arms up to indicate I don't want her any closer, but she misinterprets that and steps into my chest, throwing her arms around my neck to pull me closer to her.

"Actually, you look so fucking good. I'm in town just for tonight if you want to hang out for old time's sake," she whisper-yells in my ear. She's trying to play it coy, but that's hard to do when you're two sheets to the wind and invading someone's personal space.

I put my hands behind my neck to extricate myself from her arms. It's just my fucking luck that, when I finally get her hands separated, I look up and see the shock on Charlotte's crestfallen face. I need to tell her this is not what it looks like, but it's certainly not helping matters that Naomi is trying to fight against me.

I look at Charlotte, and then at Rae, who comes up behind her, then back at Charlotte as I say, "Naomi, get off me. Naomi!"

I take some steps back and break her hold, but the damage is done. Charlotte already grabbed her bag and is damn near running out of the bar.

Fuck! I grab my coat off the table and race off into the night to find Charlotte.

The air outside is frigid, and the snow that has fallen is fat and wet, sticking to my eyelashes. I see her damn near sprinting toward the hotel. I call after her, "Charlotte!" She doesn't stop, because of course she doesn't. "Damn it. Charlotte! Wait! That wasn't what it looked like!" She doesn't even turn around, so I give chase, trying to catch up to the woman who always seems to slip through my fingers.

She gets to the door and disappears into the hotel. I get to the lobby but don't see her, and the elevator shows that it's already on the sixth floor. I push the button and see it stop on the fifth. Damn it—*move slower, please.* The elevator finally opens, and a couple is making out in it.

"You guys going back up? Okay, cool, me too." I hit the button for the sixth floor. I hear them kissing behind me. Ugh.

We finally get to the sixth floor, and I hurry to our room, putting the key up to the lock and pushing the door so hard it flies open. "Charlotte! Listen."

Except she's not in the room.

Adrenaline surges and floods my veins, my breath ragged. My heart is pounding in my ears and against my ribs like a drum. Where could she be?!

That's when I hear a rustling in the bathroom.

Charlotte

CHAPTER 29

*S*o *much for not having feelings, Charlotte. You made them pretty damn clear, too.* I shouldn't have shown my hand. I shouldn't have run; I should have just turned around and walked out. Even though I can admit to myself I have feelings for him, I don't want to drag him into this. I'm sitting on the toilet in the bathroom, basically hiding in shame.

Bam! Through the bathroom door, I can hear the outer door slam open. Whatever game he's playing with this hot and cold is getting ridiculous. Why the fuck is he even here when he was just making out with that woman?

He's been an overprotective asshole all day, thinking that I didn't notice his expression when one of his friends got too close, or even when Rae was hitting on me!

"Charlotte, open the door!"

"Go away."

"Grow up. Stop hiding in the bathroom and open the damn door!"

"I'm fine. I'm just going to shower and get ready for bed."

He doesn't immediately respond, which means he might just leave me alone to process or pout. I'm not really sure which one I'm in the middle of—maybe both.

"Yeah, you're going to shower when all of your toiletries and your pajamas are out here on top of your bag. Though, I'm not saying I would deny the show if you wanted to strut out naked after your shower," he snarks.

"You're a pig."

"Oink, oink." I can hear him huff. He sounds like he's right outside the door now. "I don't remember you being a coward. Open the door."

What?! A coward? Me? After fighting for so long to stay alive. After fighting to work my way so that the guys on the ranch respected me. Is running away from someone who wants to kill you cowardly? Is walking away from a relationship where you had no value to your family except for the corporate alliance you could offer through your vagina cowardly?

No. Fuck him. The rage overcomes me.

He's leaning against the door and evidently wasn't expecting me to pull it open, because he falls right into me. That catches him off guard. I push him backward so that he doesn't block me in, and then I punch him in the gut, hard. Those kickboxing classes on Tuesdays and Thursdays back home taught me how to throw a punch—put your weight behind it, center yourself, thumb over your first two fingers' middle knuckles.

I hear the air whoosh from his lungs. He drops to one knee and tries to regain composure and his breath.

"Damn—" He coughs. "I was hoping you'd be naked, at least, when you opened the door."

He's still wheezing when I push him over. He lets me push him, I know that, but the sight of him clutching his stomach means my punch landed true.

"I am not a goddamn coward. You are! You walked away from your dad and the ranch. I finally get it. I ran away from my life in Boston. But I think I was running toward something. Something bigger than the life I was living. You willingly walked away from this. After you couldn't ski anymore competitively, you could have still had all of this with Jasper. And! AND! Even if you came back to find me, or tried to text me, if you really wanted this, you would have fought harder." I motion between us—him on the floor and me in the hallway.

At that, he stands up. "So, that's it? You want me to fight for you?"

I back up a few steps and feel my ass press up against the desk. "No, that's not…"

His voice is sharp enough to cut to the quick as he interrupts. "Yes the fuck it is. You wouldn't have brought it up if you didn't mean it. I know you."

Shit, why did I bring that up?

"You have had no one stand their ground and fight for you. Not your parents, not your piece-of-shit fiancé, not your boss and mentor." He crosses the room in just a few steps, suddenly in my space.

He's everywhere, surrounding me with the scent of freshly cut pine, smoke, and danger. His nearness is intoxicating and just as flammable as the whiskey we were drinking—I know, because I've been caught in his flame before. He made me feel like I was the only thing in the world. He made me think I could have something more; that's what makes it dangerous—he gave me hope.

"I would fight for you. You just have to tell me that's what you want. But you have to mean it." He takes another step, his body but an inch from mine. A big breath in, and my breasts would touch his chest. His mouth is so close, I can see the faintest bit of red in his brown scruff.

I'm not a coward. I look him in his ocean-blue eyes. There's depth there that would put the Mariana Trench to shame.

"You have to want it," he rasps out. God, I can't breathe. "You. Have. To. Stop. Running. Trust that Silver Rapids can keep and protect you. That I can keep and protect you until you can say that we're just holding on in a hurricane. I can give you a release, but that's all it would be."

The bit of silver in his eyes catches in the light from the sconces on the wall, and he looks like he's about to step away, but I don't want this connection to break. A breath, two, and he can see that I'm not going to give in. I can't surrender my heart or my life on a whim that this could be real.

It certainly looked real between him and the woman at the bar. My mind replays her hands winding up his neck, fingers working through his thick, wavy hair. That's enough to sober me.

As though he can sense a shift in me, sense he may lose this battle, he goes in for the kill and removes the inches between our lips, sealing mine with a kiss.

It's feather-light, a brush of his plush lips against mine—a tease, just a taste. He's leaving this for me to decide how much I let him in, for me to be brave and open for him.

My brain and heart never saw eye to eye. Before I know what I'm doing, I push into him a fraction, and that's all he needs. He presses forward, and his lips plunder mine. A soft and desperate sound escapes me as he moves his lips against mine.

His muscular hands are in my hair, pulling my head back just slightly so that I open more fully to him. His hands know my body; he knows what I like—that even with tenderness, I want to feel it.

The contrast between his grip in my hair and the softness of his lips lights up my senses. Whatever bitterness lingered just moments ago is fading. I'm lost in the way his body is pressing into mine, trapping me against the desk, and his hard, muscled chest, his thick thighs bracketing my right leg, holding me in place, practically lifting me off the floor. One of my hands is on his belt, touching a sliver of bare skin where his shirt came untucked, and the other is on his athletic arm. I can't tell if I'm holding him to me or if it's the other way around, but I can feel his growing cock pressing into me, and my traitorous pussy is screaming, "More, more, more!"

He kisses along my jaw to the sensitive spot between my ear and my neck while his hands explore, roving all over my body. The trail of his touch is electric.

I can't breathe; he's stealing all the goddamn common sense from my head and the air from my lungs with his ministrations. I break the kiss and manage to remove myself from the vise-like grip of his thighs. "I—am so disgusting. I haven't showered." I grab my pajamas and underwear from the top of my bag. "I'm going to jump in the shower first, okay?"

I don't stick around to see if that's good with him or not because I need some distance and to figure out how we went from fighting about him in an intimate state with another woman to me basically riding his leg.

I rush into the bathroom and slam the door. Who am I kidding? I ran so fast we're probably going to have to pay for carpet repair! Raising my fingers to my lips, I find them tender and puffy. I dare to look in the mirror and, yep, my hair looks like a bird of prey tried to nest in it. I look thoroughly wrecked.

I bang my head against the door. What am I doing?

"You all right in there, Little Bird?"

"Yeah! I'm okay." I am so not okay...I just kissed Maverick. This is going to complicate things—but only if I let it. It's just a kiss.

I put my sleep dress on the counter and start the shower, blasting it to max heat. Undressing, I put my clothes in a neat pile on the towel shelf. I look for my toiletries bag and realize I forgot to grab it...again. This hotel doesn't have those little travel sizes stocked, and so I had to use his shampoo yesterday. I carried the scent on me all day, and I could smell it even under my perfume. The wind would blow, and I would catch a scent of pine, and that hit below the belt every time. I am not using it again.

I call through the door, "Can you please hand me the blue toiletries bag on top of my pack?"

He doesn't answer.

"Maverick, please?" I brought a robe, but not into the bathroom with me. I could go out in a towel, but I can't have only one layer of clothing between him and me right now. The wetness between my legs is indicative of my body betraying my mind; this is not the time to be throwing my kitty-cat at him.

A tiny knock-knock at the door gets me out of my head and makes me jump.

"Open the door if you want this, Charlotte."

I crack the door open and hide behind it, sticking my hand out, waiting for him to put the bag in it. Billows of steam escape from this little hell.

His fingers don't brush against my open palm when he places a silicone bottle in my hand. It's heavier than my shampoo bottle. "I can help rub it in if there's a spot you can't reach," he says.

I pull my hand back, and it gets stuck—*ohh, fuck*. I yank it through and yelp when my knuckles hit the metal doorframe. I slam the door closed and lock it.

Why did my hand get stuck? Because what he handed me is not a shampoo bottle or my toiletries bag. Like a slow-motion shot in a movie, my eyes go to the object in my hand.

Oh, my God! That asshole riffled through my bag and found my vibrator! My vibrator, which was in my overnight bag, under the toiletries bag. Kill me now. Seriously, who the hell did I piss off that this is my life?

"You snooped in my bag?! What kind of animal are you?!" I scream.

"I didn't snoop. It was right on top, under your toiletries. I know you're a kinky little thing, but on a work trip with an employee? Damn, Boss."

"Don't call me 'Boss'—it's weird. And we were supposed to have our own rooms!"

"Charlotte, I am always available to scratch that itch. That's not the pink one." I hear the taunt in his voice. "Did that one die?"

Please let this bathtub fall through the floor and take me with it. "No!" I don't say that the pink one reminds me of when he used it on me. I haven't really used it since, so when Q and I got drunk, I ordered a new friend. "Please give me the toiletries bag!"

"If you want it, come and get it." I hear his footsteps walking away from the door.

"I am naked! Just give me the damn bag."

"No, I think I like the idea of you smelling like me. Besides, I've seen every single inch of your body. I've touched and licked every inch of your body."

I bump my forehead against the door. "Yes, indeed, you have," I mutter.

Enough time has passed that I don't think he's going to give me my bag. I suck it up, turn the water down to not-quite-scalding, and get in the tub. Rather than putting the stopper down, I let the water pour over me.

I sit there in my feelings for a minute, with my new favorite vibrator in my hand. That kiss got me going. It was all the things a kiss should be. I am mortified and more than just a little turned on, thinking about the fact that he is on the other side of this wall and likely thinking I'm using it right now. The hot water is helping melt away some of the tension, but the part that's turned on really could use a release. That same part also wants to fight fire with fire.

What would be great would be to be loud as fuck while I get off in here and let him squirm while listening to me. I put the toy in my lap while I wash my hair and body with a washcloth. I definitely want to tell the front desk receptionist that they forgot shampoo in this room, but am grateful there's a little bottle of conditioner and body wash.

Once I'm thoroughly washed, I condition my hair and put it up in a twist so it can act as a mask. Maybe more of the scent will linger, so I don't smell the pine and snow scent of Maverick's shampoo. I lean my head against the tiled wall, close my eyes, and scoot back further so that the water from the spray hits my abdomen. This particular vibrator has temperature settings, so it can be warm or cold; the sensation combination is seriously the most amazing feeling.

I set the temperature to the coldest setting. My skin is already heated and flushed from being under the water, and I have grown to love temperature play. Taking one breast in my hand and teasing the nipple of my other breast with the tip of the toy, I let out a gasp. Perhaps slightly louder than I normally would.

Knowing he's on the other side of the wall, and that this isn't appropriate behavior for whatever kind of working relationship we have—all of it has wetness pooling in my core. Kneading my breast and remembering exactly what Maverick did to them with his tongue and mouth, I exhale again. I spread my legs so that one is propped up on the corner of the tub and the other is up and over the side. Slowly, I trace the toy down my body and feel the weight of my breasts as I pant. Pushing the toy through my lower lips, down to my center, and up, over my clit, the invasion of the feeling—the ice and the hot water now pouring over my exposed core—makes me flutter and pushes a sinful moan from my throat.

I haven't even turned on the vibration, and I can already feel the beginnings of my orgasm tingle in my spine. The toy is slick in my hand. I put it on my favorite setting; the deep vibration feels like a rumble that starts from my clit.

"Fuck!"

I don't actually mean to voice it out loud, but it feels so good. Feeling it down to the nerves in my feet, my toes curl, and my breathy moans get louder and more frantic. It's not even a show anymore; it just feels that good. I squeeze my nipple between my finger and thumb and throw my head back as the stream of water hits just right on my pussy.

"Oh, my God!" The sound tears from my throat as I pant and come so hard that I see stars. I clutch the vibrator to my chest, the vibration still going as I try to turn it off. *Damn.*

I wash up again, stand, and rinse the conditioner from my hair. I will not be embarrassed. He had a roommate. I'm sure he's jacked off with Jude in the apartment at the same time as him—this is no different. I dry off and towel my hair. My brush is already on the counter from when I brushed it out earlier, thank God. I do not need to go to bed with unbrushed hair; that would just make getting ready tomorrow morning that much worse. I get into my nightdress and square my shoulders. Reaching for the door, I hesitate only a moment before swinging it open, but I can't get my feet to move. I look down. Did I step in superglue? *Be brave.*

The bedside lamp is on, and the window sheers filter the light from outside, everything else blanketed in darkness except for him. When I look over at Maverick, his face calm and unaffected, head propped in his hand, I can clearly see his eyes trained on me, taking in my appearance—from the wet hair spilling over my shoulders and skimming beneath my silk-covered breasts down to the lace hem of my nightdress.

"Naughty fucking tease, Little Bird. What am I supposed to do with this?" He motions down to an impressive bulge going on in his sleep pants. I know just how big that dick is to make a tent so noticeable.

"The shower can help," I offer. I take the toy back to my bag. I cleaned it off with body wash, but will properly clean it with the cleanser I brought later. I get a pair of fuzzy socks, sit on the edge of my side of the bed, and slip them on. I try to appear as cool as he does right now, but I have never masturbated while my one-night-stand-turned-enemy-turned-kind-of-employee-turned-I-don't-know-what was on the other side of the door. My heart is beating so loud I think he can hear it from his side of the bed.

I move to stand, but he's pulling me back and leaning over me in an instant. "I love a good tease, but I do the edging, not you."

With that, he crawls over me, his impressive erection grazing against me. He grabs some stuff from his bag and goes into the bathroom. I hear the stream of the shower seconds later.

I don't know what I was expecting, but at least I got a reaction from him. Wriggling to get under the covers, I replay the day and still have so many questions.

I don't hear him get out of the shower or get into bed. I don't feel him in the night, and I sleep peacefully for the first time in a long time until I realize I'm the one spooning him come morning.

"Good, you're awake." He flips over so he's facing me. I try to move my arm away, but he grabs it and keeps it in place against his bare ribs—his muscular, warm, bare ribs. "Let's talk about last night."

"I don't want to." I yank my hand back, but he tightens his hold. "Let go."

"It was nice to see you having fun with Rae. But what you saw, me with that woman, was someone who didn't want to quite let go."

"You and she have that in common. Let go of my arm."

He's using my own words against me. "I don't want to." He grips more firmly, but not enough to hurt, just enough to make me look at him. "It's been over for a while, and I would have told you that if you would have listened to me instead of running back here to the hotel. I'm not mad at how the night ended, though." His body is so hot; he must be boiling. Or maybe it's my blood that's boiling.

"It's fine. You can move on; it's for the best."

"If it's for the best, then look at me and tell me that little show wasn't for me. Wasn't meant to make me jealous. Wasn't meant to make me go out-of-my-skin crazy."

"It wasn't a show."

"Just an appetizer, then? Let me remind you, I've already had a taste, sweetheart. And seeing you with Jude and Sutton—hell, even Rae—did something. Not having you in my sight for just a moment since you told me what was going on has made me feel uneasy. And it took a while to recognize what I'm feeling. I don't know if there will ever be a day when I won't want to devour you. You're trying to leave, and I want you to stay."

"I told you, I don't want this hanging over my head when it comes to a relationship. Just look at us: we're in close quarters for two days, and we want to kill each other."

"I want to do lots of things to you. Kiss you, taste you. Smack that pussy for you teasing me, spank your ass so red you can't sit—but make no mistake in thinking that I want to kill you."

"Mav, I don't want—"

"Back to lying. You do want it," he moves closer to me, "but, for whatever reason, you feel like lying to yourself. I'm done. I'm done fighting this. I've wanted to both throttle you and drop to your feet since I saw you next to my dad's bedside. Charlotte, I'm glad that he had you, even if for a short while. I'm jealous of my father because he saw a side of you that took me too long to see. But I know you gave him a peace that I never did, or maybe never could. I know it seems that I hated him. I didn't. I disappointed him when I got drunk and fell out of the hotel on the anniversary of my mom's death and tore my knee to shit. I disappointed him when—" He breaks off.

This feels like a confession, a baring of his soul, and it's breaking my heart because I know Jasper felt like he was the one who let Maverick down. He told me as much once, before I knew Maverick was his son, and he died thinking that his son hated him.

"And maybe, in that, I did grow to hate him because it was easier for me. What he did for me and what he carried with him to the grave—I'll never get that back, and it needs to stay dead and buried." He lets go of my hand.

"Mav," I whisper. He's breaking through my defenses. I feel like I'm seeing what could have been all those months ago. I push my arm through his hold and pull myself closer to him. I hope he sees this for what it is, because I can't give him more than this. I can give him my body, but I can't give him what's left of my heart again.

He nuzzles against me. "Did you think of me?" he asks. "Did you think of the way you told me secrets? The way I pulled every single orgasm from your body? The way you screamed my name over and over and over?" He looks at me, and I hold his gaze. I'm not shying away from this. "Because I thought of you. Every single time."

"Yes, I thought of you," I admit.

He pulls me the rest of the way against him, his gaze hooded despite the intensity of the conversation.

"Wait. Before we go any further, tell me who she was."

"She was a stand-in; she was just your placeholder. There isn't anyone else who could ever compare to the sun."

Shit—well, definitely not the most romantic thing I've ever heard, but also...maybe it is? Because I want to be someone's first choice.

I know I've been missing some good dick for, well, my entire life—but I've been craving his body since he left me that morning in May. I know I need therapy because I seem to be fixated on that day. Like it was the day to change myself.

His eyes are burning with a hunger that threatens to ruin both of us. Gruffly, he says, "Fuck it."

In a move that shouldn't shock me, he pulls me so that I'm laid flat against him, bracketing me with his knees on either side of my hips. His hot hands bring my face to his in a brutal kiss. It's scorching and messy, all tongue and clashing of wills. He hooks his leg over mine and rolls us so that he's on top.

My hands roam over his bare chest and to his strong back, and his are in my hair. God, he feels so good, his weight on me anchoring me to the bed. He pushes up with one hand and trails his mouth down to the base of my throat. His tongue leaves a fiery trail from where he licks the side of my neck to my jaw, his mouth closing over the tip of my ear. I squirm beneath him, and he moves his other hand to my bare leg, lifting it and bending my knee.

He works his mouth over my heated flesh, kissing down my breasts through the silk. He pulls down the fabric and exposes my peaked nipples, flicking one with his tongue and gently biting and sucking, then the other. I moan in pleasure when his hands creep up my thighs, massaging them as he goes higher. His eyes are on me as he retracts to his knees.

The connection between us is too much. I close my eyes and arch upward as his hands push beneath me to my ass. He lifts my hips and ever-so-slowly strips my underwear from my body.

He ravenously looks down at my sex, and his breath hitches. I know exactly what he sees. A peek of gold and crystal catch the light where they hadn't been before, when we were together. It's just a small act of rebellion between my thighs. Something for me.

He doesn't say anything, but a dark storm whirls in his eyes. He's staring at my pussy, his jaw clenched and chest rising as though he's trying to calm a beast within himself.

"Who pierced you?" His tone is uneven, the words more a demand than a question—primal.

I don't flinch, but the part of me that savors this side of him preens. "He was a licensed professional. I checked." I know casually mentioning that the piercer was a "he" will be enough to send him over. "You do not have the right to be upset. I love it. If you don't like it—"

"I do like it," he rushes out. "I just—I would have been there to kiss it better."

Mmm. "You can kiss it now."

"Is it healed all the way?" he asks warily.

"It typically takes anywhere between two to three months, but can be up to a year. It's fine now. Just don't rip it out with your teeth," I say.

His eyes go wide when he connects with the piercing. It stimulates my clit a little, but really, it's just pretty and defiant. It was a way for me to reclaim my body, my autonomy. Someone would only ever see this if I wanted them to. And he's the first. I meant what I said to him all those months ago. I don't do random hookups, but I also realize I can't have any kind of genuine relationship while I'm trying to hide. That kind of secret between me and a partner is not something I would ever want.

He gives the piercing a kiss, light as a feather, but to have this man touch this part of my body again? I moan at the contact.

He looks up from between my legs and smirks. "Oh, the ways I'm going to make you sing for me, Little Bird."

And with that, he puts his mouth to my core and licks from my opening to my clit, up to my piercing with the broad flat of his tongue. He does this again, and again, and again, alternating between teasing flicks and his whole tongue. He inserts one finger into my core and, with his thumb, circles my clit, smearing my arousal over my bundle of nerves. He moves his thumb to my piercing—just a light pressure—and then to my clit. The stimulation of his tongue and fingers is electric. My orgasm is sharp and sudden, and it rocks me to my core.

More. I need more. "Maverick, I need more." I want to feel him in me again, though my head wars with that because this man infuriates the hell out of me.

"I'll give you more. But not until you give me what I want."

Infuriating fucking man.

He brings me to the edge again with just his fingers and his mouth. I have never come when someone was going down on me, never before this damn man. I watch him consume me. Grasping the sheets with one hand and his long hair with the other, I let my head fall back onto the bed.

"Oh my God, Mav! Yes, fuck." The second time his name rips from my throat, my back arches—strung like a bow about to snap, ready to splinter into pieces.

He kneels at the edge of the bed and crawls over me, the curls of his hair falling onto his forehead and around his ears. His smile threatens to devastate me, his full lips slick with my arousal. I pull his face to mine. He kisses me, and I can taste myself on his tongue. I move my hands down the planes of his body, toward his waistband and the impressive bulge in his pants, but he closes his eyes and stops my hands with one of his.

"No. Not like this. When I take this perfect pussy the next time, it won't be right before we have to go to a framily breakfast."

I huff, but he says, "Sweetheart, that mouth could send me to heaven. But I don't want just your hot, wet mouth."

As much as it stings that he doesn't want me, a part of me knows it's because he wants more. That he thinks I deserve more than just a quick fuck. But I can't. I can't give him what he's silently asking for.

He gives me another slow kiss, almost like a promise, and goes into the bathroom.

And even though I just came twice, I'm still aching. Still wanting. I am still starving for more of something I can't name.

Maverick

CHAPTER 30

The drive back to Silver Rapids was tense enough through the snowstorm without adding the fact that Charlotte didn't talk to me the entire drive except for when we stopped for gas to tell me she wanted to get out and stretch her legs for a few minutes. Brunch seemed to go okay. Everyone was a little worse for wear because they stayed at the bar and kept drinking. Whereas I chased Charlotte into the street like a man on a mission.

Arriving in town, we pass through the downtown area and get to Quinn's house to pick up Finn. Luke's truck isn't there, so it's just Quinn. I pull up into the drive.

"Just give me a second," Charlotte says tersely.

"It's fine. We just have to get back before it gets too much worse."

She nods, hops out of the truck, and walks up the driveway. It's pretty late, and the snow is falling from the sky in thick clusters, causing it to stick to the roads.

Quinn walks out of her brick bungalow with Finn and his overnight bag in hand. I don't know of a dog spoiled enough to have an overnight bag, but I know Charlotte has treated Finn like a little member of her family since she adopted him from Dad.

I roll down the window, being a total fucking creep and listening in to see if she tells Quinn anything about why she's so goddamn mad. I have no idea what Sutton said to her at brunch, but something set her off.

Finn runs up to my girl, and she catches him in her arms. "Hi, my big guy! I missed you." He yips and wiggles in her arms. I know she's strong, but to hold a sixty-pound dog trying to wiggle out of your hold is something. "Thank you, Q." She gives her friend a hug and grabs his bag and bed before heading back to my truck, throwing them in the cab and loading Finn into the back.

"Heya, mutt," I say as he perches between the seats, looking out the windshield.

"Hey! Don't call him that. Apologize; you hurt his feelings."

"You mean I hurt *your* feelings?"

"No, I said *his* feelings." She motions to Finn.

It's not his fault his mom's in a bad mood, so I scratch between his ears and whisper-shout, "Sorry, Finn." I get a side-eye from him and pull back onto the road.

The drive outside of town and to the ranch is uneventful, thank God. I'm not in the mood to deal with any more drama today.

Pulling into the ranch, I get a feeling—a twang of nostalgia. The scrolling metalwork sign above the entrance that says "Dappled Stone Ranch" cuts through the rays of the setting sun. My dad explained once, when I was young, that his grandpa built the original home. Dad said that his grandpa had the spirit of a painter, but the misfortune of being in cattle. He said the way the sunlight hit the ground through the trees and cast patterns along the granite "was like it was dappled with light."

It still doesn't feel like home, even though I've been back for over two months and have spent my entire life here. I don't know that it ever will.

The pasture on the right contains cattle grazing, and the paddock on the left hosts a few horses picking at grass that's peeking through the snow. The falling snow has accumulated a few inches on the gravel, and it's still falling.

Going past the main house, I pull up next to Charlotte's truck. She unbuckles her seatbelt, and I put my hand out to stop her from hopping out of the truck to avoid talking to me.

She looks down at my hand hooked over the upper part of her thigh. Seconds pass, and I don't dare move; I don't breathe. Through gritted teeth, she says in a low voice, "Don't."

"*You* 'don't.' You needed time; I gave you five hours. Fucking talk to me. What has you so upset? You were fine this morning...after."

"I'm fine." She pushes my hand away and opens the door. All the care she had shown earlier seems to have vanished in a flash, leaving nothing but disdain.

I haven't done the relationship thing for any length of time, but when a woman says "fine," I know enough to know she isn't fine. I'm not about to push it, though. She looks like a scared colt about to tear through a field with the slightest shift in wind.

It took a minute for me to realize, but I know I want her for the rest of my life. For now, I'll take her in whatever kind of capacity she'll let me have her, because that woman already got through my fingers once. I'm not letting her get away that easily. I want her to have her freedom from those assholes looking for her—but I still want her for myself.

Finn jumps out her side of the truck and she follows. She opens the cab door, and I rush around the front of the car to take her bag out of her hands. She pulls out Finn's bed and slams the door shut.

"I can't decide if you hate me or if you were the first to understand me, but somewhere I got mixed up in this mess. I don't want you to get hurt because of me; I would never want that. I didn't want Jas to get into this, or any of the ranch guys. But this—I can't do this, Maverick. I don't want a relationship with *you*." The way she can't even meet my eyes tells me she's lying. The intensity she normally carries in her voice is completely lacking. She has tells, and despite only reconnecting with her in this short time, I can read her body like a book.

I invade her space and brace an arm against the car, caging her between me and our trucks. "I'll give you some time, but sooner or later you're going to realize this is a thing and you're done running." I brush a kiss against her cheek and hear her gasp at its gentleness. "Now, get home, have a drink, and run a bath. We have that inspector coming tomorrow, right?" She gives a slight nod, and I feel the heat of her breath on my ear. "Come to the house before you start tomorrow." I raise my arm and turn to put her bag in the bed of her truck, then walk to the barn to check in with Ace.

Charlotte calls for Finn to get in her truck, and then slams the door. I hear the crunch of the gravel beneath the tires and turn to see her pulling around to drive to the cottage.

Ace walks out of the barn and toward the pasture with the cattle.

"Hey, Ace!" I shout.

He doesn't stop. "I'm working, Maverick. If you need me, you're going to be working too."

I definitely will have to make more of an effort to "rebuild the bridge" and form a better relationship with him. Charlotte herself said she loved working with Ace, and the pair of them always seem to get along pretty well. I know that I'm going to need his help. I've thought about telling him about her situation—it's really not my story to tell, but I need to know that she's going to be safe...and that she's going to be comfortable staying here.

I jog to catch up with him. "Hey, man. How's it going?"

"How's it going?" he says sarcastically. "You mean while you and Charlie were out 'observing a working ranch'?"

"This weekend was mainly just to get her out of town and out of her head. I'm not blind; you and Dad have built an impressive operation here."

He interrupts. "It was more than just me and Jas; the whole damn team has been working hard to get this place to what it is today. You'll never know how hard it was to see your dad pour himself into this place, knowing that he may have no one to leave it to. It got to where he looked like he was empty inside, and trying to bring him and this place back was no easy feat."

My heart ruptures, and the crevasse inside cracks wider. All that time that I'll never get back with him.

"I know. It hurt to see him, to see how bad life had gotten for him." It was one of the many reasons I stayed away. Out of sight, out of mind, right? "That's why I'm trying to make it right."

He leans against the fence of the paddock with his arms extended and crossed over the top rail. I post up next to him but face the cottage.

He's somber when he says, "Charlie was one of the first things in a long time to get him to smile. He saw something in her. We all see it. Her energy makes this place light up, kind of like your mom, you know? It takes more than just a woman's touch. It's a certain type of woman who can take this life and make it more. Marie had that; Charlie has it, too. And the fact that she's making moon eyes at you, and you at her...that's a dangerous path, boy. If you hurt her—"

In a split second, just a heartbeat, I've made my decision: Ace has to know. "She's in trouble."

"What have you done?" he asks, his tone low and menacing.

"It's not me. I wouldn't hurt her like this." He visibly relaxes and releases the clench of his fist. I continue, "But she's in real trouble. The kind I can't fix by myself. I have Owen looking more into it. I found a file in Dad's office that he sent with information from her life, the life she had in Boston, and Ace, it's not good. The Mob is after her because of her involvement at her firm. Her boss was a bad dude and got in bed with the wrong people, and now she's paying the price. I don't want anything to happen to her. If anyone comes near her or this place, she's going to run again.”

"No one is going to get to her. Tell me what else you know," he orders, and I tell him everything, including the plan I've been piecing together.

We're in the barn when he tells the guys to call it a day. We're not friends, and we likely won't ever be, but we don't have to be friends to keep her safe, to keep her here. She may be trading one cage for another, but I wouldn't truly cage her. My Little Bird's cage would exist within the bounds of her heart; I'll be the only one occupying that.

Ace calls out to me, and I look over to where he's walking out of the open doors. "You better watch her until we get this fleshed out. I'll do what I can to amp up the security and get more cameras and sensors placed around the property lines and by the cottage. Your old man already had this place under good surveillance, but I'll have some of the guys do some checks just in case."

"That sounds good, thanks." He turns around, and I say, "Ace? I mean it. Thank you. I can't tell how special she is to me."

He offers me a nod of his hat and continues outside into the blustery winter winds beyond the barn.

I finish cleaning up the tack and hang it on the wall. The barn is clean, and the stalls are mostly full as the team has started to come back for the end of the day and chow.

The inspector who's coming tomorrow is for an initiative that Charlotte got us hooked up with. It's an organic farm-to-table company that's interested in purchasing cattle from us to service restaurants out East. They go through an application process, then an onsite interview and inspection. Based on what she said, Charlotte and Dad had the initial application interview; this is the last step. They'll pay more for the cattle than the abattoirs or meat packing companies.

This part of the business is what I hate. I hate thinking that we are raising animals through drought and harsh elements, only to lead them to slaughter. I understand they provide food, and I'll eat a damn steak, but it still makes me uncomfortable. Growing up the son of a cattleman meant I saw death in an unconventional way. Dad took great pride in knowing we provided a good life for our cattle—pasture grazing and a good diet was the least we could do for those animals. Their lives provided me with a way to ski and for us to live our lives.

Charlotte

CHAPTER 31

The constellation that Quinn put on my ceiling with glow-in-the-dark stars is staring back at me. I don't know how long I've been up, but, judging by the lack of light, it's still pretty early. I try to close my eyes and rest, seeing that I can't go back to sleep. I stay like that for a while, taking in the weekend and the things Maverick said yesterday.

I groan. The alarm clock is about to buzz, the speaker that gives off a shrill ring winding up. It's so quiet in the cottage that I can hear it before it sounds. I try to beat it and turn it off, but a shrill ringing breaks the silence, and I pull the other pillow over my face. "Fuck. I'm up, okay? I'm up!" I yell at the electronic clock that is so offended, with its red light blinking back at me.

I slept so awfully last night—more stupid nightmares with faceless men and dogs chasing me through the forest. Only I know the men's faces; I've seen them around the office. I heard about what they did on the news. I am so grateful that Jasper taught me how to shoot, but sometimes I wonder if all that knowledge would kick in if I were to ever really need it.

I swing my legs over the side of the bed, and my feet hit the floor. That's when Finn pops his head up from under the quilt. "Let's get at it, bud. Big day ahead." I pull the fluffy robe off the hook on the door and stick my feet into my slippers. I scuff along the hardwood floors to the living room and see a shadow through the shades.

Finn's not barking, but he stalks to the front door. After Ezra showed up unexpectedly, I've been more diligent about keeping my gun on me while I've been home. I grab the pistol I keep in a lockbox safe in my room. I take a peek out of the peephole and find Maverick pacing on the porch. I re-engage the trigger safety. I'm mad at the asshat, but I'm not going to shoot him.

Whipping the door open, I yell, "What in the world are you doing?! I could have shot you!"

He pushes into my cottage, and Finn rushes past him to go run about and do his business.

"Yes, Maverick, please come in."

He smirks at that and says, "I told you that you'd ask me again." His fiery gaze leaves my face and trails down my body. My very nearly naked body that's only covered in baby-blue, see-through lace shorts and a cami.

I don't do what my brain is screaming for me to do, which is cover myself up with my robe.

"I wanted to come get you and do a walkthrough before the inspector gets here. I want it to go well."

"Oh." I definitely wasn't expecting him to say that. It's nice to hear him taking this seriously. "Give me a few. I still need to get breakfast for Finn, and then we can go over what I know."

"Charlotte?" He takes a step back and leans against the door.

"Hmm?"

"Blue is definitely your color."

My cheeks flush, and my neck heats. "Is it?" I ask. I know it is. Every shade of blue brings out my eyes, a fact my mother never let me forget. I can hear her say in my head, "No pink; it washes you out."

"Yes," he replies confidently.

"Thank you." I scurry to the bedroom to get dressed. I think it's subliminal when I pick out a navy cable-knit sweater to wear with black fleece-lined jeans. My suits were always navy, not black. It's my power color. My favorite dresses as a girl were blue or just a shade before lilac. Sometimes it made me look too sweet, with my pink undertones, rosy cheeks, and blonde curls. It wasn't until college that I really learned how to use color, cut, and different fabrics to accentuate my petite frame. Now, the only time I worry about dressing up is with Q, on the off chance we're doing something fancy. I have the wardrobe to support it, but not a lot happens in town that means we get dressed properly.

Maverick yells from the front room, "I'll feed Finn."

Surprised, I yell back, "Thank you. Two scoops and crack a raw egg from the counter. They're already washed."

He says just loud enough for me to hear, "Spoiled pup." That makes me smile. He seriously thinks I don't notice him giving Finn treats when we're up at the barn.

I hear the front door close and Finn devouring his food. I stop in the bathroom to wash my face, moisturize, and apply sun protector. I'm brushing my teeth when Maverick stops in the open door, his broad shoulders taking up a lot of space, hunger in his sapphire eyes. He's just looking at me; I'm not too eager to hurry my morning routine. Maverick is the one who showed up uninvited. He says nothing as he leans against the door. The sharp cut of his jaw is shadowed by stubble. He hasn't been shaving, and God, the look is working for him.

I realize that this is intimate, allowing him a peek into my daily routine, an intimacy that Julien and I never really shared. I get kind of grossed out watching people brush their teeth, or maybe it was just watching him specifically go through his routine. That's when you know it will not work; when the thought of watching that person go through the daily stuff makes you want to barf.

I look at Maverick in the mirror, and he's still just watching me with a smirk on his face. He looks like he's carrying the world on those gorgeous shoulders of his most of the time, but right now? He looks lighter somehow.

I spit into the sink, rinse my mouth, and replace my toothbrush in the holder. "Enough ogling—let's get going, mister."

"You've got toothpaste on your chin." He chuckles and heads toward the front of the house.

I look in the mirror and, sure enough, toothpaste is dripping down my chin. He always has to make sure he gets the last word, the ass.

The coffee maker is percolating when I walk into the kitchen. "Thank you for making coffee."

"I've seen you without it. That's a bad day for everybody," he says, all growly. There's no bite there, though.

I put a coat on Finn, pour us two coffees, and head to my truck. He rode the UTV over, but it's freaking cold. I'm not getting into that thing if I don't have to.

We load into the truck, Finn jumping into the bed. A pop song is playing gently over the speakers, and I see Maverick tap his thumb lightly on his jeans to the beat. I turn it up, and we drive in silence, enjoying the sounds of JB.

I am so ready to tackle this day. We are going to smash this inspection.

I wave goodbye to the woman who had me on my toes for the last three hours. She looked at every single nook and cranny within our ranch. *Our ranch?* I mean Maverick's ranch. She checked to make sure we humanely handle the animals, that they are well cared for. She checked the quality of the food we feed the cattle. The traceability in the feed supply chain was also integral to its data-gathering process. I got a call when the co-op reached out to our feed consultant, Joe, who gave a glowing recommendation and all the info they asked for. I feel like we were as prepared as we could have been. We didn't clean up the place any more than we would any other day; we're still a working ranch.

Maverick comes up next to me. "You did real good, Little Bird."

Ace joins us and claps me on the shoulder. "You did it, Charlie."

I look up at Ace, the stone man who doesn't like damn near anyone else here, or at least pretends not to. He's smiling, looking out over the pasture. "Jasper would be damned proud of you."

I do my best to blink back tears, thinking about how this started off as just an idea we had, and now we're one step closer to making this a reality. Just like that, the glamping is so close to becoming real.

Ace nudges me with his elbow and repeats, "Damn proud." He's nodding his head, like he's proud of me, too.

I've worked for all kinds of bosses, more often than not men, and nothing has ever made me prouder than hearing that from Ace. I can't keep them in; tears freely fall down my face.

I miss Jasper. I hate that he's missing out on what we've built. I hate that he is missing out on Maverick putting pieces of himself back together. I hate that their time was cut short. And I hate that the only man I looked at like a father is gone.

I'm not a cute crier. No, I ugly cry. I'm not wearing any makeup, so the red splotches are visible on my cheeks already, I know it.

"Charlie, don't be sad," Ace says.

"I'm not sad. I'm mad. I hate cancer."

"Me too, darlin', me too. But he's in a better place." I sense, rather than feel, Maverick move infinitesimally closer to me. I look at Ace, but he's looking at Maverick. "He would be proud," he says, then walks out of the barn and toward the bunkhouse.

I couldn't see through the tears very well, but I think his eyes were lined with silver, too. That's when I truly lose it. I damn near crumple until I feel strong, capable hands wind from around my lower back to my hips, to my middle, where my heart has sunk.

He pulls me closer, and I give in. Just for right now. I sink into his warm body and let my head hang. I let him hold me as I cry and cry. If I had any sense at all, I would not be this close to him right now. My emotions have literally crawled out of the box I try to keep them locked up in and are escaping in sobs and tears.

He's silent. He just lets me get these feelings out.

My breaths grow shallow, and I'm having a hard time getting a full breath. Maverick's arms pull me closer, and I wiggle to turn around in his grip. I let my forehead drop against his chest, the scent of pine and wild air and man invading my senses. My arms are hanging at my sides, but right now, in this moment, I want to return the embrace.

He moves a hand to stroke my hair, smoothing it down my back. I'm sure the wind has whipped it into an absolute mess, but the motion is calming me down a bit. I'm taking deeper breaths.

This situation takes me back to the summer when I had a panic attack after some asshole tried to manhandle Q and me the night I met Maverick and the guys. It was also the last time a man hugged me without trying to get laid.

I feel like I'm burrowing into his chest. I may have also inadvertently dripped snot all down his jacket. God, I'm a mess. I don't know how long we've been like this, but he's stopped stroking my hair and is just holding me to him.

"I know I don't have any right to be upset. I mean, he wasn't my dad, but I really cared about him," I say with a hoarse voice.

His chin rests lightly atop my head when he says softly, "I know. I'm so grateful he had you. This, all of it—the glamping, the co-op—it's remarkable." He takes a big breath and blows it out, tickling the hairs on the top of my head. "I've got something we can do to let loose some steam."

I try to push away from him, admonishing, "I do not want to fu—" but he interrupts me.

"Little Bird, yes, you do." I chuff, and he releases me. "And the next time we do, you're going to beg for it. But I think a good horse race will do you some good."

I dab at my eyes with my sleeve and smile up at him. His full lips are wide in a grin that reaches his eyes. Where has this Maverick been?

"Come on, let's get the tack on the horses, go for a ride. Maybe finally settle that bet, too," he says with a bit of sass in his voice.

"We did. I won that race. Fair and square, in front of the entire crew," I bite back.

"You cheated. You flashed that smile and I had a heart attack in the saddle."

"You are so full of shit. You just can't handle that I beat you."

"Let's see, then. Surely you think you can beat me again, right?"

"You and Walter are going down."

"We'll see."

I know that we're going to win. If he really thinks I cheated last time, homeboy can get fucked. My girl and I ran our race, and he lost.

My competitive streak is a mile long. He knows it, too. He knows this is going to get me out of my head. And this is just a perfect example of why I can't be in a relationship with him. He deserves someone without all this baggage.

The horses are in their stalls on opposite ends of the barn's aisle, so I'm looking right at Mav when I say, "We don't need luck, do we, girl?"

I pull the brush off the hook and go to her. Brushing before riding helps bring blood to the surface. The horses haven't been stabled long, since we used them to give the inspector a tour instead of the buggies, but it's cold, and, beyond the stimulation, it's just relaxing to brush them out.

I put on her boots and saddle pad, then the rest of her tack. I'm buckling the latigo strap to cinch the saddle to Betty White when I see Mav giving Walter a peppermint. Little things like that—they're just a treat, but it's how he is with Finn, too.

There hasn't been a big snow, so our normal trail to the glamping site will be good for a nice ride. I don't want to race, though, if I'm honest. Ice and hooves do not mix. "Maverick?" I call to him as I pull on the lead rope and walk out of the stall. He looks over at me. "No race. I don't want to risk them getting hurt. We can say you won this round, if it means that much."

He looks at me like I'm crazy. "I would never do anything to hurt them, Charlotte. But if you say I win, I'll take it." He leads Walter out of the stall, hands me the rope, and goes to open the barn doors. We walk out, and he shuts the door behind us. The sun is cresting above the mountains, the pink and orange of the sky mixing with the indigo. The Tetons cast shadows on us, rays of light shining through the pockets between clouds.

We both mount our horses and trot silently down the path toward the cabins and the yurts. The structures are up, and we're building the ancillary structures: the cold-plunge baths, the hot tubs, and the shared showers and toilets. They're all beautifully done, but we definitely want-ed to preserve the resources of the farm and the land that we sit on.

The sun is setting in the distance, but the last rays of golden light are illuminating the valley ahead of us. I turn in my saddle and look back to Mav, finding his eyes are already on me. The planes of his cheekbones and his strong nose are highlighted in a warm amber light. The pieces of hair curling from under his cowboy hat look like molten gold in the sun. His full lips are smirking at me, like he's caught me openly admiring how beautiful he is.

Gah! I turn back around to face forward in my saddle and look to the horizon.

Why does he have to be so beautiful?! Like, whatever kind of genetic lottery he won to have lips and eyelashes that most women pay for is truly wild.

Betty White must pick up on my energy because she sniggers a bit—she's laughing at me, too? I give her a gentle nudge with my heels, so she knows exactly what I need. She takes her trot to a full-tilt gallop. I give a whoop, and we take off, the wind rushing past and blowing my hair behind me, biting at my cheeks and ears, and making my eyes water, but this feels glorious. She's not going full-out, but I will never tire of the exhilaration I feel when riding.

I hear Maverick and Walter racing after us, but I don't pay any attention. This isn't a race. I'm not even pushing Betty White; she wants to let loose a bit, her hooves rhythmically pounding into the earth. I sit deeper in my saddle and give a slight pull on the reins to slow her down.

Mav says, "Whoa, boy," to Walter. They ride abreast of us, the horses' shoulders nearly touching. "I thought we weren't racing, Little Bird."

"We weren't racing. Betty White just wanted to have some wind in her hair for a minute." I scratch at her neck.

He huffs and pats Walter's neck. We come to a small enclosure in front of the cabins. I thought it would be a great experience for guests to meet some of our older, gentler horses or farm animals. Wake up in the morning, walk out with a coffee in hand, and see a horse outside your tiny cabin? Folks will love it.

I hop down from my girl and walk to the gate. Maverick gets down and walks Walter to the enclosure. I send Betty White in, too, and lock the gate. To my knowledge, Maverick has spent limited time out here, so I don't think he's seen it since the siding and roofing went on the cabins. They're so close to being done.

"Wow, Charlotte," he says as he takes it in. "This really came together. I definitely had doubts on how they would look when the cabins were completed. But this is something." His keen eyes find mine in the fading light.

The energy between us has always been so cut-and-dry. I knew where I stood with him. He hated me and wanted me gone from his life, away from the ranch; he made that perfectly clear. But over the last few days, so much has changed, and even though we haven't had "sex"-sex, we might as well have. I feel heavy under his gaze.

"The pellet stoves are going in next, and we decided on a tank system to provide water for the guests." I start rambling. Why, after all we've been through, does this man make me nervous?! "I wanted to use a rainwater collection system, but for the price of what we are going to be charging, we decided to put in a tank reservoir. I had no idea what all of that would entail at the time, but the contractors brought me up to speed real quick. It has to be below so many feet to survive the winters here. The tank would be naturally more insulated in the ground, and we will even use solar panels on the roofs to run the system." I point up to the roofs, but he doesn't look at them. His eyes are still on me, on my mouth.

"So, beyond having to have the water trucked in when necessary, it would be self-sufficient after that. We're installing composting toilets in the bathhouses, and the shower stalls will have skylights above them to feel as though you're showering outside. The floor of the stalls will be river rock that provides reflexology on your feet, and they're pretty. I always wanted an outdoor shower." Oh, my God. *Shut. Up. Charlotte.* I open and then close my mouth like a fish, turn around, walk over to one of the cabins, and sit on the porch steps. Distance is good.

He's still leaning against the rail of the enclosure, elbows bent, for all purposes looking casual. But there has never been anything casual about Maverick Bennett. He asks, "What else would you put in a house if you ever decide to settle down? Beyond an outdoor shower?"

"Hmm." I take a second to think about that before responding. I look up at the stars peeking out from the blanket of sky. "I love a fireplace. And a gigantic kitchen that opens into the rest of the house. A loft space for board games. Oh, a library with a sliding ladder, like Belle's."

He gives a short laugh. "Anything else?"

"Nope, the rest you build and collect as you live your life," I say, looking at him. "If I ever settle down, I'd hope to have a partner who helps me build that life. And if I'm single, I'll collect things from the places I travel to and make it a home."

His face goes deadly serious, and his full lips purse into a slash. "Your partner will help you build that life. He'll give you anything you want."

"Ha! Well, with the considerable fact that I thought I had that once already, I won't be holding my breath. Julien really did a great job of fucking that up for me."

"Julien is already a dead man."

"What do you mean?"

"Well, he lost you, didn't he?" he asks, deadpan. "We have that in common, I suppose."

"I guess you do. You guys can be 'bros' together." I laugh.

He makes a growling sound and pushes off the fence. Stalking toward me, away from the light post along the fenceline and with his cowboy hat, it's hard to see his eyes, but his jaw looks like he's grinding his teeth. "We are not 'bros.' I have brothers, and he wouldn't be fit for us to walk over on the sidewalk if he were trash."

I say nothing as he approaches, just watch him as he stalks toward me.

"He didn't deserve you. I don't either, but you'll be mine all the same." I blink a few times and don't really know what to say, but it doesn't matter, because he's not done. "If I ever see that man, he'll regret ever hurting you."

"Well, I don't think you guys run in the same circles, so we won't have to worry about that, will we?" I laugh it off, but right now, with how he looks, I absolutely think that Maverick would beat the shit out of Jules and not think twice about it. It shouldn't turn me on, but fuck, it does.

I confess, "I don't want to want you, but with every breath I take, you burrow deeper into every inch of me."

He growls. "You still don't get it. Do you?" When I look up at him, he says, "I've made up my mind. This—" He motions between us. "This second chance? I'm not letting go."

"You never had me! It was one night."

I'm suddenly pressed against every single hard ridge of his body. "You say that, and yet your body is telling me something very different. Tell me what it's going to take to get you back."

"It was more than just a night. That was supposed to be the beginning of our story." He pauses; the surrounding silence is deafening.

I know what he's saying. I felt it. Of course I felt it. It's why I didn't go on any dates, despite men asking since that night. It's why I felt so betrayed when I saw him walk into Jasper's hospital room. Why, even now, my body is clinging to his—knowing what he feels like over me, under me, in me. It felt right. It never felt like just one night.

"I don't want to hurt or disappoint you." I walk away, heading to the enclosure, and call Betty White over. In this moment, I'm too chicken to look behind me and see him, but I say, "It would have been a nice start to a story, though."

For the second time tonight, I feel strong hands on my hips before he turns me around and pushes me against the railing. Our breaths are puffs in the chilled air, his chest rising and falling quickly, like he's restraining himself.

"Our story isn't over," he says in a rush. "It was just—interrupted. You don't have to run anymore. I will keep you. I will keep you safe. I'm not a good man. But I'm the one who'll keep you safe. No one touches you here."

My heart explodes at his words. With a softness I don't expect, he leans in and brushes his lips over mine, like a question. I don't pull away, though I know I can. The softness of his lips and the way his hands roam up my back and cradle my head as he pushes further into me is intoxicating.

He moves to kiss me more firmly, testing to see if I'll open for him. I open my mouth, and the kiss turns heated. I finally taste him. He tastes like a decadent dessert at the end of a meal, something to be savored. Like something I've wanted for far, far too long. He can tell I don't have hesitation in this, and he moves his hand to cup my jaw, down to my throat, holding me in place. I meet his desire and curl my fingers over his belt.

He moans softly and moves his lips to my jaw, then down to my ear, where he knows I'm super sensitive. "Careful, Little Bird. Unless you're offering something else? I told you next time you'd beg me for it."

Am I? No. Yes. God, I could take this further.

If only it were just sex.

No. Definitely not.

This man reads me like a damn book, sensing the shift in my posture and releasing me.

"You know, I'm still kind of seeing Ezra, I think." Not a question. Though, being honest, I haven't thought of him in days; not because he hasn't texted—because he has—but I haven't given him a thought outside of that.

"You think you're seeing him?" Maverick chuffs. "If you don't know if you're a thing, you're not. You're the kind of woman a man would be an idiot not to claim. He would shout from the peaks of the damn Tetons if you gave him half a notion to."

"We're just hanging out. I told you, I'm not really in a place to be in a relationship."

"Put him out of his misery, tell him you're not interested," he says. So cut-and-dry with some things, and with others, he's like a full spectrum of gray.

I laugh. "It's not that simple."

"Sure it is, sweetheart. You say, 'You were never going to get it. But I found someone who can,'" he says cockily.

I shake my head, but don't respond. I duck under his arm.

He grabs my arm, stops me, and gives me another quick kiss. "You know it's true."

We get on the horses and head back to the barn, then the house. We haven't eaten, and it's well past the time we should be out.

Maverick and Walter stay ahead of Betty White and me. He's giving me space, and I do think about what he said. I don't want to string Ezra along—he seems like a nice guy, but I never feel sparks when we get together. Actually, the more I think about it, he's kind of intense. Not the way Mav is, but darker. I thought that feeling may have meant that I liked him, but the vibe is off. Other than the one chaste goodbye kiss when he walked me to the truck, nothing happened.

I remember I have a text from him that I still haven't responded to, but I don't think I want to see him again. I mean, if he's out in town, I'll be nice and say hi, but I don't want to date him.

This decision is definitely not influenced by Maverick, although what he said did make sense. Ezra wasn't the one I was thinking about in the shower. He wasn't the one I dreamt about or spent months waiting for.

Would it be so bad to give in to whatever this feeling is with Mav? Even if all I could give him was sex, would that be enough for him? Hell, would it be enough for me? I have wanted this man for months, ever since the festival. I should be happy he wants me, but my fear of him getting hurt over me is overwhelming. I can't be catching feelings for this man. I won't let that little piece of my heart admit what I've been feeling; that would be just about the worst thing that could happen right now.

Walter takes off at more of a gallop, and I watch them move further along the trail. I nudge Betty White forward, just enough to get her to match their pace. The shrill ringing of Maverick's phone pierces the night, and Walter throws his front legs up and rears on his hind legs.

No—*this* is the worst thing that could happen right now.

Time stops. I see Maverick fight to keep his seat and fumble for the reins. It's no use; he slides back and is thrown from the saddle.

Oh my God, no.

Walter bolts toward the doors of the barn, leaving Maverick's body crumpled on the ground, not moving.

I urge Betty White toward Mav. *No, no, no.* I throw my leg over the saddle and slide down to check on him. I've seen plenty of bad throws, and I've even had a few of my own, but nothing as bad as my friend who got trampled by her horse when she got thrown. She's paralyzed from the neck down.

My God, please, please let him be okay.

My knees hit the hard ground next to him, the cold earth and snow soaking into my pants. I reach out instinctively, then pull my hands back to my chest to keep from touching him. "Maverick! Maverick!"

The lights on the outside of the barn and along the paddock help me see in the night. Careful not to touch him, I search every inch of him that I can. This close, I can see he's breathing. I don't see any blood or any bones poking through his clothes.

He rolls over onto his back, his eyes closed. "Ow."

I could cry. "Oh my God. Are you hurt? Of course you're hurt. Where? Mav, please open your eyes!"

"I'm okay, sweetheart," he grits out. "I just got my breath knocked loose for a second. I'm okay. Give me a minute."

"Mav, don't be ridiculous, you're in shock. Can you wiggle your toes? Your fingers?"

"Char, I'm okay." He tries to sit up, but I push him back down. Maybe a little too hard, because he winces. "Damn."

I all but crawl over him. "Fuck! I'm sorry. Stay down. Can you move your toes?"

"Yes." To prove it, he wiggles his ankles, bends his knees, and raises his legs. "Really, I'm all right. Though if you want to give me a closer inspection, I'm not going to say no. I'll stay right here."

I smack his chest lightly, he chuckles, and we sit there for a second. He's moving his arms, shoulders, and head from side to side. He's okay. *He's okay.* I nod my head up and down. He's okay.

I don't realize I'm shaking until he reaches out for my hand and says, "Charlotte, are *you* okay?" He moves to sit up and does so with ease.

I still feel my head nodding, but my chest is tight, and I feel like I can't pull in enough air. I'm breathing, but my lungs are burning, and my heart hammers against my ribs, trying to escape its cage. That fall could have been bad—so bad. I could have lost Maverick, even if he wasn't mine to keep.

At eye level now, I can see his lips moving, but I can't hear what he's saying. All I can hear is my heartbeat and the sound of him hitting the ground. It's too loud in my head.

He takes my hands in his, bringing them up to his mouth and exhaling on them. I'm so, so cold, but it's not from the temperature or the snow that's melted into my jeans. Tears freeze on my cheeks, my eyelashes sticking together.

Maverick folds his legs beneath him and settles on the ground, pulling me onto his lap. He rubs one of his hands along my back, trying to warm me as I fall apart in his arms, the other hand on the side of my face. He wipes away tears as they fall.

I can hear him now. He says, "Sweetheart, I've got you. Breathe with me. In for four." I breathe in and hold. "Out for four." I slowly exhale. Since the bar this summer, I've been box breathing like he showed me that night. "Good, again." He moves both of his hands to cradle my head to his chest, and I wrap my arms around him. "Breathe. Breathe, love. Shhhh." We breathe again. "Shhhh."

My eyes clear for a moment, and I sit up straight, realizing I've been straddling him. Looking at him now, I see that he looks like he's in pain. I all but throw myself backward and scoot away from him. "I'm—I'm sorry! Did I hurt you?"

Charlotte

CHAPTER 32

A look of confusion flashes across his face, and he tilts his head.

"I told you I'm fine. I've had worse falls skiing. Fell from a third-story balcony, remember? Nine lives," he jokes.

"But—"

"No 'but.' I'm fine. See?" He twists his head and flaps his arms around like a used car lot blow-up guy. "You scared me." He crawls on his hands and knees over to me and helps me stand. The endorphin and adrenaline drop always gets to me badly after a terrible panic attack. He knows this. "I know you haven't had many people say this, but I'll do anything to protect you. The only thing that's going to hurt you again is me, as awful as that is."

I don't acknowledge what he says because I don't want to let my feelings go there. Maybe he actually could protect me. "Falls like that hurt, Maverick. You might not feel it now, but you're definitely going to feel it soon. We should get you up to the house and get some ice. Swelling or bruising can take a few minutes to hours to show."

He stands and pulls me up to him. My knees almost give out. Maverick doesn't give me any chance to protest as he lifts me bridal-style.

"Put me down." I try to wiggle out of his arms, but he's gripping me so tight. "Maverick! Put me down."

"No."

"Maverick Bennett, put me down right now!" I try even harder to get free, pushing away from his chest. Okay, now I know he's up and walking, but I've seen all the medical TV dramas; he has to have a broken back and just doesn't know it yet, or something.

I'm so mad I could spit. No one gets thrown from a horse and is up walking, carrying women around within minutes, right?

We cross into the barn, and he pushes the button to shut the doors. Both Betty White and Walter are in the barn already. He puts me on the bench next to Betty White's stall and is deadly serious when he looks at me and says, "Don't even think about moving from that bench. Let me get the tack off and put them in their stalls for the night." I move to stand up, but he pushes my shoulder to force me back down. "Little Bird, you stay there."

I'm so mad at him—*he's* the one that scared me half to death and into a panic attack. What in the actual fuck, though? He wants to put the horses away and push himself even further into an injury? I'm not going to stop him. Clearly, he doesn't give a shit that I was trying to help *him*.

I pout and cross my arms, leaning back against the door of an empty stall. I exhale and look up at the ceiling of the barn, allowing the heaters to gently blow warmed air on my face.

The horses know the routine: they both go on their own into the stalls as Maverick gets some feed, hay, and water and checks their legs. It's the same routine I go through when I put Betty in her stall.

I hate that he knows what I need. I could have walked through the steps of putting away my horse, but I needed to sit and focus on my breathing. He just knows.

I'm in my head when I feel the slide of the stall door reverberate along the panel I'm leaning against. I hear the clanging of the metal latch slide into place and roll my head toward the most stubborn man. His movements are rigid, like he's upset or angry, as he walks to Walter's stall and locks it up. Warm enough, I stand up, less like a newborn colt this time, and walk over to him.

He whips around to face me. "I told you to keep that pretty ass on that bench."

"I do not have to listen to you."

"You may be the boss here, but," he steps into me, "do not make the mistake of thinking I will not go absolutely feral when you do not take care of yourself. There will be punishment for when that beautiful mind of yours doesn't take your health and safety seriously."

My mouth goes dry, but my pussy...she's drowning. This is him showing me he's fighting for me.

"I think I know what's best for me. I could have helped put the horses away. You very well could be injured!"

"You could have, but I had it handled. Why not let me do that for you? Let you take a minute and let your nervous system reset?"

"Sure, when you could have a broken back or something."

"There is nothing wrong with my back." He takes another step forward, and I back up. "Or my legs." Another step. "Or my neck." At this point, I'm backed against the outer office wall. He flicks the light switch next to my arm, and the bright overhead lights turn off, the softer night lights flipping on. The amber glow gives him a sinister look. I'm not afraid of him, though. Other than what he can do to my heart, I know he wouldn't hurt me.

"We should get up to the house and check," I say shakily.

He leans in close, half of his beautiful face in shadow, and says, "If it means that much to you, you can check here or not at all." He flicks my earlobe with his tongue. "I." Flick. "Am." Flick. "Fine." Then he licks from the base of my neck up to my jaw, and bites. A moan escapes me. He knows that's my kryptonite.

"I was—and am—so scared. I saw Walter, and then you were on

the ground, not moving." I'm shaking again, even though I know he's standing in front of me, caging me in with his powerful arms.

"Does that mean you would care if I were trampled to death?"

"Of course I would care!" I push hard against his chest with both hands, but he doesn't budge. "How can you say that?! I care if you're hurt, trampled, or otherwise. I..."

"You what?"

I shake my head, refusing to say what is on the tip of my tongue. I take a breath. "I care about you. About this place. That's why I want to leave. Once everything is up and running, it should be self-sufficient, and you guys won't need me here to run—"

He puts his hand against my mouth. "Do not finish that sentence, sweetheart."

I shake my head, and a tear leaks from the corner of my eye. He kisses that spot so tenderly, then sighs and looks up at the ceiling. There's a hook dangling where we fix up the scale when needed. He looks down at me, and there's heat in his eyes.

"Do you trust me?"

I nod my head yes.

He removes his hand and wipes the tear with his thumb. "If I ask you not to move, would you listen this time?"

Again, I nod my head. I slump back against the wall.

Satisfied, he walks into the office and returns with a blanket and two pillows, which are kept in a closet in case we have to pull an overnight out here. He lays them down on the ground, goes into the office again, and comes back. If he grabbed something else, I'm not sure what it is.

I'm not stupid; I know where this is going. I'd be a liar-liar-pants-on-fire if I said that *my* pants aren't on actual fire for this man. I can't give him my heart, but...I know full well I'm about to give him my body, and I don't feel bad about it at all. *I am totally lying to myself; I know I caught feelings.*

He walks over to the blanket. "Little Bird, come here."

I want to, but my feet are lead, and I don't move from my spot against the wall.

He walks toward me, his long legs eating the distance between us. "Same rules as before. Green, yellow, red. If you say 'Red,' we stop immediately. Everything we do is in your hands; you're the one in control here. Yes?" He takes my hands, his callused thumbs running over my knuckles.

I nod.

"No," he says. "With your words."

"Yes, this is in my hands."

"And you trust me with this?" He moves his hands to my sides, running them from my ribs down to my hips.

"Yes."

"I hate that I caused that." He looks back toward the path. "But I think I know of a way to get you out of your head. If you'll let me."

"Okay." It sounds more breathy than I meant it to. I don't know what he's got planned, but I am all for whatever he's got. I am so tired of fighting against this pull toward him.

He backs up to the blanket and pillows and stops at their edge. Careful not to step on the blanket, he pulls me toward him, one hand still on my hip and the other behind my neck. Maverick kisses each of my cheeks. "Close your eyes."

I roll them instead.

"Close."

I oblige, and he walks behind me and covers my eyes with some type of fabric. A bandana, maybe? It's warm and soft against my closed eyelids. It smells of him—like wild storms, pine, and caramel. I open my eyes. The blindfold completely covers my field of vision, but the fabric is red:

definitely his bandana.

He wraps his arms around me and unzips my jacket, then moves from behind me, my body immediately missing the warmth of his. I instinctively put my hands out, trying to feel for him, and find him at my feet. He lifts my leg and tugs my boot off. I use his shoulders to steady myself and immediately get déjà vu. He's been in this position before.

He moves to the other boot and tugs it off. I giggle as I almost topple over. "Careful, there," he warns.

He runs his hands up over my calves, around to the front of my knees, and up my thighs, giving a little squeeze just above my knees. His fingers work to get my belt unbuckled and, so damn slowly, pull the tab of my zipper down. The last time he did this, he couldn't find the zipper and threatened to cut the pants off of me.

"You found the zipper this time," I say huskily.

"With all those dangly strings, I needed your help." He pauses and works the denim down my legs. I step out of them and hear him toss them somewhere. "I don't need your help this time, Little Bird."

I don't wear as much lingerie as I did before I started this job. Someone else might think it's the vainest thing, but I wear lingerie because of how it makes me feel. That no matter what I seem on the outside, I feel me underneath. Certainly not because—on the off chance I'm naked in front of a man—he would appreciate it. All that aside, because of some wild theory my sister posited about dying and becoming a ghost stuck in what you died in, my bra and panties always match, even if they're just plain gray cotton Calvins like I've got on right now.

Maverick's muscular hands snake under my jacket, push the shoulders back, and drag the sleeves down. It drops to the floor. He puts his hands on my bare skin under my thermal and sweater, tickling me with his touch as he runs his fingers along my ribs. Fluidly, he lifts my sweater and shirt over my head, careful not to disturb the bandana covering my eyes, and drops those at my feet, too.

As he traces his hands along my body, his mouth meets my ear. "You are so fucking beautiful." I gasp as he gives the fleshy part of my shoulder a little bite. He moves his lips to my other ear and sucks the lobe into his mouth. "Watching you with the inspector was masterful. This may not have been what you planned for yourself, but you've done so well here. I was a damned fool to think of you as anything but a blessing for this place." Then, he kisses my mouth, urgently and desperately.

Time stretches all around us, our hands exploring each other. Our tongues tangle, slick and heated, as he deepens the kiss. With just his mouth, he claims me. I unzip his jacket and unbutton his flannel.

Being deprived of my sight means relying on my other senses. Everything else is heightened, and it thrills me. I find the cold metal of his belt buckle and slide the leather free with a slow, deliberate pull. Untucking his shirt, I run my hands underneath the band of his jeans, his bare skin warm against my fingers. I push my hands up to his chest. The hardness of his taut abs sends my pulse racing. His heartbeat matches mine. He hitches one of my legs around his hip, and his solid hands squeeze the globe of my ass. I pull my hands down his front, trailing my nails lightly down the ridges of his stomach.

"Ah, ah. This is about you," he says, his hands gripping the swells of my hips, then my ass, wandering over my body. One moment they're at my waist, and the next, without warning, there's a smarting smack against my ass cheek. Then another.

I gasp. "Maverick!"

He rubs the spot tenderly, smoothing away the sting from the spanks he's delivered. "Color?"

I pant out, "Green."

"Good girl."

When he says that, in that soft yet gravelly voice, rough with desire, it does something to me. No other man has ever made me feel so alive and brought my body such pleasure as this man has. Ex-boyfriends, past lovers, my ex-fiancé—they all balked when I wanted to introduce things into the bedroom—but that night with Maverick, he let me explore all the things with no hesitation. I told him some of my darkest desires. He helped them come alive.

I wouldn't have normally been so bold to tell him—a man I just met—that I wanted him to handcuff me, but we had such a good connection and he was gentle and took his time with me. I think ultimately that's why I gave myself to him, and why I'm giving myself to him now.

He's gone from rubbing the sting of his slaps away to tracing underneath my panty line, across my buttocks, over my hips, and right to the conjunction of my thighs. He takes his thumb and rubs it over my panties where my thighs meet. Surely he has to feel how wet I am. Slowly, he pulls my underwear to the side and slips his fingers between my folds. I know he likes this part, the teasing. He knows it drives me wild.

He slips one finger inside me and pulls it out so slowly. "You are so wet for me." He repeats the motion several times before adding a second finger. His thumb slowly circles and flicks my clit, bringing me higher and higher. All the while, his mouth is exploring, sucking, teasing, pulling my breast into his mouth. He's not properly taken off my bra, but has pulled down the cups, and my heavy breasts, aching for his touch, spill over. I moan his name when he hits a sensitive spot inside me.

Quickly, he pulls his hand away from me and says, "Open your mouth." I do as he asks, and he sticks his fingers, dripping with my essence, into my mouth. "Suck my fingers like you would suck my cock." He moves them in and out of my mouth, pushing them a little further back, just enough to make me gag, then pulling them back out.

I never thought that sucking on fingers covered in my juice would be erotic, but I think it's the fact that this man has taken control over me and is getting me so wet. There may be no hope for these panties.

With his free hand, he unclasps my bra and lets my breasts free. The barn, though heated, is still chilled, and my nipples pebble at the sensation of his hand rolling one between his thumb and forefinger.

He asks me, "How do you feel?"

Breathily, I reply, "So, so good."

He wraps both of his sturdy arms around my body and lifts me from underneath my ass. I wrap my legs around him. He kisses me, and I run my fingers through his unruly hair. His jeans rub against my inner thighs, and the rough material of his field jacket rubs against my sensitive breasts. He lays me down with care and my head hits a pillow.

He kneels between my thighs, kissing along my jaw, down between my breasts, all the way to my abdomen. I try to push his jacket off. He's wearing far too many clothes. He kneels above me, takes my hands, and grasps them together. "Keep your hands above your head, Little Bird; you won't like the consequences if you move them." His tone is rough, but it elicits a shiver down my spine for a different reason altogether.

I put my hands above my head and arch my back when he licks a line from my inner thigh to my center. My hips lift, almost involuntarily, as he drags the waistband of my underwear down. I bend my knees on both sides of him and fight the urge to close my legs. With the blindfold, I can't read any of his facial cues.

He must see hesitation on my face because he says, "What's it going to take to get you out of that head?"

I'm panting because this is what I want: to get out of my head. I want to enjoy the pleasure I know is coming.

He grabs my thighs and pushes my legs wide. A gasp or a moan escapes me, and he says, "I've been dreaming about this pussy. I close my eyes and see this little gem." He flicks the top of my piercing and growls, "This thing has kept me up at night.”

“Ah!” I exclaim as he kisses it, my soaked core exposed to him, leaving me completely bare. I feel everything so much more like this.

He throws my legs over his shoulders, and I feel his breath on my body just as he takes a long lick from my opening up to my clit. He does it again, and again, and again. Like a cat licking up cream. Slowly driving me mad.

I so, so badly want to reach for him, to run my hands over his broad shoulders or through his hair. When he inserts a finger and then another and scissors them in me, faster and faster, I damn near scream his name. He sucks my clit into his mouth and reaches that spot that makes me see stars.

“Ah, oh my god! Yes!”

He pulls his head away, and I immediately miss his tongue. He pushes down just slightly on my lower abdomen as he moves his fingers in and out of me quickly. I feel a tingle down to my toes, and a rush of liquid escapes me. “Yes, fuck. I fucking love when you squirt.” He takes a long lick from my inner thigh up to my piercing, and he moans.

“Oh, my God!” I yell into the night, moving my hands to reach for him. I feel for him and try to bring him closer to me. I’ve only ever squirted when I’ve had sex with him, and before him, I didn’t know that I even could. I was so embarrassed that I wanted the damn kitchen counter to spontaneously combust and burn me to ash. But he made me come so many times that night that I didn’t feel ashamed at all.

“What did I say?”

“Please. Please, I want to touch you.”

“I told you to keep your hands above your head. This is about your pleasure; I want you to come so damn hard you forget your name.”

I reach for him again. “I want you, please, Maverick.”

“You want this cock in your mouth? In your pussy?”

"Yes." I squirm, immediately wishing I could have the friction of him over me, in me, filling my cunt.

"Get on your knees for me."

I do and hear rustling, like he's reaching for something. I sit back on my heels and wait for him.

"Beg me for this cock."

"Please, Maverick," I beg. "Please let me have your cock."

"You're not to touch me until I say. Do you understand?"

"Yes."

"Good girl. Open your mouth." I hear him unzip his zipper. "Now play with that pretty pussy."

I pause for just a moment. I may be a good girl and willing to play, but I'm still a brat. I cup my breasts and roll my nipples between my fingers and thumbs. I feel saliva pool on my tongue as I wait for him to put his thick cock in my mouth. I keep one hand on my breast and trail the other down to my core. Pushing my folds open and playing with my clit, I feel my slickness already dripping out of me.

"Mmm, fuck. You look so good like that. I could come just like this, watching you fuck your own fingers."

His words spur me on, and I insert a finger into my opening. I love knowing what I'm doing to myself is giving him pleasure. I insert another and moan, and that's when he puts his hand on my neck and guides his dick into my mouth. His pre-cum is salty and sweet; I hum in appreciation. This man is so thick.

I know I'm not super experienced with a lot of past sexual partners, but I know enough to know that he's not embarrassed when he puts on those skin-tight ski racer outfits or changes in the locker room.

"Fuck, Charlotte, yes."

I run my tongue up and down the length of him. Giving head has always turned me on, but with prior partners, it always seemed like a chore.

"If it's too much, tap my leg. Remember?"

I manage only a quick nod because I'm currently choking on his dick. His hand in my hair, he moves my head up and down at a fast pace, pushing me to my limit. Drool drips out of my mouth, spilling onto my tits. He groans my name, and that makes me preen on the inside. I want him to use me. I wish I could voice that I want him to wreck me for anyone else. I feel like he already has.

"You're so God damn beautiful with my cock stuffed in your mouth and drool dripping down your face." He knows I like the praise. I try to take him further, deeper, but I can't get him all the way in my mouth.

I swirl my tongue around his tip, paying special attention to the underside. I continue to fuck my hand, finding a perfect rhythm. Between his appreciative moans, his praise, and my fingers stroking the perfect spot, I'm so close.

He pulls his dick out of my mouth, leaving me panting. "Yes, Little Bird, come on your fingers."

As though his order was what I needed, I come apart on my fingers, but with his name on my lips. "Maverick!"

He lifts me up, his hands under my arms, helping me stand. The bandana is slipping after he's had his hands in my hair. I can see that he's taken off his clothes. His erection is thick and hard and damn near flat against his belly.

I still have drool dripping down my chest—he licks it off, his eyes on mine the whole time. Okay, new kink unlocked, I think.

He takes the fingers that are still coated in my cum and...Licks. Them. Clean. My knees damn near buckle, but he catches me. "We can't have you falling down with those shaky legs." He has a devilish smile on his face that says whatever he's thinking is anything but angelic. He picks up the rope we usually keep in the tack room for roping cows and takes my hands.

Is he...? Yes, he's binding my wrists in an intricate knot that I've not seen before, then gives a little yank and tosses the rope up—and, of course, it lands through the hook on the first try. He pulls on the long end, and my hands go up in the air above my head.

He pulls on the rope until I'm almost on my tiptoes. He then sinks to his heels and pushes my feet wider apart. With the rope in one hand and his other opening my folds, he takes one long lick from my center all the way to my piercing. He does it again and nuzzles against my sex.

I throw my head back and groan at how good this feels. At him between my legs, and me stretching on my toes. He lets the rope go with a bit of slack, so I can put my heels down. Looking at him, I see my wetness on his lips. *That's hot as fuck.*

"Get down here, Little Bird."

I sink to my knees, and he grabs my head to give me a bruising kiss. He puts his hand around my throat and squeezes slightly. "Mmm, turn around and show me that ass." I swivel my hips more than necessary as I twist around. He positions himself behind me. "I'm going to fill that pink pussy so full of cum you're going to drip for days."

My pussy clenches at the thought of being used like that.

I'm bent over, but not all the way. My hands are still bound with rope above my head, and he slaps his cock against my ass cheek with a *thwack*. His friend is big—I remember the day after, I was sore in the best way.

"Oh my God, you're a tease!" I groan in frustration. "Fuck me, Maverick."

He smacks my ass so hard but doesn't rub it this time. He does, however, run the head of his cock through my folds and wetness. "You are soaking my cock, and I'm not even in you yet. You like being my good girl, don't you?"

I am so ready for him, and thank God because he pushes his cock into my pussy and pulls it out. Again, deeper, and again, even deeper.

"That feels so damn good," I pant.

"Yes, damn, sweetheart. You're taking my cock so well."

"Fuck, it's stretching me."

That sends him over the edge, and he loses his restraint. He thrusts faster and faster, his hand gripping my hip so hard I may get a bruise.

He drops the rope, and I almost fall forward, but he keeps me upright. I can finally use my hands to help me balance against his ministrations. Leaning over me, he reaches between my lips to find my clit and circles. That bundle of nerves sends lightning through my body, and I come apart, screaming.

"Shit, you're milking my cock with that grip." He doesn't stop and keeps fucking me through my orgasm. I come so hard that I see stars. His rhythm stutters, and with both hands on my hips, he pistons into me. "That's it—take every," thrust, "fucking," thrust, "drop." Thrust. He roars his climax into the night.

Maverick is still inside me as he tugs me up and wraps his arms around me so that my back is to his chest, our bodies dripping with sweat. He pulls himself out of me, and I can feel the combination of our cum slowly trail down my inner thighs. He gives an appreciative moan deep in his chest and runs his fingers up my thigh to catch it, then pushes those fingers inside me.

I don't tell him he probably just pushed more out by doing that.

He falls forward, and I fall with him, right into the pillows. I turn in his arms and look at him, taking in the long lashes of his closed eyes and the sex-addled smile he's sporting.

That bliss doesn't last but a moment, because two seconds later, he's up and putting on his clothes. He grabs my clothes and rushes out of the building without saying a single word.

"What? Maverick, where are you going?"

What the fuck?!

Maverick

CHAPTER 33

I know it's going to chap her ass, but I'm not going to have my Little Bird get back into frozen, dirty clothes after I just worshipped her body. The snow is really coming down now and sticking to the ground. It must have snowed at least three or four inches since my fall. I have absolutely no doubt that I will feel that soon, but I feel on top of the goddamn world. I had my face and dick buried so far in her pussy... She doesn't realize yet, but she will—she's mine.

I run up the stairs to the house and shake the snowflakes free from my hair. I stomp my boots and run them through the brush next to the door before entering. I drop her clothes at the door to the laundry. I don't bother taking off my boots and rush through the living room, put some logs in the fireplace, and light a fire. I see movement in my periphery and think it's her walking naked into the house. I would absolutely smack that perfect ass so damn hard it would hurt if she walked here in that snow without clothes or shoes!

A little yawn escapes the mound under the blanket on the couch, and Finn pops his head out from beneath the quilt. I send a silent thanks to God that he deserted me long ago.

"How did you get in here, Finn?"

He cocks his head to the side like he's trying to tell me something or thinks I'm an idiot. Both are probably true.

"Stay here, be a good boy. I need to get Mama some clothes."

I rush up to my room. Going to my dresser, I pull out thick socks, sweatpants, and a thermal tee, and get a thick coat from my closet. I also pick up a pair of mud boots for her. They'll be too big, but it's fine.

I rush to get back to her because she probably has cursed me out five ways to Sunday. I pull open the door and find her pacing back and forth in the office, wrapped in the blanket.

"You fucking asshole!" she screams as she throws something at my head. It shatters against the wall. Fuck, and she doesn't have shoes on. I look to the ground and see that it was a glass jar. "How could you just fucking leave me here?" She's been crying. Her eyes are red, and her cheeks are flushed.

"Your clothes were soaked and filthy." I push the door open further and show her the pile of clothes and boots dangling from my hand.

"You couldn't say that? What does that even matter? I can go home and put them in the wash!"

"You're not going back to the cottage."

"The hell I'm not." She walks toward me with complete disregard for her bare feet and the broken glass on the floor.

"Stop!" I yell, and she freezes. I cross the distance in a few steps, pick her up, and take her to the couch.

"Put me down! You fucking caveman!"

"If by caveman you mean I will absolutely protect you because you're mine, yes."

"No—"

"Yes, you are. If you don't want to admit it to yourself right now, that's fine. But actions speak louder than words, and you were terrified I was hurt when Walter threw me."

"Just because I care for you doesn't mean I'm yours, or that I'm staying, or whatever you've convinced yourself of."

"Ha, no, sweetheart. It does. You're just a little late to the party." In a smooth motion, I drop to my knees at her feet.

She just crosses her arms and pouts her bottom lip out. I want to bite it. I wipe off her soles and put socks on her feet.

"I can do that, just give me the clothes."

"I want to do it. Let me," I say. I look into her eyes and hope that she can see this for more than just the fact that I want to dress her; I want to take care of her—all of her. "Don't you get it? I want to burn your touch into my skin, brand it into my fucking soul. You have ghosts, but you fucking haunt me."

Silver lines her eyes. I don't know that this beautiful woman has ever had someone want to put her first. Not that I'm decent, but, fuck, if I wouldn't kill myself trying to be worthy of her love.

"Mav," she says so softly that I almost don't hear her say it.

She doesn't say anything else as I put her legs into the sweatpants and pull her up to standing. She silently raises her arms when I slip the thermal over her head, and she's still looking into my eyes when I put the thick, hip-long field coat on her. She slips her feet into the boots and hugs herself.

"Did you know Finn was in the house?"

"Ha! No, Ace probably let him in."

"Spoiled dog. He's the real boss around here." I look at her lips and wipe away the tear stains on her high cheekbones. "He's going to be upset if he doesn't see his mama soon. Can I make you some dinner?"

She nods and says sheepishly, "Sure."

I grab a dustpan and broom from the tack room and sweep up the glass she threw at my head. I toss the glass into the trash can under the light switch and hold out my hand, waiting for her to take it.

"I'm not sorry," she says from where she's still standing.

"I wouldn't expect you to be," I reply.

She walks to me and takes my outstretched hand.

"It was a dick move, but hopefully you see it as a gallant gesture because that's what it was." I smirk when she looks at me, guffawing. I look at her beautiful face, lift her hand, and raise it to my lips. "I'm sorry, Little Bird. I was more worried about you freezing than a post-orgasm cuddle." I glance away. "I thought you just wanted sex out of this. You've made your stance on a relationship pretty clear. Are you saying you want me for my big arms to cuddle you, too?" I sneak a playful peek at her.

She smacks my chest playfully and hesitates, then says, "Maybe."

"You'll come around." I grin and grip her harder to me. "I'm sorry I couldn't read between those lines. Cuddles next time. What do you want for dinner?"

She licks her full bottom lip. "Mmmm, buttered cheesy noodles?"

"Eh, I don't think we have mac and cheese," I say. Now I wish we did, though.

"No, like actual buttered noodles. I'm sure you have some type of cheese. You sprinkle it on top with some salt and cracked pepper, *et voilà*!" She does a chef's kiss.

Let's see what we can whip up.

After she helped me with dinner, we found something suitable for Finn to eat and went up to my room. I made a note to get some food for Finn, because if nights like last night continue to go my way, she'll be here all the time, if not always.

We went at it all night. Maybe around 2 or 3 a.m., we finally fell asleep. I knew she was a cuddler, but her arms were wrapped around me tighter than an octopus.

We have our first skijoring competition today in Jackson. Even though it's one of the smaller skijoring events, there are going to be well over a couple thousand people there. We don't have to travel as far, but I don't want to drive back late and trek back tomorrow, too.

I look down to where she's rested her head against my chest and push back one of her curls that's fallen across her face. She's so fucking beautiful. And not just like this, naked and full of my cum, but dressed up, dressed down, in jeans, chaps, and a field coat—she's beautiful all the time. I watch her sleep for a few moments, but I know we have so much to do that she would be pissed if I let her sleep for much longer.

"Wake up, sweetheart." I give her a kiss.

"Nooo, five more minutes," she begs.

I look over at the clock, wishing I could stop time. "It's already six a.m." She groans and pulls the blankets above her head. "We are probably going to leave here at, like, one or two p.m. to get checked in for tomorrow. Did you make arrangements for Finn?"

"Yeah, Ace is going to let him in and out of the cottage for me," she says, voice muffled under the blanket.

"Just have him stay here; we can grab his food and toys, or whatever else he needs. It's closer to the bunkhouse."

She considers. "You're just trying to get Ace back on your side."

"I'm just trying to get Ace back on my side," I agree. "Besides, waking up with *my* woman naked in my bed is fucking incredible."

She throws the covers down and sits up. "Just because I lost count of how many—"

"Six," I gloat.

"Whatever. This—"

"My barn, my rules." I see it the second she realizes that I'm never going to quit; it's inevitable. *This* is inevitable. She's been mine since I saw her ride that goddamn bull. She's been mine since she said, "Go in like a wrecking ball."

"I don't want to hurt you," she murmurs.

"The only way you're going to hurt me is if you keep lying to yourself." I roll over and pin her to the bed with my lower half, holding myself above her. "You begged me to tie you up and fuck you. Me, not him, not anyone else. If you want soft and sweet, you're not going to find it on this ranch. If you want real…" I take her hand and place it over my heart. Steady beats pound from my heart, through her hand, and into mine.

"I've been broken for a long time," I say. "Whatever is left in here is yours." A tear slips free from her sky-blue eyes. "You don't understand the lengths I would go to to keep you safe."

Another tear falls, and her plush, full lips open in a gasp. I would kill anyone who tried to tear her away from me. Ace would too. She's wiggled her way into the stone hearts of every bastard on this ranch.

She nods—and that's all I need. I lower my head to give her a kiss. She moves her hands to my face. It's slow and soft, how a good-morning kiss should be. But she deepens it and strokes my tongue and sucks it into her mouth. Her hands roam my body, over my shoulders, down my biceps, where she squeezes and moans into my mouth. My dick is harder than a damn pipe, and I'm exactly where I need to be.

She breaks the kiss and says, a little sheepishly, "I probably have morning breath, but you don't seem to care. I do, however, need to take a raincheck on that monster." She looks down to where our bodies touch at the hips. Her cheeks flush the prettiest shade of pink. "I've had more sex in the last twelve hours than I have in five years."

That throws me for a loop, because what the fuck? "You were engaged. How is that possible?"

"He didn't like sex. Well, no, that's not true. He didn't like sex with me. But he loved having sex with half of Boston. Hell, maybe more. And before him, it was guys in college and some boyfriends here and there. I told you in the summer, I wasn't—eh, still am not really experienced in this. But I probably need therapy," she says under her breath. "I think I like it rough. I mean, I know I do with you. Last night was so hot."

"You don't need therapy because you like rough sex. But if you think it would be helpful for you, maybe it would be good to get some stuff off your chest. You've got a lot bottled up in that tight body of yours." I smile. "We go at your pace. And if there is something you want, or want differently, or more of, you tell me. I can read your body, but I can't read your mind."

"Okay, thank you," she says. The sun shines through the windows, and in this early morning light, she's fucking glorious. "One more thing—I don't want anyone here to know about this."

My smile falls.

"Just yet," she amends. "Technically, I'm still the boss of these guys, and I've worked really goddamn hard to get them to respect me, to get on board with the new direction of this place. And—I don't want them thinking I slept my way to the top."

"Charlotte, they wouldn't think that."

"I've seen things like this play out at the firm and with friends; it doesn't look good."

I sing, "I can be your dirty little secret."

"I'll say I fell asleep on the couch to make sure you were okay after that fall."

I don't tell her no one is going to believe that. I smirk. "You got it, Boss."

"Ugh." She groans and pushes me off of her, and I laugh. She stands up and is about to pull on the sweatpants she wore last night when I stop her.

"I washed your clothes while you were making noodles. They're probably wrinkled, but I put them in the dryer."

"Wow, thanks."

"You can shower up here. I'll get your clothes, and I can shower downstairs. Towels are in the hall pantry just right here." I motion to the pantry next to my door. "We can pretend you got an early start, and no one will know." I turn to head downstairs.

"Mav?"

"Yeah?"

"Thank you."

"You're mine; there's no 'thank-yous.'"

I'm in the hallway next to the downstairs bath when I hear Charlotte's voice in the office, talking on speakerphone with Quinn.

"I'm planning on meeting up with Ezra later this morning."

"Uh, okay, hussy! Two baes," I hear Quinn say.

I know we're not naming this, and I don't need to scare her off, but fuck, I *literally* just had sex with this girl.

"Not for an afternoon delight—gross. I just want to tell him to his face that I don't want to see him anymore."

Thank God. I don't want to kill this man for laying eyes or a hand on my girl. I would absolutely kill anyone who ever thought they could touch her.

I take the stairs two at a time, knowing that I've got my Little Bird right where I want her.

She's on speakerphone with Ace when I get to the kitchen. "Okay, great. I'm headed to the bunkhouse now. We'll knock that out quick and we'll be in a better position for when we get back Sunday evening."

"Charlie, I told you, we've got it handled. The guys and I will wait here for ya."

"Okay, there in two," she says.

The coffee is already brewing, and she's made eggs. Little Bird is already making herself at home, even if this doesn't feel like my home.

She has two thermoses on the counter and a plate of eggs on the table. She turns and says, "I need to get stuff ready before we leave. Ace is taking care of Finn. There's no creamer for coffee, so I had to use milk. And you take longer showers than I do. I have to go."

"I heard."

She whistles, grabs a thermos, pats her leg. Finn pops his head up from the leather couch and goes right to her. "Let's go, bud. We'll need your coat today; it's damn cold." She's about to walk past me when I stop her with an outstretched arm. She looks startled for a second.

I grab her shoulders and say, "Have a nice day at work, sweetie," and give her a kiss on the forehead.

"Ha! Funny, Ranger Rick. You're helping us repair that fence and check on the herd. You've got ten minutes to get to the bunkhouse."

"Better get going, then."

She and Finn head out the door, and I marvel at the fact that this woman spent the night in my bed...in my house. *My parents' house*, I correct myself.

My Little Bird made me breakfast. She yielded to me yesterday. This feeling that's been growing within my chest, expanding and beating against my ribs...I'm afraid to give it a name. Afraid that if I name it too soon, that may be the one thing to push her away for real this time.

I could face the whole of the Irish Mob if it meant that she'd be okay. I know that I'm not facing this by myself; Owen and Ace and the crew here will absolutely do their best to keep her safe. If I had half a brain, I would try to keep her out of the spotlight, but no one from Boston is going to think to look for her here.

I'd eat dirt if she put it on a plate in front of me. My dad said that once, and I've never forgotten it. *When someone takes their energy and puts it into preparing your meal, never be ungrateful; eat it with a full heart.* I heard she's a superb cook—at least, that is what some of the hands said when she planned an entire appreciation lunch for them just after Dad passed. It was for "all employees," but I knew that didn't mean I was invited. Or maybe I was, but everything was too raw, too real. I was an orphan, and I was being such an unbearable dick to everyone on this ranch. No one wanted me there.

But the hands still talked about the damn chili days later.

We get to Jackson with some time to spare. There's a registration table and a parking area designated for the participants. I pull the horse trailer through to the area for participants and hop out to get our registration packet with our numbers, racing bibs, and wristbands for the weekend's activities.

"I'll go get us checked into the hotel," Charlotte says.

"Sounds good. I'll grab our bags after I get this settled," I say, motioning behind me to the activity around the registration area.

"All right." With that, she turns and heads toward the hotel I pointed out to her when we pulled in.

There's not any real money in skijoring, but I have to do this. I can't describe it. There's a drive that I used to think was pounded into me by my parents and the folks in town. But maybe it was all me; I hate failing.

The West is a prideful place, and I have to be the best. Even when I destroyed my racing career, I did it in spectacular fashion. And besides, we—both Charlotte and I—made a promise to Jude that we would do a race this year. If she likes it and wants to keep doing more, I'm for it. I don't think I would deny her anything that was in my power to give her, and even then...

In the practice trials at home, Betty White has been great—she hasn't minded having a rope tied to the saddle or having to drag my ass across the frozen fields. There's a lot more action here, but Charlotte knows how to ride, and I'll ski any course you put me on.

I haven't had enough time to get out on a real mountain lately and feel the wind on my cheeks or the glide of my skis through the snow.

The check-in process takes longer than I thought it would, but the buzzing energy is infectious. It's like my old racing days, but there's a sting knowing that my dad isn't in the crowd. I'm alone, save for my friendships with the guys and whatever this is with Charlotte.

Navigating through the crowd and into the hotel, I try to call her, but it goes to voicemail. She wouldn't have gone far.

My eyes track her; she's standing in the lobby bar, and there's a man talking to her. Her normally jovial face is closed off, her lips pursed, her spine ramrod-straight. She must not like what he's saying. He moves to put a hand on her arm when she takes a step away. Just then, the bartender brings a paper bag over and puts it in front of her.

Did she order food? What would she be picking up at the bar?

"Hi, are we good here?" I say to her as I place my hand in the small of her back and step between her and the man.

"I was just asking this young woman what brought her to town." He motions to reach for her hand, and I grab wrist fast enough to throw him off kilter.

I squeeze when I ask, "What brings *you* here?"

"Ah—" He grimaces, and I let go. "Son, I'm doing what old men do in ski towns." He smiles ruefully.

Ew. He means he's looking for young ass. And there's no shortage of women who wouldn't take him up on his offer.

"Right, well, happy hunting."

"Wait," he says before I can pull Charlotte away. "I think I recognize your face. Do I know you?" He snaps his fingers and points at me. "Yeah, weren't you that skier who fell out of a hotel window?"

"A balcony, actually."

"Well, I'll be. Boy, don't you know you're supposed to stay on the fenced side?"

I see red and can feel my face flush with rage. Who the fuck does this guy think he is?

"Mav, let it go. Come on." Charlotte links her arm through mine and intertwines our fingers. Her skin on mine is an instant balm, like a blanket that dampens the world. "Excuse us," she says to the man. To me, she asks, "Do you know who that was?"

I shake my head. "That used to happen a lot after the accident. It used to make me so mad. Dad tried to get me to let go. There was a lot of fighting back then." I look at my hand, the one currently entwined with hers. She lifts it to her mouth and gives it a feather-light brush of her lips. "Dad was the one who taught me how to breathe through my anger. What's in the bag?"

"I don't really feel like going out tonight. Is that okay?"

"That's not a problem for me. I'll settle into my room and can go grab some food—"

"I got us burgers and a can of beer. I also told them we would only need the one room." She's facing straight ahead, but her eyes flit to me.

I stop her from taking another step and turn her to look at me. She's got a sparkle in those azure eyes and a smirk on that shapely mouth. "Why waste company money on a room I may not use at all?"

"That's why you're in charge." I pull her in for a kiss and haul ass to *our* room. She said no sex, but there are so many things I could do to her that can get her to scream my name.

"Mmm," she moans around her burger.

Fuck—I never would have thought that watching someone eat a cheeseburger would be erotic, but my dick twitches in my pants at the sound she makes, at the way her lips stretch wide around her sandwich.

She notices me watching her. "I'm a classy one, I know," she giggles.

"The classiest," I say as I lean forward and lick ketchup off the corner of her lip.

"I shouldn't eat any more. This burger was as big as my head. I'm stuffed."

"You're not stuffed just yet," I say, not looking at her. "But you could be." I sneak a conspiratorial glance at her. She just sits there and glares at me. A grin breaks across my face. *Is this happiness?* Whatever feeling this is, I haven't felt it in forever. "I've waited this long for you. I suppose we can take a night off; we have the rest of our lives, after all."

"You're delusional."

"You're beautiful."

A slight blush creeps across her face and throat.

"Did you bring a silicone friend with you on this trip?"

She chokes on her beer, her face fully flushing now.

I pat her gently on her back. "I'm just fucking with you. But did you?"

She swats me away and gets off the bed. "I did not, but I'll keep that in mind for next time. I'm exhausted. I'm taking a shower and getting ready for bed. Okay?" She grabs her things from her bag and heads to the bathroom.

I stand up and walk over to her. "I'll join you."

"No, that's quite okay." She puts her arm out to stop me, her hand landing on my chest. "I don't have any need of your services. Thanks, though. Maybe next time you can help me wash my hair."

I reach out and tuck a lock of curls behind her ear. She's still keeping me at arm's length, close enough to let me have her body but still not close enough.

She emerges after a short while in a white, baggy tee and satin shorts. Her hair is wet and soaking her shirt so that it clings to her body. My eyes laser in on her visibly peaked nipples, and, as if she's just now noticed what I'm looking at, she goes to cross her arms.

"You never have to cover yourself up unless you want to," I say. "Your body is a fucking work of art. Charge me admission to the museum."

"Okay, Casanova, get your own work of art in the shower. I'm getting into bed."

I grab her and pull her body flush to mine. She smells like sandalwood and honey. I kiss her neck, up her throat, then grab her jaw to make her look at me. "Fucking. Art."

Her eyes are wide, but not with fear—with desire.

She wanted me to fight for her. I'd fight to the death for this woman.

I kiss her forehead and gather my kit to shower. I close the door, turn the shower on, and go through the motions of washing my hair and body. I'm not a savage, but I'm only a man and find myself stroking my hand up and down my shaft. Her eyes and lips on my mind, I come so hard I have to bite my lip to stop a groan from escaping.

Maverick

CHAPTER 34

I wake, thinking of sandalwood, honey, and gold. No, that's her hair. The woman I want for the rest of my miserable life is shaking in my arms. "Charlotte?" I give her a gentle squeeze. "Charlotte?" Now, a little shake. "Charlotte." I say her name a little more sternly and shake her shoulder more firmly. "Wake up, sweetheart."

I sit up over her to see tears trailing down her high cheekbones. Her brows are scrunched, and her lips are tightly pressed together, as though she's in pain. "Wake up, Charlotte!" I shout at her, but she's in a place I can't reach.

She blinks her eyes and starts crying when she finally wakes up and pulls herself out of her nightmare. I reach out to her, but she screams and backs away from me, pulling her knees to her chest. The look in her eyes, normally so full of life and feisty, is hollow and dead. She's shaking like a leaf clinging to a tree in the fall, about to blow away in the breeze.

"It's fine, just give me a second. Please." She's still shaking and puts her head on her knees.

"Where'd you go, Little Bird?"

"I have the same three nightmares on rotation most nights. I have them so often. This one stars my ex, Julien. He rarely lost his temper with me, but this one time, he had a few drinks, and I overheard him talking to a woman. I confronted him about his cheating. He told me I was crazy. I screamed that I wasn't crazy for wanting to be enough for my future husband, for him to not cheat on me. He slapped me so hard that I saw stars. Then, he locked me in his condo while he left to meet with whomever he was meeting. He had building security and a driver in his pocket, so I guess I could have left the actual apartment, but I wouldn't have been able to go anywhere without him finding out. I didn't have anywhere to go, anyway. I swear, I even thought he bugged my condo. I never found anything, but he seemed to know what I was doing all the time."

A rage I've never felt before overcomes me. "He's a fucking dead man."

"I don't ever plan on seeing him again. He and that life are in my past. I plan to keep him there."

"Charlotte," I say tenderly as I put my hand out to her. "I will never, ever hurt you like that. I would sooner throw myself off a damn mountain than hurt you." Tears spill from her eyes, and I make a note to reach out to Owen and see what her piece-of-shit ex is up to now.

I pull her to my lap and let her fall apart in my arms. I'm gently cooing to her to quiet her mind when her breathing steadies, and she says, "I'm so tired. When I wake up sometimes, it feels like I didn't sleep at all. I see them in color; they're so vivid. They can say we don't dream in color, but I do. It's like when they say people can't see colors or taste words. They can; I believe them." She turns her tear-stained face to me when she says, "I actually thought sleeping in your arms might keep them at bay. That's funny, right?"

I vow, right here, I will keep those damn dreams from haunting her like this.

She gives a huff and says, "Ready to skijor?"

"Yes, ma'am." I kiss the apples of her cheeks. "Let's see if these knees still work, eh?"

We push through the crowd in the lobby and see the street cordoned off, ready for the races. There's a different kind of energy here than at the race I took her to in Salt Lake.

Her reaction to her nightmare has me seething, but I'm trying not to let it show. I don't want to upset her.

He hit her. I don't care if he was drunk. I don't care that it was only once. He raised his goddamn hand to her, and that was a mistake. No man should put a hand on a woman.

We get to the competitors' area, ready for the parade that kicks off the festivities. We're the last pair to race in our division, so we observe all the racers ahead of us.

"Nervous?" I ask her.

"Just a little, but we've got this. Don't we, girl?" She strokes Betty's mane.

When it's our turn to get to the racing line, she does a final check on the harness, the buckles, everything before mounting. A race volunteer hands me the heavy rope that's tethered to Betty and I take it and the small baton she extends to me. She clears the area and I signal to the race official I'm ready and in position.

The shot rings off, Betty and Charlotte take off, and I follow soon after. Holding on for dear life and trying not to fall on this first run. The first obstacle is a small jump with a ring hanging from a stand; I pierce it with the baton and it slides back on my arm. I cross the track to the other side and repeat. This is such a rush. I collect several more rings, and before I know it, we've crossed the finish line.

I squint, trying to read the time on the digital time clock, and see the numbers: 22:16. It's a higher time than the former first-place holders; they missed a ring, and I sure as shit did not miss a single thing. I had control on every single turn, and Betty White was flying down that course! As long as the judges don't penalize us for anything, we're in first!

I throw the rings from the ring grab and the baton up in the air as I click out of my skis. The crowd is cheering, but I'm laser-focused on

Charlotte. Up ahead, she's patting Betty White's neck. "Good job, baby. Good job!" she says as she dismounts from her saddle and gives Betty a hug. I clip out of my skis and run, as well as I can in my boots, over to them. Charlotte's face is full of joy, and I scoop her up and lift her off the ground.

"Goddamn, that was amazing. You guys were flying," I tell her. I look up at her, her long hair wild and windblown. Somewhere between jumps two and three, she lost her cowboy hat. I pat Betty's neck. "BDub, you were hauling some serious ass down that stretch. Good girl."

"Oh my God, that was incredible! I want to do it again!" Charlotte laughs and puts her hands out and palms-up toward the sun. "Let's do that again."

I put her back on her feet and settle my gloved hands on her face, leaning my forehead against hers. "I'll find us another race, Little Bird. Anything you want."

"Practicing on the course definitely helped. I don't think we would have done as well if I wouldn't have seen the other race in person or practiced at the ranch. You were right."

"I'm sorry, I couldn't hear you over the sound of my ego thumping its chest. What did you say?"

"You were right, Ranger Rick." She smiles a smile that reaches her eyes.

I used to hate when she called me that. Now, there's a glint of lust in her eyes when she says it, as though it's a term of endearment.

We walk to the staging area by the gates as the judges deliberate on time and to make sure we didn't miss anything—or, if we did, what the penalties would be.

We set up by the posts where the contestants are waiting with their horses. Charlotte's removed the tack and has Betty stripped down to her halter so that we can put on her blanket.

There's nothing we can do but wait. No matter what happens, I'm happy that I kept my promise. If I were actually racing competitively, it would have been reckless and wild. But, God, it was such a rush—and with Charlotte; we did it together. Now we wait.

A judge's voice comes over the loudspeaker. They announce the standings. In third place, "Jacobsen and Smythe." In second place, newcomers "Stone and Bennett." And the champions, in first place, "Jennings and Keller!"

Hot damn! "Second place!" I'm not even mad about it; I came here with no expectations of what to expect from us as competitors.

"Fuck, yeah!" Charlotte whoops.

I pick her up and twirl her around. Her head is thrown back, face to the sky, arms wide, and a smile stretching from ear to ear. I put her down, and she captures my mouth in a gentle kiss.

Wait—I pull away to look at her. "Stone?"

"I didn't want to use Adler, and couldn't think of another name. It fit." She smirks. "Come on, let's get home. I can think of a way to celebrate."

She doesn't need to tell me twice. "You take care of Betty and I'll go to the judges."

I watch her from a distance, getting settled with the race organizers. She brushes out BDub, but her motions are awkward. Did she pull something when she was riding? I can't explain it, but every hair on my body is standing up, and my need to go to her is overwhelming.

I interrupt the organizers. "Gentlemen, I apologize, but I have to get to my girl real quick." I walk down the stairs of the grandstand, not waiting to see their reactions to cutting off our conversation so abruptly.

Charlotte's back straightens, going ramrod-stiff, and I see that a man came from behind Betty White and put his hands on Charlotte to turn her around to face him.

Whoever this is, she does not want this. I sure as fucking shit do not want him touching her. I race down the rest of the bleachers and cross the narrow pathway to get to her.

"Charlotte," I say sternly—not because I'm angry with her, but to pull her out of where she is in her head.

She snaps her head around to look at me and takes a big breath in. *That's it, sweetheart.*

"Mav." She all but sighs my name in relief, worry and dread heavy in her eyes.

The man clears his throat. "Charlotte, I'm talking to you." He knows her, or at least learned her name when I said it. *Fuck.*

"I told you, Julien. I have nothing to say to you." Charlotte is shrinking in on herself; the woman who goes toe to toe with ranchers and my stubborn ass is slowly diminishing in front of this man. Her body language has gone from confident to uneasy.

Julien. This is her ex-fiancé. He looks like a typical finance-bro asshole. He'll be a dead asshole if she asks it of me.

"Your parents think you're in Thailand, and Georgina claims she hasn't heard a word from you in months. So unlike you two." He *tsks*. He picks a piece of straw off his coat and flicks it away; he looks at it like the very thought of it touching him is offensive. "No one at the firm knew where you went. Allister said there was a whole mess with every single one of your clients because you left the way you did."

"I—I tried to tell you that something was going on at the office for months. I asked you for help."

"So, you just decided to take off and never thought it through." Julien scoffs. "You were always impetuous like that."

He moves his hand toward her elbow, and faster than a lightning strike, I grab his wrist and squeeze. When he hit her, he lost that privilege to ever touch her again. With my other hand, I push Charlotte behind me, and she puts both of her hands on my belt under the hem of my coat.

Even through the gloves, I can feel her trembling. I. See. Red.

In a tone I've never heard come out of my mouth, I say, "Do not touch her."

"This is a conversation between my fiancé and I, pal. Go shovel out the horse stalls or whatever the fuck else your job is." He looks at me, then at her, then back at me, and his eyes darken.

That's right, you piece of shit. I know what she tastes like when she moans my name.

"Aren't you going to ask him to leave, Char?" He looks at her expectantly.

"No, that was you," I snap. "*You* were just leaving."

"She's *my*—"

"She's not your anything. She made that pretty clear when she left you the first time." My grip on his wrist tightens, hard enough to make the fucker's bones crack. He flinches—not much, but I see it. And he knows I see it. "Sweetheart, take BDub to the trailer. We're done here today."

That's all she needs. She puts her forehead on my back for just a moment, then unhooks the carabiner keeping Betty tethered to the posts and walks toward the trailer.

Only when she's a few feet from us do I release his wrist. I take several steps into his space. "That incredible, brave, and radiant woman? She is mine. And if you so much as ever look at her again or put a hair on her head in danger, I will find you. I will drag you back here and feed your eyes to the pigs before I bury what's left."

His Adam's apple bobs as he swallows, betraying the swagger he's trying to project. But he doesn't break eye contact. "I didn't catch your name." He grabs his wrist and rubs it gently.

"Some names come with consequences," I say menacingly.

It's a paraphrase from Dante's *Inferno*, but Dad used to say it to me as a child when I lost a race or got into trouble. "Names are consequences of things. All things, just actions and consequences, kiddo. Good and bad."

Julien smirks at me, and it turns into a full grin as he walks away, back toward the bandstand.

This dickhead is going to find out real quick what the consequences will be if he puts Charlotte in danger.

Maverick

CHAPTER 35

Charlotte hasn't said a single word while she packs Betty White into the trailer. I want to shake her, tell her not to let that piece of shit take up any type of real estate in her brain any more than he already has. And, normally, I would. We jab at each other, even when we're intimate. That's how I know I've fallen for her. It's in the way she laughs when she mocks me. It's in the way I want to tear down every memory of him with my bare hands. She doesn't need that side of me right now.

I approach her with trepidation, the way one might approach an injured bobcat—cautious, quiet, with respect for an animal that could claw my eyes out. I know better than to mistake her silence for softness.

She speaks so quietly that I almost don't hear it, as though she's talking to herself. It's barely a whisper. "I hate him. I hate him so much it's actually eating at my soul." Charlotte turns to face me, not with tears in her eyes but rage. Pure, undiluted fury. "I was finally fucking happy. I didn't dare admit out loud that I wanted to stay in Silver Rapids. To see what I could build from scratch instead of falling into a good job that my dad set up. That I wanted to stay with you and your stupid, perfect face. We have to go home; I need to pack, or just get Finn." She looks like she's about to break.

I reach for her, and she runs to me. She pulls me into her, exactly how she pulled me into her orbit all those months ago. We're in each other's paths, colliding. Her touch is desperate, like she's anchoring to me one last time, afraid to get ripped away.

Charlotte *wants* to stay, *wants* me, and she called Dappled Stone "home." She's not leaving, she's not running, and she sure as fuck isn't abandoning me to live this life alone.

I would have killed him where he stood if I could have.

She's not crying, but she's shaking. I stroke her hair and grip her tightly to me, not just to keep her here, but to remind her I'm not going anywhere, and neither is she.

"He's stolen so much from me. I don't know that I could ever love again. Why would you even want me? I'm broken."

I push her away just far enough to get her to look up at me. "You are not broken, and if this is you broken, I will pick up every piece of you and help you put yourself back together."

She shakes her head no, but her fingers dig further into my jacket, clinging to the words she knows to be true. The breath she exhales is the letting-go of a lifetime of breath she's held in.

"We're going to call Owen and see what he can do. Then we're going to call Ace and see if there's been any movement at the ranch. Okay, sweetheart? I'm not letting you go. We should get on the road. You ready?"

She nods. "I need to, um—" She looks nervous. "I have to pee," she giggles. "And I don't want to be alone...will you come stand outside the door?"

I crack a grin. "Yes, babe. I won't leave your side."

Sheepishly, she says, "I don't want you to."

While she's in the bathroom, I call Owen and tell him everything about the exchange with Julien. He tells me exactly what we may have to prepare for and says he thinks we should get Ace on board. I agree; he cares for Charlotte. He will let nothing happen to her, either.

She comes out of the restroom, some water dripping from her chin. I wipe away a droplet with my thumb. She turns her face into my palm.

"I talked with Owen."

"And? What did he say?"

"He's trying to track Julien for any flights, but if he left Jackson, he's not on any manifests."

"He has a private plane. Well, his family does."

"The pilots still have to record who's on board. But we'll know more when he calls me back."

She nods, processing that we may not know what his next move is. I hate that this is causing one ounce of uncertainty for her.

She takes a big breath, and I see her hold it before she releases it, and then she hits me with the biggest surprise. She takes my hand in hers and gives it a squeeze. I've been inside this woman and have used her body to bring her and myself pleasure, but we've never shared *this* type of intimacy. I squeeze her hand back and walk her to the truck, open the door, and place a kiss on the top of her hand before closing the door.

The whole drive home, I'm in my head, thinking of all the ways this could go. I hear Dad's voice in my head: "Identify the threat, analyze what you can do to control the situation at hand, then eliminate all other variables." He meant it more for when I had mental blocks about skiing, but it applies here.

I text Ace. I don't want her to have to relive her past, but I *need* her prepared for whatever may come next.

We're home in just an hour, greeted by Ace sitting on a rocking chair on the porch next to Finn, who is munching on a femur. "Figured I would come to you; we don't want the hands to overhear. They're good people, and I don't want them to get involved in this. Welcome home."

"Agreed. Little Bird, you head up and take a bath, cuddle with Finn. I'm going to stable Betty and talk with Ace."

"Okay, a bath and cuddles sounds nice." She walks past Ace and puts down her bag to give him a hug. To him, she says, "I'm so sorry to cause all this drama."

"Charlie, this ain't on you. But we'll make sure to be prepared, just in case. Trespassing is a thing we take damn seriously here." He winks at her. He winks! I've never seen him so much as smirk.

"Thank you." She keys the code into the lock of the house that I pray to all the stars above she'll let me turn into a place worthy of being called home. Finn picks up his bone and walks inside with her.

"Charlotte?" I call out to her, and she turns around. "Lock the door and close all the curtains. Where is your pistol?"

"In the lockbox in the cottage."

"There's a lockbox in the study. Do you want the code?"

"No. I need to go get some clothes, so I'll go—"

"I'll go," says Ace. "You should stay up here and stay in the house."

"I can go; it's fine."

"Charlotte, let him. Please, sweetheart, go try to relax for a bit."

"Okay—it's in the top drawer of the built-in cabinet in my bedroom, next to the closet." She flushes. What else is in the top drawer, I wonder? "If you can get some *essentials*, I would appreciate it. I feel so gross. I'll get this laundered tomorrow. Can you take this with you?" She hands him her overnight bag. "Thank you, Ace."

"No 'thank yous.'"

Goddamn, now I have to like this guy.

She closes the door, and Ace and I unload Betty and figure out the next move.

I'm locking Betty's stall when he says, "I have a bad feeling."

"Me too. She looked as though he snuffed out her flame, and he tried to put his hands on her. I wanted to cut them off."

"You are just as protective of her as your dad was over your mom. That apple came from this orchard."

"If this is our bonding moment, I'm going to lay it all out there: she's it. I think Dad knew somehow."

"It wouldn't surprise me."

"No one is taking her from us. This ranch is her home now."

"No complaints from me. If he steps foot on this property, he's not leaving."

I nod. "Owen still hasn't gotten back to me about the asshole's whereabouts, so I have to assume he's still in Wyoming. The only saving grace is that we took the new truck without any identifiers, so he doesn't know where the hell she could be."

"I'm going to go grab her clothes and her piece. It will give her some peace of mind to have her own gun."

"Don't go snooping."

He points at me. "I'm not; that's a gross invasion of privacy. I respect boundaries. And besides, she's not my type."

I actually don't know what his type is. For as long as he's worked on this ranch, I've never seen him with anyone. "Whatever."

"I'm taking the side-by-side. I shouldn't be but a few minutes," he says as we shut the door to the barn.

"I'm going to find her something to eat. Let me know when you're back up here, and I'll grab her stuff from you."

"Should I take my time?" he asks pointedly.

I know what he's asking, and I think about that for a second. I want my woman every moment of the day, but I'm not above putting her safety first before getting my sweet girl off. "No, not long."

We part ways, and I go off to scour the kitchen for something to eat.

I'm boiling noodles when Charlotte comes into the kitchen, wearing my Team USA hoodie and a pair of wool socks, her long, bare legs on display. It's not heat in her gaze, but static—frenetic and restless, ready to erupt. She doesn't say anything as she walks toward the stool closest to me. She sits, and the hem of the sweatshirt rises, revealing her bare ass, and she opens her legs just an inch so I can see her pussy.

This is not the time; she's processing trauma. But, fuck, if seeing her in my clothes hasn't short-circuited my brain—the water boils over and causes the flames of the burner to sputter, and the timer for the chicken tenders in the oven goes off. "Shit."

She laughs. "I wasn't trying to Sharon Stone you. I don't have any clean underwear."

"You can wear mine. You are not to open that door when Ace comes back with your stuff."

She gives me a salute. "Buttered noodles?"

"And chicken tenders."

"Yummy and not at all a girl dinner."

My phone buzzes with an incoming call. I pull it out and say, "We're a little short on groceries, darlin'." I look at the screen, and Ace's name flashes across it. I answer and put it on speaker. "Ace, I told you, no snooping."

"Mav, we've got a problem."

Instantly on alert, Charlotte stands up and comes over to stand next to me. "What kind of problem?"

"A six-foot blond man problem."

"What?! Oh my God!" she exclaims. She brings her hands up to her mouth, and her eyes brim with silver.

"Charlie, he's not going anywhere, but I think you should get over here, Mav."

"What do you mean, he's not going anywhere? How did he find me? Oh, my God," she sobs. "I should have left as soon as I got back here."

I hesitate. "Give me a little more than that, Ace."

"I went to get her stuff and put it in the cargo box of the UTV. I was going to go back and check the lock because all I could do was shut the door. And he was walking around the side toward the front of the cottage, trying to look into the window. I can only assume it's your guy because I'm an ask-questions-later kind of guy. But if he's not who we're looking for, we have bigger problems. I knocked him out with a two-by-four that was in the UTV and used the zip ties from the field repair box to tie him to a chair." Damn, that was way too easy. "Switching to video call now."

The video connection goes live and I see Julien tied to one of Charlotte's dining room chairs, knocked out cold. His head is dropped to the side, blood trickling from his temple and down his face.

"That's him. Do not let him out of your sight; I'll be right there."

"Me too," Charlotte says.

"The fuck you are. You're not going anywhere near him. You stay here."

"I'm going!" She looks adamant.

"I will tie YOU up and leave you here." I look into her eyes. "Please, I'm begging you, stay here. I can't do what I may need to do to keep you safe if I have to worry about you anywhere within arm's distance of him."

She pauses just a moment, but it's enough.

"Ace, I'll be right there." I hang up the phone, take her face in my hands, and kiss her forehead. "I will get on my knees and beg you—please stay here."

She pushes away, and I find her hard to read. I look her over: her face, her curves. She's as familiar to me as the pages of my favorite book that I've read a hundred times, and I hate that I don't know what she's thinking.

She doesn't say anything, just goes to the couch where Finn is.

I pull out the tenders from the still-beeping oven and pour the noodles into the strainer in the sink. I approach her where is on the couch, drop to my knees, and pull her hands into mine. "Charlotte, please let me take care of this. Ace and I, we've got this. Eat your girl dinner, and I'll be back before you know it."

The tears falling from her eyes kill me. I kiss each cheek and say to Finn, "Protect your mom." Then I race for my truck and tear down the path toward the cottage.

When I walk in, Julien is grunting from the wicked punch Ace just delivered to his ribs.

I close the door loudly enough to let him know I'm here.

"He won't talk. So, we're just getting to know each other," Ace says as he straightens to his full height. He's taken off his coat, working up a sweat even though the cottage is chilly.

Julien coughs.

"Well, Julien. Turns out that your name comes with consequences. And it demands action."

"Fuck you."

Ace punches; Julien groans.

"We just want to know who you told that you saw Charlotte. You seem like the kind of guy who likes to run his mouth. Who did you tell?" I ask.

"You have no idea what you're getting into. She'll be coming home back to Boston with me," he grunts.

"You know, I don't think she will. In fact, I don't think you will be, either. You know, she told me that you hit her, locked her up in your apartment while you went out and cheated on her. It broke her heart and trust in men."

"We had an arrangement."

That earns him a punch to his face. His eye is definitely going to swell shut.

He groans. "Fuck. He's going to come for her, even if I don't bring her home."

"Why?"

"She found something, and they don't want anyone to know."

"I see," I say. "And do you know who he is?"

"That you don't says you're in way over your head, Farmer John. He won't stop until she's either back in Boston with me, where I can control her, or she's dead."

"She's never going back with you. You'll never be able to harm another hair on her head. Let alone see her again."

"Not only is she going to come back with me, but I'm going to have her pregnant, popping out heirs to the McAdams-Adler fortune one way or another. Her father has already agreed to a per-grandchild sum. He's the one who helped me put out the contract for her retrieval."

That's fucking disgusting—like she's no better than a broodmare for these people. I don't even know if Charlotte wants to have kids; I don't doubt that this asshole would neglect to take that into consideration. I shudder at the thought of what would have happened to her in a different life if she were still with him.

I look at the angle of Julien's broken fingers. *Ouch!*

Ace slams his knife into Julien's thigh, and the kid screams so loudly that I don't hear someone enter the cottage.

"Maverick." She whispers it, but I hear her as clearly as if she were shouting.

I whip my head around. "Charlotte."

Her face is frozen in terror. She looks at the man she was once supposed to marry. What a sight she must see. Broken fingers, busted face, eyes swollen shut, Ace's knife sticking out of his thigh, and a puddle of blood accumulating on the wood floor.

"Jules..." She raises her hands to cover her mouth. She looks devastated. "How? How did you find me?"

"I put an AirTag in your coat pocket, you dumb bitch. Call off your dogs. Be reasonable, Char! I called your dad on the way here. He can work it out with Allister to let this blow over if you come back home with me."

I look at her bag next to the front door where Ace had dropped it. The coat she wore during the race is on top. My gaze returns to the dead man in front of me.

"You—you told them where I was?" she asks.

"Yes! What the fuck, Charlotte?! You disappear in the middle of the night without a single trace. Your parents are looking for you, and I'm going to get that money owed to me when we get back."

This time, I punch him in the mouth. I hear bones crack, and his jaw hangs at an odd angle. He screams. "You brought this fight to my home. To *her* home."

"Why?! It wasn't enough that you broke me? Why couldn't you just let me go?!" she screams. "What did it even matter? You didn't even love me in the end, did you? I was just a means to an end for you—a brokered deal in my father's boardroom."

"You were a means to an end," he manages to get out through labored breathing. He's being cruel in these last moments simply because he can. "You were just a dumb slut."

I take a step toward him.

Bang! A shot rings out into the night.

I look at Ace; his hands are bloody but empty.

Then I see her: Charlotte. Pistol out—the one my father taught her to shoot with—still perfectly aimed at her ex-fiancé's head.

Charlotte

CHAPTER 36

I heard everything Julien said and everything he didn't. It finally hit me that he was just going to kill me slowly if we had continued our lives together. I saw the lockbox next to the bag in the cargo bed of the side-by-side and I had to get my gun. I felt better knowing that I had it on me, some type of protection.

The shot rings out, clear even through the cacophony of things in my head. Julien, Allister, my father. Years—no, *decades* of betrayal, of ownership, of control. I've been reduced to nothing. My father sold off his youngest daughter in a power-hungry money move.

I've tried and spent so long trying to attain their love and approval. But to have Julien and my father conspire together, with Allister? I know I just killed a man, a man I thought I loved once. But what makes me fall to my knees and scream is the utter betrayal executed by the men who were meant to keep me safe.

There's still noise, distant and broken. It takes a minute to realize it's coming from *me*. I'm screaming, sobbing into my hands. I shot my ex-fiancé. I'm a murderer, an awful human who has just taken a life. I'm no better than any of them.

Rough, callused hands cradle me and hug me to a broad, flannel-covered chest. Maverick's pine and bourbon scent clings to him. He's saying something to Ace, maybe? I can't hear over the shot echoing in my head.

I've shot hundreds and hundreds of rounds with Jasper, but never at anything or anyone. It was only ever a safety precaution. I'm still sobbing when Maverick kneels in front of me, then stands, with me in his arms, my own arms wrapped around his neck, holding on for dear life. Even though I don't want to be touched, I have no fight left in me right now. He angles me so I don't have to see the body. Julien's body.

"Maverick," Ace says.

I forgot Ace was here for a minute. But how could I have? His knife is sticking out of Julien's leg. His hands are busted up from torturing the ex who tortured me.

"In a minute," Maverick hisses. He's carrying me to the bedroom.

I know—I know I shouldn't have come. He told me to stay at the main house.

"I'm sorry. I'm sorry. I'm so sorry." I repeat it over and over as Maverick places me on the bed and takes off my boots. I scoot back on the bed and hug a pillow to me as tightly as I can, eyes scrunched tight.

"I'm not going to say it's okay. You know I'll take care of this," he says. "Eyes on me, Charlotte." I look into his eyes, the same shade of blue as the night sky just before dusk. "Sweetheart, I'm right here. I'm not going anywhere, but Ace and I need to talk. I'm on the other side of this door." He backs out of the room and closes the door behind him.

I can't hear what they're saying beyond a few grunts. It's all a mess and so, so staggering.

He's gone long enough that I wonder if he's ever coming back.

But he does. Maverick returns to my room, and the first thing I see are the streaks of blood staining his clothes. He sinks to the side of the bed, his voice low as he says, "A few things are going to happen now, okay?"

I shake my head, trying to stop his words from hitting my ears. I don't know what he's about to tell me, but in my bones, I know that I'm more trouble than I'm worth. He's going to say that I need to leave, and that he doesn't want me here anymore. That I made a mess that I can't possibly clean up. And while there's no blood physically on my hands, it's all I see when I look down at them.

So calmly, he says, "We had to move the body. Ace is moving it right now. I had to help him load it in the back of the truck."

I am so mad and numb. I am every single emotion as rage and sadness flow through me. We're talking about Julien as an "it."

"We're going to pack up your clothes and everything you need for a little while."

This is it; he's sending me away. I shake my head again. *No, no, no. Please don't send me away.*

"I talked with Owen. He said there's still a contract on you, and he doesn't know if he can make it go away. I know it's hard, but Julien placed it. Supposedly, it was just for retrieval. And because the only one who can close it is dead, it's not safe for you just yet. So, you are going to come stay with me at the house. Ace is going to be calling in some favors for some extra hands to help us with security."

"You're not sending me away?"

"No." He tugs my ankles, and the rest of my body follows. He buries his head in my lap. "No, Little Bird. I'm not."

I feel the tears finally begin to fall. I'm not crying over Julien—I'm crying because, the time I need someone most, it's the man I want to love me who is showing up for me. His touch and words ground my soul to his. For the first time in over a year and a half of running away from something, his words have rooted me to my core.

"And Owen, he thinks he can get the contract canceled somehow?" He nods. "Yes, but what about Allister or my dad?"

He pushes hair away from my face. "Don't worry about anything else other than focusing on you." He pauses. "The land that the team leveled last year—that's where Ace is taking the body. He can get in there with the backhoe, and we still have the equipment to re-level. We just have to be careful about when we pour the concrete for the foundation for your event venue and barn. It has to be the right temperature outside and on the ground, or the foundation could crack."

"You want to bury him here? At the ranch?"

"Yes, I think it's actually the perfect justice."

"How?"

"Because he'll have to see all the lives you're going to bring joy. All the happy couples and people who will be starting their lives here, gathering here." He points down, indicating the ground.

I feel the weight and gravity of this moment, of his words, of all the things he's doing for me. I know—I have known what this feeling is, and this just makes me feel it so much more.

It is fitting that Julien will be trapped in a land that I have come to love, and one that has my heart. "He'll never get the life he wanted. Even if I were just a trophy, he'll be the one trapped. He tried to steal my life, Maverick." I sob again.

"He'll rot on this land that he tried to take you from. And one day, I'm going to marry you out there, with him beholden to watch as I make you deliriously happy. I'm going to make you my wife and give you everything you deserve, or die trying." His words are resolved and decisive—both a promise and a salvation.

It stirs in me something deep and hopeful: that we can one day build our lives together through the shroud of what I've done. But, deep in my soul, I'm just as dark as the night sky. This reclaiming of my body, my life, my freedom—it's vengeance.

"I don't want the first time I say it to be tied to all this. And it's not just the heightened emotions; you have to know how I feel about you. But when you're ready to hear it, know it's consuming me not to tell you." He kneels and places a soft kiss on my mouth. His lips are both soft and sure.

"I—"

He interrupts me, saying, "You don't have to say anything. I know." He smirks and stands, then pulls me up with him.

We stand there for a heartbeat or two. *Just say it; you know how you feel about this man!*

"I know," he repeats, and goes to the closet and starts pulling out clothes. When I stand and move toward the door, he jerks around. "Wait." He pulls the comforter off the bed.

"No. I want to see it." I don't say it's because I want to know that I'm free, or at least one step closer to being free. When we walk out of my room and into the main room, I steel my strength and look at the pool of blood, the chair in the middle like an island.

There was a living, breathing man there not too long ago. A man who, at one time, I thought I loved. I didn't know what that love would turn into and how he would utterly betray me. I guess I didn't realize the different ways he manipulated and abused me. The wounds he inflicted were some of the worst—the psychological abuse, the gaslighting, nothing but absolute control dressed up as care until I was too far into the cage that I couldn't see the bars.

I'm not saying this excuses anything, and it doesn't mean there isn't a part of me that mourns what I did, but I finally put myself first, just like he always had.

Logically, I know if there are still people out there trying to capture me, I *still* don't have my freedom. I just don't want to run anymore. I finally want to stay and put down real roots. But I know that we have to be smart about this. The illusion of safety is just that—an illusion.

Under a cloudless sky and glittering stars, Maverick guides me back to the house. I suppose I should feel relief when we shower together. When he washes my hair tenderly, scrubs my body when I just stand there and stare at the tiles, or when he wraps me in a fluffy towel and brings me to bed. And, though we're touching, skin to skin, in the safety of his arms and in this house, Finn sleeping at the foot of the bed, I don't sleep. I'm too afraid of what the nightmares will bring. I'm afraid Julien and a host of other characters will be waiting for me.

Sleep offers no escape, only a dark, unyielding nothing, leaving me utterly drained. I don't think Mav sleeps at all. But we hold each other all night, his heartbeat steady, mine struggling to find its rhythm. His hand trails up and down my back in soothing strokes. My arm is thrown across his chest.

I don't know if I have ever, in twenty-six years, felt this safe, despite everything. How awful is that? I killed a man and have a bounty on my life, but being naked in this man's bed brings me some type of peace.

"Good morning, sweetheart." He kisses the top of my head.

I close my eyes and breathe him in. "Mmmm." I stretch and sit up, not bothering to cover myself. He sits up and scoots back against the headboard. He's the first one, maybe the only one, to see me naked, stripped bare. I pull my long hair to one side and let it fall over my breast. I don't miss the way his eyes shift from sleepy to enraptured with that one move.

"Do you know how beautiful you are?"

I am shit at taking compliments, even when I know I'm doing something well. I guess that's why I craved some type of praise from Julien and never got it. Mav, though—when he calls me his "good girl" or, fuck, even when he had me bound and blindfolded in the barn, I *know* he's got me.

"I have to tell you something. And I didn't tell you before because—" He pauses and breaks eye contact, looking away. "I haven't told, well, anyone that wasn't there, or my dad, or Garrett's dad, or Owen." He glances back at me; there's terror in those sapphire eyes. "I killed someone."

Maverick

CHAPTER 37

"I was driving home from the bar with the guys. I wasn't drinking. Garrett and Luke were hammered. Caleb and Jake had already gone home. Owen was visiting with Dad and they were getting ready for a fishing trip the next day to Montana. Garrett's dad, Sheriff Hayes, was going to go with them.

"I had been pushing myself so hard, training to get back to skiing after tearing up my knee the first time. I fell asleep for just a second, but by the time I knew what was going on, I had struck something in the road. At first, we thought it was an animal, like a deer or a bear, or something. There was so much blood. The truck had a dent in the front of it, but the bull bar prevented most of the damage. Garrett went to lean over the fender flare on the side of the truck to puke. When he looked up, that's when he saw a man in the ditch, his body all bent at odd angles.

"All three of us freaked. I called my dad, and I had never heard him so nervous." I remember him talking to Owen in a hushed tone. "He asked who I was with; I told him and told him where we were. It was almost three in the morning during the summer—there wasn't a moon, so we couldn't really see much. Then, Dad and Owen arrived.

"Dad called Franklin, Garrett's dad. He knew that we were going to have to explain what had happened. Garrett was freaking out. He could have lost his scholarship to Notre Dame. Luke had just started his business.

"It was an accident; we didn't see him. I was afraid to tell Dad I had fallen asleep. But when Frank got there, he got the man's wallet and found out who the guy was on his computer. Apparently, he was wanted in connection with a series of rapes in the Midwest. He had skipped out on bail, and we did not know what he was in the area for.

"But the kicker is that one of Garrett's sister's friends, Janelle, had been assaulted a few weeks prior; she had lived a few towns over in Pine Valley. It's a small town; no one matched the description she gave. But she told the authorities that he had a tattoo down his chest and ribs. The guy I hit? There were tattoos down his chest and ribs.

"We let my dad, Owen, and Franklin work out what was going to happen next. Franklin would always do whatever was best for the county, within reason. He was the one to respond to the scene when Janelle made the call, and he said it was bad, real bad." I shake my head when I remember Garrett sharing some details that he found out later. "Dad said that he and Owen could take care of it. Franklin didn't object but wasn't about to be complicit either, so he turned a blind eye and took Luke and Garrett home. I drove the truck home, and it was gone when I woke up the next day. I don't know what Dad and Owen did with the body; I was too cowardly to ask." I scoff. *Cowardly.*

"They did that to protect me, to protect all of us. But at the end of the day..." I sigh. "I took that life, and I couldn't even ask what happened. After we found out who he was, I thought I had divinely delivered justice, but that's just shit I told myself to justify what happened." I take Charlotte's hands from my arm, lift them to my mouth, and give her knuckles a light kiss.

"I want you to know that I don't see that when I look at you," I say. "Cowardly, I mean. I see someone who is strong and took back her autonomy, her agency."

She's got tears in her eyes when I finally meet her gaze.

"But I understand it may change how you see me. The point is, I want you to know who you're sleeping next to. I've taken life, too."

I don't realize I'm shaking until she crawls over my legs and wraps me in her arms, straddling my lap. I'm not trying to break this moment and have my dick make an appearance, but with her so soft and close like this, it's damn hard. She nuzzles into my neck and I am completely enveloped by her.

We don't have to worry about anything, though, because my phone goes off, its glaring ringtone breaking the silence. I pick it up without having to look. I know it's Owen.

I bring the phone to my ear. "Owen," I say in place of a greeting. None of this is his fault—I'm just...exhausted.

"We need his thumbprint."

"We can do that. We have his whole hand."

"What did you do with his phone?"

"I kept it like you said, put it on airplane mode."

He continues speaking. Charlotte moves to stand up, and I grab her wrist. I squeeze and mouth, "Don't move."

She gives a playful grin and stays saddled on my lap, then grinds against my groin. This side of her—I haven't seen this side of her since last summer. She's lighter, somehow. The shadows in her eyes aren't as dark as they were last night—or, hell, as dark as they've been the past few months.

Owen finishes explaining his plan, and I disconnect the call. I close my eyes and lean my head against the headboard.

"Mav?" Concern mars her exquisite face.

I pull her close to me, kiss her throat, and work my way up to her sumptuous lips. This day is going to suck, and I don't know when we'll have another moment like this. "Let's find Ace. We're going to need his help again, and you both might as well hear the plan at the same time."

"Okay." She nods.

"I've got you, sweetheart." I kiss her again, my fingers gripping hard onto her hips, grounding her to me. It's rough, fervent. My hands travel up her ribs to her full, heavy breasts. I tweak her peaked nipples, and she moans. One hand continues to rub her breast, while the other comes up and wraps around her throat.

I groan as I say against her mouth, "Did you just trade one cage for another?"

Charlotte clings to me. Unwavering, with eyes clear and hands around my neck, she whispers, "Yes, Mav."

Fuck. I growl. My inner caveman is screaming "*Yes, yes, yes!*" I know what she's saying even without the words.

"All right, Little Bird. Let's go clean up your mess." I smack her bare ass, and she gasps. My Little Bird enjoys getting spanked; I know this shit turns her on. I smooth the sting away by rubbing her ass cheek, but I know if I slipped my hand closer to her center, she'd be wet.

She's wearing her pants, but she goes into my closet and picks out one of my favorite sweatshirts. It feels like a new day with her waking in my bed like this. And while I don't particularly lament that piece of shit dying, I feel somewhat responsible for the fact that Charlotte was the one to pull the trigger. Who knows what kind of trauma this could cause.

"Can we make coffee before we meet with Ace?"

"Anything you want, sweetheart." I didn't really know how she was going to process everything in the light of day. I'm quite surprised that she's taking this new reality so well.

We make coffee, and she mutters something about not having Nutella, but that's fixed with a trip into town. If that's what it takes for that smile, I'll give her coffee. I'll give her the whole goddamn world.

I call Ace, and he answers on the second ring.

"Hey," I say. "Can you come to the house? It'll be easier to do this in person."

"Tell him I made coffee."

I roll my eyes. "Charlotte said she made you a coffee."

"I'll be there in a few," he says, then hangs up.

We sit at the kitchen table, and Charlotte blows on the top of her coffee to cool it down. Lifting the mug to her lips, she blows so hard that some splashes onto her fingers. I know she doesn't mean to look so damn seductive when she licks them clean, but my dick twitches in my pants nonetheless.

There's a sharp knock at the door. Charlotte gets up to let Ace in, and I take the opportunity to adjust my pants.

"Hey," I say as he comes over and sits opposite me at the table. Charlotte pours him a cup of coffee and places it in front of him before sitting back down next to me.

"What do we know?" he asks.

"Owen's on his way here. We need Julien's finger."

"At the moment, he's in the back acres, in one of the sheds. I didn't know what to do with him until we got some more info. I was just going to bury him," Ace says gruffly.

"We are still going to bury him, but we need his fingerprints first. Based on how Owen explained, Julien put the retrieval contract out on a dark web site, and he likely had a token so that he could turn it off." I look at Charlotte. "Do you think he would have kept it at his place or at work?"

"No, I don't." I sigh, but then she continues, "He would have kept it on him. He was paranoid as hell and too arrogant. But I don't know how he would have known I was in Wyoming. His family would come out here and ski, but he likely had it on him. We used biometric tokens for work all the time. Sometimes it was a series of numbers, and sometimes it was a thumb or fingerprint. Most of the time it's small, the size of a flash drive, and gray, gray or black."

"You know what they look like?"

She nods her head.

"Okay, so we look in his pockets," I say. "Ace, do you still have access to his vehicle?"

"Maybe for another hour, but not after that. It'll be on a train."

"Owen is already on the way here from Norfolk. He had a layover in Dallas. So, about four more hours. We need to keep the body dry and cold."

"He's basically on ice already. So we don't have to worry about that. It's fucking cold outside and in the shed."

"And we're just going to saw off his hands?" Charlotte asks.

I wince. I do not want her near this, but she's here, present.

We don't say anything, allowing the silence to confirm her suspicions.

"And then what?" she inquires.

"Owen has a laptop that will allow him to access the websites necessary to see what is required to cancel the contract. But that access comes from Julien. He tried to get in other ways and was unsuccessful. But he can do it from here. His VPN is private and won't be traced back to him, us, or anyone."

"Okay, so we wait?" Ace asks.

"For now, he said to just wait for him to get here. I don't know how long it will take or how long he'll be here, so I'll get the guest bedroom ready for him, in case he's here for a bit."

"Speaking of, what about the cottage?" Charlotte asks. "Am I going to have a giant red stain on the floor? I can't tell Quinn it's Kool-Aid, you know? How do we clean that?"

It's cute that she thinks she's going to be staying in the cottage after all this.

"I can take care of that," Ace says. "Owen's been here before, so it's not going to spook any of the hands to see him again, knowing who he was to your father. But I would really like to keep all of this away from the guys. Hank and Clint included."

"Agreed. This stays with us only."

"I don't mean this to sound ungrateful, but how do you even do that? I mean, can you do that, Ace?"

"Warm water, Castile soap, some elbow grease, and hydrogen peroxide can work wonders, Charlie. At least enough until we can get back in there and sand and wax again, if necessary. Soak up anything left with sawdust, and then we can burn it."

"Wow," she says, a bit stunned, her eyes wide. "Have you ever had to do anything..." She trails off upon seeing the hardened look in Ace's eyes.

I've wondered about that myself, but I've never asked. Like he would tell me anyway.

"I lived a different life before working with Jas."

It's quiet for a moment. The silence is soon broken by Finn yipping by the front door.

"I'll let him out," Charlotte says.

When she walks out the front door, putting on her coat, I look at Ace and say, "I don't want anyone from the ranch finding out what happened, I agree. But I especially don't want her to have to deal with this any more than she has to. Do you really think you can get the cottage cleaned up by yourself?"

"Don't question me now. Yes, I'll go pull some of the supplies from the stores shed. Let me know when Owen gets here."

"Will do."

We stand and move to the front door.

"Ace, thank you." I extend my hand to him.

He looks at it, then back at me, and shakes it.

I open the door and find Charlotte running around with Finn, tossing a large branch for him to retrieve. She's got a scowl wrinkling her forehead and looks like she's trying to concentrate.

I know of a great way to get her out of her head.

Ace walks down the steps and says, "Call me when he gets here. I'm goin' to look in his rental before I get started on the cottage."

"Yep," I say.

"Thank you, Ace," Charlotte says.

Ace replies, "I told you, no thank yous."

"Will you settle for a hug, then?" Without waiting for his answer, she walks over and gives the big brute a hug.

He's stunned, like he hasn't experienced a gentle touch before in his life. He pats her back, nods at me, then gets in his truck and drives off toward where we keep supplies near the pole barns.

"Charlotte," I say, and she turns her head toward me. "Let's go for a walk while we wait for Owen to get here."

"Finn can come?"

"Let's leave him here; we'll be back soon."

"Okay. Come on, Finn. Inside." She motions toward where I'm standing on the porch.

I let him inside, close the door, and enter the lock code.

Charlotte has her Dappled Stone Ranch beanie on, but her hair swirls in the wind, and she pushes her gloved hands into her pockets.

"Warm enough?"

She nods, and I pull my own beanie and gloves out of my pockets before walking down to her.

Just getting out and being surrounded by the snow and the cold, fresh air is refreshing. It feels like a reset. We don't say a word on our walk, just listen to the sounds around us and the crunch of the snow beneath our boots.

Back in the cabin, Charlotte falls asleep on the couch, curled up with a blanket, Finn's head resting on her lap. She turned on the TV before passing out, streaming some type of jazz from my phone. In the time we've been back, I've managed to prepare the back guest bedroom with fresh linens.

Now, I'm making a bacon grilled cheese and trying to dress up some canned tomato soup when I hear a knock on the door.

Finn gives a few barks, and I say, "Easy, killer." Charlotte stirs but doesn't wake. I go to the door, look out the peephole, and find Owen on the other side. I swing it open, and Finn jumps around excitedly.

"Heya, kid," he says as I close the door. He puts his bags on the floor and gives me a big hug. Besides Charlotte and Mrs. Wright, I don't think anyone's given me a hug in a long, long time, not even Dad.

I embrace him tightly. "What a mess, huh?" I chuckle.

He pats me on the back and shakes his head, smiling.

Maverick

CHAPTER 38

I take Owen's bags to the guest bedroom, except for his satchel. He follows me, and we drop off his satchel in the office.

He gives me a sad smile. "The last time I was in here with you, you were having a hard day."

"I remember. I was telling Dad that I didn't want to be smothered and that I was strong enoughto get back out there." I pause and close my eyes. In my mind, I can see Dad sitting in the chair, Owen sitting opposite him, and I'm standing in the exact same spot. I think Dad knew I wasn't ready, emotionally. Physically, I was fine. A few months later, I had fallen off a damn balcony, sad because my mom wasn't alive to see me compete in the Olympics. "I was so mean to him."

"He knew you had a lot going on in that head of yours. Only you were going to be able to break yourself out of it."

I shake my head, ashamed.

"So...have you fallen in love yet?" he asks sarcastically, repeating his words to me from months ago.

I don't answer, but I hold his gaze. "I wouldn't do this for anyone else. I wouldn't ask you to do this for anyone else."

"I'm damn happy for you, Mav." He claps his hand on my shoulder. "Let's get to it, then."

He goes to the breakfast nook, and I go to wake up Charlotte. Some curls have fallen across her face. I push them off her forehead and give her a gentle kiss. "Wake up, Little Bird."

She yawns and stretches her arms above her head.

"I made food, and we have a visitor."

"He's here? Oh my god, why did you let me sleep?!"

"You needed the rest."

She wipes the sleep from her eyes and stands, a little uneasy on her feet.

"Mav, the soup needs basil and more pepper," Owen calls from the kitchen, where he's currently stirring the soup.

Charlotte giggles and says, "There should be some dried basil in the cupboard on the right."

I roll my eyes at these two, making themselves right at home.

We walk into the kitchen, and Charlotte says, "Hi, I'm Charlotte. Thank you so much for helping me with this. Well," she pauses, "and from before. I didn't know Jasper asked you to do that for me."

"Lottie—is it all right that I call you Lottie?" He shakes her hand.

She gasps when she hears the nickname, the one my dad used to call her, and nods. "That'd be nice."

"I feel like I've known you more than just a few minutes. Jasper thought very highly of you, young lady. He didn't throw around compliments much, either."

She brings her hand to her chest and smiles.

"I'm glad you tamed this one." He points at me. "He needed a reason to stay put."

I bristle. "All right, let's eat and figure this out."

After we've finished eating, I text Ace to meet us outside the storage shed. We take two of the UTVs, with Charlotte driving Owen. I can only imagine what the hell they're talking about.

Ace is leaning against the structure when we get there. Owen walks up to him and says, "Grayson, how've you been?" then shakes his hand.

Charlotte and I look at each other, both marveling at the discovery that Ace's name is not Ace. He looks like an "Ace."

"Never a dull day, ya know."

"Let's take a look," Owen says.

"Wait!" Charlotte exclaims. "He's really in there?"

"Yes," I say. I look at Ace, whose face 99.9% of the time is unreadable, and see pity in his eyes.

"Charlie, you don't have to do anything. Maybe it's best—"

"No, I did this," she says. "But—"

I walk over to where she's become frozen to the ground. "I can understand closure, Little Bird," I say softly to her, pulling her hand into mine. "But this is something different altogether. If you want to see the body, that's one thing, but I don't want you to be here for this." I don't say, *"while we mutilate a dead body and cut off its hands."*

A tear slips from her eye, and I try not to wonder if it's from sadness or mourning. I wipe it away; Julien doesn't deserve any more of her tears, even if she has more to give him.

Owen comes up beside us and says gently, "Lottie, you've been so brave, and you don't know me from Adam, but I promise this isn't something you want to see."

Another tear slips free. "I'm not a coward," she murmurs, her voice carried on the breeze.

"Sweet girl, no one thinks that, but let us handle this."

She burrows further into my arms. "What about where you're going to bury him?"

"The area you had prepped, it's the right place to put him," Owen confirms. He continues, "No one is tearing up a slab of concrete to look for bones that won't be there, anyway. The lime will take care of it. His bones will be there, but the tissues will be gone."

She nods again. "Okay. Okay, I think I'm going to go back to the house." She turns her sky-colored eyes to me. "Is that okay?"

I give her a kiss and say, "Of course. We'll be back at the house when we're all set here. I'll bring Owen back."

After she leaves, Owen says, "She's going to need some time. I have the number of someone if she needs to talk to somebody."

I nod. "I'll let you know—she may not want to, though. She tends to keep things close to the vest."

"You, more than anybody, know what that can do to a person. To keep that kind of guilt or trauma."

"I know. I'll talk to her."

"What exactly do you need for this to work?" Ace—*Grayson*, I remind myself in disbelief—asks.

"I'll need the toggle, which Charlotte was pretty damn sure was on him, and we try it out on his fingers and thumbs."

"I looked in the rental he had, and it wasn't there," Ace adds.

"She was pretty adamant it was on his person, to keep it safe," I tell them.

"Let's clear out his pockets and pray to God that it's there," Owen says.

We open the door, and the stench is enough to knock me off my feet, which is saying a lot. Manure, feed, horses, cattle—none of it actually smells like a bed of roses, but this...this is gross.

Ace says, "I'll look for it. Here, take this." He hands me the bone saw he brought, then starts rooting around in the fucker's pockets. He finds what we're after in Julien's jeans, in the watch pocket. *Way to be original, asshole.*

I go to the workbench, get an extension cord, plug it into the wall, and then trail it behind me to the body and the saw. Crouching down, I pick up the hand I grabbed when I first met him and momentarily think about breaking his arm, if for no other reason than because he thought he could lay a hand on Charlotte. Before me, after me, doesn't matter.

I pull the wrist flat and turn on the saw. It whirs, sending vibrations up through my arm once I put it to his cold flesh. The trick with cutting bone is to do it through the joint; that I know. But I am surprised by the lack of blood that's definitely *not* spurting.

"Is this normal?" I look up and ask Owen.

Ace is the one who answers. "No blood pressure to pump a dead heart. No spurts. Gravity does its thing."

I blink a few times at his intimate knowledge of this, then turn to Owen. "Really?"

"Yeah, basically," Owen replies.

The flesh doesn't cut the way frozen beef does, with clean precision. It's a bit jagged. Owen produces a bag from his coat pocket and holds it out for me to put the hand in. I change sides and kneel down to continue on the other wrist. I notice a ring on his right pinky finger. *Douche.* Owen collects that hand, too, and I can't help but think, as morbid as it is, it was pretty easy. I mean, in the way that I don't think twice about the fact that, even in death, this fucker can't touch her. I only need to work to ensure he doesn't taint her dreams or any part of her future.

"I'll need Wi-Fi, so we have to take these with us." Owen lifts the plastic bag containing the dead man's hands. "I'll need my bag—the Wi-Fi extend out to the horse barn? I don't want to do this in the house with her in there."

"Yeah, the office in there has its own booster, so it'll connect."

"I've got to warn you." He looks at me. "We may only get a few chances to pick the right finger. Not even I can get around that."

"Fuck," I say. I look at Ace.

"Okay, so let's assume he's right-handed," he says, adding, "Only ten percent of people in the US are left-handed."

"I don't know if I want to know why you know that."

"I don't think you do, either," he replies.

"All right," Owen says, "let's assume he's right-handed. I'd say he likely would have set it for his thumb, pointer, or middle. He's not going to pick the ring or pinky fingers."

The hypothesis is sound. I take my phone out and call Charlotte on speakerphone. She doesn't answer. I call her again. Still no answer. Again, and no answer.

All right, what the fuck?

"Does she normally not answer your calls?" Owen asks.

"Normally she picks up pretty quick," Ace answers.

I briefly wonder, *How often is he calling her, that he knows how fast she answers the phone?*

"I don't normally call her; I text if I have to."

My phone buzzes, and her name and photo flash on the screen. *Thank fuck.* The photo is of her on Betty. I took it one day when I was still so angry about everything and was going to send it to the guys' chat to talk shit, but I didn't. I kept it, and when I finally got her number, I assigned it to her contact.

"Charlotte."

"I needed a minute; I was feeding the horses. Then I came back to the house and didn't hear my phone ring."

Breathe. She's fine. It's fine.

"No problem," I say, trying to hide the panic in my voice. "We needed to know if Julien was right- or left-handed."

"Right-handed," she replies.

I look at Ace and Owen, then nod. "Okay, that's what we needed to know. Thank you."

She doesn't say anything for a few heartbeats. "Is— Is everything taken care of?"

Owen says, "For the most part. Now I just need to do my thing. Don't worry unless I say it's time to worry, all right?"

"Okay," she replies.

"I'll see you soon," I say to her, but she hangs up before responding.

"That was weird as fuck," I say to them. "Are we good here? I want to get back and check on her."

"Yeah, we're good."

"When should we bury him? I know we don't really use this for anything, but we can't just leave him here and have one of the ranch hands walk in looking for something."

"We can do it two ways. We can bury him here, where you said the concrete was going to get poured. It's going to be a bitch to get that ground dug up; it has to be six to eight feet. Far enough down that when the gas from the decomposition settles in, it won't affect the foundation of the building. Or I can take him with me and—"

"Guy, you flew here. They're not going to let you take a broken body in a duffel bag."

Owen laughs. "I was going to drive, if I had to."

Ace laughs, too. He takes the saw, re-wraps the extension cord, and places them on the bench. They both look at me like it's my choice.

"He thought he could come here to my goddamn ranch and take what's mine? Fuck that. He stays. He stays and watches her be happy."

That seems to satisfy both of them. Ace says, "The sawdust needs another day to soak up at the cottage. But after that, we can burn the sawdust. It's Monday; we can't wait until some of the hands leave on the weekend. I'll need a reason to start digging up where you think we're going to put him."

There will be reason in a few months, I think to myself.

"Tell them Charlotte wants to get started on the event space right away."

"She's the boss," Ace says.

Hmph. She's the boss.

"No thank yous and all that, but it means a lot to me. And I know to Charlotte, too."

Neither of them say anything. We walk out of the storage shed, and Ace locks it back up. "I'll get started on the hole. Could be a few hours, but it's out away from the bunkhouse, near the cabins, so it won't disturb no one."

"Sounds good," I say. "I'll loop Charlotte in. Owen, want to come with me?"

He nods, and we all get into the UTVs.

Owen's quiet for most of the drive, but after a while he says, "I'm proud of you, kiddo." I give him a blatant side-eye, to which he adds, "Not because you cut off a man's hands. But you're doing whatever you need to do to protect the woman you love." He claps his hand on my knee twice. Then, he looks back out at the mountains, bearing witness to what we've done.

Love. I know that's what I feel, but I can't voice that right now. I'm almost afraid to even think it. I'd rather ski down the Couloir du Goûter with a rock collapse about to crush me. If I say it, if I speak it, it'll disappear.

I don't say anything.

I park the vehicle next to the barn and put the keys on the numbered hook. The lights are still on. "Charlotte?" I look around, thinking she may still be in here. "Charlotte?" No answer. I go to the bathroom to wash my hands. I don't want anything from that piece of shit left on me.

We walk into the house, and Finn is at the door waiting for us.

"Hey, mutt. Where's your mom? Charlotte?" I call up to the second floor, where my room is. I take the stairs up and shout back down to Owen, "I'll be a sec."

"No problem. I'm getting my bag and am going to the office in the horse barn."

"Okay."

She's not in my room, the bathroom, the guest rooms—upstairs or downstairs—the mud or laundry rooms, my parents' room, the office, the library. I take my phone out and dial her number. Again. And again. And again.

I should have checked in with her. No matter if she said she was okay. There are a few places she could have run off to here on the ranch, but what if she left? *She wouldn't have left the ranch, right?*

I don't have time to go through all the security camera footage, but I scan the last few minutes of the main house and barns. I find her hastily putting on Betty's tack. So she's on the ranch.

I get the keys to a UTV from the barn and go off to find her. The sun's starting to set, and we're going to be losing light. Other than what the headlights illuminate, I won't be able to see shit.

Think! Where would she go? Not to the cottage.

I head to the cabins as fast as the damn thing will move. I get to the sites and see her on Betty, staring at the space where we had talked about burying Julien. *Thank fuck.*

"Charlotte," I growl, "get the fuck down from that horse right now, or I will hog tie you, carry you back to the main house, spank that ass until it turns pink, and then leave you there dripping."

She jerkily dismounts from Betty and ties her lead to the fence post. She marches up to me, going toe to toe. I like seeing her find her spark, her fire, again. It's hot as fuck, even if her ire is directed at me.

"I needed to get away for a minute—just for a second!"

"Fine, but fucking tell me! Don't take off when there are people out there trying to hunt you down and kidnap you! I would never even know if you left or if they took you!"

At that, she backs up an inch. I grab her and bring her face to mine in a punishing kiss. Our foreheads knock, but I don't care. I want to devour her right now. I push her up against the fence, but suddenly, in an impressive move, she flips us around so she's the one pushing me up against the fence.

"Little Bird, are you here with me?" I say in panting breaths.

"Make me forget," she implores. "Please, Mav. Please give me this."

Whether she's begging for my dick or just to get out of her head for a moment, I'm not sure. But I'm a selfish bastard, so if she needs a momentary relief, I'm happy to let her use my body.

I kiss her and take her ass in both my hands. She wraps her legs around my hips. Not breaking our kiss, I go to the closest cabin and open the door. It's chilly in here, but not freezing, thanks to the insulation, windows, and doors being hung.

I pull her coat off, shuck off mine, and drop both on the floor. Her holster and gun next. Then, I lift my sweatshirt and undershirt over her head and find her braless. *Fuck.* I push her leggings down, and she unbuttons my flannel and tugs it off.

She drops to her knees and makes quick work of my belt with her deft fingers. My cock is so hard at the sight of her on her knees for me. She strokes me a few times and licks me from my balls all the way to my slit, where a bead of my pre-cum has escaped. Charlotte licks up my shaft with the broad, flat expanse of her tongue again. She swirls it around my head and takes me as deeply as she can.

Her wet mouth feels so goddamn good. I take her throat in my hand and continue to fuck her face as I bend over her. My dick hits the back of her throat; she gags on it. I'm not even pushing her down—she wants it all. Drool drips down her chin, and that almost makes me nut right there. I pull her off, and she finally breathes.

"Lay back," I say, gesturing to our discarded coats so she won't be bare on the floor.

She licks her lips as she lays down, knees bent, and her eyes track my every move. She's the predator here.

"Open your legs."

She complies, and I see a wet patch on her pale pink panties.

"Look at you, dripping for this cock. Your panties are soaked from you choking on my dick."

She plays with her nipples. I kneel down, lift one of her legs, and kiss her inner ankle. Slowly, I pull the drenched panties off her, and the primal savage in me is exultant at how wet they are. I wrap them in my hand and stroke myself a few times. Her pupils are blown wide, raw with greed.

"Are you hungry for this?" I stroke myself again, again, and again.

"Yes."

This is torture, and I'm doing it to myself. I want to feel her hot, wet cunt pulsating around my throbbing cock.

I notch myself up against her entrance and run my dick along her slick folds. I enter her in one long thrust, not giving her a moment to acclimate. She wanted to forget; I'll fuck his name from her memory every day. She's grabbing me and pulling herself closer, her legs locked around me.

"Yes, God, yes."

I snatch her chin between my thumb and forefinger. "No, say *my* fucking name, not God's. This pussy is mine. I will brand it on, so you never forget. Do—" Thrust. "You—" Thrust. "Understand?" Thrust.

"Maverick! Maverick! Yes, Mav. Yes!"

"That's my good fucking girl."

She's close. Her eyes are squeezed tight, and she's getting breathy. "Oh—" I tighten my grip on her chin. "Fuck, yes. Mav, goddamn, yes!" She detonates, and her legs quiver around my hips. I don't stop; I fuck her straight through it because I can't wait much longer. A few more thrusts of my hips and I come so hard I go straight to oblivion. I fall onto her, and she gasps.

I roll over onto my back. She takes a breath and lets it go slowly. I trail my fingers along the plane of her stomach and up to her cheek. I don't want to lose this woman, and she definitely won't like this next move. But the absolute panic I experienced over not knowing where she was? I don't want to do that again.

"Charlotte?"

"Mmm." Her eyes are closed; she looks like she could sleep like this. Lord knows she didn't sleep last night.

"Sweetheart, I need you to stay on the ranch. No going into town. I wouldn't even bring Quinn or any of the guys here until we figure this out. Okay?"

"I know you said I'd trade one cage for another," she huffs. "I didn't think you'd mean it literally."

"Little Bird, it's until this is done, okay?"

She heaves another exhale, her frustration evident. "And then?"

I would never let her go if I could stop it. But right now, I just say, "We live our lives."

Charlotte

CHAPTER 39

"*We live our lives,*" he said. *What does that even look like?*

I start to shiver as the sweat on my body cools in the frigid cabin. Maverick moves his body over me as though to shield me from the wind that's whipping hard outside. We should get back, see what Owen is able to tell us, what he's learned so far. Get Betty White back in the barn. I'm reluctant to leave Maverick's warm embrace, though, his heartbeat so steady and sure. I haven't asked for the details of what happened in the barn; I don't know if that's something I really need to know.

I'll give him this: Maverick sure as hell knows how to get me out of my head. I love that he takes control but still checks in with me. I feel my armor flaking off piece by piece in slow motion when it comes to him.

I shift just a bit, and I can feel him harden against my hip. He nuzzles into my hair. "You're a cuddler," I say with a giggle.

He stiffens for just a moment before he pulls me on top of him. "Say that again," he warns.

"What? It's no big deal. I'm just making mental notes for the future."

He spanks me twice, kind of hard, and I wiggle atop him. "I'm not—" Spank. "A cuddler." Spank. "I just like being close to you."

Fuck. Being on top of him like this, with my legs straddling his hips, I realize he's going to feel me drip, and we do not have time for that.

"Hmm." I stand up and start to collect the clothes that are strewn about, a smirk on my face. He just did—well, whatever he just did to Julien, and then fucked a smirk onto my face?

I think I'll really have to unpack what this means for my mental health because I have been struggling with the fact that I shot and killed a man, yet am really not as distraught as one would think I would be. Unless I'm still in shock...but I don't think that's the case because I've thought over and over again about raising the gun, pointing it perfectly at his forehead, and taking aim. I would never do it to anyone else, but the freeness I feel right now? I can't really describe it.

I pull on my pants and turn to find Maverick in his boxer briefs, looking out of the window, toward the mountains. "Mav?"

He turns, and his gaze snags on my exposed nipples before reaching my eyes.

"I'm not sad. Or mad. Or anything. I know we still have more to figure out, but I'm okay."

He crosses the space and grasps my chin between his fingers, tilting my head backward. "Charlotte. It's okay to be whatever you're feeling."

"I know," I continue, "but I am fine. Really."

"You are incredible, Little Bird. But if you ever need anyone, Owen has some amazing resources. It helps to get it out with people who don't know and won't judge."

"If it gets to that, I'll tell you." I shimmy, and he releases my chin.

He rubs his hands up and down my arms before retrieving his sweatshirt and shirt that I had commandeered. He doesn't look convinced, but I *would* go to therapy. I went when I was younger, in college, but I didn't connect with my therapist. I saw her for three years. It's hard to take it seriously when you feel like your therapist is sharing details of your private life with your mother.

"Arms up," Maverick commands.

I obey, and he tugs the shirt and sweatshirt down over my head.

"We need to get back with Owen. See what he has been able to figure out, or if the fingers worked. If not, we're fucked, right? Because after so many tries, it would likely lock itself. We're not going to be able to reset the token, right?" I ask.

"I'm not sure, but Owen said something similar, so I'm sure he's going to be working it out somehow."

"I'll ride back on Betty. You can take the UTV back." I look at the cabin, note nothing is out of place, and walk over to the fence I've tied Betty to. She's only been out here a short time, and she's wearing her booties, but I'm going to give her so many peppermints and carrots. "Extra oats for my girl tonight, ain't that right, Betty?"

I get settled in the saddle while Maverick gets in the side-by-side. He chortles, then growls. "Sweetheart, I'm not letting you out of my sight," he says, tone going from kind of playful to downright caveman.

My phone buzzes, and Ace's name flashes across my phone. The urge I have to change his contact info to "Grayson" is so real. I flip the phone open. "Hi."

"Heya, Charlie. We've done the best we can do on this. There's no stain, but it currently smells like disinfectant, and it's making my eyes burn. We can open the windows and doors, get some air circulators to get the smell out."

He says *smell*, but I'm thinking of energy. Quinn is going to want to sage the shit out of my home. Then I almost smack myself, because, my God, I can't tell her what happened.

"Eh, it's okay. I can stay at the main house in the guest room until we figure out the cottage." We both know I wouldn't be staying in a guest room, but he lets it slide.

"Right, well. The cottage is clear after tomorrow."

"Thanks, Grayson." I giggle.

In a deadly tone he's never used with me, he says, "Charlotte, it's Ace," and hangs up.

Maverick's phone chooses that moment to buzz, and he answers on the second ring. "Owen, what do we have?"

I pull back on Betty's reins. "Whoa, girl." I definitely want to hear what Maverick is talking about with Owen.

"Okay, we're on the way back now. We'll meet you at the horse barn." He looks at me. "We've got news, but he wants to wait until we're both there."

I don't even wait for him to finish. I nudge my heels into Betty's sides, and we take off into the setting sun. Maverick gives us some distance so as to not scare my horse. I dismount and take her into her stall. All the horses have their own runs so they can go in and out as they want to.

I see Clint and one of the newer hands, who was originally hired for summer but stayed on, working with the colt that I was so excited to break so many months ago. My world has changed so much since then. I feel like I never get to work with the horses or cattle anymore.

Ace is in the barn, waiting for us. Before I can say anything, he apologizes. "I'm sorry I snapped at you, Charlie. No one calls me Grayson anymore."

"It's okay." As I walk past him, I say, softly enough that Maverick can't overhear, "I like it, though. It suits you." I give him a light smile and take Betty to her stall. Getting her tack off, I brush, feed, and put her blanket on her.

I brace myself before I walk into the office, not knowing what I'm walking into. When I enter, I see Owen has a whole setup on the large, wood-top desk. His laptop, the key fob, notes written in a journal, and Julien's ring are splayed across its surface—no hands, though.

Owen clocks my scan of the desk. "You don't need to see them, Lottie." I sigh and give him an appreciative but sad smile. "But I didn't know what you wanted to do with the ring."

"I don't want it. He got it when he was in school, from his fraternity at the end of freshman year. He used to tap it on the table, or any surface really, when he got mad or irritated. I hate that thing. I don't care if you bury it with him." The one time he slapped me across my face, the sting it left…I feel it, even now. He twirled it on his finger afterward.

"We can do that." Ace takes the ring off the desk and pockets it.

"So, believe it or not, I was able to go to the lowest of low tech. I got some tape and lifted the print of the finger he used off the token. I was going to analyze it, but when I was looking for a pen, I found an ink pad."

"We use that for bank deposits or to sign off when things are processed or checked in," Ace says.

"Right, so I inked the fingers and analyzed it against the print I was able to lift, and think there's a perfect match. But there's a couple of unknowns here, and I didn't want to make a decision without consulting with you first, Lottie."

"What do you need from me?"

"We may only get one chance at this, and if we're wrong, we'll have to move to a backup plan."

"Do we have a backup plan?" I ask. If there is one, I don't know about it.

"At the moment, no, but that doesn't mean we couldn't try to make some adjustments. Move you to a more secure location. We're not sure who, if anyone, your ex-fiancé may have shared your location with. I've got a friend working to see if he can break into his phone."

"I don't want her to leave. She's not going anywhere." Maverick takes several steps forward from the corner where he's been observing this exchange and moves in front of me, trying to push me behind him—as though Owen is the problem here and not Julien's overbearing, psychotic ass.

I swat him away, or try to. His body is all muscle, and he's like a bull holding its ground. I divert and just walk in front of him, as though shielding him from something he may not want. He puts his hands on my hips.

"Mav, we may not have a choice. If we can't confirm that we are successful in this, it may be what's best—for a while," Owen says with sorrow in his eyes.

I feel Maverick stiffen, and when I look down, he's clenching and unclenching his fists.

"But you think we have a match. Right? And if we are given the option, we may have other tries with other fingers? Does it matter that the hand isn't on his body?"

"The middle finger from his right hand seems to be the most perfect match."

I give a *humph*, and everyone turns to me. "That tracks; his last middle finger to me."

Maverick turns to ask, "What the hell did you see in this guy?"

"Honestly, now I'm not even sure. We were young, and our parents were pushing for the relationship. Even from a young age, they made jokes about it."

"Go for it. I'm sick of living my life this way. I can't do it anymore."

Owen nods, looks to Ace, then to Maverick, then to me. "Do you want to be in here when I do this?"

Maverick's hands on me tighten.

"Yes," I say.

Owen lifts a severed hand, now a discolored pallor, and presses the middle finger to the scanner on the token. His face lights up.

I squeal, but Maverick pulls me back into him and squeezes me so hard I feel his touch to my toes.

Owen says, "I would deny it if any of my colleagues ever asked, but sometimes low tech is the best. We're in." He stows the hand back under the desk. *Blech.* I will need to sanitize this entire room before I sit back down to do reports.

It's agony to just wait and watch Owen do his thing, so I go out and walk around in the barn, giving treats to the horses in the stables, taking extra care of my Betty. Maverick hasn't let me out of his sight. He thinks I don't notice his eyes tracking my every move, my every breath, from where he stands in Walter's stall.

Within the hour, Owen—posing as Julien—contacts all the contractors involved and successfully cancels the contract. He explains that, even if a contract is no longer active for hire, parties who had already agreed to it might still follow through, believing it to be valid. It's a precaution—to ensure nothing else comes of it.

A simple business transaction, as if that is what my freedom and life have been reduced to.

I thought maybe I would cry, scream for joy, something. Instead, I walk over to him and give him the biggest hug. Maverick comes up behind me and gives us both a hug at the same time.

I've never seen Maverick touch anyone besides me when we've been intimate, But he's showing all the emotions now. I let that sink in. I know he feels so fiercely protective over his friends and his peace, but he's slowly letting people in. The way a lone wolf might inherit a new pack.

"Thank you, thank you, thank you," I say to Owen—to the universe. This wouldn't have happened if I hadn't been in the right place at the right time, overhearing Jasper talk about this place in the Bluebird.

"You are so welcome, sweet girl."

I pull back from the hug and see Maverick's eyes are lined in silver, but bright, happy.

"Thank you, Owen." Maverick knocks his head to Owen's.

"No thank yous, remember?"

I see Ace standing to the side. I break away from the triple hug and walk over to him. In a serious tone, I say, "This is not sexual harassment."

His eyes go wide, and I leap to give the giant man a hug and a kiss on the cheek, his scruff tickling my face.

"Boss, get a hold of yourself. You'll give that one the wrong idea, and I'm not trying to bury two men today." He pats my back and takes a wide step back.

I giggle and say, "He's fine." I turn my head to Mav, shocked to see him not flaming red with jealousy. He looks...relieved, but there's a touch of sadness in those ravishing indigo eyes.

I take a few breaths. *In for four, hold for four, out for four, hold for four. And repeat.*

I just got my life back. But what does that even mean? I can do anything now; that was all I ever wanted. So, why does the thought of going back to my old life in Boston—my friends, my family—terrify me? What if what I want now is to be surrounded by dust, hay, and a stubborn-as-a-fucking-bull, six-foot-three reluctant rancher?

With all the options equal, what is the best course?

"What's next?" I ask.

"I was going to get back to the Kill Devil Hills, but I think I'll stick around for a few days." Owen claps Maverick on the back. "Is that all right with you?"

Mav replies, "Yes, of course. I've got the guest bedroom downstairs all ready for you."

"If it's all the same, I think I'll take the cabin. I may post up here for a few days. Go ski, walk around, and enjoy the fresh mountain air."

"The cabin isn't ready yet, though, is it?"

"Technically, it's clean now, but the windows and doors are open while the air circulates," Ace says.

"I'll be okay. I have plans tonight, anyway." A sly smile and a blush play across his face.

"Uh, okay." Maverick guffaws, but I don't press. The man just saved my life; he can have his secrets.

I barely hear Owen whisper to Maverick, "Besides, I would think you would want some privacy tonight."

Maverick gives him a completely predatory smile.

I blush twenty shades of pink and pretend I didn't just hear that.

Owen pats his belly and says, "I could go for some more of that tomato basil soup." I know that he does this kind of thing all the time, but the quickness of the pivot throws me for a minute.

"Ace, want something to eat?" I ask.

"Nah. I have a body to bury, and I'm going into town after that. I'll be back for tomorrow's morning meeting."

"Do you want some time off? This goes well above and beyond what you signed up for."

"No, I need to keep these hands busy."

I step back into his space and put my hand on his arm. "If there's ever anything I can do for you, you'll tell me, right?"

"You got it." He walks into the office and returns with a black trash bag. I can only assume that it contains Julien's hands. "I'll see you tomorrow, Boss. Owen. Maverick." He nods at the guys and then walks out of the barn, like he's on a mission.

"Okay." I try not to let the hurt show in my voice. I'd love for Ace to feel like he's included, and not just when I have a body to bury or a pool of blood in my cottage. I'd like to be able to give him more salary and maybe build him a place here on the property if that's what he would want.

"Lottie, he's a complicated man," Owen states. "But I've seen him be more chatty with you than I have with any other person I've ever seen him with in twenty-plus years."

"You've known him that long?"

"Yes, I introduced him to Jasper twelve years ago."

"I didn't know that," Maverick says, a bit shocked.

Owen just smirks and walks toward the door that leads in the direction of the main house.

Maverick

CHAPTER 40

Owen, Charlotte, and I scarf down what's left of the food. Owen takes over to make the grilled cheeses, and Charlotte pours everyone a bourbon. I notice the cherries in her rocks glass. There are, like, five of them in there.

It hasn't really settled in yet that what Owen has given Charlotte is a second chance at life. *Her* life. The relief I have is nothing short of miraculous, but—but my heart is terrified at what that might mean. What if she was merely staying because that was her only option? What if she *does* want to go back to that life? Even if she said she hated it, it provided a different lifestyle for her, one that she grew up with. The city girl in her never really left. Would she be happy here in the long run?

My brain is second-guessing everything, and my heart is screaming at it to shut the fuck up. It's screaming, *"She's ours, she's not allowed to leave!"* Can I truly allow her to trade one cage for another?

I'm shaken out of my thoughts when Owen says, "Yes, you have access to everything that you want now. If you want to re-establish your accounts, banking information, phones, anything, it's all yours."

I turn around and see my Little Bird's eyes go wide and her mouth form an O. "I guess I didn't think about that. I mean, I did, but not really. That I would get all the access to my money."

Fuck. It's a fuck ton of money, too—more money that I might make in a lifetime of instructing. And she's only twenty-six.

"So, I could return some of the capital investment that Jasper put into this place for the eco-cabins?"

"That's way above my pay grade; you'll have to talk to the accountants. But from what I know, you'd be paying yourself anyway, so what you do with it is up to you. I just kill people." Owen chuckles.

"Owen!" she exclaims. "You do more than kill people. You fix things." She reaches across the table and takes his hand in hers. "And I'm so grateful. You'll never know. If there's ever anything I can do to ever repay you... I don't know what that is, but please—*please*, let me know." Tears well in her eyes. "Owen, I can't believe it. Thank you."

"Lottie, Jasper considered you family. He was my family, and that means we're family. No thank yous." He pats her hand, then looks down at his watch and says, "Hate to eat and run, but I'm going to be late for my appointment in town. Use this time, Charlotte. See it for what it is: a second chance to design your life how you want. Dream big and live the way you want, where you want. After everything you've been through, you deserve that. And know, no matter what, know that you always have a friend in me."

I swallow a knot in my throat and release a breath I didn't realize I was holding.

"I'm going to grab my bags. I'll post up in the cabin, but I'll check in with you guys tomorrow." Owen hands me his plate, smiles cheekily, and then walks to the guest room in the back of the house.

"Does it seem like he's meeting up with a booty call?" Charlotte whisper-shouts conspiratorially and then giggles. "It seems like it to me. A man doesn't book it like that unless he's getting some ass."

I never thought of that. Who would he even be meeting up with? "I have no idea." I laugh.

She stands and comes over to help me load the dishwasher.

I get an email on my phone while we are cleaning up, reminding me about the Big Sky skijoring competition in Montana this upcoming weekend. I sigh. I can't ask her to do that; I won't.

I am typing out a response for us to withdraw when she says, "What's wrong? What was that?"

"An email from the race organizers in Big Sky. I'm going to tell them that we're withdrawing."

"No, wait. Don't." She puts her hand out to stop me.

"Charlotte, we're not going. You've got a lot to figure out, and I'm not asking you to go up to Montana to do this."

"You're not asking me to do anything; I want to go. I want to live my life. I want to stop looking behind my back and around corners. I want to live a full life, wherever that is. I'm so fucking done with letting people push me around—Julien, my job, my parents, and the fucking ridiculous pressures they put on me." She slams the dishwasher door shut. "I'm so done. I'm reclaiming my life from everyone who ever thought they could take it from me."

Damn, this woman is so goddamn hot when she's passionate. Watching her come into her own as a rancher, with the tiny cabin village, and through all of this has been remarkable. The taste of the woman she was over the summer—a bit freer, sassier—is back in her eyes.

I get the feeling that she's starting to feel the same way, and it's only been a day since Julien's death.

"Are you okay with Owen staying in the cottage? We can get all new things, change it all out, if you want."

"It's fine." She gets a kind of playful look in her eyes when she says, "I want to celebrate my re-found freedom. I'm going to let him out." She points to Finn laying in front of the fireplace. "Will you meet me upstairs?"

Oh, my Little Bird wants to play.

"Whatever you want, sweetheart." I turn off the light above the sink and go to the fireplace. After spreading out the wood and embers so that they burn quicker, I close the screen. "Outside, Finn," I say. His ears perk, and he goes to where Charlotte is standing by the door, slipping her feet into her sneakers and my coat. *My coat.*

I'm so intrigued by what my Little Bird has in mind for us tonight. God, our first night together, she wanted to play. Toys, my tongue, my fingers, my cock—everything I could offer to give her pleasure, she took it all. I poured candle wax on her body and rubbed it all over her supple curves, devouring her. My dick is getting hard just thinking about all the ways I brought her pleasure. I'm so glad she picked me to open up that side of her.

And, now that I can put a face to the name that made her question herself—that made her feel anything less than perfect—I feel such a deep satisfaction knowing that he will never touch her again. She's mine, and I'll remind her again and again and again. I'll remind her all night long.

My room is chillier than downstairs, so I start a fire in my fireplace, then go to turn on the light in the attached bathroom. I'm stripping off my flannel when the recessed lights turn off, leaving just the light from the dimmed fixture overhead and the glow of the firelight.

I turn around and find my Little Bird naked, holding a bottle of whiskey. My gaze snags on that tempting rhinestone at her pussy, then travels up the rest of her curves. Finn is at her feet, and that just will not do.

I eat the space between us in just a few strides and look down at him. "I don't want to traumatize you, boy." I shoo him out, then shut the door and look back at Charlotte. "Because what I'm about to do to your mama, you'll never get it out of your eyes."

My throat has gone dry, the temperature in the room well past sweltering. I pull her into my space, grab the bottle, and throw it on the bed before I lift her, my hands cupping the globes of her ass.

She wraps both of her arms around my shoulders and whispers in my ear, "Erase him. Make it so that I only know your touch. Please, Mav." She licks my neck from just above my thermal to the tip of my ear, then bites my ear and sucks it into her mouth, smoothing the sting. "I want all of you—however, wherever you want me."

My dick goes harder than a damn steel pipe, and I can't wait to have this woman—*all* of this woman.

"I'm still dripping your cum. Fill me back up?"

I walk her back toward the fireplace and slowly drop her to her feet. As she lands, her hands begin pushing my clothes up and over my body, frenzied and rushed, like she can't wait another minute. This shift in her—is this what she was like before all this mess? What man wouldn't want a woman like this? She's practically ripping me out of my jeans and boxer briefs.

"Charlotte, let me take care of you."

"No, I want to take care of you first."

I'm not going to tell her no. I'll make sure she gets everything she wants. She's taking the reins and leading wherever this goes.

Her big blue eyes look up from beneath her long lashes that fan across her cheeks, and she licks her lips. One of her hands works up and down my shaft, while the other grips her breast. She gives one long lick, another, and then swirls her tongue along my crown.

"Yes. God, yes."

She is doing her best to take my full length, but I don't want to hurt her. I have my hands in her hair, but I'm not guiding her; she's in control.

She takes it further and further, wrapping both her hands around my length and applying the perfect amount of pressure. She takes me until I hit the back of her throat, and I fall forward and put my arms out to brace against the mantelpiece over the fireplace.

"My good girl is so greedy."

She hums in pleasure. In all of our past encounters, she's loved the praise I've given her. She scratches her nails down my abs and thighs, the sensations of her hot, wet mouth and the sharp pain of her nails exquisite.

"Fuck, I'm going to come if you don't stop."

As if that spurs her on further, she increases the tempo of that little flick she's doing with her tongue and continues to bob up and down on my dick. Thank fuck I'm bracing myself against the mantel, because I would have fallen over by now. She's about to suck my blackened soul out of my body.

She hums and scrapes her nails across my ass, and the orgasm that's been building and building erupts. She opens her throat up even wider to take me further. She doesn't stop.

"That's my good girl. Take every fucking drop." I'm still spilling into her when I throw my head back and groan, "Fuuuck."

My Little Bird is on her knees, drool dripping down her chin onto her breasts. The little bit of mascara she was wearing runs black lines from her eyes and down her cheeks. She looks utterly beautiful. She doesn't realize that, though she's on her knees, I'm at her feet—all hers. Hers to ruin. There's a bit of my cum on the corner of her lips. I take my thumb and push it back inside her plush mouth. She sucks on my thumb, swirling the tip like it's my dick, and my cock twitches.

"Oh, that's how it is, eh?"

She giggles. "I guess so."

I scoop her lithe body into my arms and carry her to the bed. "Sweetheart, playing with fire gets you burned."

She gives me a deep kiss and runs her hands through my hair. I have a good rebound time, but I'm going to need a minute before I can fuck her the way I want to.

I place her on the bed and sink to my knees on the carpet. Her blonde waves spill out all over as she props herself up on her elbows, looking down at me from a position that makes her look like a queen. I see the bottle of whiskey next to her hip.

Her eyes track my gaze, and she swallows hard.

"Fight fire with fire, Little Bird." I open the bottle and take a big swig. "Want one?"

"Yes, of course."

I smirk and take another long draw. "Open up, Little Bird—I'm going to make you sing for me." I stand and pour a shot of the whiskey straight from the bottle into her mouth. She swallows. "Another?" She nods, and I take a sip before pulling her chin down and slowly allowing the amber liquid to drip from my mouth to hers. She sticks her tongue out, and some of the whiskey drips down her chin. I lick it up, then take the bottle and pour it down her body.

I watch the golden liquid wind its way from the hollow of her neck, between her breasts, down the flat plane of her stomach, and disappear in her folds. I do it again, only this time my gaze is on Charlotte's sapphire eyes as she watches the liquid dance along the curves of her body. I cap the bottle and sink to my knees, pulling her to the edge of the bed. She smells like oak, a touch of cinnamon, and honey. Knowing she's had my cum in her already today, mixed with the whiskey, is a fucking heady combination.

I push her thighs apart and open her pink folds with one hand, while the other hooks around one of her legs and plays with her clit and piercing. She's so wet. I inhale and smell her arousal mixed with the whiskey. I slowly lick her from her opening up to her clit.

She moans. "God, yes."

"What did I tell you before?"

"Only your name."

I lick her over and over. "Say it again."

"Only your name! Fuck, yes, Mav, yes!"

I twirl my thumb around her clit while I thrust my tongue in and out of her cunt. I love how wet and responsive my Little Bird gets for me. I insert two fingers and stroke her upper walls while I continue to suck her clit into my mouth.

"*Fuck*!" My brain is screaming, "*Mine to claim. Mine to fuck. Mine, mine, mine!*"

I don't want her to think about that piece of shit ever again. When she's touching herself, I want it to be to thoughts of me; when she's crying out, I want it to be my name on her lips.

She tries to close her legs, which is her tell for when she's close to coming. I lick a trail from her inner thigh to her core and continue to ravage her pussy until whiskey drips into my tongue's path.

I look up to see Charlotte pouring the liquid down her body, and I open my mouth to catch it as it trails over her piercing. Her eyes ablaze with desire, the glow of the fire highlighting her high cheekbones and full lips. She takes a sip of the whiskey and caps it again. I don't break eye contact from between her legs while I lap up every fucking drop. The whiskey tastes like honey, toffee with a bit of spice, and 100% like Charlotte.

I continue to lick even as her legs begin to shake and she throws her head back. She's so close. I apply just a little pressure to her clit with my thumb, and she shatters against my tongue. I catch her squirt and lick up as much as I can from her body. My dick is harder than it ever has been and is begging to sink into her.

I stand over her and put my soaked fingers into her mouth, and she sucks them clean. I force her mouth open, and I spit her essence and the whiskey from my mouth into hers. She swallows and I ask, "Do you taste how fucking perfect you are?"

She's got a dopey smile on her face. "Mmm."

I scrape her body off the bed and take her to the bathroom, my thick cock bobbing against my stomach as I walk. I put her ass on the vanity and turn on the shower to get nice and steamy. As we wait, I tenderly kiss her knuckles, then pepper kisses on her palm, between her breasts, and over her heart, which is beating faster than a bird's wings.

I look her in her eyes and hope that she can see how deeply I feel for her. I wanted to say those three words the other night, but it wasn't the right time, and now it seems too raw—nevertheless, I feel them. I feel how much I've fallen in love with this woman.

Charlotte

CHAPTER 41

My body is sore in the best fucking way. We had sex on every single surface in Maverick's bathroom and bedroom—against the tiles in the shower, the sink, the tub, the floor in front of the fireplace, and the bed. We fucked like we were animals, and then we made love. There's a difference that I've never known before. I didn't realize that this is what love could be, or what it's supposed to feel like. Having the attention of this man is such an intoxicating thing. Sometimes I want to knock him in his beautiful face, but when he calls me his good girl and takes care of me, it fills me with something that I've never truly known.

Maverick's chest is rising and falling with his breaths. I watch him sleep for a few minutes. He looks peaceful. I don't want to wake him, so I peel away from him and slip into a pair of sweatpants and a sweatshirt from his closet. My clothes are still downstairs, where I took them off.

I haven't felt this confident since college, maybe during one of the breaks that Julien and I were on. My steps are lighter, not trodden or crushed with the weight of my past, but I know I have to take stock of what I want to do now.

I take one last look at Maverick's sleeping form before I shut the door. Damn, if he wasn't giving me more reasons to stay. Somewhere between getting tied up in the barn and this moment, I started falling in love with Maverick Bennett.

"Come on, boy," I say to Finn, who is sleeping on the couch. I let him out to do his business while I get his food settled, then look out the window and see another beautiful day of bright blue skies and a blanket of snow on the ground.

I left my phone on the table yesterday while we were having dinner with Owen. Checking it, I find that Quinn texted this morning about joining us for the skijoring competition in Big Sky. Damn, news travels quickly. Mav must have told Luke.

Realizing I haven't heard Quinn's voice in a minute, I call, and she picks up on the third ring.

"Hey, babe!" she says animatedly.

"Hey, back," I croak. My voice is hoarse from screaming well into the morning and from trying to take Maverick as far back as I could.

"Ooh, shit. Are you sick?"

"No, uh, I'm not sick."

"HAHA! Oh, bitch, Maverick really must have been laying down the moves then. Hmmm?" I can almost see her eyebrows wiggle.

"You could say that."

"Fuck, yasss, baby girl. You've been needing to get your back cracked like a glow stick!" She has no idea about all the activity that's been going on over here: Julien—I don't know that I ever want to tell her about that—Owen being in town, and the development between Maverick and me.

"Ha, yeah, there's been lots of that last bit."

"I'm so happy for you, Charlie. You guys had this energy between you the first day, and even when you guys wanted to kill each other, it was almost like you were going to bang it out before or after. Did you know that the heightened response people feel after a good fight is called the 'misattribution of arousal'? And that make-up sex is often considered by both parties as the best sex ever? You guys must have had marathon sessions, because I haven't heard any Maverick gossip in weeks. What else have you guys been up to?"

It's a split-second decision. I can't drag her into this, no matter how much I want to come clean. "Same old, same old. With the exception of Mav and I, it's life on the ranch." I cringe. This is this last lie I tell her.

"Damn, the downshift from 'Ranger Rick' to 'Mav,'" she says dreamily. "What a wild ride."

"Okay, well, what about you? You and Luke are coming to see us race in Montana?! I didn't realize you guys were traveling together now."

"Eh, well, we're spending more time together and, like, officially dating, I guess."

"That's great, Q. I love that for you guys."

Maverick suddenly appears and lets Finn inside. "Holy damn, it's cold out there."

I turn to him; he's in a pair of gray sweatpants and is bare-chested. I put the flip phone down and cover the microphone with my hand when I say, "You should have put some clothes on; it's winter!"

I won't say that I don't appreciate the view, though. Washboard abs and that V that dips below his waistband. I can see his imprint through the fabric, and I shift a bit where I'm standing, feeling heat begin to pool in my core. My mouth goes dry.

He just smirks, props his hip against the counter, and raises an eyebrow at me.

"You know you look like sex, right?" I say to him.

He throws his head back and barks out a laugh.

"Charlotte?" I hear Quinn say.

"Sorry—Maverick just let Finn back in the house, and I got distracted." I did *not* mean to say that out loud.

"You're in the main house? Oh, bish, you're gone. Off the damn market." She laughs.

"Okay, on that note, I'm going to make some coffee. We'll see you

Friday? Are you guys driving up separately, or we're all going together?"

"Separate. Luke wanted to stop in Bozeman and get something for his business, and I wanted to get to a bookstore and scope it out. Its Insta is so cute!"

"All right, I'll connect with you before Friday. Bye, Q."

"I don't love waking up in the morning without you in my bed," Maverick growls when I turn to face him. "Time doesn't stop just because your legs are jelly." He runs at me, and I squeak.

I run around the dining table and over to the living room, ducking behind the couch, but Maverick jumps over the back like it's a hurdle and tackles me onto the smaller sofa.

"Not jelly, it seems." He gives me a kiss that's slow and languid.

We're interrupted by a sharp knock. "Open up, Mav."

"Owen." He knocks his head against mine. "He would have just entered without knocking; he must have that spider-sense that a woman was about to get—"

"Mav, I'm opening the door."

"Come in, Owen!" I shout.

Mav sits up and composes himself like he wasn't about to maul me like a rabid bear. We're on the small chair and a half, even though there are two full couches where we could have sat.

Clearly noticing, Owen asks, "I'm not interrupting anything, am I?"

"No," I say at the same time Maverick says, "Yes."

I thwack his leg. "How was your night?" I ask Owen. "Your special appointment," I add saucily.

"Probably about as good as yours, Lottie," he retorts and chuckles.

I say nothing, too stunned at his call-out.

"I just wanted to come by and check in on you, Lottie—see how you're doing, if you're getting some of your old life back."

"Ah! I haven't even checked or done anything yet. I've been, uh, busy, and I just woke up. Haven't even had coffee yet."

"I see. Okay, well, I've decided to stay for a few more days, if that's all right with the pair of ya?"

"Yes, of course. Please stay as long as you like!" I say.

"Owen, you know you're always welcome here. How was the cottage last night? I'm surprised you have eyeballs or lungs. Ace said that the disinfectant was pretty overwhelming."

"I didn't stay there; I'm just getting back on the property and wanted to check in before I get out there to work for a bit. I'm going to do another sweep on the sites for your name, but barring complications we didn't see yesterday, we should be good."

Oh my gosh. He didn't sleep in the cottage, so it was for sure a booty call. "Well!" I clap my hands together and stand up. "I was just about to make some coffee. Do you want any?"

"Do you have any at the cottage?"

"Yes, I've got the good-good stuff there. And all the fixin's are in the cupboard next to the microwave."

"Then I'll make it in a bit."

"We have a race on Saturday and Sunday in Big Sky. Do you want to join us? Quinn and Luke will be meeting us there."

"We'll see how the week goes. I've got some reports and work to get through. But I'll let y'all know."

"All right."

He opens the door and says, "I won't likely see you for dinner, so I'll check in with you tomorrow. If you need something, give me a call. Lottie, I put my number in your phone." I must look dumbfounded. "We've got to get you a better phone, girl. Don't you miss having the world at your fingertips?"

"It's been nice to unplug and detox from the world, actually."

"Well, it's more secure, anyway. Think about it." He waves and walks out the door.

I turn to look down at Mav and say, "What now, Ranger Rick?"

"We live our lives."

I'm doing the Friday reports when Ace walks in. "Boss lady, got a minute?"

"Of course, what's going on?"

He shuts the door to the office. "I wanted to check in with you since, ya know…"

"Since I walked in on you beating the shit out of my abusive ex who I shot in the head, who Mav then cut the hands off of?"

"Yeah."

"I'm okay."

"Really?"

"Surprisingly," I say. "I keep waiting for it to hit me. Or for me to feel bad. Not that I ever plan on seeing his parents again, but I don't feel bad for them. I don't plan on seeing my parents again, either, for that matter. I'm done—with all of them. But I really miss my sister, Georgie."

"Your sister's name is Georgie? Your names are Charlie and Georgie?"

"Ha, yeah. Georgina and Charlotte. You think my parents may have wanted boys?"

"I like your names."

"Likewise, big guy." I raise an eyebrow at him. "At any rate, I miss her and didn't want her mixed up in all that shit. She's happy just living her life."

"Go ahead and get out of here. I'll finish up whatever you have left."

"Are you sure?"

"Yeah, you guys have a bit of a rough drive. Have you seen the weather report? It's supposed to be a big snow. You guys are going to have some powder, for sure."

I never see Ace let loose. I mean, never in over almost a year. "A couple of the guys are going into town tomorrow night for some band. Are you going to that?"

"Nah, I'm going to stay here. Do you want me to check on Finn?"

We were going to bring him because the hotel is dog-friendly, but that's just an added level of stress, and he would be alone in the room most of the time since we're competing. "If you don't mind, that would be great. Thanks."

"Don't mention it."

I stand up and grab my work bag, then walk toward the door. "Ace, I hope you understand what I mean when I say, in a serious *Golden-Girls* kind of way, 'Thank you for being a friend.'" I knock into his shoulder with mine.

He just nods, and I walk back to the house. Maverick was going to head out to check the defrosters in the water troughs in the fields. I text him:

> *Ace just kicked me out of the office. Finn is going to stay here with him, too. I'll be ready to leave when you are.*

He doesn't text back right away, so I text Quinn:

Let me know when you guys get into town, if you wanted to meet up for dinner. Or just to let me know when you guys get there. The weather is supposed to be bad.

Quinn: *Ok, no problem, babes. We're already in Idaho. Weather is bad. Be careful.*

Ugh, got to love the weather in the mountains.

Charlotte

CHAPTER 42

What should have been a three-and-a-half-hour drive to Big Sky from the ranch turned into six hours. We crossed into Idaho, and the snow just kept coming. And with Betty's trailer, we took it slow.

Maverick had been white-knuckling some of the drive, but I'm glad the snow let up a bit once we crossed into Montana. The road is wild; it took us from Wyoming to Idaho, to Montana, to Wyoming, finally back into Wyoming. It's beautiful, though.

So, it's well past dinner, but luckily we brought some snacks with us, and I'm not hungry. Mav, though? I can hear his stomach growling. We get to the designated spot for competitors to park and trailer their horses. We checked in over the phone because we knew it would be so late when we arrived. There's just enough room for us to squeak in and get situated.

I pull the panels out and set up a corral area to let Betty stretch her legs for a minute. I lead her out, while Maverick lays down her bedding and gets the trailer situated for the night. I check her liner and blanket, and when Maverick yells from inside the trailer, "All right, Betty, your palace awaits," I chuckle.

She nickers before she walks over to him, and he rubs her forehead.

We leave the panels set up for the weekend and go grab our bags out of the truck. I hear his stomach growl again.

"Let's get some food before we check into the hotel. I think your stomach could set off an avalanche."

He throws his arm over my shoulder and says in my ear, "I'm hungry, but not for food," then gives it a nibble.

It's been five days since Julien. It's also been five days of being completely wrecked by the man holding me. I was so worried that he was going to be the end of me, but Maverick ended up being exactly what I needed when I needed him. It's so wild, but I've been thinking about it, and this either has to be the universe giving me what I didn't know I needed, or Jasper was a damn mastermind. I've tried not to dwell on it, but the thought has crossed my mind more than a few times these last few days.

There's a hotel restaurant and bar that offers food late at night, according to the website, so rather than trying to find something, we decide to check in and see if Quinn and Luke want to meet up.

> *Q, we made it! Finallllly! Are you guys still around, orrr?*

After a few minutes, I still haven't heard from her, so we choose to eat downstairs at the bar before heading up. Sitting at the hammered copper bar, we pile our stuff under the counter. I look around and see some of the people I met at the last race. Even though it's not well known outside of the Rockies, for those who know skijor, they're dedicated. A woman smiles and waves. I can't remember her name, but she was nice, and so I wave back in acknowledgment. *God, I hope she was smiling at me.*

"I could do a charcuterie tray. Ooh, or the cheese ball. They have a girl dinner combo—Caesar salad and truffle fries. Fuck, yes." I wasn't hungry, but I am now.

"Mmm, burrata flatbread? Say less." Maverick closes the menu, and the bartender comes to take our order.

"What looks good, guys?" he says.

"May I have the girl dinner combo with a chicken breast, please, and water and a Diet Coke?"

"I'll have the burrata flatbread and water, please. Thank you."

After some chat about the eco-cabin village launch in a few weeks, we fall silent when the food arrives. It's not an awkward silence; it's kind of nice that we can just be together but not feel pressured to fill the quiet.

When we finish, Maverick signs the bill. "Are you nervous about tomorrow?" he asks as we head up to the room.

"No, I'm excited! It's a different vibe here than the last two I've been to. Each town has its own vibe, and I love it. I wish we had some more time to walk around. I'm finally getting to new places, and I don't have any time to explore."

He's quiet after that, like he is thinking real hard inside that pretty head. He's like that even after we get settled into our room. After we make love, I'm in the bathroom, looking at myself in the mirror, my lips puffy, wondering again about all the things I had to go through to get to this moment. Sex tonight wasn't hurried or rough the way I normally like it, but soft and tender, more intimate somehow.

I shut the light off before walking out of the room, where I can hear Maverick's steady breaths as I climb into bed. I'm ready for tomorrow's race. He made a comment during dinner—"I'm glad that I could do this. If you had asked me last year if I would be doing this with anyone but Jude, I'd have laughed. But with you, this is a different kind of experience." It made me realize he really meant it when he said that once he makes a promise or commitment, he sees it through.

I drift into a deep sleep and dream about riding horses on the beach with Maverick.

I wake up to him trailing his hands up and down my thigh. "Good morning, Little Bird. It's time to get up."

I yawn and stretch. "All right. Let's go kick today's ass."

"I texted Luke, and they're already downstairs eating breakfast. We can have breakfast with the other competitors."

"Okay." I give him a kiss and get up to go to the bathroom. When I come back out, I see him moving things around in his overnight bag. "All yours," I say, and he startles.

"'Kay." He gets his Dopp kit and goes into the bathroom.

I get dressed in weather-appropriate clothes and throw my hair into a loose braid—I didn't wash it because I definitely didn't have time to dry it.

When Mav emerges, I see he's shaved his face, his jawline even more pronounced without his stubble. *So. Hot.* But now, we barely have time to eat.

"Come on, slowpoke," I joke.

I look for Quinn and Luke when we walk past the restaurant, but I don't see them. I text Quinn:

> *I'm sorry we missed breakfast with you guys! We're headed to the competitor's area, but I'll see you after we race.*

> Quinn: *It's alright! I was hangry and needed bacon.*

> *OMG bacon sounds so good!*

Breakfast with the competitors was good, but quick; we didn't really have time to interact with anyone. We hurry over to the trailer to get Betty for the race.

"Good morning, BDub," Maverick says as we lead her out to her small, makeshift pen. "Who's going to be as surefooted and fast as the wind today?"

The energy is frenzied as we make our way to the racetrack. I look at Maverick, and he's whispering something into Betty's ear. He's not hurried—he's used to this type of energy, a lifetime of competitive skiing behind him. No, he's methodical, calming Betty and me with his smooth shift into competitive Mav.

When it's time for the start of the event, we get to the racetrack and watch the parade. We're in the second position, meaning we wait for everyone else to beat the times of the riders before them. Not that I need someone else's time to push me, but I do better when it's not just against the clock.

We get into position on the track's starting line. Maverick snaps into his skis, puts his goggles and gloves on, and, once he's settled, yips, signaling that he's ready to take off.

The buzzer sounds and Betty and I take off. The wind rushing is so exhilarating, the crowd is cheering, and after a few feet, I feel when the slack of the rope snaps, going taut between us and Maverick as he trails behind us. We navigate the course easily enough, but this race feels different than last time; we don't go as fast, but the experience is amazing all the same.

Riding on Betty's back, I turn to see Maverick whooping and pumping his fists in the air. I dismount Betty and, just as he did at our first event, he comes running to me and lifts me off the ground. "Fuck, yes, Little Bird."

What a rush! I can't even hear myself think with the pounding in my ears. But I swear I can hear Quinn whooping and whistling all the way from her place in the spectators' village. I look over and see her decked out in a vintage fur coat and cowboy hat with a red, chunky scarf around her neck. Luke is in all black snow gear and a beanie.

"I know we did amazing. Whatever we place, we place. Let's go celebrate with our friends," I say. We walk Betty back to her trailer so we can get her tack off and put some food in her belly.

We head up to the spectators' area and receive plenty of congratulations on a good first run. It wasn't as clean as the trials we did at home before the race in Jackson, which is just wild to think was a week ago. It feels like a lifetime.

If I'm honest, as much as I tried to get my head into it, my brain kept replaying the same scenes—Julien after the race. Then, Julien tied up in my cottage. And then, Julien with a bullet hole in his head, one that I put there.

"You all right?" Maverick asks as we wind our way through the crowd.

"Yeah, I'm fine. Yeah." I try to paste a smile on my face.

We find Luke and Quinn, and she runs over to give me a hug.

"Charlie, you guys were so dang good! I had no idea that I needed to see you pull this one down the street on a piece of thirty-foot rope, but I did. I get the excitement!"

"Bro, this is amazing. I can't believe you've never done this before. Horses and skiing—you were made for this!"

We don't watch the other competitors race right away, but we don't leave the area either. Instead, we spend the next couple of hours catching up with our friends. We won't race again until tomorrow, so we spend time with them and watch the later races. It's a full two days of different categories—novice, sport, and snowboarders.

After seeing the times that we're up against tomorrow, I know we won't place, but at least we finished the course, no wipeouts. I tell them I'm going to go feed Betty and get her settled in for the night.

When I get back to the group, they're laughing, and the sound of it is so nice. "What's the plan for tonight?" I ask, looking at Quinn and Luke.

"Dinner? Drinks?" Luke says. He claps Maverick on the shoulder and knocks their heads together. "I've missed you, asshole."

"Back at you, dickhead." Mav laughs and walks with Luke ahead of us back toward the hotel.

Quinn and I turn to each other and laugh.

After dinner, I ask the bartender to snag some rosemary from the kitchen to make Quinn and me rosy lemon cocktails. Time passes quickly, and day wears into night.

"We should turn in," Maverick says. "We've got another early start."

"Okay, let's get the checks."

The guys take care of the bills, and we go our separate ways, since our rooms are in different wings of the hotel.

"You really looked magnificent out there," Maverick says, cornering me in the elevator. "It's kind of funny, the symbolism of all this. I'm tethered to you out there." He points to his chest, then to mine. "I'm tethered to you in here. No matter how long the rope, I'll still chase you." He moves his hand up to my throat, under my jaw, and pulls me to him for a kiss. It causes a tingle to spread from my scalp to my toes.

"Mav." I'm not sure if it's a plea, a question, or a statement. I just know that I need him. I want to tell him, *"You don't have to chase me, I'm right here!"*

I push my hands in the back of his pants when he kisses me again, squeezing his ass and pulling his body flush to mine.

The elevator dings, and I pluck the key card out of his back pocket. His eyes darken. Emotion crosses his face, a thundercloud ready to deliver much-needed rain to the plains. The electronic lock's light blinks green, and I push the heavy door open. I damn near trip over myself when strong hands pull me into a warm, broad chest.

I smell the hay and sweat, and, despite wanting this man, I definitely need a shower. He likely does, too; slick and sore, both of us could stand to let the water sluice over the muscles we used today.

"A hot shower sounds nice, doesn't it?" I say, backing away and starting to strip off my coat. I suck my bottom lip into my mouth and bite down on it.

"Little Bird, are you trying to get me naked?"

I offer a cheeky shoulder shrug. "Do I need a reason?"

"No, I don't think you do." He kicks off his shoes, and I walk backward until I fall onto the bed. I catch myself in a smooth motion, sitting while I watch him slowly undress. "But you're right, a shower sounds fantastic."

He's naked except for his socks and boxer briefs, the bulge showing just how good of an idea he thinks the shower is. He walks toward his bag, grabs his kit, and kicks off his socks and briefs. I'm already salivating for the impressively thick cock hanging between his legs, though it isn't even fully hard yet.

He sees me eyeing his dick and says, "My eyes are up here, sweetheart."

I blush so damn hard and feel the red creeping up my neck to my face. He walks toward me and gives me a kiss on my cheek. His dick hits my knee when he bends down to kiss me. I want to touch it.

He leaves me there, stunned for a second, and heads into the shower. I stay on the bed; my feet and body won't let me stand up. This all feels like something we would do every day for the rest of our lives. It's intimate yet ordinary, this interaction.

I must have been lost in that thought, because he calls out my name, voice muffled from behind the door. "Charlotte, are you coming?" I can't miss that hint of sarcasm.

I stand, kick off my boots, and strip down to my lacy bra and thong, leaving them in an unceremonious pile on the floor.

"Done so quick? Must have been a good highlight reel," I say sassily.

"Actually, I was coming out to get you and didn't want to fall on the damn tile."

I'm still in my bra and panties, but I get a look at him. He stands there, dripping wet, looking way too fucking fine, that slutty little white towel barely holding onto his hips. My mouth goes dry despite the steam billowing in the space. I want to lick the water rolling down his chest more than I want to breathe.

"Get that perfect ass over here."

With my clothes still on, I walk into the open shower stall.

My panties are soaked, and not from the water dripping down my body. One gentle tug of the towel causes it to fall. He lifts me, and I wrap my legs around his hips, our lips crashing together as he backs me up against the cold tile. His mouth plunders mine, a tangling of tongues. With the wall at my back supporting my weight, he rips through my lace thong and tosses the scraps on the floor.

I grind against him, his dick between us, desperate for whatever kind of friction I can get. He gently pushes his fingers between my folds, gathering the wetness that's been pooling there, then brings his fingers to his mouth and licks. *Oh, my God.* Then he says, "Taste how sweet you are for me, Little Bird." He pushes his slick fingers past my lips. I lick them, tasting myself. He then pushes them into my center and fucks my tight cunt with his deft fingers.

My orgasm is building; I'm coming too fast to a crescendo. He cradles his head in the spot between my collarbone and neck and runs his nose along the column of my neck. "You smell like honey. Fuck, you always smell so damn good, like heaven."

Goosebumps break out all along my body, and I shudder. He licks a trail along my exposed skin and bites down the slope of my shoulder. That sends my body soaring, and I come all too soon.

He's not even inside me, and I've come all over his cock pulsing beneath my ass.

"You made a mess, sweetheart. Clean it up."

I slide down to my knees, and he unclasps my bra. I lick from his base to his tip. I look up at him, and his eyes are on my mouth, watching me take as much as I can.

He pulls my hair to one side and guides my head down until I start to gag. I want to please him. I want to give him whatever he wants. I want so much for him to call me his "good girl." He pushes again and puts his hand around my throat as he does, just enough to apply pressure. "Touch yourself," he says.

I move my fingers to the apex of my thighs, circling the bundle of nerves there. I hum around him at how sensitive I am.

"Fuck, that mouth will be the death of me," he groans.

I push a finger inside myself, already slick with arousal.

"Are you going to come again?"

And, fuck, yes, I am so close. I nod, and he releases my throat and pulls out of my mouth.

"Give me your fingers."

I'm so close; I don't want to stop.

"Give. Me. Your. Fingers."

I withdraw them from my body, raise them to him, and he sucks them clean.

"Good girl. Get on all fours, Little Bird. Show me that pretty pussy."

I do as he asks, the tiles warm on my hands from the hot water, so my ass is up in the air, my greedy cunt waiting for him, water droplets running down the backs of my thighs.

He steps out of the stall, and I track him through the frosted glass of the shower divider. He grabs something from the counter, then comes back into the stall, standing while I'm on my knees.

"Tell me what you want."

"I want you," I say breathily, turning and twisting my body so I can look up at him. "I want you to fuck me."

"How, Little Bird?" He languidly strokes his cock, up and down. Up and down.

"However you want me. I trust you, Mav." I face away from him, hoping he knows I mean that with more than just my body.

He comes up behind me and rubs the globes of my ass, then—*smack*—his hand comes down hard. My skin is already heated from the shower, and the spank sends waves through my body. It's not painful, but the sensation radiates. The contact between his hand and my skin is feverish; the rubbing soothes away any lingering sting. He smacks my ass again, and again rubs the burn away.

"I fucking love seeing my marks on your skin. You've left your mark on my soul. It's only fair, right?"

I moan at the sensation, aware of where his body presses against mine. "Yes."

"If you want to stop at any point, you say so."

"Yes."

He runs his thick length between my folds and smacks it against my pussy.

"Ahh!" I cry out. My clit, already sensitive, begs for more contact.

He lines his dick up with my entrance and doesn't give it to me soft. No, after a few thrusts, he's all the way seated inside me. Filling and stretching, the pleasure and burn are so equally driving me wild. I exhale a breath to scream, "Mav!"

"You're going to take every fucking inch. Aren't you?"

"Yes, please, Mav," I beg.

He's gathered my hair into a ponytail, which he grips at the base of my neck, helping keep me upright. He pulls out, dragging against my walls so fucking slowly I feel like I'm going to combust. He maintains this rhythm, and it's the most delicious torture I've ever felt. I come so hard, stars dance around my vision, and I actually push him out of my body. I immediately miss the fullness of him. I cry, "No, no!"

"That's my good girl, give me one more. Fuck—you're so tight," he says with a laugh as he tries to fuck me through my climax.

My body finally relaxes and allows him to rock into me. I can feel him shift behind me; he releases my hair and holds onto my hip. His pace is punishing.

"Yes, Mav. Fuck, harder!"

I hear a buzz. I turn to look at what is making the noise, but I can't see it and he doesn't show me. He does give me a wicked smile and says, "I ordered you a new toy." He's still moving inside me when he hooks an arm around my hip and holds something to my clit.

"Ah. Fuck, that feels so fucking good." I put my hand out to brace myself against the wall in front of me—anything to keep me steady as whatever toy Maverick is holding to my clit brings me closer. I'm on my knees, holding on for dear life while he continues to piston into me from behind, one hand holding the toy and the other with fingers hooked in my mouth. It's rough and everything I asked him for.

"You're always beautiful, but seeing you stuffed full of my cock is the most beautiful sight I'll ever see."

Those words, this feeling that's been building...all the yearning, the fighting, the teasing, the jealousy—everything has boiled down to the way he makes me feel. I feel tears, hot and wet, not water from the shower, trace down my cheeks, every damn feeling I've kept bottled up for him spilling forth.

He drops the toy and extracts his hand from my mouth to stroke down my spine softly. I come, and this time, he comes with me. He comes with the force of a damn avalanche that could bury everything in its path.

"Are you with me, sweetheart?"

I shake my head, and he pulls out of me and leans back on his heels, turning me to face him. He looks devastated when he sees me crying.

"Charlotte. Fuck, fuck, I'm so sorry. You said you wanted it—"

"It's not that. That was great."

He looks confused, and I can't blame him, but I'm not confused; I'm in love.

He gathers me in his arms so that we are standing. "Hang on." He walks out of the large shower stall and comes back with a plush white towel. He lifts me up and walks me over to the vanity. I am shaking, overwhelmed with all kinds of sensations and emotions. He steps in between my legs and holds me to him in a grip so firm, I don't think anything could tear him away.

He pulls away just enough to look at me, and the look in his eyes... I can't keep this in anymore.

"I love you," I blurt out. "I didn't realize that this is what love is supposed to be. You make me feel so many things. That being safe can be both vulnerable and relinquish control. I told you before that I wanted you to fight for me; in my own way, that's what I was asking you for."

He doesn't say "I love you" or anything in return; he just holds me as I fall apart in the comfort of his arms.

Maverick

CHAPTER 43

I love you. I love you. I love you. Her words ring in my ears louder than anything ever has. She's falling apart in my arms, and I don't know what I can do to help her.

I should have said those words back. I feel them. But I don't dare voice this out loud yet. The only woman I have ever loved was ripped away from me. The small boy from that day, still living inside me, is afraid that if he admits this is love, he'll wake up tomorrow and find Charlotte gone, too. Maybe not from cancer, but definitely from something. And yet—and yet, the resounding part of me wants this more than I ever wanted a gold medal.

This fear I have of her leaving isn't just because of what she said, but also because there's nothing holding her to Silver Rapids now. She's free to go and live her life wherever she wants, and what if what she wants isn't the life of a cattle rancher?

I hate what I've become—the doubt and fear that come with caring for someone; it's crippling! I worry about her every day. *How do people live like this?!* Owen had mentioned that if Charlotte ever needed to talk to someone about her trauma, he had the number of a great therapist. Maybe it's time for me to unpack all the pent-up feelings about my mother and father, all the feelings of guilt and pressure I put on myself to be anything less than perfect. I have been carrying all that with me since childhood, and the bags are getting heavy.

Charlotte's gone quiet, and while her breathing is still a little ragged, she's no longer crying.

"Hi, sweetheart. Are you with me?"

"I'm so sorry. I didn't mean to just blurt it out like that. And you don't have to say it back. Like, really, I'm not just saying that to get you to say it back. I was just in my head, and in the moment, it felt right."

"You don't need to apologize. You're valid, however you're feeling right now."

"Thank you." I'm about to interrupt her when she says, "I know, no thank yous. But let me fucking say it."

I chuckle. "All right, sweetheart, let me hear it."

"Thank you, Maverick."

I take her face into my hands, skimming my thumbs along her cheekbones, wiping away her tears.

"The thing is, I'm not even sad." She laughs. "Even if you never say it back, I know what love is."

Say it. Fucking say it, you idiot!

I say nothing and kiss her temples, then her mouth. Towel and all, I place her on the bed.

"I have feet, you know."

"Yes, and what fine feet they are. Let's start there." I lay her back and open the towel. She immediately closes her knees, and I say, "Uh-uh," as I lift her legs up. I kiss the inner parts of her ankles, a kiss for each side, then work my way down to her center. She runs her hands through my hair—not hurriedly, but as if she wants this to last as long as I do.

Her sex is still swollen from the absolute pounding in the shower. It was primal, raw, transcendent. I place a soft kiss upon her piercing, which glitters from the light of the lamp next to the headboard. I work my way up her body, peppering her with kisses and nips before settling above her breasts—those perfect peaks. Going back and forth between them, I lick and suck her pebbled nipples. Her legs are on either side of me as I hover over her. She's watching me explore her body, and the weight of her eyes on me—I feel it to my core.

I make my way to her magnificent lips. "You have beautiful lips," I tell her. "Every inch of your skin is keeping heaven in one place."

I spend the rest of the night buried in her heat and fall asleep to the sound of her deep breathing.

The next morning, I roll over, expecting to find Charlotte in bed, a mass of honey-colored hair surrounding her. But she's up and pacing the room, my long-sleeved T-shirt dwarfing her frame.

"Little Bird?"

"So, let me just get this out. I know that, logically, I shouldn't be freaking out because I've said those words before. But—"

I move to sit and bring my knees up to my chest. "Charlotte, I—"

"No, please. I have spent the better part of my adult life feeling unlovable. Or thinking that love was a transaction, just a tit for tat that if I were good enough, or smart enough, or anything, that it would make it easier for my parents, my partner, my boss, or Julien to love me. And then you come in with your fucking gorgeous face and throw all of that on its side. I think about all the times I've been broken-hearted by almost every single man that's been in my life. None of them have cared for me the way your family has cared for me. Your dad? He didn't have to take me in and show me kindness or compassion. I was nobody to him, a stranger on the street."

That's a punch to the gut I wasn't expecting from this. *Dad, you crazy man. I bet you knew all along who she was to me.*

"Ace? He could have been resentful as fuck. He didn't have to show me the ropes when I could barely lift a bale of hay. Owen? I don't even have words for what he's given me. And then there's you." She points at me. "You have pieced back together bits of my heart that I didn't realize were broken. I don't even know if it was ever whole. My life made sense before—the job, the car, the guy, where I lived—but it shouldn't be so hard to try to make 'perfection' work.

"I know that there's a difference now between what I had with *him* and what I *could* have with you. He said I was just a means to an end; you said I was heaven. Every time—even the first time—I have been with you, there's been love. Whether rough or soft, whatever last night was, there's always been love." Silver lines her eyes. She wipes the tears away before she goes to the bathroom and locks the door.

Feeling like a right asshat, I bury my face in my hands.

We raced, but I couldn't tell you what happened. I'm so far in my own head that the entire day is a blur. We didn't medal, but I'm okay with that; I set out to do what I promised Jude I'd do this season, and somehow I feel like I've fucked up the best thing I have ever found in this world because I couldn't say anything when the time was right.

We're loading Betty into the trailer; Charlotte's been quiet since she came out of the shower. I've tried to talk with her, but she seems to be processing some things, too.

Soon, Luke and Quinn come to say goodbye to us in the competitors' area.

Quinn asks Charlotte, "Baby girl, you good?"

"Yeah, just in my head about some stuff. We good."

"It's still kind of early—do you guys want to do dinner on the road, or maybe pick something up when we get back? Maverick, can we come to the ranch and hang," Quinn proposes.

I like where she's going with this. "For sure, that sounds great. I'll get ahold of Caleb and see if he and Kennedy want to join. Maybe some pizza from Flour Child?"

"Bro, I will always be down for pizza," Luke adds.

Charlotte locks up the trailer, and everyone helps load it with the rest of the gates of Betty's pen.

"You're following us?" I ask Luke.

"Yeah, I've got your six, guy. We'll be pulled over on the side of the road; you'll see us."

"Thanks." I clap him on the back, and they head off to get in Luke's truck. We check the hitch one more time before getting in.

On the road, I start and stop a conversation in my head a dozen times, and finally think I have something to say to try to explain myself after an hour of silence, when suddenly Ace's name scrolls across the dashboard and my phone rings.

"Hello, Ace." Our relationship is slowly changing: he's been there when I needed help for Charlotte, and he's earning my respect.

"I'd really like to not have to clean up another body," he says.

I sit up straight, and so does Charlotte.

"Ace, what the hell are you talking about?"

"Another of your lovestruck fans showed up today, Boss."

I look at Charlotte, baffled, and she returns the same look of bewilderment. "Ace, what do you mean?" she asks.

"I mean that I just chased off Ezra. He looked like he was still drunk from last night. Or he is just crazy. Either way, I may have implied that he would be tangling with me the next time he steps foot on this property."

"What do you mean you *implied*?" I grind out.

"I told him that someone else was taking care of Charlotte."

"Ugh, did he say why he was there, or what he wanted?"

"No, I was letting Finn out, and we were playing the frisbee, and he drove up."

"You let him leave drunk?!" Charlotte shrieks. "He could hurt somebody if he were drunk and driving."

"I called the sheriff as soon as he left."

"Ah. Okay. Maybe I should try to call him. Explain. He's a nice guy, but it was never going to be him. It's always been Maverick." She says it out loud, but I don't think she meant to, because as soon as the words leave her mouth, she looks like she wants to take them back.

"I wouldn't, Charlie. Leave it be. He can either lick his wounds or get on with it, but either way, the guy gives me the creeps."

"For real," I say, glancing in her direction. "I don't trust him to stay away even if Ace did manage to chase him off this time. Who could stand to stay away from you?"

I give her a wink and she rolls her eyes before looking out to the trees beyond.

"Seriously, Ace. If he doesn't stay away, we *will* have another body to bury."

"Just letting you know. I'm going into town for a bit. Are you guys on the road?"

"Yeah, about another hour and a half until we get back to the ranch."

"All right, I'll get Finn out one more time, and then I'll be back tomorrow."

"Ace, take the night off. Please," Charlotte implores. "Take tomorrow off; we got this."

"All right, then. I'll see you in a couple of days."

We exchange goodbyes, and with the break of silence, I grab her hand that she's been running along her denim-clad thigh and say, "It's going to be okay."

She looks at my hand and then at me. "I know." She gives my hand a squeeze.

"It's going to be nice to get the gang together; the last time was Jasper's service. We need to start creating more happy memories."

I take a big breath and say, "This weekend is a happy memory. I texted Jude a photo Luke took; I think he's a little jealous. But he's the kind of guy that just gets even more motivated by that shit."

"Ha! His whole family is competitive!"

"They are, but that's what makes them Cortlands."

"You should give Caleb and Jake a heads up if you're wanting them to come over."

I call Caleb, and he answers on the second ring. "Hey, Mav!"

"We're doing a family dinner—you guys free tonight? Jake too? I know I haven't been around much. But it'd be really good to get the crew back to Sunday dinners."

"Hell yeah. Kennedy and I are in; she was just asking about dinner. But Jake's actually moving in with his girlfriend. He's there now."

"Ahhh! That's so exciting!" Charlotte exclaims.

"Yeah, they're so damn cute together. I'm happy for him."

"That's good news. I can't wait to meet her. Maybe next time."

"Caleb, any chance you can bring some of your mom's pizza?"

"We could definitely work that out. Our usuals?"

"That sounds good." I turn to Charlotte. "Any requests? Our usuals are meat lovers and luau."

"A Kevin McAllister special for me, please!"

"A cheesy pizza for Charlie, got it."

"We'll be home in about an hour and a half, but give us two so we can get beer."

"We'll be there!"

We get to town, stop to grab beer, and arrive home just in time to stable Betty and enter the house just as Caleb and Kennedy pull up the drive.

Finn greets us at the door and jumps into Charlotte's arms.

"Ahh. Who's my good boy?"

He jumps down and runs right over to Quinn.

"I miss you, too, little man."

Charlotte pulls the plates out, and I get some paper towels to put on the table. The girls start talking about some book they've been reading, while I crack a beer with the boys, moving to sit around the fireplace. Finn comes of his own free will to sit next to me, demanding pets.

The girls soon join us, and I pull Charlotte onto my lap.

I watch her with my friends. Her smile and laugh are easy. The way she has embraced this life means more to me than I ever knew I needed.

I slip away and head to my parents' bedroom, to a drawer in the center of the chest with a pull-out hideaway section, and grab something that's been burning me up.

Everyone is on their second round of pizza and beer. I come up behind her and say, "You look rather beautiful with a smile on your face."

She turns around and knocks her head against my chest.

It's only a short while later that Luke says, "Well, I have an early morning. I've got to get to the bookstore to build a flying library."

"No, I told you, rolling library ladder!"

"Who has a library ladder?"

Quinn and I say at the same time, "Belle!"

We all laugh, and Kennedy says, "It's okay, we should get going too. I've got an early shift at the Bluebird."

They all make their way to the door. The girls hug and Caleb, the goof, gives me a hug just as animatedly. Luke follows and we wave goodbye to our friends as they get in their cars and drive down the path to the main road.

I'm tired; this day has been a different kind of exhausting. But also, I don't want to forget exactly how I feel at this moment.

Finn is curled up in his favorite spot on the couch, and Charlotte's loading the dishes into the dishwasher. She closes the door and faces me.

Without hesitating, I say, "I've been wanting to say something for a long while." I sit her down on the bench.

Now it's my turn to pace.

"Are you happy here? Truly?"

"Yes!" She laughs, uncomfortable with my question. "Why?"

"I don't have anything that can compete with the life you had in Boston. You can literally travel the world over with the amount of money you have, and I'm just trying to process that you want to stay in Wyoming."

"I like my life here. I want to be here. Is this because of what I said?"

"No, this is because I'm a fucking idiot for not saying it earlier. I love you."

She gasps—clearly she thought this was going a different way.

"I just want you to have the life of your dreams," I continue. "Last May, you said your biggest dream was to travel the world. To live the life of a wanderer."

"I can do that with you."

"What if you get sick of this place and want to leave?"

"Then we go on vacation and come *home*."

Home. The house does finally feel like home. I think that with her, I'm ready to make this house even more of a home. It's so weird to think about, but Charlotte deserves better than my room. My parents' room is so much bigger, and she will definitely need closet space. But not yet; we need to make it our own, and for the love of all things, we need a new bed. All plans for the future—a future I want to build with her.

I kneel before her. "This love, my love for you, it's like a snowstorm. The kind that hypnotizes you as it winds down from the sky, torn between fury and tenderness. It can freeze you to the bone, but that's the risk you take—to be surrounded by it, damn near consumed by it. I've spent my entire life chasing that feeling, chasing the peace I feel when I'm skiing. Loving you, being with you..." I take her hands, "is like chasing snowfall and hoping to heaven I never find summer." I kiss each of her hands. "But if I do, at least you'll be by my side.

"This—" I pull the object from my pants pocket. It's been in a velvet bag, and I'm so nervous that I almost drop it. "This is something precious to me; it was my mom's. We can take all the time you want, but you're mine, sweetheart. You've been mine since I saw you riding that damn mechanical bull." I take my mother's Montana sapphire ring Dad had custom-made for her out of the blue velvet pouch. "Would you take this? Make it and me yours?"

She looks at my outstretched hand for several long heartbeats. This may seem rushed considering all that we've been through, but I don't want another day to come and go without her by my side—without her knowing how much I love her.

"We can take all the time you need or want," I say again. "We don't even have to get married. I just want you to have it."

She nods. "I want your ring on my finger; I want the world to know we belong to *each other*."

I slip the ring onto her ring finger, and it fits perfectly.

She looks at it and then her gaze is back on me as she smirks. "But, technically, you're still my employee—"

"I quit," I tell her.

She gives me a slap on the arm. "You interrupted, but I was going to say I can give you a promotion to partner."

I laugh and lift her into my arms. She wraps her legs around my hips and I lay her out on the first flat surface I can find.

We make love on the kitchen table of our home, and when I've finally spent myself inside her, I roll over and look out the window. The two-month calendar on the wall catches my eye; I notice an important date at the end of May and smile.

I look at the love of my life, take her left hand and kiss her knuckles, and, with my full chest, tell her, "You know, I can't wait to match your time on Brutus this year."

She swats me away and says, "It'll never happen, Ranger Rick. You'll have to catch me first!" Then, she peels herself off the table and runs up to our room.

So chase her I do; I'll never stop chasing her.

Maverick

EPILOGUE

The setting sun casts a golden glow on my Little Bird, my wife. It's just us, our small family of friends, and the mountains. The fireworks for the Summer Kick-Off Festival will be going off soon, but we won't be watching them. It's a year to the day since my own firecracker changed my life.

Charlotte's hair is unbound and wild in the wind, a hairpiece tucked to the side of her head. The long, floral black gown flows behind her as she stands with Quinn, Rae, Kennedy, and her sister, Georgie, alongside her. She invited Georgie out with the provision that she doesn't tell their mom and dad where she is. I support her decision to go no-contact with her parents, if it helps her heal.

It's been easier for her to live her life since submitting her findings and documents to the SEC, effectively closing that chapter of her life. Georgie's been staying in one of the finished cabins for the last week or so and it's been great to see Charlotte reconnect with her sister.

There's a floral archway that we were going to use as an altarpiece that Charlotte decided to place over my parents and grandparents. She placed pictures of them on a stand underneath the arch. I hope I make them proud—I hope they see what I've become and know that it was because of them that I'm able to live this life.

Tears blur my vision; I try to fight them back, then decide, *Fuck it, I can cry at my wedding if I want to.* A breeze lifts my cowboy hat off my head and I swear I can hear a chuckle. I know it's Dad coming to tell me he's here with me—with us. As I pick it up and dust it off, I catch a glimpse of a shadow in the treeline just at the crest of the hill. I squint and it has disappeared; it must have been a trick of light in the shadows.

Charlotte actually took all of the old photos Dad had in that shoebox and put them in frames to hang all over our home. My girl has no problem flexing her money now, and I shouldn't be amazed at how quickly she and Quinn were able to plan this wedding in just under two months. So much so that when we decided on Thailand for a honeymoon, she insisted we all go on a group night out in Vegas because we were going to have to connect anyway through Vegas and LAX to get to Bangkok.

Luke, Owen, and all my boys are a wall of black suits as they talk animatedly about what we're getting into tonight. The girls were squealing about going to an all-male revue because they were denied a bachelorette party, to which the guys, myself included, said, "No." We joked about giving them a repeat karaoke performance, complete with a strip tease, if that's what they really wanted to see.

Mrs. Wright cries out, "All right, kids, if you're going to make your fancy flight, time to get going."

Charlotte has chartered a private plane for the trip. No, my wife definitely has no problem flexing money now.

Owen comes up and gives me a bear hug that lifts me off the ground. "You've done real good, kid."

The Next Morning:

I made sure my wife would be tired this morning. We made rough and tender love throughout the night; we didn't even sleep. We showered and caught a rideshare to the airport. She looks dead on her feet and the caveman in me is smirking, knowing the reason why. We'll both sleep soundly from LAX to Shanghai, where we'll layover before Thailand. It's a short flight from Las Vegas to LAX, so Charlotte pulls out her new phone and scrolls through the ranch's new social media DMs.

"Ooh, this clothing brand wants to come do a shoot at the ranch!" she says spiritedly. "So many people have been reaching out, interested in what we're doing. We have a meeting when we get back with a chef from New York."

"Whatever you want to do, sweetheart. You're the boss." I kiss her hand, above her ring.

We're about to take off. Before I put my phone on airplane mode, a notification for the "Gold Not Silver Rapids Boys" group chat pops up with a new message.

> Luke: *I fucked up. I don't think this secret is going to stay in Vegas.*

Want one more scene with Charlotte & Quinn? Find it on Anastasia's website! www.authoranastasiawilder.com for a bonus epilogue featuring your favorite Silver Rapids besties.

ACKNOWLEDGEMENTS

To my darling husband, the wrangler of my life, the glue that keeps our little family together, and the one who helped put me back together, there is no love story without you. Our adventures will be forever an inspiration. Thank you for every single one of the late nights you've suffered through on my behalf, the inane conversations, and the dissection of characters that exist only in my head. I don't deserve you, Bunny, but I'm so fucking happy I can call you mine.

To my grandparents, I am all that I am because of you. It is no small thing that you have afforded me. Thank you. A special thank you to my Papa—the man who taught me how to spell, how to read, and how an entire world opens for you with just twenty-six little letters...thank you!

To the FBS, thank you all for pushing me to be a better writer! To the Scream for Peens, you girls are incredible, and I am so damn lucky to call you friends. I cannot wait for more shenanigans.

To Ruthi, you have been in my corner since day fucking one, and I am so grateful for your support and friendship! We are just getting started, lady! More adventures to come. This book would not exist without you!!! To Rachel, your guidance and willingness to answer all my questions is no small thing; thank you from the bottom of my heart. To Mads, you will always be my first PA. Thank you for getting this off the ground with me! I can't wait to see your author career take flight. Chelsea, a bit of your story has come to life on these pages. I love you.

To my editor, Erin, your kindness and support is nothing short of remarkable. Thank you for helping me shape this story.

Sincere thanks to my beta readers: Casey, Kandace, Brooke, Heather, and Megan. Thank you for caring about these characters as much as you do!

To my street team, the Little Darlings, thank you for staying with me and for your support! You were all such good girls for patiently waiting; I hope I didn't edge you too hard.

To my illustrator, Valentina, you took stick drawings and some descriptions of my characters and turned my words into works of art. Thank you! To Emily, a book is often judged by its cover, and I'm so damn lucky to have your incredible talent helping me capture my readers from the very first glance. Thank you for designing something that perfectly represents my story.

To the many author friends who have supported me, words aren't enough. To the many authors who have inspired me and will never know it, your words have got me through the hardest of days and the worst of times. You will never know the impact you have had on my soul, but thank you all the same.

To the Silver Rapids characters that kept me in a damn chokehold longer than a Sleep Token song, thank you for being my first. You weren't gentle, but, fuck—you got the job done and let me flex my writings skills on you so that I could get ready for my OGs.

To you—yes, you, the reader: time is irreplaceable, and if you made it this far. Thank you for supporting a debut indie author. I hope you enjoyed your time in Silver Rapids, but you're going to have to hang up your cowboy boots for just a little bit because we're going to New York City next.

Finally, to coffee and to Writers' Tears whiskey, thank you.

ALSO BY THE AUTHOR

Curious to learn how Charlotte and Maverick met?
Find out in Midnight Heatwave. Available on Amazon, Barnes & Noble,
and my favorite indie booksellers listed on my website.

ABOUT THE AUTHOR

Anastasia Wilder is a dark romance author whose passion for storytelling and reading began at a young age. Her love for dark romance, suspense, and romantasy fuels her writing, bringing a unique blend of intensity and emotion to her stories.

Anastasia lives in the Midwest with her husband and two furbabies. When not simping over morally gray characters, wing leaders, guys with wings, or the villain, she enjoys skiing, traveling to new places, finding great Thai restaurants, and swinging in her hammock with a cocktail in hand.

For other upcoming projects, art reveals, shenanigans, or to sign up for Ana's newsletter, visit her website: www.authoranastasiawilder.com. You can also follow Anastasia Wilder on Facebook, Instagram, and TikTok: @authoranastasiawilder. Email your thing? You can reach her at anastasia@authoranastasiawilder.com. Or join her reader group on Facebook at: Anastasia Wilder's Little Darlings.